Spi

by
Leslie Jones

Published by CompletelyNovel.com

For Mum and Dad

Prologue

The fence wire digs into the back of his legs. As he leans back, it gives a little, before becoming taut again. An innate fear of heights causes his heart to pound painfully and his breathing becomes rapid.

The drop is hidden, masked by a narrow stretch of curved ground extending in front of him - first grass and then smooth rock, glistening with damp from melted frost. Perhaps one step forward, or two at most and he will be able to see what lies below waiting to engulf him. Only a few feet of hard granite between this life and oblivion.

He is sure that, as soon as he steps onto the slippery surface, his legs will shoot from under him and he will land on his back. From there, he will slide unable to stop the momentum. How long would the terror last? Four or maybe five seconds, perhaps? What will follow? Nothing, he hopes. This life ended - no more guilt.

'Don't think about it - all your thinking is done now.'

He bends forward - enough for gravity to take hold, but then jerks back, needing safety again. 'Soon,' he murmurs, 'just a few more minutes.' With a trembling hand, he fumbles for the packet of cigarettes in the pocket of his jacket. He lights one and draws in deeply, focusing on the horizon, a momentary distraction.

His focus turns inwards. Scenes depicting aspects of his life cascade through his mind. While some are happy, most emphasise his failure.

The corners of his mouth twitch into a sardonic smile. *Is this my life flashing in front of me before I die?*

The voices start - not for the first time - he's heard them all before. But this time, there is a sense of finality. They appear to deliver the same fundamental message but in different ways:

5

'Understand this for sure - you are no longer welcome in this life.'

The owner of each voice takes turns to convey meaning, reminders of his wasted existence. Words are accompanied by visions - some hazy, half-remembered, others lucid.

'How could you?' a voice implores. 'Why? What have I done to deserve this? What sort of man are you to be so cruel and heartless?'

Her words were etched into his memory. She had been very angry, her words resonating with hurt and disbelief. Now, the anger seems to have subsided and her eyes reflect a different emotion: profound disappointment. Her face hovers a few feet in front of him. He reaches out wanting to touch. She takes his hand and brings it up to her face, regarding him with a sad smile.

'I'm so sorry,' he whispers.

No sound comes from her moving lips - but he can sense she is saying, 'I know you are.' The remembered features start to fade. 'If I could turn the clock back, I would...'

'Too late now,' a voice whispers as her face vanishes.

A different voice. Her face is close to his. She is looking at him, her eyes wide as if in sudden realisation. 'I can't do this anymore. I wish we'd never started.' He feels again the tug deep in his chest - one of unexpected loss. But a flurry of images causes him to react exactly as he did then - sadness is replaced immediately with gut-wrenching panic.

Another voice, this one an older man: 'You betrayed them, and now they don't want you. If it were possible, I'd pity you. For Christ's sake, you had everything, and you threw it all away.'

The face of the man who once respected, even admired him and, most importantly, welcomed him into his family, now scowls at him as he might at a cockroach found in his kitchen.

Another man's voice, this one stirring loathing and an urge to lash out: 'You're not wanted here. Nobody wants you - now go on, get lost!'

He takes a drag of his cigarette, which is almost finished. As he inhales, he reminds himself this is the last time he will enjoy the calming effect of tobacco. He studies the butt, beginning to radiate heat into his fingers. Then, with a deliberate, aimed flick, he propels it forward. He watches as it arcs and disappears over the cliff top.

There is one last scenario to endure - this one more significant than the others, and the reason he is here on the precipice, preparing for his final moments. The scene is as sharp as though playing out in front of him.

'Granddad! Oh, my God, what have you done to him?'

The young woman is crouched down cradling the old man's head. Blood is trickling from a ragged gash in his forehead. Her eyes turn to him.

'You've killed him!'

He gazes ahead of him towards the sea. Once again, he gently eases forward in readiness to leave the security of the wire.

'Come on,' urges a voice somewhere unseen in front of him. 'You can let go now. It's time.'

PART ONE

"RISE"
(OCTOBER 1959 – APRIL 1960)

Chapter 1

"ONE CAREFUL OWNER"

(23rd October 1959)
'I need this sale,' Gregory muttered. 'No, you really need it!' his inner voice reminded him.

He started his new career as a car salesman three months ago, buoyant with optimism. It was to be a fresh start, an opportunity to prove he could achieve something and was not completely useless. He worked hard, but his efforts so far had resulted in only one sale, this achieved through offering a discount, which, announced Mr Ramsay, the manager, and proprietor of *Ramsay's Autos*, was way under the threshold to make any meaningful profit and had been, therefore, 'a complete balls-up.'

A woeful lack of sales and the fact he was a 'bloody liability,' in his manager's opinion, led to a first and final warning. Even though that exchange had taken place several days ago, the memory was still raw, savage in its intensity. Few words had passed between them since that unhappy episode.

Gregory busied himself cleaning and polishing the cars parked at the front of the forecourt, enjoying the unseasonable warmth of the late October sunshine. This activity kept him clear of the small office building where he visualised the glowering presence of his boss, sitting at his cluttered desk, working on whatever he did in there. At that moment, the Number Eleven stopped outside the *Golden Lion* opposite the garage - an hourly occurrence of no particular interest, but it provided a momentary distraction from a tedious and, given that the cars were all gleaming, pointless task. He paused, leaning on the front of a year-old Ford Consul he had been polishing. The bus drove away in a billow of diesel fumes having disgorged one passenger, a man, who emerged from the fug and walked across the road.

A small tinge of anticipation. *The first customer of the day - in fact, the only one in - how long? My God, two days! Now, if Mr Ramsay doesn't spot him...* He threw a worried glance at the office window. *He's likely watching through the window - he'll want to manage this one himself because he'll think I'll make a mess of it. I need this sale - please don't come out!* A tinge of panic.

The man raised his hand in a brief wave and walked towards him with what Gregory assessed to be a sense of purpose. 'He's here to buy,' the voice of optimism whispered to him. But an insidious voice of doubt added, 'But perhaps he only wants to ask for directions.'

'Come on,' he urged himself, 'have confidence!'

He studied the man's appearance: smart and business-like, wearing a sports jacket over a country-style shirt with a woollen tie; flannel trousers, well-pressed, and brogues, highly polished and expensive-looking. 'You can judge a man by his shoes,' said the wise voice of his mother. 'Looks like someone with money - cash to spend,' he whispered. Another glance at the office and no sign of the boss. With a relieved smile, he assured himself: *He's mine - and if I can sell a car to him... well, I might hang on to my job. He looks like a genuine punter, not the usual time-waster. What does Mr Ramsay call them? Oh yes, "tyre-kickers". No, this chap is a bona fide customer for sure - a professional.*

As he got nearer, the man's face broke into a broad, friendly smile. He extended his hand in greeting. Gregory smiled in return, fumbling with the can of polish in his hand, placing it on the roof of the Consul. He wiped his hands on a rag and accepted the handshake. A firm grip.

'You can tell a man by the way he shakes hands,' the voice of his mother said again.

'Good afternoon. You have a Healey for sale, I believe?'

Gregory grinned, and his heart leapt with excitement. *A prospect for sure!*

'We do indeed. Came in the day before yesterday,' he said, pointing to a group of cars in the corner of the forecourt, trying not to sound too excited, and failing.

The man smiled at him and nodded.

He stared back, sudden panic overcoming him. 'Bloody hell, not now! 'Scuse me a mo', he wheezed, pulling out an inhaler. A sharp inhalation of cool, medically enhanced air, and he was in control again. 'Sorry about that - a spot of asthma.'

'No problem.'

'The Healey's over there, behind the green Zodiac.'

'Let's have a look-see, then.'

Gregory detected an edge of excitement in the man's voice. His confidence returned. After a few moments, he followed him.

In his mind, a Yorkshire accent, belonging to Mr Ramsay, advised him, 'Don't go diving in! Let the punter examine the motor first. Keep an eye on him - if he kicks the tyres, he'll be a time-waster. He won't be buying!'

Gregory observed the man from a respectful distance, noting the way he ran his hands like a caress across the polished paintwork. 'He's not kicked the tyres, so he must be interested,' he muttered. 'Mind you, I've seen no one, real or otherwise, ever kick them.'

For several minutes, he stood silently as the man conducted a detailed examination of the car's exterior, first one side followed by the other, with an occasional pause to inspect a feature.

'He knows what he's looking for,' he murmured.

'Perhaps he's from "The Trade",' the voice of doubt whispered inside his head. *If he is, I'm going to have to call the Boss; I'd be out of my depth. No way am I going to negotiate.* Mr Ramsay, he knew, would sooner lose a sale than sell at a cut-down price to the competition.

The man turned and beckoned to him. Gregory walked over, his heart pounding, expecting a barrage of detailed questions about the Healey, which he knew he wouldn't be able to answer, at least not with any credibility. This was not because he lacked knowledge about cars - he had worked hard to learn the specifications of all those on the forecourt. In his jacket pocket, he had a self-made aide memoire of filing cards on which he had listed the key points of every car. The Boss always banged on about the necessity to understand the "unique selling points"– "yoo ess peez".

'You need to get this off pat for every motor!'

He could recite details verbatim, but he acknowledged his lack of any real understanding. His technical knowledge was veneer-deep. Within hours of the Healey's arrival, he had produced a card listing the "yoo ess pees" and the features - but, he hadn't had time to imprint these on his mind.

'She's a beauty, isn't she? Came in two days ago. Don't suppose she'll be here for long: there's likely to be a lot of interest!' He realised he was prattling.

'Very nice,' answered the man, in a neutral voice. 'Can I have a shufti inside?'

'Oh, yes, of course.' Gregory moved over to the driver's side door. 'I think you'll find it's... yes, unlocked.' He opened the door with a flourish, relieved there was no need to collect the key from Mr Ramsay's office.

The man's expression when he sat in the driver's seat of the Healey was telling.

He wants this car - I can see it on his face. He loves it!

'What do you think? Is it what you're looking for?' he asked as the man emerged a few minutes later.

'Oh, for sure! She's in mint condition and...' He paused, and his face creased into a smile. 'I'll need a good deal on it, though.'

Gave yourself away there, chum, he told himself, savouring a hint of triumph. *Tread carefully, though - don't blow it!*

'You know what you're looking for in a car,' he said, attempting flattery and trying to elicit a clue as to the customer's identity. *Please don't be from "The Trade!"* He spotted the quizzical expression on the man's face.

'I noticed the way you examined the Healey, the same way we do at an auction.'

He prayed his patter sounded convincing as he had never been to a car auction and had the vaguest idea of what happened at one.

'Can't say I've been to a car auction, but you're right, I know what I'm looking for. Can I ...'

Gregory made a mental note: *Don't try and hoodwink this bloke: he understands cars!* 'Which is a damn sight more than you do!' his inner voice said in a mocking tone.

'...have a look at the engine?'

'Of course, there should be a....'

'...a lever down here. Yes, I know.'

The man reached down inside the driver's door. The bonnet jerked up in response. He moved around to the front, slid his fingers under the gap and, with what looked like practiced skill, sprung open the lid. With the safety arm clipped under the hood, he tucked his tie inside his shirt and bent down to examine the engine. Gregory hovered behind him, glancing over his shoulder, instinct suggesting he should stay silent as he couldn't think of anything sensible to say.

But after a few moments: 'You know something about engines, then?' He winced as soon as he uttered the words, sensing he sounded contrived and awkward.

13

The man ignored him and continued to scrutinise each part of the engine. After a few minutes, he glanced up.

'Yes, I know about engines. I was a driver in the army - a few years ago, now'. He shut the bonnet as though he had done this several times before.

'For a colonel. I was his driver and did the day-to-day maintenance. Learnt a lot about cars and how they work. Self-taught you might say.'

There was silence for a few moments. He sensed the man was studying him.

'Aren't you due for National Service?' asked the man suddenly.

'Failed the medical - asthma–that's why I need this.' He pulled his "Medihaler" from his pocket again. 'I suffer badly. They said I would never cope with the physical training.'

His face reddened as the familiar wave of guilt, embarrassment, and shame awakened. Mention of National Service reminded him of how often Mr Ramsay, who had served during the Second World War, used his affliction as a weapon.

'The Army might have knocked some sense into you!'

He glanced at the man's face, expecting a look of disdain, perhaps disbelief. Instead, he nodded and smiled. He fished inside his jacket, pulling out a packet of cigarettes.

'Hard luck, but you might have had a lucky escape. I couldn't wait to get out. Taught me too many bad habits.' The man laughed then flipped a cigarette to his lips, offering the open pack. Gregory feigned shortness of breath. The man smiled.

'Sorry, of course, you don't smoke. Okay, why don't you talk me through the features?'

Gregory nodded, pulled out his aid memoir and started to recite the details, praying he wouldn't be asked to elaborate on any technical point. He spoke with more

14

certainty about the aesthetic qualities, which he remembered from the car magazine studied that morning. The technical aspects, however, he read out with little understanding.

The man seemed to be listening. He gave an occasional nod as though acknowledging the correctness of what he was being told.

I'm getting away with this! He glanced up from his notes and saw the man was smiling. *He doesn't need me to tell him anything about this car - he knows the details already. Is he testing me? Or is he letting me do my job?*

***

The man was only half listening. In his mind, he now owned the Healey and envisioned himself driving it. He anticipates the vibrancy of the steering wheel, recently caressed, the responsiveness of the gear stick, the smell of treated leather, and the roar of the 3-litre engine.

'Just one careful owner...'

He wakes from his reverie to and notices the young man again.

'... a lawyer.'

He pondered this detail for a moment, wondering whether it had any significance. None whatsoever, he concluded.

'This is the car for you!' the young man continued.

He sensed a growth in confidence and smiled, recognising the attributes of a novice. The salesman adopted a wise and knowing tone.

'You have excellent taste! I bet that applies to the ladies as well!'

He bit his lip to stop himself from snorting with laughter.

'I can see you now: a lovely young lady in the passenger seat and a picnic basket on the boot rack!' The salesman said this with a dramatic sweep of his arm.

Clumsy sales talk, but the lad's doing his best. He acknowledged to himself that the vista being evoked was much like the one playing in his mind. The vision of the girl in the passenger seat, even the wicker picnic basket strapped to the chrome luggage rack, reflected his imagining. In fact, his own version included a blanket: red and white checked. As for the young lady - he visualised her and smiled. *I want this car! She would want to be a passenger in it!*

The salesman, he noticed, was staring at him, his smile gone, replaced with an uncertain and embarrassed expression. He felt sorry for him.

'I'll need a test drive - put her through her paces. But before I do that, what price are you looking for? The advert suggested one - but I'm hoping we might negotiate?'

The uncertainty vanished in an instant from the salesman's face to be replaced with an eager, hopeful look.

He grinned when he was offered a figure, lower than the advertised one but still hefty. It was a game with which he was familiar, and he played along.

'Hum - a bit on the high side - I was looking to pay much less than that.'

'I might be able to offer some discount.'

He smiled as the salesman pretended to do a mental calculation. Another figure was suggested - lower but still higher than he expected.

'Still too much! Come on, you can do better than that!'

'Perhaps I could include one or two little extras?'

He noted the uncertainty in the voice. He had to stop himself from suggesting what the salesman might say.

'What little extras? I would hope they would be significant given the price you're asking!'

Once again, the smile is replaced with a frown, and a perceptible shadow of doubt drifts across the salesman's face. Is he panicking?

***

16

Gregory was struggling to keep control of the sales process - he was fighting a growing sense of panic. The limits and ability of his negotiation had been reached. He convinced himself he was failing and would lose the sale. With a sinking heart, he acknowledged he needed Mr Ramsay's help.

A vision of his boss's red, perspiring, angry face appeared in his mind - critical, ready to rebuke and berate. 'You couldn't sell a bag of toffees!' the image shouted at him. He hesitated, dreading the thought of going into the office but aware the man was expecting a response.

'I'll need to have a word with my manager about that,' he said after a few moments.

I must seem like a right Charlie! he thought, with a growing sense of frustration at his inability to progress the sale - one that was so near and yet...

'Better go and speak to him then,' the man replied.

Is he laughing at me? The voice of doubt had returned.

***

He chuckled as the salesman retreated to the office. *The lad's doing well enough. Yes, the sales patter is contrived, predictable and, let's face it, quite funny! Not a lot of confidence. He's new to the game. Rattled off the technical details far too rapidly and it was obvious, he didn't understand them. But - perhaps with a little direction, he might become a real salesman!* Able to judge now, he considered himself to be an expert in sales. At twenty-four, he had achieved the accolade of *"Area Salesman of The Year"* not once but two years in a row. Although selling vacuum cleaners door to door was not his profession of choice upon leaving the Army, a chance meeting launched the career he was now in - and he was flourishing. The challenge of sales stimulated him. His natural charm and ability to persuade won him custom and favour. Doors

17

opened for him. But he achieved his expertise and confidence through hard work and determination to overcome obstacles. Perhaps it was the anticipation of owning the craved for Healey that gave him a feeling of munificence - but he felt empathy with the young salesman who was clearly out of his depth.

Alone on the forecourt, he stared towards the small office building, and then glanced at the weathered sign above the entrance. *Ramsay's Autos*, read the motif in faded letters. A shadow fluttered across the window overlooking the forecourt, and a face appeared, pressed to the dusty pane - ruddy, mottled, and flushed. He noted the face was looking at him as if sizing him up, like a prize fighter about to enter the ring.

***

'But Mr Ramsay, it's just that...'

In the office, a one-sided, heated exchange between Gregory and his manager was taking place. Mr Ramsay was being unhelpful. He cut his only salesman off in mid-sentence, not allowing him to explain. He banged the desk with his fist.

'Hells bloody bells, what have I told you about letting punters dictate price?' He got up and turned to the window behind him, lifted a slat of the venetian blind and stared out for a few seconds before letting it drop. Then he turned and glared at him.

'Right, this is what you do,' he said in a loud, blustering voice. He fired off instructions, striking one palm with a slicing motion from the other hand to add emphasis. Then, without warning, he pushed him aside.

'If you want a job done properly, do it yourself!' he muttered with menace in his voice.

***

18

In the brief, few moments his eyes locked onto those belonging to the large, flushed face in the window, he sensed antagonism. He shrugged when the face disappeared, and then shivered. The appearance of the face evoked a memory of a sergeant from his army days, who exhibited the same aura of bovine belligerence. That man had made his life a misery during his weeks of basic training.

Deleting the scene from his mind - that life is long gone - he turned to the Healey - a flush of anticipation again. The reassuring bulge created by the wad of banknotes in his jacket pocket reminded him price would not be a problem. A vision of his mother appeared. 'Burning a hole, is it?' For a few moments, he was a child again being admonished for spending all his Christmas money in one go. He smiled at the memory. 'I can afford it, Mum,' he assured the image.

The cash came as a windfall, an unexpected and most welcome boost to his modest wealth, the result of a final settlement of his aunt's estate, an aunt whom he had never met and, until the letter from the solicitor arrived, never realised existed. The Healey was his prize - a reward - an acknowledgement for his hard work and success.

A new suit and shoes, befitting a man "on the up," had made a small dent in his inheritance. Plenty left to buy the object of his desire. The polished body of the Austin Healey 3000 Roadster glimmered in the early autumn sun, seductive like an attractive girl preparing for a date.

'Good afternoon to you, sir!' said a voice with what he guessed to be contrived friendliness. He turned to see a thickset man approaching. The face he recognised as the one seen staring at him from the office window. The salesman stood behind him looking uncertain and unhappy.

'Alf Ramsay, owner, and manager!' He extended a meaty paw which Frank gripped with little enthusiasm.

He noted how the northern accent seemed out of place, unexpected in this small outpost in the Home Counties.

'Nice little motor!' said Mr Ramsay, nodding towards the Healey. 'Understand you want to make an offer.'

'Frank - Frank Armstrong. Your salesman's done a great job in trying to sell me the car, but he seems to be stuck with coming to a price meeting my expectations. Perhaps you can help?'

A brief, grateful smile appeared on the young man's face. He was sorry for him again, guessing an angry exchange had taken place in the office. Maybe it was the association with the bullying sergeant who made his life so miserable in those early army days, or perhaps it was the sure knowledge this man treated his young salesman with little respect; whatever it was, he experienced an immediate sense of antipathy towards this over-sized individual.

'Oh yes, I can certainly help you with that. Gregory here - well, he's new and won't have any idea of the true value - particularly when it comes to the high-end sports range. I hope he hasn't confused you in any way?' he said, shooting an angry glance at his novice salesman.

'No, he's been most informative and helpful. As I said, he's done a great job. We can't agree on the final deal and, quite rightly, he's asked for your help with this.'

He saw another brief smile of gratitude on Gregory's face.

'Gregory suggested a price that, to my mind is a little on the high side. But he mentioned one or two extras might be thrown in? I'm paying cash, so I want the best deal possible.'

He turned and addressed Gregory. 'So, what's it to be?'

The flash of anger on Mr Ramsay's face at the affront was almost imperceptible, but it was there, and it pleased him.

20

'You suggested two fifty, Gregory. How about two hundred? For cash,' he added.

Gregory smiled, stepping forward into the scene, the focus now on him, not his manager. 'Two fifty is our best price, I'm afraid - but, well, as you're paying with cash, I think we can offer a small discount, say five percent.' That would be okay, wouldn't it, Mr Ramsay?'

'Come on, you can do better than that. How about twenty percent? I've got the cash. It's here, look!'

Mr Ramsay eyed the wad of banknotes and licked his lips, then said dismissively:

'I would be giving the car away at that rate. My margin's small enough as it is! I can give you seven and a half percent that's my best deal - take it or leave it.'

He stared at Mr Ramsay, then at Gregory, and shook his head. 'No,' he said and turned as if to walk away.

'Hang on!' he heard Gregory's voice raised with a clear hint of desperation. He turned around, noting the sudden reflection of fear on the young man's face as if he knew he had spoken too loudly.

'I think we can do you a ten percent discount - that would be fair wouldn't it, Mr Ramsay, as Mr Armstrong is paying cash?'

Mr Ramsay seemed agitated, and he guessed he was about to contradict Gregory's offer. He stepped forward quickly and gripped the young man's hand.

'That's agreed then - but I'll need a test drive first - just to make sure she runs okay - if she does, I'll pay you the cash today - you'll have your sale.' He smiled at Gregory. 'We'll be needing the car keys.'

Chapter 2

"GREGORY"

Gregory's lack of self-esteem was profound - a serious impediment causing him considerable unhappiness. Had fate not intervened, he might have been a very different person: happier and, yes, more successful.

His early years in Fairfield were happy and carefree. Boyhood adventures would be remembered in vivid detail - they were wonderful years. Alex had been alive then. Alex was always the leader, but being five minutes older than his brother, both accepted this as right and just. Then came that fateful day when a rash decision changed everything. 'Let's take the shortcut over the railway line,' Alex suggested.

The memories would never leave him, his recollection of the events leading to the catastrophe, as vivid now as if they happened only yesterday. He would see himself and his twin brother enjoying a day of fishing at the river. The August weather had been glorious, the fish plentiful. For the eleven-year-old twins, this seemed like Heaven. Time stood still - until the realisation they would be late home dawned on them both at the same time.

'Bloody hell, Dad will murder us!'

Weighed down by baskets, rod holdalls, nets and other paraphernalia, they made slow progress. The shortcut presented itself as their only chance of getting home in time for supper and avoiding a potential good hiding. Alex, the bolder spirit, crossed first. He walked across the first set of tracks then turned, beckoning to him: 'Come on Greg, stop being a chicken, no one will see us.'

The gap in the fence leading from the meadow to the railway line led to the north-bound London line, which ran dead straight, allowing warning of a train. The opposite line curved, offering only seconds warning of danger.

'Come on!' Alex urged. 'Look right, then left, then...'

Gregory decided to follow but his fishing basket, heavy and unwieldy, slipped off his narrow shoulders creating a momentary distraction. Later, when coaxed to relate what happened, he described how he felt the approaching train before he heard and became aware of it. The last enduring image of his twin would be seen in his mind many times, and in the regular nightmares that still troubled him. Alex, clowning as usual and acting out a parody of the road-crossing code, was looking the wrong way. Gregory screamed a warning, but too late. As if appearing from nowhere, the locomotive engulfed his brother with a shrieking of brakes, metal grinding on metal, and the frantic hooting of its siren, coming to a shuddering halt three hundred yards further on.

Shortly after the tragedy, Gregory started at the secondary school alone. 'Far too early, he's not ready, he's still in shock,' his mother said. But his father insisted.

'He's got to come to terms with it. There's no point in letting him feel sorry for himself.'

His first asthma attack followed soon after. 'More than likely psychosomatic,' the doctor suggested. His father agreed. 'All in his mind!' For whatever reason, imagined or otherwise, the affliction took him in its grip.

Now an only child, his mother devoted herself to him and he became, in his father's view, cosseted and enfeebled. Gregory grew quiet and withdrawn. He left school at fifteen with no qualifications. There followed a series of meaningless and boring jobs devoid of prospects.

His father, a travelling salesman, spent much time away from home. Even when he returned from his travels, he preferred to spend evenings in the pub rather than with his wife and son. In his favourite boozer, *The Wagon and Horses*, he made the acquaintance of Mister Ramsay – Alf, as other regulars called him. Both he and Alf shared a love of drinking and flirting with the ladies.

Alf offered to hire Gregory as a salesman. After several pints of ale - a celebration following a win on the horses - he was inclined to be generous. Gregory's father had been bemoaning the fact his son had, once again, lost his job, leaving a dent in the family's income. His dad would never have accepted the fact Gregory had sacked himself because the job had become too much for him. A grocer's boy, responsible for house-to-house deliveries, he rode an ancient, mammoth of a bicycle, with a huge iron rack on the front. The iron monstrosity, precarious with its heavy loads, often left him gasping for air to the point of near collapse.

Kind at first, in a blustering indelicate fashion, Mr Ramsay instructed Gregory on sales technique and showed him how to manage the administration involved in selling cars. Although slow to learn, his confidence grew. Alf, who previously managed his small business on his own, was secretly pleased with the progress of his protégé, congratulating himself on his decision to help his pub friend, particularly as he paid his apprentice a nominal wage with the vague promise of a commission.

Alf had been in the car trade since his demob from the Army. He used his "War Gratuity" to buy the garage and established his business. The sign over the forecourt announced in faded and difficult to decipher words, the motif: "Ramsay's Autos - Quality Cars and Service."

The business failed to flourish largely due to Alf's inability to discern a good sales prospect from a "dog" at auction. He made disastrous purchases, shiny like glittering jewels on the outside, but rotten inside, their mechanical innards beyond permanent repair. Several of these had been parked on the forecourt for over a year, wallflowers at a dance, no chance of attracting interest. His business was just about breaking even.

As with his relationships with people, his dealings with cars lacked understanding and subtlety. He compounded his inadequacy and burgeoning money problems through a compulsion to gambling. Regular flutters on the horses became an enduring habit, often causing him to lose vast amounts of cash on rashly placed bets. More recently, all-night poker games contributed to his losses. Booze helped to ease the pain—but only for brief interludes.

His attitude towards Gregory changed from gruff kindness to open hostility and apparent resentment. He never gave praise or encouragement; instead, his apprentice provided an easy target on whom to take out his many frustrations and increasing bitterness with life. The mistakes, and there were several, encouraged Alf to escalate the level of bullying. But, had he taken the time to examine critically and impartially the background to Gregory's latest apparent "disaster," he might have understood the significant part he played in it himself. His incoherent ramblings were confusing, and often he couldn't be found when his young charge needed help or advice. With more knowledge and experience, Gregory might have seen through his boss's belligerence and realised he represented the real source of incompetence and failure.

***

Gregory accompanied Mr Armstrong on the test drive. They spent a few minutes working out how to fold back the cloth car hood, which caused amusement to them both.

'Call me Frank,' his customer insisted as soon as they climbed into the car.

Gregory found the drive exhilarating. Frank handled the car well and pushed it to its limits within the bounds of safety with apparently assured confidence. They said little, but Frank's comments, difficult to hear above the throaty roar of the 3-litre engine and the rush of the wind, were friendly. Gregory smiled and nodded, conscious his lack of technical knowledge might let him down at any moment. But there were no questions, and he grew more confident and relaxed. He sat back, enjoying the ride, a smile of satisfaction on his face. Success at last!

On their return, Frank switched off the engine and then seemed to ponder for a moment before turning in his seat. 'Ten percent discount, you said?' Gregory nodded. He sighed with relief when he heard the words: 'I'll take it.' They shook hands on the deal.

***

Mr Ramsay was not in his office - this came as no surprise. He'll be at one of his "business meetings," Gregory thought, knowing this to be a euphemism for the bookies. I can handle the paperwork myself, he told himself with his newfound confidence. He set about managing the sales administration, careful not to miss a single detail: a signature here, a name there. Mr Ramsay would use any mistake as an excuse to criticise him, which would spoil his own sense of achievement and triumph.

Frank pulled out a wad of bank notes and counted out twenties and tens before handing them over to him. He counted the money with care, shooting an embarrassed glance back.

'It's fine, I'd rather you checked it. Save any misunderstandings later.'

'Thank you, Mr Armstrong, I mean Frank,' he added in acknowledgement of their familiarity. 'Congratulations, by the way, you've bought a fantastic car.'

'I know,' he replied, grinning in obvious delight.

With the sales administration completed, Gregory stood up and held out his hand. Frank responded with a firm handshake.

'Stick with it Gregory, you're a promising salesman.' He nodded at the manager's office door as though to add gravity to his words. They walked back out to the forecourt and the waiting Healey which shimmered seductively in the faint autumn sunlight.

'Enjoy the car, Frank. It has been a pleasure doing business with you.'

He grinned as Frank gunned the Healey into life. It was, he thought, a most satisfying noise and matched his current mood. Frank shot his hand in the air and waved without turning back as he drove the car onto the main road.

A satisfied customer - Gregory smiled at the thought.

On returning to the office, he picked up the neat pile of banknotes lying on his desk. He knew the money should be secured. Had the boss been there, he would have handed the wad of notes to him - but as he was nowhere to be found, he would have to deal with it himself.

With a weary sigh, expecting he would be in the wrong somehow, he walked into Mr Ramsay's office where the safe was. As he entered, he saw the key sticking out of the shut door. He turned it, then the "T" handle, and pulled the heavy door open. He tutted. Inside was the cash float for the business and several sets of car keys. Mr Ramsay's sense of security was woefully lacking, one of the many examples of ineptitude he had seen in his boss. He placed the banknotes in a neat pile on a shelf and closed the door. The temptation to spin the combination was strong, but his instinct told him not to bother: the boss wouldn't be happy - he only secured it properly when he left for the day.

Later that afternoon, sitting at his desk and waiting for the clock to register 5 o'clock when he could go home, his mind played through every step in the sales process, examining each stage, looking for errors, reasons why he might be criticised and rebuked. He was ever conscious he could, it seemed, do no right: The "Sword of Damocles" hung over his head in the form of Mr Ramsay's wrath. *I'm going to have to defend everything I did.* Self-doubt returned, dulling his recent euphoria.

***

Mr Ramsay was not at the bookies but at the bar of the *Golden Lion*, the pub opposite his small business. Three pints of ale, downed in quick succession, were slow to take the desired effect. He watched as the barmaid pulled a fourth.

'Pour me a Bells as well while you're at it.'

He needed alcohol to dull the thoughts rushing through his head, prodding, and taunting, reminding him of the sure fact he faced financial ruin.

Less than hour ago, his life had been on track - well, bearable at least. But then, he had not been aware of the disaster waiting to fall crashing around his head. He downed half of the whisky - the brief comforting numbness it created was extinguished by the clear image of the brown envelope with the official wording "Inland Revenue" that had filled him with dread. The remembered scenes, thoughts, and emotions of less than an hour ago, were fresh. It might, he reminded himself, have remained undiscovered had he not been so full of bitterness and resentment following the scene on the forecourt.

He recalled how he stomped away from Gregory and his customer - furious and, for reasons he could not fathom, humiliated. *That little shit has undermined me - and in front of a customer! Well, he'll be bloody sorry when I sack him! And as for Mr Sodding Armstrong - smug bastard!*

His mind presented the image of his desk, seen from where he slumped in his chair - it is strewn with paperwork. His rage had reached a crescendo by then and he was planning the tirade of abuse he would give to Gregory later. With an irrational gesture of anger, he had swept his hand across the clutter on his desk, sweeping a swathe of unopened envelopes, unpaid bills and grimy invoices to the floor. The official-looking envelope was revealed in the detritus remaining on the surface. He remembered how he picked it up - the slow movement of his hand, his hesitancy as if the object were alive, dangerous and might bite. As he stared at his pint, he felt again the sense of painful foreboding - the contents meant trouble. The temptation to screw it up unopened had been tempting.

'Oh God,' he muttered, reaching for his beer with a shaking hand, spilling some it down his shirt.

Alf avoided paying tax wherever possible, convincing himself he was merely playing the system, being clever, finding loop holes. *I need the money more than they do - and I'm the one who earned it,* was how he justified his blatant dishonesty. The terse words in the letter had advised him otherwise. A large sum of money - an insurmountable figure - was demanded with a threat of further investigations to follow.

Sod it, I need more of the hard stuff. He ordered another Bells. Ignoring the disdainful look, the barmaid gave him, he downed the whiskey in one, wincing as the burning liquid rushed into his gut, reaching at the same time for his half-finished pint. The rush of alcohol fuelled his deep feelings of self-pity. Not one to acknowledge his own failings or to feel guilt, instead his thoughts raced to identify targets whom he could blame for his dilemma. A suspicion his wife may have betrayed him to the authorities flickered in his mind? 'Bitch,' he muttered to himself, but loud enough for the barmaid to overhear him. She glared at him. He shook his head as if to say, 'Not you,' and focused on the jug of beer in front of him, aware she was watching, judging, and despising him as a drunk.

Could it have been Gregory? No, he thought, he wouldn't have the brains or the balls to drop me in it. Despite the intrusion of his alcohol-fuelled musings, he reached the sure conclusion that the cause of his impending downfall was entirely his own.

Half an hour later, he staggered across the road to the garage. He brushed past Gregory, who appeared to be eager to talk to him, and blundered into his office, slamming the door behind him. Slumped in his chair, not bothering to remove his coat, he stared at the mess on his desk appearing in and out of focus. Soon, he drifted into unconsciousness.

***

Gregory gaped for several moments at the door through which Mr Ramsay stumbled.

Flipping heck, I've never seen him that sozzled before!

A successful sale, the first in days, had been achieved, and Gregory wanted this to be acknowledged. He was realistic, with no expectations of any form of direct praise - but even simple recognition would be welcome. Perhaps this might help to lift their relationship from the depths to which it had sunk.

He avoided the temptation to knock at the door, returning to his desk instead where he sat brooding. With nothing to do - the administrative details around his recent sale now complete, tedium kicked in. He looked at the clock on the wall. Almost shutting time - might as well go home. With a final glance at the door, through which he could hear loud snoring, Gregory put on his duffle coat, searched in the pockets for his bicycle clips and left the office, closing the door behind him.

***

Mr Ramsay woke in darkness, disorientated and confused. It took several moments to realise where he was. The dull thump in his head and the sour taste of stale alcohol augured the approaching hangover. As he reached for the desk light, his hand knocked a glass ashtray onto the floor, spilling cigarette butts. The wall clock showed it was nearly 7 pm.

The recollection of his predicament hit him with a series of taunting images each depicting aspects of his impending ruin. 'Fuck,' he muttered as he raised his head from the cushion of paperwork, 'what the hell am I going to do now?'

He forced himself to think. A vague plan formed in his mind, incoherent and unthinkable at first, but after much internal debate, shaping into a course of action.

'I've got no choice - it's the only way,' he murmured.

Chapter 3

"FRANK"

Frank hated the full version of his name and never used it. His mother, with vague leanings towards socialism but with no real understanding of politics, admired the American President of the time and considered him to be a perfect icon after which to name her only son. Franklyn lived in New York, alone with his mother. He never met his father, a jobbing actor who made scarce as soon as the results of his ardour became apparent.

They shared a poky flat on the west side of Manhattan above the small café where his mother waited on tables. These early years, Frank would remember as happy times despite the threadbare existence in which they survived. His mother, disorganised and chaotic, presented as one of those rare spirits who exuded genuine warmth and happiness. Although unable to recall much detail of his early years, he could remember the laughter and pervading sense of fun.

Melissa, or Missy as everyone called her, had a shambolic, ill-planned approach to everything, including her love life. With a myriad of ill-chosen, random lovers, each bringing an empty promise of salvation that invariably led nowhere, she made many mistakes. Several "uncles" would appear in Frank's first years, only to disappear without a trace.

He was five years old when a British merchant seaman met and fell in love with his mother. Unlike the other men in his mother's life, this one stayed. Albert's character: level-headed, organised and serious-minded proved the adage that opposites attract. They were married just a few months after meeting and, with Albert having a sister in

England, and Missy having no close ties in the USA, they embarked on a liner bound for Southampton.

Albert accepted Franklyn as his own son; however, he refused to call him by his birth name, insisting instead on calling him Frank. It was 1939.

Their arrival in Southampton coincided with the outbreak of war. The privations of rationing did not cause too much of a hardship for them - being hungry was not a new experience for Frank and his mother. But in contrast to their life in Manhattan, he realised new emotions, bleak and unhappy beneath a thin veneer of optimism. His mother seemed less happy-go-lucky, her sense of fun disappeared, replaced with pensive worry. Her husband of fewer than six months was now at sea, absent for long periods.

Years later, Frank would learn about the Atlantic and Russian convoys - Albert's ships, all fuel tankers, took part in both.

He started at infant school in September 1939. Soon after, the order came from a concerned government to evacuate children from cities and towns, the targets for German bombers. Separation from his mother, difficult at first, was soon overcome. He learned to make the most of the situation. His temporary family, a childless couple running a small farm in Bideford, north Devon, looked after the young boy like their own. He would remember this time as happy and carefree. Apart from the regular drone of German bombers, transiting to or returning from their city targets, the war seemed to be at a safe distance.

In late 1941, with the worst of the bombing believed to be over, he returned home to Southampton. Life settled into a routine of normality, at least as far as the war would allow, with school, friendships and adventures in a redefined urban landscape, ravaged by the many thousands of bombs dropped on it from German planes. Bomb sites with hidden treasures of spent, and sometimes live ordnance, to be traded like cigarette cards, were playgrounds of choice.

Life changed forever in March 1945. He would always remember the day, not long after his eighth birthday, when his mother opened the telegram. He would recall how she made no sound, but ran upstairs, closing her bedroom door behind her. Later, she sat him down and told him his father would not be coming home.

***

Frank grinned, thrilled with the sense of ownership. As he pulled off the forecourt, he shot his hand in the air in a triumphant punch upwards where the roof would have been. Although early autumn, the afternoon sunshine felt warm, so he left the hood down. The image of Gregory in the rear-view mirror waved to him with a grin that matched his own.

As he turned onto the main road heading away from the town towards the coast, he slipped the car into top gear and accelerated. The throaty roar of the engine and the rush of air as he gathered speed seemed in perfect harmony with his mood. 'Bloody brilliant!' he shouted, smacking the steering wheel with the palm of his hand. The action sparked a memory of a few years earlier when he had experienced a similar sensation of unrestrained excitement. In that scene, he drove an army staff car collected from the Motor Transport Section at the base.

'Needs running in - but don't overdo it!'

He could recall in vivid detail the Humber, olive green with plates denoting a General still on the front bumper. 'Used to be Monty's car,' the mechanic confided with a serious look on his face. True or not, the thrill proved real: open topped, leather upholstery, the steel rimmed dials and, above all, the assured hum and throb of a powerful and well-maintained V8.

The Colonel, to whom he was assigned as a driver, seemed young for one of such a senior rank, he recalled. But his instruction left no doubt what he wanted: 'Drive as fast as you like, but make sure I arrive in one piece.'

He enjoyed putting the car through its paces, ignoring the instructions to take it easy on the first run. The sudden reminder of what happened later: the accusation followed by an investigation brought him back to the present. Remembered images of that fateful day revealed itself to him at inopportune times and could shatter, like now, the most euphoric of moods. Even though the subsequent enquiry showed he was not to blame, guilt overwhelmed him.

He glanced at his watch. Still plenty of time. A quick mental calculation - yes, time enough to get to Southampton and back along the A27. An hour later, he was stuck in traffic and becoming both impatient and worried. 'If this doesn't start moving soon, I'll be late,' he muttered.

Chapter 4

"INFERNO"

Gregory sat at the dining table staring at his unfinished supper - he had little appetite. A black pall of despondency enveloped him. What's wrong? What's bothering me? He sensed his mother watching him from the chair in the corner near to the small fireplace, her knitting needles clicking and clacking. In the background, a lively dialogue played out from the ancient wireless. He recognised the voices behind the "Navy Lark," a programme that always made him laugh - but not this evening. With a deep sigh, he shoved his plate away and leant back in his chair, gazing at the ceiling.

'Penny for them.'

He sighed and attempted a smile. 'I'm fine - been a rotten day, that's all.'

'Think yourself lucky you've got such a good job. Mr Ramsay was so kind to take you on; you know after...'

'Yes, Mum, I know.'

Small stabs of doubt and anxiety joined his depression. The memory of his boss stumbling into his office and slamming the door behind him flashed through his mind. This is troubling, he thought, but why? At first, he could not decipher his thoughts, but then it came to him with crystal clarity: the root cause of his worry. He remembered the green safe in the corner of the room. The heavy iron door would be shut, as he left it earlier, the key, still in the door. It wasn't locked, he was sure of it.

His mind created a picture of the safe's contents. The cash from his sale that afternoon lies in a neat pile on the shelf where he had put it. Some cheques, banker's orders

- and the keys to the cars on the forecourt were all on view - all unsecured.

A vision presented itself in his mind: the drunken man blundering disorientated to his feet, lurching out into the fresh air. *I bet he forgot to lock the front door as well!*

Gregory possessed an ingrained sense of responsibility - but he balanced this knowing, should a break-in happen, he would be blamed. He imagined the scene: youths spilling out of the *Golden Lion*, their inhibitions dulled through alcohol. *What a gift - an open door! Easy takings!*

He stood - realisation what he must do now certain. 'I've got to go out for a little while, won't be long.' He grabbed his jacket from the stand by the door, ignoring his mother's protests.

Soon, he was on his way. After ten minutes of furious peddling, he narrowly avoided a collision with a car that hurtled from the opposite direction, the driver having failed to see him. *Should have bought batteries for the lamps,* he admonished himself as he wheeled the bike off the grass verge onto which he slid. A few minutes later, he pedalled the last hundred yards to Ramsay's Autos, wheezing and dizzy, falling off the saddle in a heap, gasping to regain his breath.

After a few seconds, he stood. While brushing grit from his trousers, he realised a glow of light emitted from the Manager's office. *Strange,* he thought, how it seemed to pulse and grow, dimming and then intensifying again.

At first, he experienced a sense of relief: *He's in there, probably still asleep.* A gentle shake, some careful handling and an offer to secure the building and the problem would be resolved. *Might even get a "thank you." Well, perhaps that's too much to hope for.*

The front door was unlocked as he feared. He took a step inside. The acrid smell of burning assaulted his nostrils and throat making him cough and splutter. His eyes streamed as he fumbled for the switch and flipped on the lights. A thin fog filled the interior.

With mounting horror, he looked towards Mr Ramsay's office. Smoke eddied through the gaps in the door frame. *He's still in there!* he concluded, panic and uncertainty paralysing him momentarily. *Got to get him out!* He acted on impulse, tearing off his coat and covering his head with it - something told him this might provide some protection. *Better be quick. Got to do it now!*

He stumbled the few paces to the door and, gripping the handle, pushed it open. A sudden blast of air jerked him off his feet and blew him backwards against the back wall where he slumped. He drifted into unconsciousness. The flames, released from the inner office, continued their inexorable destruction of the rest of the building.

***

The proprietor of *Ramsay's Autos* sat ensconced on the same bar stool at the back of the pub where he wallowed earlier that afternoon. Hunched into his car coat, he puffed on a cigarette which only exacerbated a throbbing headache. He took a glug of beer, casting a furtive glance at the door through which he entered twenty minutes before.

'Too bloody late to worry now, Alf,' he muttered.

But he was intensely worried, and his heart thumped in fear. Although far from sober, a sane voice somewhere in the recesses of his inner soul suggested what he had started was nothing short of insane.

He stared at the remaining ale in his glass, his thoughts drawn inwards, piecing together and struggling to rationalise his actions. A series of scenes played in sequence through his mind. He tried to focus his thoughts, to make sense of them – but they seemed confused, seen through drunken eyes.

A dull ache in his shoulder reminded him how he fell against the door frame as he lurched out of the bar and into the car park. He winced as he recalled the frantic hooting of a car horn as he staggered across the road. 'You blithering idiot!' the driver who swerved to avoid him, had shouted.

A brief picture of the outer office area appeared. Gregory is raising himself from his seat at though wanting to talk to him. Next, his memory presented a blurred vision of his desk, covered in debris, and there, right in the centre, the cause of his misery. The brown envelope with the word "Inland Revenue," seemed like a taunt. A sudden blur as his hand swept everything on the desktop to the floor.

'Bloody hellfire, I was arseholed! Probably still am,' he concluded.

He knew he had slept for some time, head down among the detritus on his desk. His next recollection, as he sat leaning on the bar staring at his glass, was a strong impression of being disorientated and nauseous as he woke. His heart thudded again as it did in the office when he experienced panic at the reminder of his financial disaster. He recalled standing too quickly and having to grab the corner of his desk to stop himself from keeling over. When the room finally stopped spinning, he remembered registering the time on the wall clock, and then staggering to the door, flinging it open and looking in to the outer-room. No Gregory - he must have gone home. This was significant, he reminded himself because at this point his plan had germinated.

'Another one, sir?'

Snapped back to the present again, he nodded. 'Yes - pint. Whisky as well - make it a double.'

The drinks in front of him, he drifted back into his semi-dream. His mind presented a depiction of himself back in his own office again, sitting on the corner of his desk as though deep in thought. The incorporeal spectre vanished, and he witnessed imagery as though seeing them for the first time. His déjà vu vision focused on the bin by the side of his chair - it is overflowing with litter. The image disappeared, replaced by another. As though drawn by an undeniable force, he follows himself walking to the corner of the room where the green monolith of a safe stood.

'That's my money, and the flaming Taxman's having none of it!' He looked up with a guilty start, worried the barman might have overheard him - but no, he was busy serving drinks.

He thrust a hand in to his jacket pocket and touched the reassuring roles of banknotes, separated into denominations, each bound with elastic bands. The fact there had been a fresh stack of cash inside had confused him until he remembered Gregory's sale. The thought he had of Mr "Smug Bastard" Armstrong's money brought a momentary smile of satisfaction to his face.

One of his trouser pockets bulged against his thigh. He patted it and frowned. 'Oh yes,' he murmured, remembering the small, square tin with the lid depicting a happy festive family gathering: memories of a Christmas many years before. His fingers took in the scene again - how he flipped off the top and emptied half crowns, florins, shillings, and sixpences into the palm of his spare hand. Some coins, he recalled, dropped to the floor. It was too much effort in his boozed-up state to bend and pick these up.

I could have walked, just buggered off. Plenty of money to escape and lie low with. Maybe go abroad and start again. What made me do it?

'You had no choice,' he whispered as quietly as he could, needing the sound of his own voice assuring him. The bar was filling, he noted, before drifting back to his introspection.

As though being played a film as evidence, he observed the image of himself, perched on the corner of his desk, lighting a small cigar. Once again, he imagined himself back there again, witnessing the scene. The waste basket, full to the rim with screwed-up paper and other litter, is in focus. His cigar is smoked down to the last inch - the tip glows red. The hand - his hand - thrusts the still burning butt deep into the heart of the ready-made bonfire.

The figure of him leaves the office now. It pauses at the door, as if thinking, and turns back, retrieving a half bottle of Bells from his desk drawer, kept for emergencies. He thrusts this into his pocket, switches off the desk lamp and exits, shutting the door behind him.

A welcoming vista presented itself: the warm glow of light from the *Golden Lion* beckoned across the road. But for a few moments, he turns back and surveys the front facade of his business. His final recollection of the events was the sure knowledge of finality.

He gulped greedily from his pint glass followed by a large sip from the chaser. His nerves have calmed a little now, and he thought about the possible outcome of his ruse. *Will it work? And, if it does, is there anything I did or didn't do that might point the finger at me?*

A sudden commotion towards the front door jolted him from his reverie. An elderly man was shouting from the doorway, 'Ramsay's is on fire! The whole place has gone up!'

His heart lurched as he watched punters spilling out in their eagerness to see the catastrophe for themselves. In a few minutes, the pub was empty, except for him. He sat immobile, craning his head to decipher what was going on.

'Someone call the Fire Brigade,' a voice yelled.

'They're already on the way!' shouted another.

He felt a jolt in his chest as the realisation of what he had done hit him. A myriad of emotions rushed through his head dominated by panic. He grabbed the glass of Bells, his hands shaking so much he spilled some of the contents. Downed in two gulps, the desired effect was instant but momentary.

The sound of approaching fire engines, their sirens blending in a cacophony of noise, added to his growing sense of unease. He slid off his seat and lurched to the front door, compelled to witness the results of his deed. He heard muffled shouts - someone screamed.

'That's your gaff, isn't it?'

He shot a frightened side-look at the man, grunted a non-committal response and brushed past him.

'Oh, my God,' he uttered, his shock and fear convincing because it was real. The enormity of the disaster created by his own hand flashed in front of him in startling Technicolor. The main building was an inferno. Huge flames leapt into the night sky with blinding intensity. A car on the forecourt was also ablaze and, as he stared in frozen horror, it exploded with a pop followed by a thunderous bang. The fire engine lights cast flickering shadows through which he could see figures silhouetted: firemen fighting with charged hoses - onlookers getting too near - a policeman arriving on a bicycle, dismounting, waving his arms: 'Get back! Now! Get back!'

Another blast, louder than the first, was accompanied by a reverberating shock wave causing those nearest to stagger backwards. A group of fire fighters were knocked off their feet, the hose they were grappling with dropped and whipping uncontrolled like a demented snake. The eruption lit up the scene, the flash intense, the panorama captured in stark, lucid relief.

When he uncovered his eyes, he registered the image of an Austin Healey 3000, parked at the entrance to the garage. He frowned, distracted for a few moments from the reality unfolding in front of him. *What's that doing there? Did Gregory mess up the sale?* Then he remembered the neat pile of banknotes in the safe - he is confused.

Chapter 5

"THE HERO OF THE MOMENT"

The *Crows Nest*, a popular haunt for holidaymakers during the summer months, offered a warm welcome, a fine selection of ales and spirits, and an extensive menu. The pub garden stretched almost to the cliff edge, bordered by a stone wall on which drinkers would support their drinks while looking out to the sea. Some of the bolder, or perhaps more stupid ones, sometimes sat on the top, dangling their feet over the vertical drop.

The bar opened for the evening trade at 6 o'clock - too early for the main cohort of regulars who would arrive later but perfect for the small number who, having finished their day's work, needed a drink before going home. A group of Council workers stood at the bar - they had spent all day repairing potholes in the coast road. They talked loudly, laughing and in high spirits, enjoying the start of their weekend. As they drank, they cast occasional surreptitious and appreciative glances towards the young woman sitting alone at a table near the entrance.

Helen, conscious of the looks aimed at her, smiled, unable to stop herself. Careful to avoid eye contact, which might lead to an unwanted invitation to join them, she allowed herself a tinge of satisfaction. Men found her attractive, a fact of which she was well aware, and which she found both assuring and pleasing. A glance at the time - a quarter past six. Still early - he's not late - yet.

'Your drink, miss.' The barmaid placed a glass of white wine on the table.

'Thank you. Keep the change,' she said, handing her a shilling.

A sip of wine evoked pleasant thoughts. 'Wonderful,' she whispered, although not in response to the taste but to the memories it evoked. Frank introduced her to wine - German wine, like this one. She found herself day-dreaming about him.

He brought me here on our first date, she recalled, that was back in early March when it had been warm enough to sit outside in the small sun-trap in the pub garden. That first proper date! How wary we seemed of each other - like walking on egg shells!

It took ages before he plucked up the courage to ask me out. She smiled, remembering how he would look at her across the office, his eyes lingering a little too long, giving away his interest and then averting his gaze as if caught out. His approach had been careful - he seemed shy at first - but then, being the boss's daughter might render her, in his eyes, "off limits." No wonder he took his time!

Yes, something about him attracted me to him right from the start. It wasn't love at first sight - nothing so simple, but...

She pondered what had drawn them together. He's a good-looking man for sure. Plenty of girls have made "glad-eyes" at him. This thought prompted a small twinge of jealousy. But it was me he wanted, it was me he singled out, she reminded herself - this sure fact made her smile with satisfaction.

One of the men walked past her towards the jukebox. As if in tune with her thoughts and mood, the *Everly Brothers* started singing "...'til I kissed yah." The song was one of her current favourites.

She smiled, her thoughts turning to Frank again. He has natural charm - not put on in any way. Mind you, he's charming to everyone - but in different ways. You might describe him as being almost old fashioned but with no airs and graces. I'm sure that's what drew me to him.

Her mother's voice whispered to her: 'You've found yourself a Bobby Dazzler there, Helen!'

God, what an awful term! But Mum would have liked him.

Fastidious with her own looks, she saw and appreciated how he took great care of his appearance. He's always dressed well without being flashy. Or is that what a Bobby Dazzler is? Well, whatever it means, I know he's a catch.

Another glance at her watch: just gone half-past. She took another sip of wine and decided not to fret his lateness - he would be here soon enough. The surroundings, even the raised voices of the workmen at the bar, dulled into the background as she slipped in to a daydream again.

We met only ten months ago - gosh, we've come a long way since then - and so fast! Her mind presented brief scenes from their early dates. Those first meetings were separated by days, sometimes by over a week. He worked a sales pitch in Southampton, over forty miles away from Fairfield - too far for daily meets. But every weekend he would return to see her. As their relationship developed, he took every opportunity to visit Head Office on the pretext of meeting with various managers - in reality, to court her. He negotiated a good deal on a room at a local guesthouse on the outskirts of town. From there, a short bus ride took him to the venues where they would conduct their clandestine meetings. The *Crows Nest* perched on the cliff top was quite a way along the coastal road. We both love this place, she reminded herself.

She wondered - not for the first time - about his previous life, of which she had little knowledge. He offered brief snippets such as the fact he had been in the Army, but nothing of substance - it was as if the past was not important - it was the "here and now" that counted for him.

'Not much to tell, really,' he said once when she had pressed, 'Nothing that interesting.' But, when he was relaxed, usually after a few drinks, he would offer tantalising titbits of his former life - an amusing anecdote here - an observation drawing upon his experience there - but no detail to paint a full picture.

Although much of his background remained a secret, this did not worry her. His hidden past would reveal itself over time, she assured herself. In the meantime, a little mystery added to his charm.

During their recent dates, she had raised the subject of marriage. He agreed they should be married, but he appeared non-committal - this was both frustrating and annoying to her.

'I'm all for it, Helen, but what about your dad?' Or, 'Perhaps it might be too early to tie the knot? I mean, shouldn't we leave it a bit longer? After all, we've been together for less than a year.'

She could acknowledge the sense behind what he said - but her certainty they were meant to be a couple made her impatient.

It was now ten to seven. Where on earth is he? He's never been so late before - in fact, he's a stickler for being on time. A small tinge of anxiety - perhaps something's happened? Don't be silly, she rebuked herself, he'll be here any time now. Maybe he's been into London, buying the ring I showed him the photograph of in *Bride's Magazine*. But then no, he wouldn't do that - he'll need me with him to choose the right one - he could never manage that on his own. Could he?

Then again, he hasn't actually proposed, at least not in the conventional sense.

This thought presented itself without warning. *Am I forcing him into this?* Dad's the issue. We both know he's a potential problem. And Frank's more concerned about it than I am. He's been so desperate to keep our relationship under wraps.

She remembered a recent conversation: 'Your dad will sack me if he finds out,' he had said. 'I think he might expect you to raise your sights, Helen. I'm just a bloke who sells vacuum cleaners - he wouldn't want someone like me as a son-in-law.'

'It's not true - Dad thinks the world of you - and as for that social climbing nonsense - for Heaven's sake!' Although this had been her reply, she guessed he wasn't convinced. I'm not exactly sure myself, she thought, as she looked at her near-empty glass.

There was no doubt her father held Frank in high regard. 'He's going places, that young man, you mark my words!' he said on one occasion. But, she acknowledged, Dad may not be so effusive in his praise if he knew his top salesman was courting his daughter.

It's time to come clean - I'm not going to have Dad deciding my future for me. If he sacks him, he'll have to sack me as well! We're going to have to tell him - and soon.

She downed the remaining wine in her glass and nodded as if to affirm her conclusion.

***

With how to react to her father's potential reaction to their marriage plans decided, at least for the time being, Helen's thoughts turned to another nagging worry: the unexpected return of her younger sister, Vee, from university.

Dad's convinced Vee's abandoned her studies, Helen reminded herself. This would never fit with his single-minded determination and focus on achievement.

'She's throwing away such a great opportunity. It's madness. A degree would set her up for life!' he argued.

'But Vee's not giving up university, Dad - she's...,' and this was where she lied, 'simply taking a leave of absence to catch up with her work with no distractions. She'll go back in a few weeks.'

Vee's studies had fallen behind schedule - but this represented only a small part of a much bigger story. Helen knew the real reason for her return home.

'Please don't tell Dad, Helen - he'd have a coronary if he found out the truth.'

What happened to my little sister? The thought made her sad. We've always been very different - but in one year - well, she's transformed into almost a new person, and I'm not so sure I like this version.

When she met her at the railway station two weeks ago, they didn't go home straight away. Instead, she took her to a hotel bar and inveigled the truth from her. The details presented as shocking and troubling - how could she have let this happen? At the same time, she allowed her natural maternal instinct to kick in and promised to support her.

The sound of the door opening disturbed her reverie. She glanced up as a couple entered chatting noisily. Still no sign of Frank!

A sip of wine took her back to thoughts of Vee. In fairness, she is working hard, she acknowledged, catching the bus to the library in town every day except Sunday. And, she reminded herself, Vee had asked her opinion on some of her essays she was working on, and to proof-read her dissertation.

But Vee often returned home after midnight. What on earth could she be getting up to after the library shut? For Helen, her younger sister's welfare created significant worry, magnified by the fact that there were genuine reasons an imminent return to university may not be possible.

A sudden draft of cool air brought her back to the present. She looked up and smiled, half standing as she crooked her arm around his neck and kissed him in greeting.

'At last! Where have you been? I was beginning to think you'd stood me up!'

'Sorry, darling, I got waylaid.'

His face creased in a grin. He's very pleased about something, she thought. Her heart leapt with anticipation. *Is he going to tell me – no, ask me something?* She recalled her recent thought he might have been up to London buying a ring. *Maybe...could he be about to...? Wouldn't that be so perfect?*

She watched him as he walked over to the bar to buy drinks for them, returning a few minutes later with a glass of wine for her and a beer for him. He sat down next to her, the grin still present - the look of eager excitement bursting from his face.

Please, Frank, get on with it! she pleaded inwardly, convinced he was about to propose to her at last.

Her impatience increased when, instead of reaching into his pocket and bringing out a tantalising velvet box, as suggested in her imagination, he engaged in small talk. He's teasing me, she thought, noting that, not once did the grin leave his face.

'Come on,' he said, 'It'll be dark soon and I want to show you something.'

An instant vision of the table in the pub garden, the one at which they sat on their first date, flashed into her mind. *He's going to do it - at last!* She stood and turned towards the rear door.

'No, this way,' he took her arm and guided her to the front door.

A surge of disappointment made her want to cry, knowing the small scene suggested in her imaginings was not to be. As they emerged into the pub car park, he placed his hand over her eyes and with the other orientated her on the spot.

'What do you think?' he said, dropping his hand.

She stared, uncomprehending at first, at the sports car in front of her. The realisation that this object and not the one she hoped for was the root of his excitement hit her with crushing clarity. The car seemed posed, she noted, parked at an angle, its silver-spoked wheels turned as if to create a pleasing image.

'What do you think? Isn't she a beauty?'

She detected hesitation in his voice and sensed her reaction was not what he expected.

'Is it yours?' Her voice pitched the words as if in accusation.

He nodded, frowning, the grin now gone. 'I got money from an inheritance I didn't know I had. So, I bought it as a present for us. I thought you'd be happy.'

She heard the doubt in his voice, knowing he expected her to share his enthusiasm. For the briefest of moments, she felt almost sorry for him. But then an image of the small velvet box appeared and then evaporated. Her own feelings of disappointment overwhelmed her.

'How could you? How could you waste money on this, this...?' She waved her hand towards the car. Not waiting for a response, she turned away from him and stormed back into the pub.

In the brief moments, it took for him to follow her back inside, she had retrieved her coat and was putting it on.

'Come on, Helen, let's sit down and talk about it over a drink.'

'No, I'm going home and, and I suggest you think about why I'm so upset about this.'

He looked at her as if unable to comprehend.

'We need money for our future, can't you understand that?' Her voice was raised. She glanced towards the men at the bar, conscious they were watching the scene with interest.

'Dad can't be expected to pay for everything, you know that!' The tirade within her erupted - she couldn't stop herself - heads turned, curious to know what was going on. Time to go before I embarrass myself, she thought, lifting her handbag from the arm of the chair.

'I'm going,' she announced, walking towards the door. 'And I suggest, you...,' she left the sentence unfinished as she walked through the door and into the car park.

Moments later, the door crashed open and Frank appeared. 'Hang on, for Pete's sake, let me at least give you a lift home!' he shouted after her.

'In that thing,' she spat the word, 'I'd rather walk.'

'But...' he began, 'you can't, possibly...'

'There's a bus in five minutes,' she snapped back, 'I'm going to get that.'

***

Frank leant against his car, fumbled in his pocket for a cigarette and lit it. He eyed the bus stop across the road where, in the shadows thrown by the gathering twilight, Helen stood looking away from him. The bus arrived at 7 o'clock; she disappeared inside, and it drove away.

His smoke didn't provide the desired calming effect. Confusion at Helen's reaction turned to anger. 'Sod you, then!' he muttered, grinding the butt into the gravel of the car park with his heel. The thought of re-entering the pub and ordering a beer was tempting - but his recollection of the amused expressions on the faces of the workmen at the bar quashed that notion.

He stepped back from the car and surveyed it, realising the excitement and thrill of ownership had dissipated. 'Bollocks!' he exclaimed to the empty car park. The urge to leave the scene of his humiliation was strong. He climbed into the Healey, gunned the engine and, moments later, wheels spinning on the gravel as he turned the car into the road a little too quickly, he started his journey back to town.

Evening twilight merged into darkness, which matched his mood. 'I should have known she would spoil everything,' he said out loud, slapping the steering wheel in his frustration. 'Wouldn't be the first time, would it?' he muttered, his anger simmering. 'For Christ's sake, I can't be in the wrong all the time, can I?'

The fond feelings for her that stirred his heart earlier in the day were gone - now darker thoughts dominated.

It's always the same: I do something wrong - at least in her view - she goes into a huff and we don't speak for days. Of course, once I've grovelled to her satisfaction, everything's fine again. Well, not this time! Why shouldn't I own a sports car? I work hard and damn well deserve a reward. Oh yes, I don't suppose it would have been an issue if it wasn't me but one of those well-bred, educated types her dad wants her to take up with. They would be entitled - but not me - not with my working-class background. I mean, who the hell do I think I am buying a decent car?

As he drove, he created an inventory of occurrences in their ten-month relationship, providing evidence of her unreasonableness. A rush of images appeared in his mind taunting or perhaps challenging him to justify why he always caved in to her. As each scene played, his bitterness grew. His inner-voice refused to be silent.

Sometimes, she takes umbrage because my reaction on seeing her after a few days of separation is not sufficiently enthusiastic. Oh yes, and she got in a right old strop on the one occasion I didn't telephone at the exact time she expected me to call her - I mean, come on, I came up with a good excuse why I didn't. A small voice of reason suggested his excuse had not been entirely true - but this reminder was extinguished - he didn't want to be reasonable, not now.

The memory of a recent event prompted more bitter thoughts. They were in a restaurant.

'Do you find that waitress attractive?'

Although said sweetly, hidden venom lurked. 'Am I not enough for you?'

'Oh, come on Helen, I was just being nice to her.'

'No, Frank - I saw the look in your eyes - you were *undressing* her.'

'And the birthday present!' Frank was talking aloud again, remembering a different scene. 'Oh yes, we won't forget that occasion in a hurry, will we?'

He said this to an invisible partner sitting in the passenger seat - where Helen should have been. The remembered scene played through his mind.

'Come on, Helen, hurry up, the taxi will be here any minute!'

A table at an expensive restaurant awaited them and he was becoming anxious.

'Won't be a moment, I'll be with you in second.'

She struggled through the door, balancing a large, elaborately wrapped box in her hands. 'Happy Birthday, Frank,' she said smiling.

He had torn off the wrapping to quickly, impatient, conscious the taxi might be waiting outside - he hated lateness.

'Careful, it took me ages to wrap it up so nicely. You could at least take care and not just rip it open.'

The briefcase smelled of treated leather and there were shiny brass reinforcements on the bottom corners. The clasp bore his initials "FDA" engraved in copperplate letters. It was, without doubt, an expensive gift and given, he knew, with the best of intentions. Helen must have seen the look on his face - not the one of radiant joy and gratitude she expected to see.

'You can throw out your tatty old one now,' she said with an edge of doubt in her voice.

'But I like my old one, my mother...,' he protested. He remembered the look on her face - first confusion then hurt.

'Come on, you needed a new case,' her voice rising now, 'you can't hang onto your old one forever - for heaven's sake, the thing's falling to bits.'

As he drove, he recalled his sense of guilt, knowing how ungrateful he sounded, and sensing her disappointment at his reaction. But, he reminded himself, she did not seem to understand what that old briefcase meant. To him, it represented heritage and therefore significance.

'I'm so proud of you, Frank,' he could hear his mother's voice, her American accent still strong. She gave it to him - a present to celebrate his passing of the "Eleven Plus" examination, which marked his entry to the grammar school he would attend until he reached fifteen. Old, battered, falling to bits - it made no difference to him: the case meant a great deal and he would not allow it to be discarded as a piece of unwanted rubbish.

Frank remembered his response: salt on the wound: 'But there's nothing wrong with my old one.' He couldn't stop himself.

She had turned away from him, but not before shooting him a look filled with emotion: disappointment, hurt, anger; her eyes glistening with tears. He apologised moments later - but too late - the damage had been done.

Wouldn't talk to me for days after that, he reminded himself. Five quid, I paid for those flowers - almost half a week's wages! And she still made me agree to throw out my old one!

Recollection of their past disagreements combined with his thoughts about this latest falling out. His anger and frustration would not subside.

'Is this what I want? Is it really?' he asked himself, frowning, troubled by the thought. He shivered, wishing he had taken the time to put up the hood before driving away. The air rushing across the top of his head felt cold, and his hands gripping the leather-bound steering wheel were feeling numb.

The headlights, carving a swath into the night, reflected in the eyes of animals, probably foxes, peering from the undergrowth at the side of the road. As he entered the town again, the driver of an approaching car flashed his lights at him. He frowned for a moment before realising his own were on full beam - and he was speeding. He slowed down, breathing heavily.

'Come on, get a grip - no point in killing yourself,' he told himself.

He spotted the sign for *Ramsay's Auto's* lit by his headlights. Without knowing why he felt compelled to slow down and then stop the car outside the garage entrance. With the air no longer rushing across his head, everything seemed strangely still. He sniffed, detecting the smell of burning. He cast a glance across to the right where the *Golden Lion* was illuminated from within. Probably coming from the chimney - damp wood, maybe. A vision of a warming fire and the calming effects of a good pint of real ale presented itself. No, it's not the pub. He looked to the left, back towards the garage.

A pulse of light appeared to throb from the office building beyond the row of cars at the front. That's weird - something's not right here. A wavering glow, as if from a candle but much stronger, could be seen through the window - the one through which the large red face of Mr Ramsay had glowered at him. The stench of burning stung his nostrils.

Then he realised. 'Oh, bloody hell, the place is on fire!'

He turned the Healey into the garage forecourt and got out, surveying the scene in front of him. His immediate thoughts suggested he should run over to the pub and raise the alarm. But he made out the shape of a bicycle on the ground next to the office door, which, he noticed, hung open. Even though the darkness was thickening, he could see wisps of smoke emerging through the doorway.

Still uncertain whether he should run across the road, he shot a frightened glance in the pub's direction. A man was passing, walking his dog.

'Hey, you! Yes!'

The man stopped and turned.

'Call 999, will you - the garage is on fire.' The man raised his arm in acknowledgement.

'Tell them to send an ambulance as well - I think someone may be in there,' Frank shouted.

He hesitated for a few moments, still undecided as to his course of action. Then, his decision made, he pulled the handkerchief from his jacket breast pocket and, clamping this over his nose and mouth, approached the open door. When he reached the entrance, his eyes were streaming, and he stopped to wipe them. He poked his head through the gap and appraised the situation. Smoke was billowing from a door to the right - Mr Ramsay's office, he remembered. Hungry tongues of flames licked across the ceiling - the heat, apparent to him for the first time, felt intense.

With streaming eyes, blurring his vision, he looked around the outer area. Through the haze, he made out the shape of a body sitting in a slumped position against the wall to the left. He took a tentative step inside, feeling his hair scorching - the heat was becoming unbearable.

'Got to move - fast - before it's too late,' he murmured.

A memory, one he had tried to bury, returned, reminding him what he must do - what he had not done then: act now! For a few moments, he is back there again, lying bruised and bleeding on the road, staring at the staff car with its open top in which the young colonel, unconscious, as if asleep, sat in the rear seat. The recollection of the sudden flash of blinding light as the car exploded made him wince. He had lain immobile, paralysed with fear. A few seconds, the briefest of opportunities to save a life - and he had failed.

'Not this time!' he shouted. Holding his breath, he ducked into the office, covering in seconds the few yards to where the body slumped. The acrid fumes made his eyes stream, and he stumbled blindly, stooping low to avoid the rippling flames rolling across the ceiling. He reached out in front of him and fumbled to find the body now obscured by smoke. There was a leg - he worked his way up, seeking somewhere to grip so he could lift the weight onto his shoulders. The fumes and intensifying heat almost overwhelmed him - it was impossible to breath - he choked and coughed. Instead of attempting to raise the body, he grabbed both legs, knowing he had seconds to achieve his task. With what little strength and consciousness he had remaining, he dragged the body backwards to where he guessed the door was. Later he would recall being aware that others were present, helping him to pull the body clear.

He heard the shouts, the sound of engines and pumps, the urgent ringing of sirens and bells as he drifted in and out of consciousness.

'Well done, mate, looks like you were just in time. You saved that young man's life!'

Frank nodded, smiled, and then passed out.

Chapter 6

"ALF'S REGRET"

The first light of dawn crept in from the eastern skyline. A swirling mist carpeted the ground, obscuring everything under waist height. The cliff top was deserted except for a solitary car and its occupant. It was too early for the first of the dog walkers, who would not arrive for at least another hour.

The car, a grey two-tone Rover 100, stood parked with its engine running. Inside, the figure of a man sat immobile, hunched into his car coat, gazing unseeingly at the windscreen misted over in front of him. He shivered - the warmth offered by the heater feeble.

Mr Ramsay, the once proud proprietor of *Ramsay's Autos*, delved into his scrambled thoughts. Although not sober - he had taken several nips of Bells during the long, uncomfortable night – with his reasoning now less befuddled from alcohol, the flaws in what he considered yesterday to be the perfect solution to his troubles, now seemed obvious.

'You idiot, Alf - what the hell have you done?' he muttered.

The images appearing in his mind were intense, and the most devastating scenes presented in graphic, accusing detail. Once again, he witnessed the flashing lights of the fire engines, the flickering silhouettes of men busy fighting the inferno engulfing his business. He squeezed his eyes shut, remembering the blinding flash of exploding cars.

'They've found someone inside!' someone had shouted. 'He's lying on the ground. They're trying to bring him round.' A short pause and then the voice had added, 'He's in a bad way.'

He knew straight away who that person must be. In confirmation, someone else yelled: 'It's a young lad. They think he works there!'

He relived the sense of panic, paralysing him with fear - and recalled how an urgent desire to distance himself from the scene of his lethal folly swept through him. His head down, he had slunk away, hoping no one would notice, not wanting to be recognised or challenged.

The memory of his inebriated stumble to his car, parked at the far end of the forecourt, played again. He followed the remembered image of his hand trembling, struggling with the effort of inserting the key in the lock - his other hand joining it to steady the aim.

Once again, he experienced the same sensation of crushing guilt that overwhelmed him as he sped away, desperate to distance himself from the disaster.

When he exited the town at the end of the illuminated High Street, instant darkness registered the fact his headlamps were not on. Unable to see, fear of crashing caused him to brake suddenly, stalling the engine. He remembered how he turned his head, expecting to see a blue flashing light behind him.

It had taken a nip of Bells to sooth his agitation. After gathering his thoughts and wits, as much as a drunken man was able, he started the car, driving with exaggerated care, headed towards the coast road.

As he drove, he recalled how he wanted to witness the results of his ruse - to confirm it was working. At first, it seemed everything would go to plan. When he emerged from the pub, the intensity of the destruction he'd caused had shocked him - but this was accompanied by murmurings of satisfaction at the success playing out before him. He imagined himself looking aghast and devastated as the Police informed him his business had burnt to the ground. 'Kids, probably,' the imagined policeman said.

But everything had gone devastatingly wrong.

As he drove away as fast as he could, he was following a vague plan suggesting he should drive to Portsmouth, or Dover, or anywhere that a ferry might be boarded for France. But the futility and impracticality of this idea soon became clear. 'No bloody passport!' a rational part of his mind reminded him. On top of this, it did not take long to acknowledge to himself he was drunk, panicking and irrational.

The "Parking" sign had beckoned to him a mile along the road and he heeded its call, turning in and parking his car near to the fence marking the cliff edge.

Almost as soon as he applied the handbrake, he had fallen into a fitful slumber. But the respite from reality gained through sleep was disturbed throughout the long night. Bone-numbing chill prodded him awake before he could escape into slumber and after this, he only dozed for minutes at a time. In his waking moments, scenes of the evening before taunted him.

He could not stop shaking: cold, anxiety and the effects of alcohol all combining to grip his body. A sudden thought: he fumbled in the glove compartment through the detritus inside. Relief - there it was, a battered pack of Embassy Number 6. He shook it into his palm and two cigarettes dropped out, one of them broken, the other pinched and bent but still offering a full smoke. Best keep that one for later. The partial cigarette once lit, provided the small comfort of a drag or two before burning to the filter.

'Oh God, what have I done?' he murmured, not for the first time.

That he would be accused of arson presented as an irrefutable fact. On its own, this might not have been so bad - he might have rationalised it - planned a way to divert the accusation. That issue shrunk into insignificance as he pondered what he had done. What was Gregory doing there when he should have been safely at home?

'I killed him - I murdered that boy.'

He spoke aloud, sure in the knowledge what he said was true, acknowledging the full weight of his guilt.

'I'm sorry Gregory - I'm so sorry - I never meant this to happen.' For the first time since he was a child, Mr Ramsay wept.

After a few minutes, he composed himself and, feeling the need for some calming sustenance, reached into his coat pocket and pulled out the bottle of Bells. Relieved there was still sufficient whisky left to help numb the pain, he leant back in his seat allowing himself a momentary hiatus of satisfaction. After extracting the remaining cigarette from the packet, he lit it and inhaled, welcoming the familiar dizzy sensation as the smoke entered his lungs. He unscrewed the top of the Bells and took a long sip, savouring the taste for a moment before swallowing, sighing as the comforting warmth slipped down to his belly.

Time to face the music. This thought came to him with unexpected clarity as if buried in a rational part of his soul, a small remnant of whatever good remained within him.

No point in running away - nowhere to run to.

For all his many faults, Alf Ramsay was not a coward - a Military Cross hidden in his sock drawer could attest to that fact. In another life, only to be remembered in his nightmares, he risked his life to save his platoon by providing covering fire for them as they retreated from an advancing German patrol, leaving him alone in the dugout.

With his sleeve, he wiped the condensation from the windscreen and stared blearily at the scene revealed. The fence marking the cliff edge was, he noted, only about twenty feet away, much nearer than he thought. He raised the bottle to his lips and emptied the rest of the fiery liquid into his mouth, at the same time slipping the gear stick into first, pressing down the clutch and releasing the handbrake.

The pain ripped from his jaw down into his chest. He cried out, choking as he inhaled some of the whiskey. His hands left the steering wheel and flayed the air. His right foot flattened the accelerator to the floor of its own volition.

The Rover shot forward. For a few seconds, the loose wire slung between the fence posts halted the momentum of the car - then it snapped, allowing the car to continue its inexorable journey to the drop just beyond.

He did not feel terror as the car toppled, then plunged to the ground a hundred feet below. Nor did he experience the last moments before his car, and his body entombed within it, smashed onto the rocks to be engulfed by the incoming waves. Mr Ramsay was already dead.

Chapter 7

"THE AWARD"

(Wednesday 18th November 1959)

'If I might have your attention,' yelled the Mayor in a high-pitched voice, standing at a lectern, trying to make himself heard above the hubbub of conversation, laughter, and general background din filling the Town Hall.

A council clerk, by nature quiet and taciturn, but his spirit fuelled through several glasses of rum punch, clinked his glass with a spoon a little too hard, shattering it. Eyes turned towards the noise. Someone cheered. 'Sack the juggler!' shouted another voice.

'Thank you, Arnold,' said the Mayor, scowling at the clerk who blushed with embarrassment. With all eyes now upon him, he coughed and addressed the room, his voice quavering - he had never got over his fear of addressing crowds.

'This is a very special occasion,' he started in a hesitant voice. He surveyed the room seeking encouragement. A bird-like woman waved from the crowd. He focused on her as if no one else existed in the room. Now oblivious to everyone other than his adoring wife, his confidence grew. With words rehearsed in his private room while adorning himself with the finery marking his office and status, he launched into his speech.

'We are here to acknowledge the bravery of a member of our community.'

What followed could only be deciphered by those standing a few feet from him. The Town Hall thronged with people who, more interested in imbibing free alcohol than hearing the Mayor's discourse, would be happy to celebrate anything. Raucous cheering, scattered applause, and sporadic whistling drowned out the details of the speech.

***

Frank stood a short distance from the lectern - the Town Clerk told him to stand there in readiness to be called forward. He stared at the parquet floor between his feet, standing in a form of relaxed attention, as the Mayor began his oration. How he wished the ground might open and swallow him.

It was just over two weeks since the incident at the garage. He spent the first week in a hospital bed - but then boredom and a desire to return to work took over. Despite the doctor's protestations, he discharged himself. Their row forgotten it seemed, Helen pleaded with him to remain in Fairfield. 'You need looking after. Come and stay with us - there's plenty of room - and Dad...'

He guessed she had admitted their relationship - this worried him - another reason to go back to Southampton and let things blow over. The thought of being ensconced under the same roof as his boss filled him with horror. Things were happening too quickly. He needed space to think.

A few days ago, having returned to Fairfield for a meeting at the depot, he arrived at his digs to find a scrawled note from the landlady pinned to his bedroom door. 'Shit!' was his response when he read the message: *"You need to phone your boss straight away - urgent."* An imagined conversation, a one-way discourse, Bob to him, culminating in: 'You're sacked!' played through his mind as he dialled the number. But that didn't happen. Instead, Bob's raised voice announced: 'Wonderful news! You're being awarded a medal!'

Frank felt relief rather than excitement when he put the phone down. 'I'm not going to be given the boot after all!' But, as he sat in his favourite dockside pub back in

Southampton later that night, enjoying a second pint and smoking a cigarette, he warmed to the prospect of being acknowledged as a hero.

Mind you, I'll need to buy a new suit if I'm going to the Palace. His conviction he would be invested by Royalty evaporated when, on the following day, he received the official notification forwarded on from Bob in which he learned he was to be honoured with a local, civil award by the Mayor of Fairfield and not, as he imagined, a more substantial gong by the Queen.

Helen chastised him for his ingratitude when he expressed his disappointment to her: 'It will be useful in so many ways. Dad hasn't stopped talking about you and...'

'You've told him about us, haven't you? I knew it. I thought we'd agreed that...'

'Well, yes, we did. But, I thought it time - and with, well, you know, your new status, and...'

'But...'

'It's fine. Anyway, I'm pretty sure he'd guessed we've been seeing each other.' She hesitated, and he detected a shadow of guilt flicker across her face.

'Did you tell him, we're...'

'Planning on getting married? Sort of - but...'

This conversation took place in a pub the night before the ceremony. Helen, he recalled, seemed evasive. This worried him. He had lain awake for most of the night worrying, convinced he would be sacked if her father found out the true extent of his relationship with his daughter.

***

The Mayor persevered in his oration, oblivious to the fact few could make out what he was saying. At last, turning to face the focus of communal gratitude, he smiled, nodding, beckoning Frank to step forward.

65

The urge to run and escape became almost overwhelming. Conscious all eyes in the room were upon him, and aware the cheers and claps were, in most cases, far from genuine, he felt embarrassed and self-conscious.

The Mayor coughed, reaching for the card lying on the silver tray on the table in front of him. With his glasses now perched on the end of his long, angular nose, he emitted a pompous sounding 'Ahem.' A ripple of laughter erupted from a small group of young men, enjoying the occasion through alcohol-fuelled lenses. Annoyed shushes from the surrounding crowd silenced them - for the time being.

'It gives me great pleasure to award Mr Franklyn Delano Armstrong...' The Mayor's voice was high-pitched, and he sounded comical, at least from the perspective of the same cluster of drunken youths hushed a few seconds before. Hoots of laughter drowned out what he said next.

Frank groaned, focusing on the parquet floor again, wishing it might open and swallow him.

'… in recognition of his conspicuous courage,' the Mayor continued, glowering at the young men and making a mental note to have strong words with Arnold, his clerk, who appeared to be the ringleader, '…this civic award.'

He held up the small medal in its velvet box like an exhibit at an auction. The room exploded in a roar of clapping and shouts, drowning out his attempts to complete his carefully prepared speech.

The Mayor handed both the frame and the box to him. More applause and cheering. An awkward shuffling of items enabled a handshake. A paternal arm was placed across Frank's shoulders and he was propelled around to face a waiting press camera. He creased his face into what he hoped reflected a suitable "I don't deserve this," type smile.

A flash - he blinked, releasing the limp and sweaty hand. The formalities were over at last. He mumbled polite thanks and moved away, looking around him for a drink.

'I'm so proud of you!' Helen said, taking his arm and steering him away. He smiled, relaxed now he was no longer the centre of attention. He showed the medallion to her, a small silver laurel leaf-shaped badge nestling in purple velvet.

'I'm not sure what I'm supposed to do with this!' he said smiling.

'Perhaps you could wear it on your tie, or on your lapel,' she offered.

'This can go on our loo wall!' he said, referring to the framed certificate.

'We'll need a house with a loo first,' she said laughing.

He smiled at her, glad they had put their previous disagreement behind them. His act of heroism had extinguished any animosity she harboured towards him due to his purchase of the Healey - at least for the time-being. 'But, I wonder how long the peace will last,' an internal voice of cynicism whispered. 'What will the next argument be about?' Such thoughts faded to the back of his mind - at this moment, he needed a drink. He looked around him for one of the tray-bearing stewards.

'Congratulations Frank, you're a credit to the company!' Helen's father had appeared.

'Thanks, Bob. It seems - well - over the top! I didn't do much - just in the right place at the right time.'

'No, that's not the case - you showed real courage. Not everyone would have done what you did. Give yourself some credit and stop being so damned modest!' He put his arm around his shoulders and squeezed.

'Let's put those things away somewhere safe. Free up your hands - I'm guessing you could do with a drink!'

Frank slipped the box into his jacket pocket and placed the framed certificate on a nearby table. Bob beckoned to a hovering steward. They each took a glass.

'Can you make a toast, Dad?' Helen asked with an expectant expression on her face. Bob laughed, coughed then raised his glass.

'To a brave man,' he said, looking him in the eyes - 'one who I will be proud to call my Son-in-Law.'

Frank shot a glance at Helen, who, at that point, appeared to find something wrong with her right eye. She fumbled in the depths of her handbag and withdrew a handkerchief, then, muttering something about 'going to the ladies to splash my face,' walked away in what seemed like unseemly haste.

'I'm guessing I put my foot in it, Frank - sorry about that,' said Bob smiling. 'Come on, though, I'm not a complete idiot, you know. I didn't need Helen to tell me you and she are an item. Everyone in the office knows I should imagine.'

'We agreed not to say anything yet. There are a lot of things to sort out before we make any announcements. But, since the cat's now out of the bag, are you okay with the idea? I mean, shouldn't I be asking for your permission?'

Bob laughed, 'Well if you're asking, the answer is yes, I'm delighted! Let's drink to it!'

They chinked glasses, and both downed the sickly concoction in one. 'Christ!' said Bob, 'We'll need something stronger than this gnat's piss!'

Frank nodded. 'I'll drink to that!' he agreed.

Bob surveyed the room - the crowd had thinned. 'I reckon things are wrapping up here; the Mayor's already gone, so I reckon we can escape to the pub now and get a decent drink.'

'I would put money on quite a few people nipping across the road,' said Frank. 'Seems like the community's in the mood for a party. Hang on, Helen's on her way back.'

Bob took charge, much to his relief. 'Come on, Helen, we're off to the pub for a proper celebration.'

He went off in search of his coat, leaving them regarding each other.

'Sorry, Frank. I told Dad - last night when I got in after seeing you. I thought he should know - didn't seem right keeping the news from him. Anyway, as you've no doubt gathered, he's delighted - especially now you're a local hero. He's jumped the gun a little, though - I said we're *planning* on getting hitched.' She held up her hand and wriggled her wedding finger with exaggerated meaning. 'Not that we are *actually* engaged.'

'Okay - hey, I'm fine with it. You have no idea how relieved I am. I thought he'd flip and sack me on the spot! Come on, we might as well celebrate, then!' He paused before adding with a grin, 'With your dad.'

He could see Helen was about to protest. 'What's up, Helen?' he whispered. 'A few drinks will do us both good.'

'Here it comes,' said the knowing voice in his head.

'Alright - yes, of course. It's your day after all. But let's celebrate your bravery award, not the fact we're going to be married - we'll celebrate that when we get engaged - I mean, once you finally get around to putting a ring on my finger.'

He nodded. 'Okay - listen, Helen, we can go up to London on Saturday, once I've sorted things out in Southampton. Let's make a day of it - choose a ring for you; maybe take in a show or a film. Perhaps we might stay overnight in a hotel together?' This was said with the full expectation of a rebuff.

'I like the sound of that. Come on, you deserve a drink,' she said, much to his surprise.

He saw the happy smile on her face and that pleased him.

***

'The thing is, you're a good salesman - actually an excellent one - you've proved that. But...'

Bob, well on his way to being drunk, tapped Frank on the chest as if to emphasise his words.

'You're wasted on the door-to-door nonsense. You need to move up, take on more responsibility.'

Frank, pacing himself, and, more experienced than the older man in imbibing volumes of alcohol, remained coherent and in control of his faculties.

'So, what do you have in mind?' he asked, feeling he was humouring him but trying to give the earnest impression he was listening seriously. He glanced at the nearby table where Helen, having encountered a girlfriend, chatted animatedly. No chance of rescue from that quarter. Bob swayed slightly. Frank held out a steadying hand.

'I want you to come and support me in Head Office. We're growing the business, diversifying our product range, and I need you to help me.' He nodded emphatically in an exaggerated way as if wanting Frank to nod in unison, signalling fervent agreement.

A surge of excitement made his heart beat faster. But then the voice of doubt dulled his sudden enthusiasm. Although ambitious, he retained a realistic view of his prospects. His lack of qualifications remained a real obstacle to his career progression; he could see no way of moving up, other than to increase his income by selling more. But then realisation dawned - he was being offered a leg up - his current hero status, and the fact he would soon be hitched to the Boss's daughter being significant factors in this.

'I'm not sure, Bob.' Let's test this out, he thought. 'I'm just a salesman at the end of the day, and I've no idea how a head office works - all that administration stuff.'

'I'll teach you!' Bob stabbed his index finger into his chest again, talking a little too loudly. 'You'll be my right-hand man. I'll show you the ropes - won't take a bright lad like you long to pick it up,' he said clapping him on the back and grinning.

'Come on Dad, I think we should go home now.'

Helen appeared at his shoulder. Frank noted the look she shot him - her eyes raised, questioningly.

'It's been a long day,' she whispered, 'I need to go home. Sue will give us a lift.' She nodded towards her friend who waved from her table where she and Helen had been in conversation.

'I'm going to stay for a while if that's okay with you. I'll catch the bus later. Just need to relax - especially after the ear-bending your dad's been giving me!'

Helen seemed to be about to protest - but, at this point, Bob stumbled into them both. Frank grabbed him, almost falling over with the unsteady weight pressing on him.

'Think we'd better get him out before he causes a scene,' he said pulling Bob's arm over his shoulder, holding him upright.

Sue joined them and together they helped Bob out of the pub and into the car park. After several moments during which he threw up, apologising and groaning in equal measure, they persuaded him into the back of Sue's car where he slumped and fell asleep.

Frank tried not to look pleased there was no room in the car for him.

'Don't stay too long, Frank - don't forget you're driving to Southampton in the morning.'

'I'll only stay for one - I need to think about what your dad said. Listen - I'll tell you about it tomorrow night when I phone.'

***

With five minutes of drinking time left, Frank was both drunk and penniless. The young men, the same ones whose noisy behaviour caused annoyance at the reception earlier in the afternoon, had welcomed him into their midst. Frank bought all the drinks, which seemed to enhance his hero status. An hour passed in raucous joking and laughter - and then he ran out of money.

'Last orders, ladies and gentlemen!'

All eyes turned to him, expecting yet another free drink. But they were to be disappointed.

'Cheeky bastards - how about one of you lot getting the last round in?'

Inebriated, yes - but he knew when he was being taken advantage of. The mood changed. Dark looks were exchanged, glasses emptied, and, within a few minutes, the young men drifted away leaving him alone at the bar. But not entirely. One of their number, Arnold, lay face down on a plate of sandwiches. A full jug of ale stood in front of his submerged head.

'Nice one,' Frank muttered, lifting the pint and downing half of it in three huge gulps, conscious of the barman's look.

'Time, please! Come on, haven't you got homes to go to?'

He placed the empty glass down with an unintended bang and, waving goodbye to the landlord, lurched toward the door.

The last bus departed half an hour ago, and a long walk to the guest house didn't seem appealing. He considered driving. The Healey seemed to beckon to him from its parking spot outside the Town Hall where he'd left it. He stumbled across the deserted road and, after several unsuccessful attempts to insert the key in the driver's side door, he gave up and allowed common-sense to kick in.

He turned and began his unsteady walk home. It would, he knew, take the best part of an hour to complete his journey - but so what?

'Things are working out just fine and dandy,' he said aloud, smiling as his mind conjured up images of a bright and successful future.

Chapter 8

"VEE"

Virginia, or "Vee", as she preferred to be known, applied the final touch of bright red lipstick and, with a small adjustment to the beret perched on her cropped black hair at a rakish angle, surveyed the finished product in her dressing table mirror. 'You'll do,' she said, nodding to her reflected persona.

She rummaged through the drawer and took out a tin containing the secret stash of tobacco and cigarette papers hidden inside, dropping it into her canvass shoulder bag, decorated with a large CND badge etched in biro, in readiness for the day ahead. The "roll-up" represented an essential accoutrement supporting the alternative front cultivated at university. Helen hated the image and everything it stood for - being unconventional was an attitude her elder sister could not, and never would understand. This thought made her smile. But then, as she glanced at her reflection again - her smile faded to a frown.

As she ventured onto the landing, she heard movements downstairs. It would be Helen, no doubt busying herself around the kitchen. 'Bugger,' she whispered - her plan to escape the house without having to face her sister and the inevitable questioning, thwarted.

Tiptoeing down the stairs, she recalled how keen Helen had been for her to be at the award ceremony.

'But surely you can spare an hour or two, Vee – Dad will be there and, well, I know Frank is so looking forward to meeting you.'

'Sorry, I can't, Sis - if I don't finish my essay in time for the late post, I'll miss the deadline,' she said. Helen's face showed both disappointment and a hint of disbelief.

'Well, okay. But try to join us in the evening - we're bound to go on somewhere - a pub or a restaurant. I'll phone early evening - tell you where we are - assuming you are at home?'

'Sure - that would be great - look forward to it.' It was difficult to feign enthusiasm knowing she wouldn't be in the house to pick up the call.

She passed the bus journey to the library trying to think of a credible excuse why she would not be sharing the celebrations that night. If it were not for the fact her work really was pressing, she would have put in a token attendance at the Town Hall - enough of a sacrifice to keep Helen happy. As for attending in the evening - well, that would mean foregoing her date with Richard.

Later, Vee wished she had stood him up and met up with them instead. Oh yes, hindsight would be so useful! The assignation did not go quite the way she hoped. Brother to one of her girlfriends, they were introduced at a party. In a few days, he would return to Sandhurst to continue his officer training. The fact he was an embodiment of the most alien part of the "Establishment" - the "Military," made them an unlikely match. But, contrary to her values and beliefs, it surprised her when they seemed to hit it off.

'Let me take you out for dinner. I might not agree with your politics, but I think we could have fun together - what do you say?' he offered.

The rendezvous turned out to be an unmitigated disaster. During the two hours, they spent in each other's company in the hotel lounge, he talked about himself and the glittering career lying in front of him. She smiled and nodded, wondering when he might show interest in her. By the time he did show awareness of her, he was inebriated and leery. His sudden focus on her, it became clear, did not reflect the intellectual kind.

'I've booked a room,' he said with a conspiratorial wink, 'I can order champagne to be sent up if you like.'

Vee poured the rest of her pint of Guinness over his head and walked out. She returned home earlier than expected, in a foul mood and with a thumping headache - too late to receive the phone call from Helen. All she wanted was to climb into her bed and sleep, shutting out the misery caused by her confinement in Fairfield.

Later, she dozed off only to be jerked awake by the sound of the front door opening, raised voices and bodies stumbling into the hallway. A crashing noise made her sit bolt upright in her bed.

'Careful, Dad. Oh, I'm sorry, this is so embarrassing!' Helen's voice sounded strained.

'It's not a problem,' said a female voice, Vee didn't recognise.

The sound of heavy, laboured footsteps came up the stairs. 'Open the door can you, Sue - yes, that one. Can you help me get him on top of the bed? I'm so sorry, he's never been this drunk before.'

***

As Vee entered the kitchen, Helen looked up from where she sat at the table, reading the "Gazette" and nibbling on a corner of toast.

'Where are you off to so early in the morning?'

'Only six months overdue!' she replied pulling a library book from her canvas bag and waving it in the air like a trophy. 'Borrowed when I was last home and forgot I had it!'

'That'll cost you! You'll be fined at least five shillings. You'd be better off telling them you lost it - might be cheaper to pay for a replacement.'

'Got to spend my student grant on something,' she said laughing, studying her sister and wondering whether she might be able to head for the door and avoid a detailed examination of what happened to her last night.

Too easy! Helen lay the newspaper down on the table and adopted a familiar expression. Her glasses perched on the end of the nose - the eyebrows raised in place of an articulated question, reminded her of the history teacher at the grammar school, who did not need to speak to make her views very apparent.

'I'm sorry, Helen. Yesterday seemed to be just one disaster after another. That essay took longer than I thought and - well, by the time I finished it, it was too late for the last post. I had to catch the bus to the main post office in Fareham. And.....'

She dropped her eyes in the face of Helen's stare. 'Well, to tell the truth, by the time I got home, I felt so awful with a headache, I went straight to bed. Sorry, I missed everything.'

'I'm surprised we didn't wake you - we made quite a racket - well, Dad did. I can't recall ever seeing him drunk let alone legless. He knocked over the hat stand in the hall, then he fell on the stairs when we - Sue and I - tried to help him up. Later, he got himself undressed, took himself to the bathroom and threw up everywhere - then he collapsed into the bath - stark naked. I needed to get him out - so embarrassing!'

Helen's face, she noted, registered a hint of a smile. This provided an opportunity to divert the focus away from her failure to attend the celebrations.'

'Well, I didn't hear a thing,' she said, lying. 'I would have come and given you a hand with Dad. Wish I had been woken in fact. Falling in the bath, drunk and starkers - gosh, that would be a sight to remember!' She chuckled and, with relief, noted Helen's face break into a smile.

She sat at the table, helped herself to a slice of Helen's buttered toast and poured a cup of tea. Her face creased into a frown. 'Can't we throw this old thing out - it's grotesque,' she said, taking a pinch of the tea cosy shaped like a bizarre exotic bird, the spout forming an elongated beak.

'I agree, it really is horrible - but Mum made it, so Dad will never part with it.'

The crisis appeared to have passed. Helen seemed relaxed - a ghost of a smile on her face. Perhaps she was remembering their mother? Vee pulled out the tobacco tin from her canvass bag, prised off the top and extracted one of her pre-prepared rolled cigarettes.

'Please, not in here. Dad doesn't like you smoking those things.'

'I don't suppose we'll see him this side of midday - he'll wake with one hell of a hangover.' But, she put the roll-up back, hoping this placatory gesture did not go unnoticed.

'So, tell me about yesterday. What happened at the Town Hall?'

Helen related the events of the day before. Her face creased into smiles when she described the unintended hilarity of the proceedings. Vee laughed with her, cringing when hearing about the Mayor's pompous speech and Frank's obvious embarrassment.

'So, how did Dad end up so drunk? I mean, he's not a big drinker.'

Helen rolled her eyes. 'The booze was flowing - a real party atmosphere. I think he tried to keep up with everyone else - but, he can't drink that much, and it didn't take long before he was sozzled. He latched onto Frank - gave him a right old talking to. Poor thing - he needed rescuing.'

'How on earth did you manage to get him home? Not in a taxi, surely?'

Helen frowned as she described in graphic detail the journey home.

'Dad crashed out in the back of the car. I worried all the way home he might be sick again - that would have been awful.'

'So, Frank wasn't with you, then?'

'No, I left him in the pub. He needed time to himself, he said, after Dad had pounded his ears for much of the evening.'

Vee noticed the sudden frown - there for a moment then gone.

'Sue and I got Dad into the house and up the stairs - eventually. God knows how we managed! He'll be mortified when he wakes up and remembers.'

'If he remembers!'

'Yes, maybe. Oh well, I suppose it was a special occasion.'

Helen remained silent for a few moments as if deep in thought - then she smiled. 'He seemed happy - the first time I've seen him looking relaxed since Mum passed away. And it was so nice to see how well he and Frank bonded.'

Vee could sense that, as so often happened when they talked, Frank was emerging as the central theme. She had learned much about her sister's boyfriend already. Helen had taken her into confidence, mentioning him in the letters she sent to her at university, and during the many conversations, they shared since returning home. She knew Helen wanted to keep her relationship with Frank secret from their father. They never discussed the reason, but she guessed Helen was concerned about the probable reaction of their dad, who was protective of his eldest daughter.

'Frank wasn't happy when he found out I'd blabbed about our plans.'

'Oh? After all this time? He was bound to find out sooner or later. You've kept him under wraps; what's it been, eight, nine months?'

'Almost a year,' Helen replied. 'Well, eight months since we went out for the first time. And Dad knew, apparently, he just said nothing.'

'So, Frank meets with Dad's approval then?'

'He does indeed. When Frank saved that boy's life - well, Dad was so impressed. A Park Domestic Products salesman turns out to be a hero! But, I wish I'd warned Frank I was going to tell him.' she said looking rueful. 'Frank's got a hang-up about the fact he's a salesman–and that Dad might consider him not good enough for me. Silly, isn't it?'

Vee nodded. A sudden vision of Jonny appeared in her head - Dad would not have approved of him!

'Frank was convinced Dad would sack him if he found out,' Helen continued. 'We've been meeting in secret all this time - and he knew all along.'

'So, how did he react when you told him - officially? I'm guessing he was okay about it?'

Helen shrugged and smiled, 'Dad was delighted. He likes him - quite a lot, in fact. He's convinced he's wasted as a salesman - reckons he could go much further in Parks. The incident at the garage helped to elevate Frank's standing with him. Dad sees him as a hero which he is, of course, and therefore fit to marry his eldest daughter. Well, don't look so surprised, Vee - we're getting engaged.'

'That's great! So, when's he going to put a ring on your finger?'

'Soon, I hope. Perhaps now everything's out in the open, he'll sort out an official engagement. I don't want to press him - he needs to fix things - show some commitment. Actually, he's agreed to take me up to London to choose a ring, so I suppose that shows he's ready to get things moving.'

Vee detected an edge of doubt in Helen's voice. Was Frank as enthusiastic about the thought of marriage as Helen? she wondered. Having never met him, she was in no position to judge. But, he seemed to be dithering. Time to change the subject, she decided.

'Anyway, looks like everything's turned out well.'

'Yes, most definitely. Dad wants to tell the world - he seems so pleased with the prospect of having a son-in-law. He's told Frank he's going to promote him, which means he'll be in Head Office, so I can see a lot more of him. He won't have to disappear off to Southampton so much and...' she paused as if for dramatic effect, 'you can meet him at last Vee!'

Vee smiled. Helen had not appeared so positive and contented for a long time, at least not since their mother died. She lifted herself from her chair and hugged her.

'I'm pleased for you, sis!' she said, 'you deserve to be happy.'

***

Twenty minutes later, Vee sat in her usual seat on the bus at the front of the top deck, deep in thought. As so often happened when on her own, her mind taunted her with comparisons between the apparent order in Helen's life and the chaos that characterised her own.

Everything - well, almost everything, seems to have fallen into place for Helen. She had a secure and happy future ahead of her. A brief vision of a smug-looking Helen with two young children flashed into her mind. There will be two, her sister had informed her, a boy and a girl. Frank's image, at least the one she created, stood in the background - smiling - dependable - ruggedly good-looking.

'Stop being so jealous,' she murmured to herself in admonishment, knowing she *was* envious. Helen deserves to be happy. *Look at the sacrifice she made, foregoing university to stay at home and support Dad. And what did I do? Well, that's a different story, isn't it?*

'My life's a mess - a complete shambles.' She whispered these last words as if to emphasise and confirm their veracity. An embarrassed glance behind her. *Is someone listening?* A young couple sat several rows behind, immersed in their own world and paying no intention to her. They looked happy, at ease with each other. She turned back around and stared unseeing out of the window.

Helen's been an absolute brick - hasn't criticised me or made me feel ashamed - not once. Oh well, today I'm going to plan a new life - put all my mistakes behind me and start again - away from bloody Fairfield!

This decisive thought prompted the memory of the tearful phone call to Helen that took place a month ago: 'Please don't tell Dad - it will just make things worse. I'll tell you everything when I get home - can we keep it between us?'

On the day, she returned to Fairfield, laden with a heavy suitcase and backpack - her entire collection of belongings from halls - she didn't see Helen waiting for her at the station exit. She recalled the scene.

'Come on, give me that case,' Helen commanded, prising it from her hands. 'Let's have a chat before we go home - you need to tell me what's happened. Then we'll sort out what needs to be done.'

She remembered how her heart sank at the prospect of relating her sorry story to her elder sister. On the train journey down from Manchester, a litany of criticism and accusation played through her mind - the imagined chastisement to be endured:

'For Heaven's sake, what were you thinking, hooking up with a man like that? How could you be so stupid, so irrational? Why couldn't you find someone normal - someone, who wouldn't destroy your life? Surely you could see the risks you were taking? You do know it's a privilege to go to university, don't you? Others - and that includes me - would give their right arm to study for a degree. Few women get the opportunity as it is - and what did you do? You've risked everything - and probably thrown your chance of success away.'

But the actual discourse took a very different tone and direction. Helen led her into the lounge of the *Station Hotel* - a most unlikely occurrence given that Helen would never contemplate entering a drinking establishment during the working day. Even more surprising was when Helen ordered without demur a pint of Guinness for her, opting for a glass of wine for herself.

'So, what's happened?' Helen asked as they settled into the corner of the bar.

Vee had talked, hesitant at first, then with more confidence. Her sister listened without interruption, only encouraging her when she hesitated. Perhaps the result of the third Guinness, or maybe the act of unburdening herself, triggered a growing sense of relief. She told most of the story - at least enough for Helen to understand the seriousness of the situation. An hour later, they took a taxi home.

'Okay, like you said, Vee, let's keep this between us. There's no point in telling Dad - he'll only get himself upset.'

Helen hugged her in a sisterly embrace. 'Don't worry, everything will be fine - you'll see.'

Vee was not so sure.

Chapter 9

"JONNY"

Vee's arrival at the University of Manchester in October 1957 heralded a new and exciting change in her life, one that offered a level of freedom and expression unimaginable during her late teenage years at home. Unlike many new students, she never once suffered from homesickness - there was too much going on to dwell upon thoughts of home. In moments of reflection, she could acknowledge that being a student provided an escape from the stultifying restrictions of suburbia. Compared to Manchester, Fairfield appeared backward, suburban and so boring.

Within days of her arrival, she became immersed in the many and varied facets of student life. The freedom university offered created invigorating and exhilarating distractions from mundanity and she embraced her new experiences with full-on enthusiasm.

An intelligent girl, she maintained a semblance of credibility, achieving acceptable grades for her work. But she knew she could do better - a fact her tutor confirmed on several occasions. Her examination results at the end of the first year were disappointing.

'You have so much potential, Miss Park - and it is abundantly clear you are not realising it. Freedom of expression is all very well, but a certain amount of conformity, such as meeting work deadlines, is an essential part of your degree.' Professor O'Donnell said this with a smile on his face - but the significance of his message could not be ignored. The wake-up call could not have been clearer. 'Continue in this vein, Miss Park, and you are likely to risk failure.'

But returning for her second year of study after a stultifying period spent at home during the summer vacation, she appeared to forget how tenuous her survival at university might be. There were too many attractive diversions - so much going on! Student parties were regular features in her social calendar and she shared these with like-minded students. She adopted the counter-culture image of the beatnik, although, like others favouring this alternative lifestyle, she hated the term, preferring to be described as a member of the "Beat Generation."

Unlike many other student members of her social milieu, she did not succumb to radicalisation - but she enjoyed being on the periphery of radicalism, engaging with activities protesting the nuclear arms race. She had been an enthusiastic participant in the recent Aldermaston marches with other protesters of the "Bomb," and wore her CND badge with pride. Like others, she railed against the "Military Dictatorship," she believed was taking over the country.

The style underpinning the Beatnik movement suited it her because it offered a different perspective, a unique image and fashion, and a stimulating ethos of "alternativism."

English literature had been her passion and winning a place at university to study the subject presented like a dream come true. Her studies opened a new world of literary exploration. A series of lectures and seminars on post-war American literature introduced her to several new idols, and she became immersed in the works of, amongst others, Lucien Carr, John Clellon Holmes, and Neal Cassidy. However, Kerouac and Ginsberg stood out as her favourites. She read their works many times and could quote lines of text word perfect, which she often did when meeting with her friends at the various social haunts they frequented.

***

What did I ever see in him? This question would haunt her in the years following.

She met him in one of her favourite café bars, where fellow 'beatniks' gathered to share their ideas, talk politics and listen to poetry. Like everyone else in the room, she listened to his impassioned speech about the "Bomb", and his fervent exhortations to join a demonstration against it. His passion was matched with his earnestness, his hands gesticulating to emphasise his words, his eyes searching the room for affirmation. An adoring group of students, both male and female, surrounded him. She remembered the faint, involuntary shudder and the strange sensation of excitement when his eyes, Rasputin-like, locked onto hers and drew her in.

Jonathon, or "Jonny," as he called himself, masqueraded as a post-graduate student. He claimed to be working on, or at least thinking about writing, a dissertation on the "Growth of Socialism in the Post-Modernist World." Like her, he was a keen proponent of the counter-culture associated with the Beat Generation - but for him, the alternative lifestyle opened a door to something more radical, exciting and, as she would become aware in a short space of time, far more dangerous.

His mind attracted her, not his looks. He presented a bizarre, what some might describe as a disturbing image. Long black hair, straggly and unkempt was topped by a black bohemian-style beret. Much of his face was obscured - the lower part by a thick black beard, the top masked by black plastic rimmed glasses behind which his eyes glinted. He always wore a black duffle coat, despite the claustrophobic warmth of the crowded coffee bars and pubs he frequented.

He projected a working-class image reflected in the words he spoke when holding forth, surrounded by his acolytes with their eager, nodding faces. His audience would be infected by his enthusiasm, accepting every word he uttered without, she guessed, knowing why. He could pull the crowds, developing a not insignificant following among certain circles of the student fraternity: those bored with the conventional and seeking something different, and alternative.

'Complete and utter claptrap - you don't really think he understands what he's twittering on about, do you?' a young man had asked her, his voice filled with scorn. In the early stages of her relationship with Jonny, she felt compelled to challenge back.

'I think he talks perfect sense - you should listen to what he's actually saying.' But, the more she listened to him, the harder it became to understand his diatribes. Nonetheless, her fascination for him grew - she found herself attracted by his magnetism and aura of mysticism. In a short space of time, a connection between them developed, which she encouraged.

His alternative view of the world, explained to her in patient detail, bordered on the extreme. Later, she might admit to being drawn into his way of thinking, at least the parts she could make sense of. His powers of persuasion were strong. Later, she would acknowledge how much she had fallen under his spell without being able to understand why.

He lived in a small, dingy terraced house which he shared with several others, his only private space a tiny room with a single bed. Despite the apparent grubbiness of his existence and the fact she knew nothing of substance about him, she shared his bed willingly.

In her mind, this was always meant to be a temporary arrangement - not a protracted affair. 'I'm living for the moment,' she explained to Helen in one of her infrequent letters home, the one in which she admitted the existence of a boyfriend but offering no details about him. Helen would be horrified if she found out the true extent of her boyfriend's strangeness.

Her association with Jonny started during the weeks leading up to the examinations at the end of her second year at university. Their meetings became regular occurrences, these assignations mostly coinciding with various political gatherings in cafés and pubs where Jonny appeared as the key speaker. Overnight stays in his untidy digs across the other side of Manchester, quite a distance from the main university buildings, caused her to be late for several morning lectures and tutor sessions. The realisation she was neglecting her studies in favour of spending time with him became clear.

It didn't take long for doubts about her relationship with this enigmatic man to trouble her. Perhaps it was the growing understanding that what at first, she considered to be harmless platitudes and political posturing, hid a darker side to his character. Maybe it was the realisation they shared little in common other than a liking of the unconventional. But the intensity of their individual passion for an alternative lifestyle differed markedly. She enjoyed the trappings of the "Beat Generation": the fashion, the poetry, and music. Her politics leaned towards the "Left" - but largely due to her abhorrence of the "Bomb." His views, although incoherent, presented as far more radical. His dream of a "new world order," a term he used a great deal, was underpinned by an anarchic leaning bordering on the extreme.

Soon after their relationship began, she recalled how his eyes shone with pride when he showed her the press clipping covering his recent offence for disorder. He got off with a caution on that occasion. Soon after this, a second incident might have resulted in her being prosecuted.

A small peaceful demonstration in St Peter's Square turned into a scuffle with the Police. Jonny knocked off a policeman's helmet, an act she witnessed. His action was more than a mischievous student prank - she remembered noting the glint of venom in his eyes. She had picked up the helmet and handed it back to the very annoyed representative of the law, who arrested them both. Only her charm and acting ability convinced him to let them go. Jonny's lack of gratitude for saving them both from arrest and a probable fine, if not something worse, irritated her. He appeared frustrated by what he called her 'appeasement to the capitalist pigs.'

His penchant for violent affray became a real issue for her; although she welcomed peaceful protest, any action that might be considered as overstepping the boundary remained unthinkable. But by this point, she had become tired of him from several viewpoints. His politics bored and confused her, and his view of the world most definitely did not match her own.

But, as well as his toxic political views, she realised another side of his character, one that worried her more: he was becoming obsessively possessive. Hints of this manifested whenever anyone, male or female, showed an interest in her when in his company. Frequently, he grabbed her by the arm and pulled her away from a conversation. He would never offer a reason - nor would he apologise. But despite this strange behaviour, and her growing doubts about him, she remained in his thrall.

It was at the end of term garden party, the last of the second-year examinations completed that morning, when Jonny went, in Vee's view, too far with his obsessive behaviour. He had insisted on accompanying her, despite her protestations that he would find it boring. During the party, he became jealous when a photographer, hired to cover the event, appeared to flirt with her when taking their photograph.

'If he looks at you like that again, I'll ram that camera down his throat,' he said in a low voice, full of menace.

'Oh, for God's sake, he's just being friendly, that's his job. What's wrong with you Jonny?'

He strode away, his face projecting simmering anger, leaving her alone. Glad to be free of him, she was walking towards a group of her friends when Professor O'Donnell intercepted her.

'Not good news, I'm afraid. Sorry to break it to you here - but it's the only opportunity I'll get before you all disappear off home for the vacation,' he said. Vee's eyes filled with tears when he informed her she had failed two of her examinations.

'Well, I did warn you,' he said gently. 'You have so much potential, young lady - but you seem to lack focus. And, I must say, during the second half of term, you have appeared more distracted than usual. If something is troubling, you - if you need help, then you should talk to me. Is anything the matter?'

'No, nothing's wrong — I just ...' Her excuses sounded lame to her, and she guessed Professor O'Donnell did not believe her. He advised her the re-sits would be scheduled for the end of September and she would need to return early from her summer vacation to sit them.

'These are important exams, Miss Park. If you fail them, the re-sits, I mean, you may not be able to complete your degree.'

These words from her tutor prompted her to review her relationship with Jonny, and the extent to which he had begun to dominate her. Jonny, she admitted to herself, represented a significant and detrimental distraction. At this juncture, any vestige of attraction vanished. Later, she would chastise herself for not having the courage to end their association right there.

With Professor O'Donnell's warning resonating in her ears, she determined to "buckle down" as her father would describe what she must do. Through most of the summer vacation, instead of going home, she stayed in her hall of residence, so she could spend time in the university library. In a phone call to Helen, she explained why she would not be home, although avoiding any mention of the underlying reasons for her failure. The re-sits were towards the end of the vacation period; this would leave a week or two for her to return home before starting her third and final year.

Determined to avoid any distractions while focusing on ensuring a clear pass in her re-sits, she told Jonny to stay away. At first, he pleaded with her, attempting rational reasoning: 'I can help with your revision,' he insisted. But, as he knew nothing about English Literature, his offer was an empty one. She sensed his wanting to control, and this made it easy for her to be firm.

When faced with rejection, he became petulant and then angry. She decided appeasement would be the best approach and allowed herself to be coaxed into agreeing to meet him again once her re-sits were over. This wasn't what she wanted - but what choice did she have? Perhaps he'll lose interest, or find someone else to focus on, she reasoned, recognising and hating herself for her weakness.

Later, recalling the details of their brief affair, she realised this should have marked the point where she ended the relationship. However, absence from him for nearly a month dulled some of her negative feelings. She could never explain why - maybe it was the exhilaration and knowledge of a sure "Pass" - or perhaps she missed his company - but within minutes of finishing her last examination, she phoned and arranged to meet him. Instead of going home, as she had promised Helen, she stayed in Manchester with Jonny, a decision she would regret.

Vee believed herself to be worldly-wise, but one with more experience of life might consider her to be naïve and vulnerable. Despite Jonny's many obvious flaws, she had convinced herself their liaison, although not based on love or affection, might at least be described as honest. A chance encounter in one of the backstreet pubs they frequented revealed the true nature of his attitude to her.

They sat a table towards the back. He was delivering a diatribe to her. She pretended to listen to him but studying the other people in the café interested her more.

The girl, enveloped in an over-sized army greatcoat, caught her eye. She was sitting at a table, looking around her as if in search of someone - a date - a friend, perhaps? Her face, pretty, she noted, without makeup, was topped with voluminous red hair, wild and unkempt.

'You're not paying attention, are you?'

Vee, stifling a yawn, realised she had been caught out. She fixed him with an attentive stare and encouraging smile.

'I am, Jonny, really. Sorry, I'm just a bit tired, that's all. What were you saying?'

'I was saying,' he said with exaggerated emphasis as if talking to a recalcitrant child, what we need is a ...'

Neither of them noticed the girl, the one who attracted her attention, approaching. The memory of the next few seconds would be played again many times in her mind.

'Hello, Jonny.'

They both looked up. She registered that, although the girl smiled, her eyes blazed anger.

'What's going on?' said Vee, sensing danger. She stared at him. He stared back, his eyes wide behind his glasses. Surprise? Or was it fear?

With a speed and ferocity, frightening and impressive in equal measure, the girl plunged her small fist into his face. Her aim true - his nose exploded in a crimson spray and a loud scrunching noise.

'Take that you bastard!' she said smiling, clearly pleased with the result of her violence.

Too shocked to speak, Vee gaped in disbelief and fascination. The girl turned to her and said in a pleasant voice, incongruent with the circumstances: 'Good luck with him - you're going to need it.' With a last withering look at Jonny, her face registering satisfaction as she surveyed the damage to his face, she spun on her heel and left the pub.

Jonny grabbed a handful of paper serviettes, which he fumbled with, trying unsuccessfully to stem the flow of blood from his nose.

'What the hell was that about?' she whispered, oblivious to the many pairs of eyes focusing on them. He mumbled a hurried explanation - illogical, contradictory and, she concluded, untrue. A small crowd had gathered around their table watching, some smiling at the unexpected entertainment. Despite the shock, she surprised herself by laughing. The image of him with several paper napkins in a huge crimson wet bundle clamped to his face, combined with the empty, meaningless words that emanated from his mouth, was comical. She half-listened to his self-pitying ranting - but her mind was already made up about him. Someone burst into applause when he announced to the gathering crowd that monogamy represented the "chains of modernism."

He appeared oblivious to her presence. With shocked amusement, she realised he was turning the incident, which would have been humiliating to a normal man, into an opportunity to pontificate his political platitudes. She stood and replicated the girl's stance, leaning across the table, her face a few inches from his.

'We're finished! Kaput!' she said. Her hand reached for his beer glass, almost full, and poured it over his head. A loud cheer erupted from the crowd - this made her smile - it was a most satisfying experience.

She left the pub with her head up, conscious all eyes were upon her. Soon after, as she sat on the empty top deck of the bus smoking a roll-up, she cried, but only briefly. Then she giggled, recalling in vivid detail Jonny's public humiliation.

***

This had taken place a few days before the start of the new term marking her third and final year at university. Her belief Jonny could now be forgotten proved short-lived. As she exited the library, he emerged from the shadows and grabbed her by the elbow causing her to drop the armful of textbooks balanced in her arms.

'Come on Vee,' he remonstrated and implored, 'let's talk - you owe me that much at least.'

'I don't owe you a sodding thing. Now bugger off and leave me alone!'

She gathered up her books, pushing his hand away when he tried to help her. 'You're making a fool of yourself. Go away - please!'

A small group of onlookers collected. 'You heard her - go on beat it,' commanded one gallant, squaring up to him.

He shot her a malevolent glance, turned on his heel and strode away. But this was not the end of the problem - he would not stop hounding her. The next day, he confronted her as she came out of a lecture. This time, she was with a large cluster of female friends.

'We've got to talk!' His words were an instruction. He grabbed her arm, his grip strong and determined.

'For God's sake, can't you understand? I don't want to be with you.'

'You can't go on ignoring me. I'm not going away - you're supposed to be with me - you know that.' He seemed to be oblivious to the mocking, cynical stares of her companions. She wrenched her arm free.

'Get lost!' she spat the words, defiant and angry and walked away, quickening her pace, desperate to escape him, sensing his eyes boring into the back of her head.

After that incident, the suspicion he might be watching her, unseen, waiting to confront her, became overwhelming.

Still in her first week, asleep in her hall of residence, she awoke with a start and sat bolt upright in her bed. What was it? She stared fearfully at the door, imagining someone - no, not just someone, it would be him - twisting the door knob.

A glance at her bedside clock: 3.15am. Her sense of foreboding intensified. Then a loud tap on the window caused her to turn towards the curtains. Another distinct chink, then another - this one a little louder. Although very frightened, she felt compelled to creep over and peep out. Perhaps the fact her room was on the first floor provided a modicum of protection. Determined to stay concealed, she pulled the edge of the curtain aside a few inches, enough to peer out.

She knew it would be him. Like a ghost in the light of a nearby street lamp, he stood looking up. As she watched, praying he hadn't seen her, he stooped and picked something up - another stone, she guessed - and in a careful underhand motion, he cast it upwards.

When in the morning, she reported the occurrence to the Warden, he seemed to dismiss the event as trivial.

'Did he get in? Did he break the window? No harm done - probably drunk too many ales.'

'But this is harassment - you need to do something!'

Well, what do you expect me to do about it? If you feel *that* aggrieved why don't you contact the Police? But I don't suppose they'll be that interested. As I said, no one's been hurt. Why don't you forget about it and...?'

She shot a look of disgust at him and left his office, slamming the door behind her.

***

'I'm not coping,' she said, embarrassed, unable to prevent the sudden flow of tears.

Professor O'Donnell nodded and smiled. 'Go on' he said - take your time.'

She told him her story - the one made up following her visit to the Warden - the one suggesting pressure of work had become too much. He said little as she spoke, concentrating, apparently, on clearing out his pipe and refilling it with tobacco from a leather pouch. But he listened - she could see that.

'Interesting,' he said when it was apparent she had finished her story and was expecting a response from him. He lit his pipe and puffed at it for a few moments, staring at the ceiling as if lost in thought. Then he leaned forward and studied her face.

'Miss Park, you are more than capable of coping with the academic rigours of your course. We've spoken about the need for you to focus - but I believe you've heeded that advice. Your results in the re-sits reflect your true potential - they were excellent in fact.' He paused and looked at her meaningfully.

'Now,' he said, leaning back in his seat and looking at across the rim of his spectacles, 'tell me what's really going on here.'

Her defences crumbled. Vee told him the true story. Tearful at first, but realising he wasn't judging her, she told him most of the details about her relationship with Jonny. He laughed when she described the scene in the café where the girl in the greatcoat assaulted Jonny.

'Good for her,' he said, 'sounds like he deserved it – a complete bastard!'

This shocked and pleased her at the same time.

'Get yourself away from Manchester. Take a leave of absence: let the dust settle,' he said. 'I'll speak to the Dean and arrange a work schedule for you. A dissertation and some essays should make up for the lectures you'll miss. What do you think?'

She left the study with a smile on her face.

Chapter 10

"GREGORY'S VISITOR"

(Sunday 8th November)
Gregory lay on his back motionless, staring at a point on the ceiling. With the ventilator removed the day before, he could breathe unaided now, although his chest still ached, and he would be wracked with coughing fits.

'You're a very lucky, young man - a minute longer in there and you would be dead,' said the doctor. 'Welcome back,' he had added more cheerfully.

His mother, he learned, had insisted on staying at his side for much of the time since being admitted to the hospital. She appeared haggard and exhausted but determined to stay with him.

'You were unconscious for almost two weeks - I thought you'd never wake up,' she said between stuttering sobs. After a while, she calmed down.

'Dad says hello, by the way,' she said sniffing.

His mind conjured a vision of his father in the pub, raising his pint of ale in a "cheers" motion. Do I care he can't be bothered to come and visit me? he asked himself. Not really. But part of him acknowledged this wasn't entirely true.

His mother told him about Mr Ramsay's death. Shock overwhelmed him for several minutes. How can he be dead? Then, as incoherent flickers of memory reminded him of the inferno, his immediate conclusion was he must have died in the fire.

'They think he committed suicide - drove his car off a cliff.'

'What? No! How? He...' His train of thought halted as he struggled to breathe.

'Apparently, yes,' said his mother when, after taking a few gasps of oxygen from the mask dangling next to his head, he felt able to pay attention again.

'The police believe he did - kill himself, that is.'

'But why?'

She couldn't answer him.

Unable to gather his thoughts, and anxious to make sense of them, he wanted desperately to be alone. 'Mum, you need to go home and get some proper rest - you're done in.' It took a good deal of persuasion but at last, she left, leaving him to his contemplation.

A policeman visited early in the afternoon. The interview continued for almost an hour.

'So, you went to the garage to lock the safe and the building.'

'Yes, Mr Ramsay - well, he liked a drink but - but I've never seen him so drunk. Later - supper time - it occurred to me he could have forgotten to lock up properly. I mean he seemed so out of it! I went back - to check - to be sure.'

'And it was unlocked when you got there?'

'Yes, I...'

'And you didn't realise the place was on fire when you went in?'

'No - at least not at first. But then I smelled burning - and I noticed a light in Mr Ramsay's office. I panicked, I think... I thought he might be inside.'

Spasmodic rasping. The policemen handed him a glass of water. 'I opened the door and then...well, I remember nothing after that.'

Gregory glanced at the policeman who scribbled in his notebook. Worry he was under suspicion gnawed at him.

'Well, investigations show the fire started half an hour or so before you arrived on the scene. Your boss, we believe, did it himself - trying to pull an insurance scam. There were money problems - the usual story: gambling debts - and he owed the Inland Revenue unpaid tax - a lot.

So, he'd been drinking during the afternoon, you say? A boozer, was he?'

'Yes, you could say that.'

'He was in the pub across the road from the garage soon after it started. He might have been looking for an alibi. We can only guess you returning and getting yourself trapped in there didn't feature in his plan. Lucky for you, um...' he viewed his notes, 'Mr Armstrong was passing and detected smoke. If he hadn't got you out when he did, we wouldn't be talking now.' He paused, the tip of his pen poised. 'Here, have a sip of water,' he said kindly.

After a few moments, during which Gregory emptied the glass - his throat was parched - the policemen continued. 'We found the safe open and empty. Later, once we'd recovered the body from the wreck at the bottom of the cliff, we found a few rolls of banknotes in his pockets. So, it seems likely he did plan on burning his business down, making it look like an accident so he could claim the insurance money. The fire was started in his office - we definitely know that.'

'But why would he want to kill himself? I mean, he wouldn't do that - that doesn't sound like the Mr Ramsay I know - I mean knew,' Gregory said, unable to understand the logic.

The policeman paused. 'He came out of the bar and stood watching - several bystanders confirmed that. And, we gather, based on what onlookers told us, he realised you were inside. A witness reported seeing him walking away from the scene after you were dragged clear. One witness said he saw him getting into a car and driving away at speed. We can't be sure what he was thinking or doing - but when he discovered it was you being pulled out, perhaps he panicked, believing you might be dead and, well...'

Another coughing fit erupted, and Gregory struggled to breathe. A nurse rushed in and placed a mask on his face.

After a few minutes, his breathing settled down again and he lay back on the bed. The policemen, he noted, had left.

***

Later, Gregory lay staring at the ceiling trying to make sense of the unexpected news. Relieved he was not under suspicion, he nonetheless began to worry again. Feelings of guilt troubled him - but, as his thoughts clarified, he allowed himself to dismiss them as irrational. Mr Ramsay was a drunk, and he gambled his money away - is that my fault? And, I knew the business was in trouble - but, other than the fact I couldn't sell his cars, - can I be blamed for that? No, his death is not down to me? But the policeman suggested he might have killed himself out of guilt - because he thought he had killed me. This thought nagged him.

If only I'd stayed at home, he would still be here. Suicide, though? Driving off a cliff? His memory of the blustering, ill-tempered man did not tally with the profile of someone willing and capable of committing suicide.

Alone with grief, his mind conjured scenes involving himself and his boss. He accepted their relationship could never be described as a happy one. But, try as he might, he could not draw himself away from the fact his boss had treated him in an abusive and bullying way. *He made my life a misery - and for no reason.* But nagging doubt persisted - things did not add up.

Would he kill himself? It did not seem right; he would never do that. His heart told him the Police had got it wrong. Any bitterness he may once have harboured about his boss was forgotten - instead, he experienced an overwhelming sense of pity. *Poor Mr Ramsay if only someone had given him a break.*

Muffled voices outside the ward suggested someone had arrived.

'Just a few minutes - he's exhausted and needs to rest.'

He dabbed at his eyes with the corner of his bed sheet and, feigning a yawn, turned over so he faced the door. It was Mr Armstrong - Frank. He recognised him straight away.

'Hello old son, thought it about time I dropped by to check how you're getting on.' He squeezed his hand in way of a greeting. 'Frank, you remember...?'

'Yes, of course. Hello.'

Shyness kicked in - self-consciousness made it difficult for him to put words together appropriate for the occasion.

Frank sat down in the chair by the bed and grinned at him. There was an awkward silence.

'You risked your life, I will always be in your debt.' This sounded lame and contrived to his own ears - remembered, perhaps, from some film, or maybe a radio play. But it did the job well enough.

'Anyone would have done the same. I happened to be in the right place at the right time. You're welcome anyway. Oh, I thought you might like these.' Frank placed a large bag of "Pic n Mix" on the cabinet next to the bed. 'And here's some reading material for you. I guess it must be pretty boring being stuck in here.' He dropped some magazines on the bed.

'You've been talking to my mother,' Gregory said smiling, picking up the copy of "Aircraft Modellers World." 'Thanks, Frank, that's kind of you.' He frowned and then laughed when his eyes fell upon the second magazine, the latest copy of "Playboy". 'Stick that one in the drawer will you. I dread to think what the nurses would say if they found that–and as for my mum, well...'

His visitor grinned. The ice had been broken.

He expected to be asked questions about the fire and investigation but was relieved when, instead, Frank talked about his Healey, which he did with great enthusiasm.

'I'll take you out for a run in it as soon as they let you out of here. Oh, and we can stop on the way for a few beers.'

'That would be great, I'd like that - but...' He was about to add he did not drink beer or any other form of alcohol, but he stopped himself. '... but I'll need to take the doctor's advice on what I can and can't do.'

They chatted for a while longer. Gregory yawned involuntarily.

'I'd best be off,' Frank said, 'You need your rest old son. Get your strength back.' He stood and turned towards the door. As if it were an after-thought or spur of the moment, he paused, fished in his pocket and took out a card.

'I guess you're going to be looking for a new job. This has got my office number on it. Call me once you're well enough. There's an opening in my business you might be interested in.'

Alone again, Gregory looked at the card, emblazoned with the motif "Park Domestic Appliances" and his saviour's name under the title "Operations Director." He placed it in his private drawer, together with the copy of "Playboy." Life is looking up again, he told himself - it has to!' Within seconds, he fell into a deep sleep.

Chapter 11

"THE RING"

Despite his natural disinclination to be the centre of social attention, Frank found he rather liked his new local hero status. People nodded to him and smiled; some even stopped him to shake his hand, murmuring congratulations, engaging him in conversation, wanting to hear the details about his heroic act.

Soon after the award ceremony, he was interviewed by a young, and, in his opinion, rather attractive journalist from the *Gazette*, gushing in her admiration and playful in her unashamed flirtation with him. The interview took place in a backroom of *The Three Feathers*, the main hotel in Fairfield. He went alone - Helen needed to be at the office. 'Try to feed in the news about our engagement,' she said as her parting comment.

He arrived early for the assignation which he dreaded. A couple of beers helped to allay his nerves - and his inhibitions. Later, when he read the resulting article, published in the newspaper, he flushed with embarrassment.

'You should be proud of yourself - you're a brave man,' Helen said, admiring the picture. She would be furious if she ever found out the detail hidden in the photograph.

Frank studied the picture of himself, noting the inane smile on his face, and the fact he was standing a little too close to the girl. She smiled as well - but in a tight-lipped way as if something had displeased her.

'Get your hand off my backside!' she whispered as soon as the photographer signalled he had finished. 'You can sod off,' she said when he invited her to have a drink with him.

Helen, much to his relief, registered nothing untoward in the picture. She commented, though, that he might have ensured some reference to his forthcoming marriage to the daughter of a local successful businessman.

'You missed the opportunity for some good PR.'

He nodded - 'Sorry, she didn't give me the chance to say much.' He threw her a glance, looking for indications of suspicion.

***

Helen knew precisely the ring she wanted. 'Isn't it beautiful?' she said, opening her "Brides' Magazine" and pointing to the page advertising an array of engagement rings.

He sipped his third pint and, feeling relaxed and mellow, guessed she had picked this moment so he would not become too excited about how much it might cost.

'Lovely, Helen - really beautiful.' His voice reflected an enthusiasm he did not feel. Instead of absorbing the details of the image, he scanned the page for an indication of price. When he saw none - just an address in Knightsbridge, he groaned inwardly. It will be expensive, he told himself.

On the following day, a Saturday, they drove up to London in the Healey. Although too cold to drive with the hood down, they both enjoyed the journey which set the tone for the day. Frank parked the car in Richmond and they took the Tube from there to the West End. He tried not to think overmuch about the price of the ring. Helen's worth every penny, he assured himself. And, since she knows what she wants, there'll be no need to spend the day traipsing around all the jewellers in the city.

Later that afternoon, after finding the shop in an expensive-looking arcade, they sat in front of a smartly dressed salesman wearing white cotton gloves. He nodded with a knowing smile when she pointed to the ring in her magazine.

'Ah, yes, a perfect choice if I may say.' With a jangling of keys, he opened a glass cabinet and withdrew a tray with glistening rings embedded in turquoise velvet. He prised one of them from its groove and held it up for her to examine.

'Yes, that one!' she said, her voice rising with excitement. 'Can I try it on?' The man nodded. Helen's face radiated a vision of happiness as the jeweller handed the ring to Frank. She extended her hand, waving her wedding finger.

He tried to squeeze it on. His smile and hers changed to frowns. It was too small.

'I'm afraid, I only have this one in stock.'

Helen's joy crumbled in an instant.

'I'll get another one made for you, of course - shouldn't take too long. I can have the ring sent to you by courier.'

Frank detected Helen was not placated, and he guessed the lunge in her mood might spoil the day. Perhaps the reminder of his recent indiscretion with the journalist prompted an urge to make some form of hidden recompense. Within a few minutes, he added a not insignificant addition to the bill by negotiating enhancements to the ring to be made for Helen. The additional flourish of small diamonds around the central jewel put a smile back on her face. With the promise it would be despatched by special post within the week, they left the jewellers.

The rest of the day proved to be a great success. They had lunch in Covent Garden at a French restaurant where an expensive bottle of wine helped pave the way for a relaxing and enjoyable afternoon. They visited the theatre in Drury Lane and watched the "Crucible" that had not long opened in London. Much later that evening, tired but happy, relaxed in each other's company - no disagreements on that day - they returned by Tube to Richmond, where Frank had parked the car.

They booked in as "Mr and Mrs Smith." Helen giggled like a schoolgirl at the chicanery of their shallow deception as he led her up the stairs to their room.

That night, they slept together for the first time.

Chapter 12

"VEE MAKES A DECISION"

'Listen, I've told no one yet - not even Dad. I wanted you to know first.'

Helen had seemed so excited and, despite the lack of a ring, her face radiated happiness. 'As soon as it arrives, we'll make a formal announcement - but in the meantime - well, I needed to tell someone. Gosh, I can hardly believe it - he's finally got around to committing.'

'Fantastic! I'm so pleased for you. So, when am I going to meet your fiancé?'

'Oh, sorry, Vee. You're like ships passing each other in the night. He went back to Southampton yesterday - he's handing over his sales area to one of Dad's reps. After that, he'll be back here in Fairfield - for good this time. You'll meet him soon - I promise.'

Later, as she sat on the bus on her way to the library, Vee's happiness for her sister dissipated - in its place sadness descended at her own plight.

Yesterday, at the moment when she pushed the brown envelope containing her assignments for the week into the letter box, the realisation had swept over her. I'm wasting my time - fooling myself I might go back soon. Working from home was only supposed to be a temporary arrangement. *But, how can I ever go back if he's around?'*

No work would be done at the library today. *There's no point, I'm not going back.* A germ of an idea formed in her head based on a recent conversation with one of her female acquaintances. 'It's a fab way of finding yourself and meeting other people, who will be just like you - adventurous spirits.' She had never heard of a "kibbutz" - but today she would find out at the library. Sitting in her accustomed seat on the top deck, staring unseeingly out of the window, she wondered whether she was doing the right thing. Her thoughts spun and twisted in her mind.

Am I running away like a coward? What will Helen say when she finds out? She'll no doubt consider me as a disappointment - a failure - a fool? She would never have behaved like I did, she told herself. *And of course, Helen sacrificed her own chance of university to look after Dad. She'll make the most of that - and so will he. I went to university for both of us. And now - what am I doing? Throwing it all away. But how can I go back when Jonny's there? I can't finish my degree from home. If I don't go back in time for next term, they'll chuck me out, anyway.*

She stared ahead of her, her eyes misting. All lost because I wanted to be... oh yes: alternative. Then a voice in her head that sounded like that of her Dad added to the turmoil by remonstrating: 'Well, look where your lifestyle has got you now, young lady!'

God, what's Dad going to think? What's he going to do? The thought of his probable reaction filled her with dread. He would never understand. She imagined what he might say - something like: 'You're throwing the towel in. How could you be so weak and foolish?' No doubt he'd play on the fact Helen gave up the chance of university - oh yes, he would make the most of that! But Helen's always been his favourite, hasn't she?

She shook her head as if to throw out the shameful thought. A stronger voice of reason advised her that what anyone thought was no longer important. Nodding at her own wise council, she muttered to herself: 'I've got to get away - I can't stay around here any longer- this place is driving me mad!'

***

The bus was late. Dense drizzle filled the air adding to the evening gloom and matching Vee's mood. The tiny flame of optimism flickering as she entered the library that morning lay doused in the recesses of her mind, replaced with a sense of hopeless directionless, leaving her with the unfathomable question: 'Now what?'

Her research earlier in the day left her deflated. What, at first, offered an exciting prospect of living cheek by jowl with like-minded free spirits, did not quite measure up to reality. Her mind compared the ethos of communal camaraderie with her former life in Manchester. University came up trumps every time in the excitement stakes.

By the times she climbed the stairs of the bus and found a vacant seat, a black pall of depression enveloped her. As she sat hunched into her reefer jacket - a size too large but it matched her beret - she extracted a roll-up, lit it and looked through the gaps in the shoulders and heads sitting in front of her. 'Sod it,' she whispered.

She missed the freedom left behind in Manchester - no doubt about that. Although not subject to any significant restrictions, life at home did not compare.

'God, I wish I could go back,' she muttered under her breath, her mind playing images of the world she longed to be back in again.

Perhaps a distraction from her desperate thoughts, she pondered Helen's relationship with the, to her, mysterious Frank. Helen gave the impression of being besotted and eager to advance the wedding plans - but something's not right. Their recent conversation played through her mind together with the memory of the sudden, almost imperceptible shadow of doubt reflecting for the briefest of moments on her sister's face.

She remembered how Helen's regular letters always included updates of the developing relationship. News of the engagement came as no real surprise. But Helen divulged only the broadest detail about her fiancé. She would not be pressed: 'You need to talk to him yourself. I'm sure you'll both get along famously!'

As she stared unseeing out of the bus window, the fact she knew so little about the man, now the centre of her sister's life, didn't seem right. She conducted an inventory of how much she knew about him.

Not caring if anyone might be watching her, she used the fingers of her left hand to count off what she had found out about him. One: he works for Dad as a salesman. Two: he worked a sales pitch in the Southampton area, and this was where he grew up. What else? Oh yes! Three: he's done something brave and been awarded a medal.

I know the barest details about him, and he's going to be my brother-in-law!

She tried to form a mental image of Frank from the scant detail gleaned from Helen. Not much to go on. In her mind, she imagined a handsome man, in a rugged sort of way - that's how Helen described him, didn't she? Oh, and he's fastidious about the way he dresses. And he's recently bought a sports car. Helen was none too pleased about that, she recalled.

Sounds like a "Flash Harry" to me, an uncharitable voice in her mind suggested. This thought led to another. *What is my sister, a girl once destined for Oxford, doing getting hitched to a man who probably lacks a decent education? Wasn't he a common squaddie?*

Don't be such a snob, she admonished herself, you don't usually think like that? You're supposed to be the new generation, putting class-driven nonsense back where it belongs: in the past.

But something seemed not right, she thought. Again, the remembered image of Helen's face - a sudden hint of doubt registering on her sister's face at something said.

The fact she had not yet met him did not surprise her or cause any concern. Days spent in the library - evenings trying to capture some excitement akin to that at university

111

in the confines of Fairfield and the surrounding area - left little opportunity for an introduction. And, he appeared to flit in and out of Helen's life spending sometimes over a week away in Southampton. Lost in thought, she almost missed her stop.

Chapter 13

"UNEXPECTED NEWS"

Helen looked up from her desk at the Park office to see the sinewy figure of Hugh O'Driscoll, the Production Manager, grinning at her from the doorway.

'The top of the morning to you – and, if I might add, you're looking radiant today!'

'Oh, get on with you, Hugh.'

Used to the unrequited flirtation from the man leaning against the door frame, she could not be annoyed. His Irish lilt seemed a little out of place in the essential Englishness of the depot - but he added colour with his wit and charm.

'Your dad said I'm to remind you we're meeting at 10 of the clock and you're not to be late - otherwise he'll smack your bum.'

Hugh's grinning face disappeared seconds before the Parks brochure smacked into the door frame with an accuracy that surprised her. Cackling laughter accompanied the sound of his steps retreating down the corridor. She smiled and returned to the daydream that evoked shivers of pleasure.

The weekend passed in a flash - but the memories remained to be savoured. She replayed scenes in her mind, each one evoking shades of happiness. Impossible to work - and anyway, what can I do in twenty minutes - except dream?

Perhaps it was the brief conversation with Vee earlier that morning - but for a while, she found her thoughts diverted away from the happy ones associated with the weekend and her wedding plans.

There was something in Vee's face - a clue, maybe? I didn't register it then - but now? Funny how these mental prompts come after the event, she mused. An idea presented itself: she's going to give up university.

Vee's story of stalking and harassment was troubling - easy to understand why she might be afraid of going back. But that's the point - how can she go back? She's refused to involve the police - convinced they'd consider the matter to be trivial. Nothing will change her mind over that - although she's wrong in my opinion.

Thoughts turned to their father. He'll flip his lid if she gives up her studies - and if he knew the real reason behind it, God knows what he'd do! He must be told though–and soon. Let's face it, he's supplementing her student grant. And, I wonder if she's given any consideration how I might feel if she jacks it all in?

A scene remembered from Helen's last day at school played through her mind.

'Please think about what you're doing. I understand life's been hard for you since losing your mother - but to throw away your place at Balliol - that is unthinkable - madness!'

As the memories revisited he troubled mind, Helen experienced the same emotions as those she felt in the Head's office all those years ago - it was if the meeting had happened just a few hours ago.

'I have to Mrs Valentine; I need to be with my dad - he's not coping you see.'

She remembered her determination. Nothing the Head Mistress could say would shake her conviction she must stay and support her father. That was seven years ago. Dad had been so depressed, she reminded herself.

Her mother's illness presented suddenly. The diagnosis of lung cancer came as a sledgehammer blow to them all. She died within six weeks leaving a massive gap in all their lives: one moment there, loving, energetic and supporting and then snatched away. Their father almost lost his business - his frequent absences leading to loss of control, a decline in sales, and a plummet in customer satisfaction. It took a supreme effort on her part to coax and cajole him to move forward.

Up to the time of her mother's sudden illness, a career in law beckoned her. But this vision evaporated - instead, she set about helping her father save his business. By the time her A Level results arrived on a postcard - four A grades, she was established in her self-appointed role of Marketing Director for Park Domestic Appliances.

As for Vee - well, in many ways, I've taken Mum's place. I have a responsibility towards her. With this understanding, she determined to sit with her that evening and sort things out.

***

Vee arrived home damp and dejected. It had been tempting to stay in town: a few pints of Guinness might raise her spirits a little - but it was only Monday - and this wasn't Manchester. The unnecessary reminder of her incarceration in Fairfield now added to her feelings of restriction - once again, she longed to go back to the free existence offered at university.

She slung her jacket on the coat rack by the door and pulled off her shoes - leaking she noted, staring in disgust at her wet socks squelching on the floor tiles. The telephone rang - its loud ring startled her.

'Fairfield 2359.' God, I sound just like Dad! She smiled at the thought.

'Vee, is that you?' said a female voice, high pitched and urgent.

'Fran?'

'Yes, it's me! Listen - oh damn! Hang on a sec' - need to shove some...' The sound of beeps - then Fran's voice

115

returned. 'Look - got to be quick - running out of money. Your boyfriend - I mean your ex...'

'What about him?' Vee's heart pounded. For a few seconds, she saw a vision of Jonny, sitting on a train heading to Fairfield, intent on tracking her down. Then, she heard the unmistakable sound of a car crunching on the gravelled driveway and shot an anxious glance towards the front door.

'He's been banged up - got four years for - what was it? I'm reading the *Manchester Evening News* - violent disorder and actual bodily harm to a policeman. You know what that means don't...' The phone cut dead - Fran had run out of money.

'Oh yes, I know what that means,' she whispered. Only the clatter of the door opening prevented her from dancing and whooping on the spot. Helen and their father spilled into the hall in a flurry of raincoats and umbrellas.

'Are you alright?' said Helen.

Chapter 14

"THE ALHAMBRA"

(Tuesday 1st December 1959)
Tuesday night and, although still early for the main body of revellers - they would arrive later when the pubs shut, the club was already busy. The air was thick with cigarette smoke. A jukebox blared somewhere in the background - a mix of soulful ballads and rock n roll. No one listened - but it created a pleasing ambience.

Two men sat opposite each other at a bar table, heads close together so they could converse above the din, deep in conversation. Older than most of the clientele, they might have seemed out of place - but no one paid them any heed: just two old mates gassing.

Frank did not have a huge network of friends. Although sociable by nature, his friendships were not enduring - not because he fell out with anyone - he simply moved on and would lose touch. Joe was different though - they had shared the experience of army life - both having served together in the same unit in West Germany. They had been drivers by trade - he a staff car driver - his mate a heavy transport specialist, what Joe called a 'proper man's job.' Now, making a living driving long-distance lorries, he spent his life on the road. His peripatetic lifestyle reflected a character with no intention of ever settling down.

Earlier that afternoon, just as he placed his travel bag on his bed having returned from Southampton: 'Frank! Telephone - someone called Joe. Hurry - he's in a call box!' Mrs Bunning, his landlady, handed him the receiver.

'Right, Franky boy, listen up - I'll run out of money any moment. I'm parked up at the Red Lion - end of the High

Street. Get your arse down here for early doors, we've got some serious...'

The beeps, then the phone went dead.

He was supposed to meet with Helen that night: a drink at the *Crows Nest*, where she wanted to discuss their wedding arrangements. For a few moments, he considered calling the *Red Lion* and asking for a message to be passed - some form of excuse for not being able to make it. He checked his watch - almost 3 o'clock. Joe would no doubt be at the bar - last orders for the lunchtime drinkers. He imagined him holding court with regulars, several beers already drunk. He would sleep it off in the afternoon in readiness for the next session when the pub opened its door for the early evening trade.

A flood of images from a former life flickered through his mind. A tinge of nostalgia perhaps for the past long gone? The thought of catching up with his old mate was appealing. *I've not seen him for ages - and we're due for a catch-up.* Counter to this thought, an image of Helen appeared - she would be looking forward to the quiet drink together as planned in their phone call last night. *What if I kill two birds with one stone? Why not take her to meet him?* He dismissed the idea almost as soon as it suggested itself to him. She would not want to set foot in the *Red Lion*. As for Joe? No, she would not like him - not one bit!

He hesitated before reaching into his jacket pocket for some coins. With a heavy feeling of guilt, he telephoned her at the office where he knew she would still be working.

'The handover's taking longer than expected - I have to stay over. I'll make it up to you.'

'But you're supposed to be going up to Birmingham tomorrow - remember. You're relieving Dad on the stand, so he can come home.'

'Bugger - forgot about that! I'll have to drive up directly from Southampton. Look, I'll see you in a few days, okay? Then I'll make it up to you. Perhaps the ring

118

will have arrived by then - we can celebrate in style - book a restaurant, maybe.'

That did the trick. Helen still seemed in post-engagement euphoria. But, he hated lying to her.

The evening started very early with a couple of "snifters" in the *Red Lion*. They followed this with visits to two other pubs along the High Street and were heading for a third, one of Frank's favourites, when Joe spotted the alluring poster inviting passers-by into the delights of the *Alhambra*: "Live band! Dance to the latest numbers - Bar opens till midnight!"

'The youngsters hang out there,' Frank protested, 'we'll seem like a pair of old men compared to them. Let's find somewhere else.'

'What's wrong with you Franky boy? Come on - it'll be like the old days!'

Frank wanted to point out those days were long gone but realised the subtleties of this would be wasted on his mate. Instead, he followed Joe's broad back through the entrance.

As time passed in a blur of beer and cigarettes, the club became very busy, filled with people all intent on having a good time. Groups of young men surveyed the room, drinking and smoking, decked out in their best threads. Girls pretended to ignore the looks aimed towards them but threw occasional glances in return, raising hopes.

At some point, someone turned up the volume of the jukebox. Some couples, eager to create a party atmosphere, danced.

Joe leaned in close - he had to shout in Frank's ear above the din. 'You're making one hell of a decision, mate. How long have you been going out with this girl?'

'Helen - her name's Helen - and we've been together ten months.'

'Ten months! You must be mad! Why do you want to get tied down? The Frank I remember would never let that

119

happen to him - he would want to play the field - not be stuck with one woman. What's the big hurry? Not up the duff, is she?'

'No, she's not and - well, it's time I settled down. I don't expect you to understand that. Life's moved on - at least mine has.' He glanced at his friend. No chance of Joe growing up yet, he concluded.

'The past is behind us - things are different now - I'm not the same person and...'

'We had fun, though, didn't we? You and me - we made a great team eh?' Joe grinned in a way suggesting hidden, shared secrets. This invoked a flurry of brief memories of another world, one in marked contrast to the here and now.

'Yep, they were happy days. Unlike you, though, I don't want to be single forever. Now, seeing as you've necked that one, and I've still got half left in mine, why don't you get the wets in - and leave me in peace for a few moments?'

The expected sarcastic rejoinder did not come. Instead, Joe drained his glass and grinned back. 'You're turning into a lightweight, Frank and, last word on the subject...'

'Oh, I doubt that.'

'I still think you're making a mistake - but it's your funeral, I mean wedding.'

Joe, he noted, appeared to be a little unsteady on his feet as he swayed towards the bar. Bloody hell, not even 8 o'clock and we've seen off more drinks than I can remember! Early start tomorrow - need to slow down. Several minutes later, his friend returned and placed four pints of beer on the table without spilling too much.

'Got extra ones in - save going back for a while. Getting busy in here. Wall to wall fanny, eh Frank!'

He nodded, trying not to show his distaste at Joe's use of language. They drank in companionable silence for a while.

'Well, you won't find me getting tied down. I think you're mad - but if that's what you want, I'll look forward to being your Best Man!' Joe thrust out his hand. 'Now, drink!'

Frank conducted a quick inventory of their conversation so far. No, I don't recall mentioning anything along those lines. The logic of Joe's statement was apparent, though. After all, he is my best mate - in fact, my only mate - so it stands to reason he should be my Best Man. He raised his glass and paused. An imagined vision of Joe attempting to make a speech flashed into his mind - a look of horror on Helen's face as his friend revealed elements of the past long buried. His imagination conjured up further scenes - a nightmare!

Joe featured in a different era of his life, one which Helen did not need to know about. She could never understand. They shared many adventures during their service together in Germany, centred on Hamburg and the Reeperbahn. They were young soldiers, not old enough to vote, but their unique experiences shaped them in a profound way.

He glanced at his mate, who was surveying the room. A small tinge of guilt for thinking negative thoughts about his friend bothered him. Joe, he acknowledged, had a good side. A larger-than-life character, he matched his considerable physical stature with a big heart. His love of beer, though, usually encouraged the darker side of his soul to emerge. His language became uninhibited and his temper, often fierce, could spark at the smallest provocation. During their army days, excessive drinking landed him in trouble frequently, his crimes ranging from lateness on parade to occasional bursts of violence. Oh well - there's plenty of time to sort out the "Best Man" issue.

Their table heaved with empty glasses - the ashtray brimming with cigarette butts. Neither could say for sure how many pints they had drunk so far, but it would be enough to floor many men. Their initiation to boozing took place in the various bars and clubs in Hamburg and theirs had been a long apprenticeship.

As the evening advanced, their conversation dried up, and they sat watching what was going on around them. Frank enjoyed people-watching when drinking. At this point, both his and Joe's attention focused on a group of girls. Although their conversation couldn't be heard from where they sat, it was clear they were in high spirits. Occasional shrieks of laughter pierced through the din. The *Alhambra*, it seemed, was not the first drinking den visited by them that night.

One of the girls negotiated her way towards the busy bar while her companions made space for themselves at a table crowded with uncollected empties. It was the girl aiming for the bar who caught his attention. He could not have put a label on the girl's sartorial style, but he found the overall impression appealing and sensuous. She wore a black roll-neck sweater and tight chequered jodhpurs. Her head was topped with a black beret which perched at a jaunty angle over short-cropped dark black hair. Bright red lipstick, he noted, made her smile dazzling. She smiled a lot. With a sudden flash of guilt, he turned his head away.

'Same again, Frank?'

'My round, isn't it?'

'What the hell. I'll fetch the beers, and you can get us into that group over there. Come on, you haven't stopped ogling them since they came in - use your charm.'

'No, leave it, Joe. They don't need us butting into their party. They won't be interested in a couple of old farts like us, for heaven's sake.'

'Come on, what've we got to lose? Live for the moment - you'll be an old married man soon!'

Within a short space of time, the group accepted them into their midst. A round of drinks helped to facilitate their way in. Frank's reservations melted away as he hid behind the charming, confident persona he could slip into with ease when the mood took him. Helen drifted to the back of his mind - but thoughts of her did not disappear entirely. Occasional pangs of guilt prodded him.

The noise level in the club reached a fever pitch, added to by a small but very enthusiastic pop group who had started to perform. Shouted conversations, cheering and whistling added to the cacophony. Two of the girls joined the gathering couples on the dance floor. A pair of young men lurched after them seeing an opportunity. Others followed. The party developed from there.

He waited, biding his time, talking to the girl's companions, telling risqué jokes that raised a laugh. His magnetism worked.

Looking around, he saw Joe had cornered the girl with the beret. Subtlety and charm were not qualities possessed by his mate, who preferred a more direct approach. It worked sometimes - at least he claimed it did.

Joe had the girl pinned against a pillar - he towered over her. She looked small, trapped and uncomfortable. Frank grabbed the opportunity. The girl seemed relieved when he appeared at her shoulder. He winked at her. 'Come on Joe, give the lady some space, you're suffocating her!'

He registered the brief flash of anger on Joe's face as he turned his head. But he pulled away, releasing her. The girl leaned forward as if released from a trap. She grabbed Frank's elbow and lifted herself up on tiptoe.

'He's okay! Joe's been telling me about your adventures in Hamburg. Sounds like you and him...' The rest of what she said was drowned by a crescendo of noise. She smiled at Joe and patted his arm. Joe grinned back.

Frank stared down into the girl's eyes, studying her grinning face - tantalising and mischievous. 'I think you'd better introduce us, Joe,' he shouted.

123

Joe shook his head and pointed to his ears. The noise had become almost deafening. Then he waved and shuffled away, no doubt to try his luck elsewhere. At that point, the pop group finished a lively number. The appreciative audience erupted in applause and whistles. The girl's lips moved - she stretched up and tried to make herself heard. He shook his head to show he couldn't hear although he thought he might have heard 'Dee.'

Impossible to conduct any form of meaningful conversation, he pointed to her nearly empty pint of Guinness, inclining his head towards the bar. She nodded. He took her glass and inched his way through the crowd. He had not expected the girl to come with him, but an unexpected surge of excitement rushed through him as he felt her hand gripping his sleeve as she followed behind him, the pair of them shuffling through the good-natured punters.

The colossal din of music made it almost impossible to communicate other than through signals and body language. This didn't seem to matter: the girl was drunk, he realised. Later, they swayed in a parody of dancing - just one of many such couples crammed on the small dance floor. He glanced down. Her head rested on his chest, eyes closed, a contented smile on her face.

Although alcohol dulled his inhibitions, pangs of guilt troubled him. *What am I doing?* The realisation he was crossing a line sparked fear. Although he had never been in the club before and, as far as he was aware, neither had Helen, there was the danger someone might recognise him - after all, he had become well-known in the local community. Perhaps one of Helen's friends was watching, judging him. A fearful glance around the floor - no one seemed to pay attention to them. But who knows? He imagined her reaction when told of his transgression - the hurt, the anger - their relationship ended. It was a huge relief when the loud, mind-numbing music finished.

'Time, please! Thank you!' The ringing of a bell. The girl opened her eyes and stared unblinking up at him. She stumbled - he held her up. She blinked at him as if disorientated and seeing him for the first time.

It happened in a flash. One moment she was gazing into his eyes, and then she crooked an arm around his neck and pulled his head down to hers as if she wanted to tell him something. Her lips rammed against his. After the briefest hesitation, he responded.

The moment was fleeting. One of her girlfriends grabbed her by the elbow and yanked her away throwing him a disdainful glance. Enveloped back into the throng of her party, the group made towards the exit door. He watched as they moved away as one, the girl almost hidden in the centre. She turned as the party reached the door and with her free arm made a beckoning wave to him: 'Come on!' he saw her mouth say. Her companions bundled her through the door and she vanished.

For some time, he stared at the door through which the girl had disappeared. A part of him, perhaps more than a small part, felt tempted. His feet made a sudden move towards the door. Then an overwhelming sense of shame swept over him and he turned around, disgusted with himself. He fumbled in his jacket pocket then swore, realising he had left his cigarettes on the bar.

Joe appeared at his shoulder. 'Bloody hell, I thought you were in there! Why don't you go after her? They're probably going on to some hop somewhere. We could go with them!'

'No,' he replied, 'I don't think so. You go if you like. I'm done in - need my bed.'

A few minutes later, having cadged cigarettes from Joe, he left the club and started the long walk back to his digs. Even though his thoughts were dominated with guilt, in a small, dark area of his mind lurked the hope he might encounter the girl again.

Chapter 15

"RECOGNITION"

Helen fixed Vee, who sat across the kitchen table from her, with a level gaze - she wanted a response to the question she had just asked.

'What? Sorry, I was miles away.'

'Do you need a lift to the station?' she said a little louder, her voice expressing exasperation. 'On second thoughts, must you go today? You don't seem at all well.' She frowned. 'In fact, you look awful.'

'I'm fine, but I wouldn't mind another cup of coffee to perk me up.'

Vee stared back at her through bleary, bloodshot eyes.

It would be so easy, tempting even, to reproach, to adopt the moral high ground, Helen thought. But would there be any point?

'You had a good night, then?' She could not resist throwing a meaningful glance. 'You got in at half past five this morning! Lucky Dad didn't hear you coming in - he would've gone ape! He worries so much about you.'

Here I go, she thought, nagging, being critical.

'I went to a party. Remember those, where people meet up and enjoy themselves?'

Helen ignored what she considered being an unnecessary, petulant comment. Vee turned away as if embarrassed and ashamed.

'I don't want to sound like an old nag, but...' She left her sentence unfinished and studied her sister, who seemed to shun eye contact with her. *Why can she not understand the simple fact I care about her?*

Vee stared at a framed photograph hanging on the wall. Helen followed her gaze and studied it. The image of their mother depicted in it would always be imprinted on her mind - Vee's as well no doubt. This thought prompted an awareness of just how much she had taken on a maternal role.

'Please be careful,' she whispered, 'you may be almost twenty-one and used to looking after yourself - but I still worry about you, you know.'

Vee seemed to consider this for a few moments. 'What are you worried about? I don't take dope, and I'm not jumping into bed with every man I meet. That is what you're getting at, isn't it?'

A surge of anger almost caused her to retaliate and point out the unfairness in this response, something like: 'I had to forego the joys of being young to care for you and Dad - so cut the attitude.' But there was no need - shame etched into Vee's face.

Silence for several seconds - then: 'Sorry, sis, I didn't mean to snap - but you're right, I can take care of myself.'

'Yes, I'm sure you can,' her voice conciliatory now, 'but I would hate for you to be taken advantage of, especially when you're, well...'

'Pissed?' Vee scowled and then giggled. 'Oh, don't look so shocked - that's what you were thinking.'

Mum would never have brooked such language, but then I'm not her. She laughed, knowing Vee was trying to goad a reaction. But then she adopted a reproachful expression - no point in laughing off a serious matter.

'Yes, when you're drunk- which is quite a lot wouldn't you agree?'

Vee turned away again, once more anchoring her gaze on the framed scene. She nodded her head as if in agreement but unwilling to show acceptance.

Helen didn't need to look at the photograph to recall the details. The photograph captured a moment from ten years back. A young, pretty woman sat on a beach, leaning forward and smiling. Two little girls huddled next to her.

Helen stared at her younger self gazing back at her, reflecting her mother's smile. A junior version of Vee, profiled with her head side on, distracted it seemed, or perhaps rebelling, refusing to cooperate with a suitable pose

***

Vee studied the depiction of a now forgotten day at the beach. She could remember nothing of that day - but the vista of a happy family fascinated her - it helped focus her mind while she thought.

Helen's words, combined with a revelation of self-knowing, showed what her life had become. But admitting this seemed so difficult - pride, perhaps? Too late to change the past. University had provided an endless abundance of pleasing distractions - so many parties and new, exciting experiences. Too much fun - the line crossed into excess - a dangerous road to take. An uncomfortable truth - but perhaps it is time to take stock - be a little more ordinary. She screwed her face up at the notion.

Vague, incomplete memories of the previous night flitted through her mind - a flurry of images. Her head thumped - hangover fuelled by anxiety and something else - was it guilt? She could not remember how she got home - in fact, few clear recollections presented. A man featured at some point - but nothing happened. Did it? She grimaced, struggling to recall details fogged through the amount of alcohol imbibed during a fun-packed evening. The frivolities went on into the small hours - was that man there? She wasn't sure.

Last night had been a celebration: her "Return to University" party. No more Jonny - free to go back. A comforting reminder perhaps last night was a form of passing - casting off the old Vee with one more blow out? Lost in her musings, she forgot about Helen until she spoke.

'Have a good time back at university. I really am pleased you're going back.' She laughed at Vee's frown. 'You know what I mean! I'll miss you - but I'm glad you can finish your degree now. But take care - okay?'

A momentary pause as if considering these words and then a nod. 'Yes, you're right. I'll tone it down a bit - be more sensible and...'

'You don't need to change who you are. But cut back on the booze a little, yes?'

'Oh, definitely.'

'And if you must take a boyfriend, try to find someone - well - normal.' Helen smiled- a small sparkle of humour.

Vee nodded and smiled back, although a faint twinge of resentment at being lectured to burned like a small ember in her mind. But the lecture was over - a blessed relief. A shuddering yawn - she clapped her hand over her mouth.

'Oh God, sorry, I'm so tired.' She got up from the table and walked over to the kitchen sink, filled a glass with water and drained it in a series of gulps.

'Do you need to go today? Why don't you go back to bed - for a few hours at least? You'll feel a lot better. Go tomorrow - please. Dad will drive you to the station.'

The suggestion of some rest seemed appealing.

'Go on - you're in no fit state to travel. I'll get you up at about five, and...' Helen smiled, 'why don't you and I go out for dinner? There's a fantastic Italian opened on the High Street. Frank and I went there a few weeks back. I can update you on my wedding plans.'

Vee nodded, smiling, as though relieved to be given no choice. 'Sounds fab! It'll be nice to catch up on the details. You know, I have absolutely no idea what this bloke of yours looks like!'

Helen waved her hand in a shooing motion. 'Go on, bed! I'll get you up later.'

**

129

The aroma from the pizza oven rekindled an appetite and reminded Vee, she had not eaten for several hours. She nibbled on a bread stick, looking forward to more substantial sustenance. Staying an extra night was a wise move, she mused, glad Helen had persuaded her to stay.

The waiter, flamboyant, theatrical and an outrageous flirt, amused them both. In marked contrast to the sombre mood of their earlier talk, the atmosphere was now relaxed and happy, the focus of conversation Helen's engagement. A courier had arrived that afternoon, an unexpected but most welcome surprise it seemed.

'I'll show you at the restaurant - I want us to celebrate. You'll be the first person I've shown the ring to!'

Helen ordered for them both with evident confidence. Restaurants with exotic menus did not feature at university - this was a different, new world.

'Thank you, Gino - yes. Minestrone to start, and we'll try the Seafood Pasta as the main.'

'And wine, madam?'

'A carafe of house white - do you reckon, Vee?'

'Oh yes, that will be lovely.'

The wine arrived - glasses were charged. 'Well, here's to your return to university.'

'And to your engagement!'

She was relieved Helen hadn't insisted on ordering soft drinks. A few sips of wine hit the mark. Leaning forward in her seat, she adopted an expectant, eager smile.

'Come on, show me the ring.'

Helen smiled and delved into her handbag, pulling out a small blue velvet box, which she nipped open and held out for inspection.

'It's beautiful, Helen. Go on, put it on.'

Helen slipped the ring on her finger and extended her hand out over the table. 'A perfect fit,' she said, her face beaming. 'I can't wait to show Frank - I'll ask him to put in on - you know, make the point.'

'Isn't he supposed to go down on one knee - do things properly?'

'I somehow doubt he'd do that. Anyway, he's already asked me to marry him - or did he?' She looked doubtful - and then smiled. 'Actually, it may have been me who asked him.'

'Gosh, how very contemporary! So, when's he back again?'

'Wednesday. He will be busy at the exhibition - at least I hope he is. Cost us a packet to hire a stand there. I told him about the ring when he telephoned earlier. Typical Frank - he didn't sound particularly excited.' She paused - frown replaced her smile. 'In fact, he seemed subdued.'

'Maybe he's missing you.'

'Hum, perhaps. He promised to take me out for a celebratory meal when he gets back.'

'It really is a beautiful ring - it must have cost a small fortune!'

'But he knows I'm worth it. He was relieved I didn't need to drag him around all the jewellers in Knightsbridge because I knew exactly what I wanted - he hates shopping.'

'So, when am I going to meet your beau? He sounds quite a catch. Trust you to find yourself a hero to marry!'

'Oh, you'll see him soon enough. Such a shame he had to go up to Birmingham. It'll have to be Christmas now - I'm assuming you *are* coming back - I mean, you're not going to stay up in Manchester, are you?'

'Of course, I'll be back! I'm looking forward to your engagement party.'

'We're not going to have a big affair - Frank doesn't want a fuss. But we will organise a little family celebration.'

'So, apart from being a knight in shining armour, what's he like? Is he tall, short, fat, thin?'

Helen smiled and unclipped the clasp on her handbag, rummaging inside. She pulled out a folded card. 'This is the invitation to his award ceremony - I think I kept it in here - yes. This is the clipping from the *Standard*. Not a great photo - but that's him. Not a bad looking chap, is he?'

It was as if the man in the photograph could see her. Grainy and indistinct at first, the image blended with the one she held in her head - now much clearer. The embarrassed smile in the picture changed form, shaping into a lecherous grin. She dropped the paper as if it were red hot.

'Are you alright? You've gone ever so pale!'

'Yes - sorry Helen. I think last night's catching up with me. Give me a few minutes, I need...'

Vee stood, grasped the back of her chair to steady herself - then, conscious Helen was watching her, she ran to the bathroom.

Chapter 16

"FLEUR"

An attractive housewife with a radiant smile and wearing a floral apron stared unblinkingly from her cardboard world. The "Vaculux upright" vacuum cleaner, the latest model from Park Domestic Appliances, provided a life-changing experience - the source of her apparent happiness.

Frank sat next to the cheerful scene, his image a marked contrast to his static companion. His head drooped, and he stared at a spot on the floor between his feet. A cigarette dangled from the fingers of one hand, in the other, he held a plastic cup, the dregs of tea still in it - now an ashtray.

Bob left an hour ago, flushed with excitement. 'That daughter of mine has a fine business head on her. She said direct marketing at exhibitions would be the way forward and, by God, she's so right! There've been countless wholesale orders - and expressions of interest in opening Park franchises. Things are looking up, Frank! Make sure you give out plenty of these - get the brand name out there.'

He handed over a box of enamel badges shaped as tiny "Vaculux" uprights.

'We've entered a different era, Frank,' Bob announced as he rummaged for his car keys hidden somewhere in the detritus of brochures, boxes of promotional materials and empty coffee cups. 'No more door-to-door sales - we need to build a team of area representatives. In future, we'll sell to wholesalers, just like Helen said. If all goes well, we'll open a chain of franchises across the South of England.'

Finding his keys, he pumped his hand. 'Good luck, Frank - and bring 'em in!'

***

The journey up to Birmingham had been painful. A sizeable hangover and the relentless thoughts about the events of the previous evening combined to sap his soul. He sighed with relief when Bob left him alone.

Late in the afternoon now - the main throng of visitors had gone, leaving a few stragglers in the exhibition hall. He did his best to muster enthusiasm - to put on a welcoming smile and try to usher passers-by to the stand. One potential punter visited - but, after a cursory inspection of the "Vaculux" and a quizzical stare at him, left. Frank gave up after that. A glance at his watch - half an hour to go before shutting time.

'What the bloody hell did you think you were playing at?'

His imagination presented the image of the woman in the cardboard upright, who would be about the same age as Helen, waving her finger at him - the one not holding the handle of the cleaner. Her eyes flashed, angry and accusing - her lips no longer smiling but mouthing disgust. 'Engaged for a week and you've betrayed her already!'

He nodded in acknowledgement - the image didn't need to remind him. The fact he allowed the situation to happen even though still in control of his actions created a depressing reminder. But the most worrying thought, one that nagged and prodded, was the one that questioned his relationship with Helen.

He remembered his response to the girl's kiss - and the desire to follow her, one he could so easily have succumbed to if his conscience had not stopped him. An insidious doubt took seed within his mind and, try as he might, he could not quash it. *I'm being dragged into marriage. She wants it - but is it what I want?*

134

***

5 o'clock arrived at last. He locked up the stand and boarded a bus that would take him to his hotel.

After checking in, he telephoned Helen. She sounded happy, which came as a relief. He wondered why and then realised. The guilty part of his mind anticipated the possibility of an accusation: 'Who was that girl you were all over last night?' he imagined her asking. Instead, she told him her engagement ring arrived that afternoon.

'It's beautiful, Frank - a perfect fit. Oh, I wish you were here - I want you to see it - to put it on for me - so we can be engaged properly.'

A heavy load of guilt pressed down on him. When she suggested they celebrate on his return on Friday evening, he tried to sound enthusiastic.

'Is everything okay?' He detected her hesitation - a hint of doubt in her voice. 'Are you alright? You seem down,' she said.

'Oh, I'm fine - just a little tired that's all. Why not? Yes, let's book a restaurant - make it an occasion.'

The image of his cardboard companion appeared in his mind. Her arms were folded, the "Vaculux" gone now. She looked at him with a cynical smile on her face - as if she could sense his weakness.

Helen sounded placated and reassured. He put the phone down after promising to call again at the same time tomorrow. Returning to his hotel room, he threw his briefcase on the chair and himself on to the bed having turned off the room lights and switched on the bedside light. He lay staring at the ceiling, drained, waiting for weariness to overcome him so he could shut his eyes and escape his feelings of utter dejection.

He dozed, but only for a few moments. The sound of a man and woman arguing in the corridor outside woke him. He listened like an eavesdropper, unable to stop himself.

The female voice dominated - she sounded shrill and incensed. The male voice less vocal - occasional muffled words as if trying to interject but without success.

A clear scene formed in his mind: a young woman, wronged by the man, was remonstrating with him, and the man had difficulty in defending himself from her verbal onslaught. The woman's voice was the loudest - shrill and caustic in equal measure. Then the man's voice becomes louder, more strident. He imagines the man holding out his hands, trying to placate the woman, calm her down - but to no avail.

'Not this time!' yelled the female voice. The man makes a shushing noise. Frank sensed his embarrassment and humiliation. A door slammed shut followed a few seconds later by a loud banging that could only be the man knocking on the door shut in his face.

'Fleur!' The sound of the door knob being twisted and turned - the man sounded angry and frustrated. 'For fuck's sake!' Heavy footsteps pounded down the corridor.

He lay on his bed, unable to sleep. The argument outside his door, which on other occasions might have provided light entertainment, had intensified his gloom. A glance at his watch - approaching 7 o'clock. Faint stirrings of hunger reminded him he had eaten nothing all day. He saw fish and chips on a bed of newspaper - this presented a most appealing prospect. Perhaps a couple of pints in a local boozer as well might help to lift his spirits. He raised himself off the bed, stripped off his shirt, grabbed his toiletry bag - a present from Helen - and a towel. A freshen up first, he told himself.

He discovered an ancient looking, but functional shower in the bathroom, which offered a better proposition than a quick scrub down. No point in getting dressed - a change of clothes would be appropriate now he had freshened up. He padded back along the corridor with his towel wrapped around him, his trousers, shoes, and socks clutched in a precarious bundle under one arm, the wash bag dangling from his fingertips. As he inserted his key in the lock, he heard a click and detected a faint draft of air behind him. He turned his head around in an automatic reaction and found himself staring at the face of a young woman, her head looking out from the gap in the door, held on a chain. She frowned for a moment - then smiled. 'Hello,' she said.

'Good evening,' he replied in a polite tone of voice, conscious of his state of undress. He turned back to his door, fumbling with the key; uncertain whether he should engage in conversation, aware also that his towel was working itself loose. He pulled the door open quickly and slipped through the gap, his towel falling to the floor at the same time. The door opposite hadn't closed, and he guessed the face must have watched his inelegant and amusing entrance.

Frank grabbed the towel and wrapped it around him again and opened the door, enough to poke his head through. The young woman's face stared back at him, a trace of a smile on her face. He grinned back at her, noting she was pretty and interesting-looking.

'Sorry about that,' he said, 'a tad embarrassing.'

The girl released the chain from her door and opened it a little. She laughed then looked up the corridor, her face turning fearful.

'I think he's gone,' he offered.

Her face creased in an embarrassed smile. 'You overheard the argument, I suppose?'

He shrugged in what he hoped conveyed 'Hey, none of my business.'

'Are you okay?'

She nodded. Streaks of mascara smeared on her cheeks showed she had been crying. 'He'll be back; he won't give up.'

The words came out before he could stop them.

'Well, if you're not here, he's not going to find you, is he? Just a thought, but I'm going out for a bite to eat - maybe a drink or two. Would you like to join me?'

An inner voice whispered to him. 'That was rather forward of you, wasn't it? And what about all that self-recrimination this afternoon?'

She appeared to hesitate, but only for a moment. 'You know what, that sounds like a jolly good idea! Just give me five minutes - I need to put my face back on.' She nodded at him as if to say, 'All agreed then,' and added, 'I'm Fleur by the way.'

'Frank,' he said in return. They shut their doors at the same time.

He dressed, wondering what he would do if the girl's male companion came back in the next few minutes. His feelings of guilt returned when he realised he looked forward to his impromptu date.

***

They found a small café across the road from the hotel. He noticed Fleur cast worried glances towards the hotel's entrance - looking, he guessed, for the possible return of "the Man."

'His name's Raymond - Ray.' Fleur volunteered this information while they ate supper: mixed grill for him and cheese on toast for her. 'We've been seeing each other for a few months - we were close - a couple.'

Later, having moved on to a small, busy pub in which they found a free table, Fleur became more loquacious, helped by several glasses of port and lemon. He listened with interest as his new companion told him the story of her doomed relationship.

'Of course, I never guessed he was married. He seemed so nice, caring - perfect, in fact. I was feeling low having finished with my boyfriend. He went off to university, and he never bothered contacting me. And along came Ray - when my defences were down.'

Little by little, the layers of her story were unpeeled. Frank formed an image of her boyfriend, which made him uncomfortable. He realised he and the focus of conversation were not dissimilar in how they behaved.

'Oh, I'm a sales assistant in the cosmetics department of John Lewis in the city centre,' Fleur explained. 'Ray's a rep - he would often come in with new products for us to sell. We hit it off straight away. He was such fun, and interesting too.'

'And married,' he reminded her. He realised he had adopted a critical tone, which, in the circumstances, struck him as ironic - no, hypocritical. 'Sorry,' he added, 'Obviously, I'm not suggesting you were to blame in any way - I mean, how were you to know he was hitched?'

'You're right - he never mentioned that little fact. He gave every impression he was footloose and fancy-free. He saw his chance and grabbed it.' She gazed at him as if seeking approval. Frank nodded, showing he understood. He adopted a contrived, sympathetic smile.

'Ray was so charming, so...' She hesitated, and he sensed the bitterness in her voice, guessing there was more sordid detail to follow.

'I could kick myself. I mean, how many men in their thirties are single these days?' She stared ahead and frowned before adding: 'Unless they're divorced.' He saw the quizzical expression on her face. He ignored the unspoken question.

'How did you find out?'

'He told me,' Fleur said. 'Just like that - as if it were no big deal. He got annoyed with me because - well, I wanted some commitment from him. Perhaps I pushed too hard. I got angry because we had - well, you know...'

'Slept together,' he finished for her.

She nodded. 'Yes. I felt used - like a cheap tart. I would never have let things go that far had I realised.'

He lit a cigarette and handed it to her. She took a deep drag and blew a cloud of smoke up to the ceiling.

'Come on, Fleur - you seem to blame yourself when he's the one to blame. None of this is your fault.'

'If only things had been that simple.' Her eyes bore into his. 'Why didn't I walk away when I realised what he was about? How could I be so stupid?'

'You kept seeing him?'

'Yes. I believed his lies. He told me his marriage had fallen apart - "official separation," he said. Oh, how wronged he was, the poor darling. She had been having a fling with her boss and he found out. Well, that put a different slant on things for me - in fact, when he told me that, everything was okay again. I even felt sorry for him. So, we continued seeing each other.'

He nodded, realising he had gripped her hand across the table. A pang of guilt again. She wiped a tear from her eye, smearing mascara across her cheek.

'Of course, he was lying - I was such a fool to be taken in by him.' She pulled a handkerchief from her handbag and dabbed at her eyes.

'What happened? How did you find out?' He realised he was genuinely interested. I think I'm comparing notes with this bloke, he thought.

'I got his address from the store's admin department - I only had to ask. No one asked me why I needed it. Anyway, a couple of weeks ago, Jen, she's my flatmate, drove me down to Nuneaton, where his address is. We found his house with his car parked right outside. We pulled up a little way down the road and waited. I had no idea what I was looking for. But, after a few minutes. his front door opened and out came Ray and...' She paused - perhaps reliving the moment in her head. '...a woman. I knew it was his wife - came out behind him with a toddler in her arms, a little boy. Quite the family scene! She followed him to the garden gate - and he hugged and kissed the pair of them before getting into his car and driving away. He even beeped the horn and waved his hand out of the window.'

He made sympathetic noises and put his arm around her shoulders and squeezed.

'I wanted to get out and confront his wife - tell her the truth about her precious husband and their wonderful marriage! Jen had to hold me back to stop me getting out of the car. I was livid!'

He nodded and patted her hand. 'You poor thing,' he said with as much sympathy as he could contrive. 'Let's have another drink,' he added.

'That would be nice,' she said, smiling back.

As he made his way to the crowded bar, he thought about what was happening. A looming sense of discomfiture was fighting with an urge to continue along the route he had opened. He knew compulsion was winning. *I only met this wronged woman two hours ago, and she's confiding her deepest secrets. Where's this going to lead?*

When he returned to the table with their drinks, she was applying lipstick, manoeuvring a compact mirror to capture her image - he found this alluring. She snapped it shut and looked at him. 'I'm sorry; you don't need to hear my tale of woe. I must sound like a "Moaning Minnie." I bet you're thinking: shouldn't play with married men or something like that.'

Is she reading my mind? he thought. 'Not at all,' he lied. 'You shouldn't blame yourself. He sounds like a complete bastard.'

'Thanks, Frank, you're so understanding.' She rested her head on his shoulders - a brief suggestion of intimacy. He kept his arm around her - a gentle squeeze of encouragement. Thoughts of Helen were buried far to the

141

back of his mind. The darker side of him was in the ascendancy with a powerful grip.

'What the hell am I doing?' asked a faint voice of reason.

'So, what happened today? How did you end up with him in the hotel?'

'I wanted to confront him - challenge him face to face. We used to stay at the same hotel when he came to town. I would book the room under the names Mr and Mrs Smith!' She laughed. 'How obvious is that?'

This sparked a recent memory of his visit to London with Helen. 'To buy an engagement ring,' reminded an accusing voice.

Fleur emptied her port and lemon, shaking her head when he reached out for the glass.

'I booked the room, as I always did,' she continued, 'Ray pays cash, so there was never a problem. I had checked in, left my overnight bag in the room and gone out. We always met in the same place: a little tea shop, not too far from here. We would go together to the hotel afterwards.'

'But why did you book a room? Why not simply confront him and be done with it?'

'I live out in the countryside; about half an hour away, you see. So, I came here straight from work. I wasn't sure I would be in a fit state to go home after, well, confronting him and....' She gazed at him. 'Would you think I was wrong if I said I wanted just one more night with him?'

He shook his head as if in disbelief. 'Why on earth would you do that? I mean, after what he did to you?'

'Well, I've got my needs, and..' she paused as if gathering her thoughts, 'I wanted him to realise what he'd be missing. I was going to confront him in the morning - finish with him at that point.'

She laughed without humour. 'Well, things didn't turn out as planned. Ray knew something was wrong and, well,

I ended up blurting out everything as we were walking upstairs to the room. I think you know what happened after that.'

They sat in silence for a while.

'Do you think I'm a bad person?' she said, suddenly.

'No, not at all. But I think you learned a valuable lesson. That's life, Fleur - we all make mistakes from time to time; the key point is to learn from them and move on.'

She nodded and smiled clearly pleased with his response. He smiled back and raised his beer glass.

'To a better future, free of Ray!'

'I'll drink to that!' she said, emptying the final dregs of port and lemon. They sat in companionable silence for a few moments. Her head rested on his shoulder again, his arm squeezing her in close.

'What about you?' She pulled away from him as if the thought had just struck her. 'Are you married? I bet you are - just my luck!'

'No, and I'm not divorced or separated,' he said without hesitation.

'So, you haven't got anyone else? No girlfriend?'

The words flew from his mouth before a stab of guilt hit him in the guts. 'No, free and single!'

She smiled, pulling his arm over her shoulder again, kissing him on the cheek.

'So, what will we do if this Ray is in your room when you return? I'm guessing he would pick up a key from the Reception.'

She frowned and shrugged. 'Yes, he could do that. And, as my overnight bag is still there, he'll know I didn't go home. He'll be worried I might spill the beans to his wife. I did sort of hint, I might do that - although I wouldn't. He might be waiting for me - or maybe he'll come back later. I mean, I'm not frightened of him - he's not violent or anything like that. But I don't want to see him - he's very persuasive, you see, and I don't want to give in to him.'

'You think he'll be there?'

'Yes, I think he will be.'

'If only you'd put your overnight bag in my room.'

She paused as if thinking - then hooted with laughter. 'It would have seemed strange, though, wouldn't it? Asking a man who I've known for a few minutes to help me out!'

'And wearing nothing but a towel!' He chuckled, remembering the scene earlier that afternoon. As he drained the rest of his pint, the darker side of his mind had formulated the basis of a plan.

'Fleur, we have to do something. I don't think you should meet this Ray if he is waiting in your room. And you certainly shouldn't spend the night with him. I've got an idea that might just work.'

She looked at him - her eyes expectant - a look of trust.

'You need to go into your room and retrieve your stuff without him in there. We've got to get him out somehow.'

'Do you think it'll work?' he asked, having explained his ruse.

'Worth a try.'

She was grinning as if enjoying the prospect of an adventure.

**

His plan worked, a fact he would later regret as it opened a door through which he should not have stepped - a door named "Temptation".

He dictated a note to her, which she wrote on a page torn from her diary.

'This will be the bait,' he said. 'What we need to do is draw him out of the room, thinking he's going to meet you in the lobby. You'll be waiting behind the door of my room. As soon as you hear your door open wait for a count of ten - that should be enough time for him to head down the corridor and down the stairs out of sight. All you need to do then is nip in your room, grab the bag and get back in my room again.'

As arranged, he entered the lobby a few moments behind her to give the impression they had been on separate engagements. She was standing at the reception desk talking to the bored looking night janitor. Without raising his head, which was buried in the sports pages of the "Daily Express," he confirmed: 'Yes, Mr Smith collected the key to your room earlier on.'

They went up the staircase together. Her mood had transformed into one of merriment and she giggled - she was drunk, he realised. He stopped her before they reached the top, pressing a finger to her lips.

'Shush, we need to be quiet or you'll give the game away.'

She nodded - serious for a moment then holding a hand to her mouth to suppress a giggling fit. 'What a hoot!' she whispered.

He groaned.

The upstairs corridor, to his great relief, was silent and empty. 'Go on,' he mouthed, giving her a gentle push. In a few seconds, she had walked the few paces to his room, opened his door with his key and shut it behind her. A few moments later, he tiptoed towards the room. A pool of light shone from under the door and there was the sound of muffled music and metallic voices from a transistor radio.

Frank bent down and slid the note under the door, then tapped lightly. Within seconds, he had retreated and slipped into the bathroom adjacent to the stairwell.

The sound of a door being opened. 'Fleur? Hey, wait.' Footsteps padded past the bathroom door towards the stairwell. Frank poked his head out of the door in time to see Fleur flitting into her room - she re-emerged with her bag, crossed over and entered his room closing the door behind her. He grinned. This was going like clockwork, he congratulated himself. He turned his ear to the stairwell - no sound of returning footsteps. Seconds later, he was back in his room. He shut the door behind them, applied the latch and put on the door chain.

'Bingo!' he whispered. 'Best keep the light off for now, we don't want to attract suspicion. He'll be back soon no doubt.'

Fleur clung to him and he held her in a protective embrace. He could feel her body shaking. 'Don't worry, you're safe now,' he whispered. Then he realised she was wracked not with fear but with suppressed mirth. He found himself chuckling as well.

A couple of minutes passed then the sound of a muttering voice approaching. They both held their breath. Several expletives were followed by the creak of the door opposite being opened and then shut. They exhaled at the same time.

'Gosh, that was so much fun - that'll teach him to...' The sound of the door across the corridor opening again. He held his hand over her mouth. She gaped wide eyed up at him.

He sensed the presence of the man on the other side of the door. A light tapping.

'Fleur! Are you in there?'

They both froze, holding their breath again. Then he was gone. Fainter knocking was heard further down the corridor. 'He's going to try every room to see if you're in there,' Frank whispered.

'Bugger off!' shouted a voice. Another door opened followed by a heated exchange. Seconds later, it was clear Ray had re-entered his room.

'I think we'd better lay low for a while. We don't want him to hear us leaving. And he might decide to check out instead of waiting for the morning. We wouldn't want to bump into him in the lobby, would we?'

'Why leave at all? Look, Frank, it's late. There may not be enough time for me to catch the last train and look,' she said, flipping back the curtain, 'it's raining.'

He was about to make the same suggestion and was delighted Fleur made it first.

'I'll sleep on the chair, you have the bed,' she offered. He suggested the opposite. After a few minutes, she was in his bed having undressed with no embarrassment it seemed. Even though the lights were off, he averted his eyes. She fell asleep in a few seconds - the faint sound of snoring emerging from the bed.

Oh well, no harm done, he thought. Perhaps the beer consumed earlier had dulled his senses - but at this moment, he felt gallant, a true gentleman. He shivered as he settled into the bedside chair. His coat provided a makeshift blanket - but it did little to ease the cold. This promised to be an uncomfortable night. Less than an hour later, he woke with a groan - he had a cramp in his legs, but it was the inevitable effects of the beer that woke him. Careful not to wake her, he opened the door which he locked behind him - best to be on the safe side.

After returning, he had just pulled his coat back over him when: 'Frank,' she whispered. 'Frank!' a little louder. The sound of bed clothes rustling as she moved across to the side of the bed where he had just settled himself down. 'Look, this is silly. You can't sleep all night in that chair. I don't mind, really, if you want to share.'

He didn't need to be asked twice.

Chapter 17

"HELEN'S NEWS"

Helen felt alone and despondent. As she sat sipping a cup of tea, she tried to assure herself that her feelings must be related to Vee's departure. But no, although she cried when she returned from dropping her at the station, this was not the real reason. Anyway, she would be home again in a few weeks for Christmas.

No, the primary cause of her sadness derived from the phone call from Frank last night. He phoned much later than usual. This was not like him - he liked routines, including calling as agreed. But even his lateness might be explained by a need to work late at the exhibition. I'm being silly, she admonished herself. But something was not right. He did not sound himself: no good-natured banter - his natural warmth had been absent - he came over almost monosyllabic. And he called not from the quiet of the hotel call box but from somewhere with noise in the background - muffled conversations and music. It sounded like a pub which wasn't an issue - but he did not volunteer the fact.

Try as she might, she could not rationalise and quell her worries. Something is wrong - could he be having second thoughts about the engagement? This thought made her heart jolt. The urgent sound of the telephone ringing in the hallway startled her.

'Hello - is that Miss Park - Miss Helen Park?'

'Speaking.'

'Fairfield Clinic here. Just to let you know your results are back and...'

Her heart leapt for the second time in a matter of seconds.

'Can you tell me, please - am I...?'

'I'm afraid I can't give you any information over the phone - you must make an appointment with Doctor Scott - he'll explain everything.'

She replaced the receiver and sat down in the chair next to it. Her heart pounded in painful thuds, her breaths too rapid - she realised a panic attack held her in its grip.

Yesterday, when she said goodbye to Vee at the railway station, the temptation to confide in her was strong. But something in her sister's demeanour stopped her. Did she appear worried about something? Perhaps the thought of starting back at university again? Whatever it might have been, she kept the fact her period was over a week late to herself.

The thought she might be pregnant prompted her to go to the doctors for a test. The doctor agreed with her own assessment that lateness might result from stress. After all, she had assured herself, you don't get engaged every day, do you? Add to that the worry about Vee - and looking after Dad. She had all but convinced herself of the validity of her self-assessment. I mean what were the chances of getting pregnant the very first time?

But the doctor agreed to do the test - just to be sure.

The call from the surgery prompted doubt and anxiety. Her instinct told her what the diagnosis would be. As she tried to calm down, her mind raced. What will Dad say? He'll be so upset - he might throw me out? No, he would never do that. But... Her thoughts turned to Frank. We've discussed children. No, I told him what I wanted - he didn't express an opinion. Oh, my God, what if doesn't want kids at all? Maybe he'll leave me!

'That'll my hormones kicking in,' she announced to the room.

***

Vee's return to Manchester should have been a joyous occasion for her - the longed-for opportunity to resume the life she missed so much during her sojourn in Fairfield. Her mood reflected the grey dampness of the weather outside and the gathering darkness marking the end of the day. Instead of joy, her mind flooded with a myriad of thoughts revolving around that Monday night out.

It was him - she knew for sure. An image of the man in the photograph presented itself in her mind, remembered as if printed on her memory. She played the scene at the restaurant many times - a constant reminder. *My God, how near I came to reveal all.* The split-second realisation of what the implications would be if Helen detected something might be amiss had stopped her. The ensuing conversation would have been very uncomfortable. She shook her head at the notion - no, unthinkable. Her rapid exit to the "Ladies" supplied a perfect distraction.

'Probably seafood - I think I had a bad reaction to it.'

Helen, all concern and sympathy, paid the bill and they caught the next bus home.

Early the following morning, Vee boarded the train for the first leg of her journey back to Manchester. Tucked into a corner of a busy and smoky apartment, she pretended to read, not wanting to talk to her fellow passengers. In her mind, however, an internal debate raged creating confusion and anxiety.

Two days passed since she returned to university and still she could not decide what to do.

The recollection of her own role in the situation filled her with shame. Helen's recent advice about "taking care" troubled her. But the more she thought about that "Man" - acknowledging him as "Frank" seemed too much - the more she wanted to place all the blame on him. *I mean, why should I worry? I can do what I like when it comes to men. I didn't go out to betray my sister. He was a stranger - a random bloke. How could I have possibly known?*

Images of the "Man" kept appearing. She experienced again an undeniable sense of attraction. She shuddered as if to shake the unwanted thought away.

Why would he want to be in a place like the Alhambra in the first place? He and his friend - they were so much older than everyone else in the club. On the pull - and he'd only been engaged to her for a few days!

Her sense of outrage created a range of emotions, chief of which featured indecision. Should I tell Helen? What would that do to her? What would she think of me?

A visit to the pub with her friends later that evening provided a brief respite from her worries. Next morning, she called on her tutor, Professor O'Donnell, to discuss her studies and progress.

'A creditable piece of work, Miss Park - most gratifying.'

The award of a "First" for the dissertation completed at home lifted her spirits. Later, sitting in the library, she decided what she would do.

Helen will be at the office - I don't want to call her there. I'll ring this evening. But I need to think how I'll break the news.

***

But Helen was not in the office, she was in the Doctor's Surgery.

'Well, there's no doubt what the test shows. It's not one hundred percent accurate, but it generally works. The results are positive, you're pregnant Miss Park. So, I think congratulations might be in order?'

She was too shocked to reply - instead, she stared at Doctor Scott's bald and shiny head, not able to look him directly in the face. His question appeared to emphasise "mistake" and "unplanned pregnancy," perhaps something worse, like a judgement on her morality.

Doctor Scott coughed distractedly, perhaps embarrassed. He picked up the sheaf of Helen's medical records and made notes with his Parker pen.

'You didn't plan this, did you?'

His words sounded kind, non-judgemental. Helen shook her head. Her hand smudged a tear away - she did not want to show her emotions - not here, not in front of him.

'I take it that there will be someone to help you - the father I mean?' He fixed her with a meaningful stare over the rim of his half-moon glasses. When she didn't respond, he sighed.

'I have seen many cases like yours: unwanted pregnancies. The father runs a mile when he finds out - realises what he's taking on.'

'Frank will support me. We're already planning our wedding. This just came a little sooner than expected.' She realised her voice was raised - shrill and indignant.

'That's alright then.'

Doctor Scott rose from his desk, indicating the consultation was over. As she walked to the door, he added: 'You might want to bring the nuptials forward - you know, before you start to show.'

***

Frank packed up his stand before the official closing time. Only a trickle of visitors meandered around the hall - hardly worth staying for, and he was keen to get on the road. He slid the cardboard housewife, the last item from the display, into the back of the Park Domestic Products van, slammed the doors, climbed into the driver's seat and fired the engine. As he slipped into first gear, there was a tapping on the window - it was a security guard.

'Shit,' he muttered, expecting to be prevented from leaving as the exhibition had not yet shut. He wound the window down.

'You Frank?'

He nodded. 'Is there a problem?'

'Phone call for you. Came through to the office: a young lady - says it's urgent.'

'Oh Christ,' he muttered, knowing it would be Helen. His mind filled with possibilities, guilt burning in his gut. He got out and followed the security guard back into the hall. As they walked, he tried to elicit more information.

'Did she say anything else?'

'Said she needed to speak to you - didn't give a name.'

When they entered the office, he indicated the telephone, its handset lying on the table.

His heart pounded as he picked it up. After a moment of hesitation: 'Hi Helen, what's up darling? I'm just about to set off. Is everything...'

'Who's Helen?' asked a familiar voice.

'Oh, what a nice surprise! Sorry! Helen's the office clerk. She often calls when I'm away - likes to check up on me - make sure I'm behaving myself.' He laughed, hoping this explanation sounded plausible, experiencing a huge sense of relief at the same time.

'I'm going to run out of money any moment. I just wanted to say thanks, you know, for the last couple of days. You've been wonderful, and I appreciate it, and...' she spoke hurriedly, 'please ring me, when you can. I really would like to see you again - as a friend.' The line went dead.

The drive back to Fairfield lay ahead of him - a dismal prospect with the traffic leaving Birmingham heavy and the rain relentless. He concentrated hard on the road, his vision impaired by the windscreen wipers on full tilt swishing back and forth. By the time he reached the A3, the movement of traffic was freer, and the rain had turned to drizzle. He lit a cigarette and relaxed back into his seat. His mind now free of the need to concentrate so much on present danger evaluated the implications of the last two days.

***

The relationship with Fleur should have ended on Thursday morning when he waved her on to the Number 9 bus that would drop her at the department store. End it here - walk away - she'll get the message. It was just a bit of fun.

Yesterday had been the busiest day of the show and the Park stand had been inundated with visitors. He collected several orders - the sales figures for November would no doubt be a record high. In the brief moments when he found himself alone, he experienced deep pangs of guilt - and something else. *Have I been tested in some way? Has this experience been created for a reason?* It had been a relief when the doors were closed on the last of the visitors. He locked the stand and took the bus back to his hotel. Sitting on the top deck, smoking a cigarette, he became increasing miserable and fretful.

I'm not ready to settle - I don't want to be tied down - at least not yet. Bloody hell, Joe's right - marriage isn't for me! I've got to end it - but how?

His thoughts had been interrupted by the realisation the bus was approaching the stop nearest to the hotel. He dashed down the steps and jumped onto the pavement as it pulled away. As he walked into the hotel lobby, the cheerless janitor glanced up from his "Daily Express." 'You've got a visitor,' he said, jerking his head towards the small bar area.

'Bloody hell,' he muttered under his breath, imagining Helen waiting to confront him having suspected he was up to something.

Fleur stood when he entered, a broad smile on her face, which turned into a frown.

'You don't look very happy to see me.'

154

'No, no,' he said, putting on his best pleased expression, 'you surprised me, that's all. I thought you were going to go home.'

'I was,' she replied, smiling again now, apparently reassured. She gazed over his shoulder towards the janitor who, as usual, hunched head down in his newspaper.

Frank grinned, understanding the unspoken message. 'I'll think of something, don't worry,' he said, grinning.

Their time together followed a similar pattern to the previous evening, except they were more relaxed, and they didn't drink so much. They sat in the same bar and talked - light-hearted chatter at first, but then she turned the conversation around to them. To his surprise, and a with a good measure of relief, she told him she did not want a serious relationship. 'I just want a friend, Frank. I'm not expecting you to commit or anything silly like that. Anyway, you don't strike me as the committing type.'

Fleur and a few beers provided a splendid antidote to the frantic day at the exhibition. A sudden realisation he hadn't made his nightly phone call to Helen brought him back to reality.

'Sorry, give me a few minutes, I need to ring head office - they'll be wondering how sales went today.'

He found a pay phone on the wall on the other side of the bar. Helen answered after a couple of rings. She sounded cheerful at first, chatting as usual about their wedding arrangements. Perhaps it was the stabs of guilt or maybe the fact he knew his voice was muted and stilted, that created a nagging worry she might suspect something was not right. He tried to perk up the conversation by suggesting they meet at *Giovanni's* for a celebratory meal the following night on his return. She agreed - but he could detect no enthusiasm in her voice. Their call lasted a couple of minutes at most. When he put the receiver down, depression enveloped him. He glanced over towards the table where Fleur sat - she was reapplying lipstick with the aid of a compact. The vision cheered him slightly.

She smiled as he joined her. Within seconds, his mood regained some of the pre-phone call levity.

A relationship with no ties appealed. She gave him her address, scrawled on a beer mat. He provided that of his Southampton digs.

Later, a ten-shilling note assured the discretion of the janitor; he tipped them a conspiratorial wink as they made their way up the stairs to his room.

***

Frank was so lost in thought, he nearly over-shot the turnoff for Fairfield and had to brake suddenly. The angry hooting of the lorry that had followed him most of the way down the A3 into Hampshire showed how near he came to causing an accident. Pulling into a lay-by, he felt himself shaking. He fumbled for his cigarettes and leant back into his seat, inhaling deeply. It was several minutes before he continued his journey, by which point he had made up his mind what he needed to do.

Chapter 18

"VEE'S QUANDARY"

(Thursday 3rd December 1959)

Vee's final lecture of the day finished at 5 o'clock. A throng of fellow students headed for the ancient pub, which stood in splendid isolation in the middle of the bombsite behind the university library. They urged her to join them and expressed surprise when she declined. Hurrying to the bus stop, she jumped on the Number 82 as it pulled away.

The seat at the front of the top deck provided an ideal platform from which to observe the busy scenes of Manchester playing out below her. But the world outside might as well have been invisible. Her thoughts focused on Helen as they had been all day. If she could muster the inclination, it was doubtful whether she would recall a single idea from the lectures of the day. As the bus drove along Oxford Street, the fact some of the shops were adorned with Christmas decorations did not register.

The janitor beckoned to her as she entered her hall of residence. 'Message for you,' he said, waving a chit of paper. It was brief: *"Rang at 4 pm. Please call as soon as you get this–Helen."*

She glanced at her watch: almost five thirty. Helen must have called when she returned home from work. For a few moments, she wondered if Helen had found out about Frank's indiscretion. Perhaps someone had reported the incident in the pub, someone who recognised both her and Frank? Stay calm - there might be many reasons Helen would want to talk, she tried to assure herself. But doubt tugged at her nerves.

157

The girl in the telephone box in the foyer seemed determined to drag out her conversation, which was interspersed with giggles and occasional shrieks of laughter. Vee's anxiety and impatience reached fever pitch. A growing sense of foreboding fuelled her irritation. 'For Heaven's sake hurry, will you?' she muttered. A few moments later, unable to contain her composure any longer, she tapped on the window of the booth with a coin. The girl appeared to notice her for the first time. She nodded back and smiled, holding up her fingers to indicate she would be a couple of moments. Vee glared back at her.

At last, the girl put down the receiver and stepped out. 'I'm so sorry about that - it's my mum: she likes to talk!'

Normally courteous, Vee pushed the girl aside in her hurry to get to the phone. The call was answered straight away.

'Vee?' How one word sounded like an accusation - so full of emotion.

'I got your message a few minutes ago. Are you ok? Is everything alright? Is it Dad?' Vee's words blurted out in a rush as if she was eager to find out what would be said next. She could hear crying at the end of the phone.

'What is it? What's up?'

'Pregnant! Marvellous, eh? I'm pregnant, and I don't know what to do. What am I am going to say to Frank? And how am I going to tell Dad?'

Vee pushed a series of coins into the slot, this brief action giving her time to gather her thoughts. Relief surged through her - there would not be an accusation.

'Everything's going to be ok,' she whispered after a short pause. 'Dad will be fine, I'm sure he will. He obviously approves of him.' She was about to add something about Frank standing by her but couldn't bring herself to do that. The other end of the call became silent.

'Helen?'

'It's Frank. What's he going to say? What will he do when I tell him? This might be too much for him. To be honest, Vee, I've made all the running and I guess I sort of assumed he would be happy to fall in with my plans.' A pause followed before she added, 'Including getting married.' Another pause. '... and having children.'

Vee had to fight back an almost irresistible urge to tell her what she knew about him - her so called fiancé. She bit her lip to stop herself.

'He's coming back from Birmingham tonight. We're supposed to be going to *Giovanni's* to celebrate our engagement. I'll have to tell him then, face to face. If he leaves me, well, so be it.'

Vee nodded to herself, feeling powerless and weak, but her instinct told her to keep silent. Let Helen see how he reacts when he hears the news he's going to be a dad. A man like him would run a mile at the prospect of responsibility.

They talked for a few minutes longer. Helen sounded much calmer and a little happier. She needed someone to talk to, that was clear, and who better than her sister?

'I'll be home soon for the Christmas vacation - I'm sure everything will have settled down by then, you'll see.'

Vee put down the receiver with a heavy sigh. Only a few minutes before, fear of discovery had been paramount, now an even greater worry and dilemma presented itself. As she walked to her room, she considered various courses of action - none of them had a happy ending. If she stayed quiet and let events take their natural course, Helen would marry a man who did not deserve her, and who would betray her again no doubt. But presenting the truth - what would that do? It would destroy her - and perhaps the child yet to be born.

The image of the pub on the bombsite behind the library suddenly presented as an attractive proposition: an escape from reality in the company of her fellow students would help dull the pain. In fifteen minutes, she was back on a bus heading back to the university.

Chapter 19

"DINNER DATE"

(Friday 11th December)
'Buggeration!'
The specks of blood might not be detectable by most, but a stickler for detail, and the fact he had cut himself while shaving without noticing, annoyed him. Frank stopped the process of knotting his tie and glanced at the travel clock next to his bed.
'Sod it!'
He ripped the tie off followed by the shirt, flinging both onto the back of a chair.
'What's the flaming point?' he asked his image in the mirror.
For several moments during which he studied his reflection, the temptation to stand Helen up presented itself as a real consideration. 'The traffic was a nightmare, I didn't reach Fairfield 'til midnight.' The lies would come easy. And she would believe him. Instead of the awkward, perhaps dreadful conversation expected, he could lose himself in contemplation and peace at the small, smoky pub a few yards from the guest house.
'Everything's happened so quickly, Helen. I'm not ready to settle down - not yet.' These words, when tested, seemed so empty, meaningless and - true. *What if I say nothing? Perhaps I can put off the wedding. I might persuade her to wait awhile before we get married - give us time to save money for a deposit on a house. No, that won't work - for a start, Bob has promised to pay that - and anyway, she knows I'm not short of readies - I've had a rise and then there's the cash from...*

'You're a liar, a cheat, and a coward,' his inner voice informed him. He looked at his image in the mirror and nodded.

'Yes, I am - all of those,' he muttered.

It took several minutes to iron another shirt and choose a tie to match. He was late - Helen would be at the restaurant by now. The idea of ringing *Giovanni's* and asking for a message to be passed didn't occur to him until he took his seat on the bus. He smoked a cigarette, gathering his thoughts. The nagging notion he would be sacked if he mishandled the crisis worried him. Perhaps not tonight - but soon, I need to find a way of prolonging the engagement - at least until I can think of an escape plan. His guilt, although not diluted, was for the time being buried somewhere at the back of his mind. He focused now on seeking a practical solution, one that would not burn all his bridges.

***

Helen waited with mounting impatience outside the restaurant. He was already fifteen minutes late. 'It'll be the traffic,' she muttered to herself, 'it's Friday evening after all. He'll be here soon.' But it was not the lateness that bothered her: a credible excuse would be offered, and her irritation would be forgotten. But things were not so simple - her anxiety about how he might react to her news nagged and prodded.

It had started to rain, which was turning to sleet. A glance through the window - most of the tables were occupied. She decided to enter alone, anxious not to lose their table for two.

The restaurant was festooned with festive decorations, which she considered distasteful. Even worse, in her view, Christmas carols and Jingle Bells replaced the Italian opera that had created such a pleasant ambience on previous visits. Not the right atmosphere in which to

162

discuss the important issues that must be addressed tonight.

A waiter took her coat and ushered her to a table. She sat feeling self-conscious and isolated among the couples and groups who filled the tables all around her. She poured herself a glass of water from the jug on the table and tried to quell her growing anxiety. *Please hurry, Frank!* She glanced towards the door wishing he would appear and put her out of her pent-up misery.

The stab of pain in her abdomen made her cry out.

'Are you alright, dear?' The woman had her arm around Helen's shoulder. 'You've gone very pale. Where is it hurting?'

Helen moaned softly, 'Please, no,' she whispered, and then cried out as the pain hit again. 'My baby - I'm losing her.'

'Try to stay calm. John, go and bring the car around'. A man nodded and headed swiftly out of the door.

'Everything's going to be alright, you'll see,' said the woman in a soothing tone, 'We'll drive you to the hospital. No point in waiting for an ambulance - we can get you there quicker. Listen - I'm sure everything will be okay, but best to be on the safe side.'

***

Frank walked up the High Street, his steps rapid, conscious of his lateness. He quickened his pace as he neared the restaurant, expecting to see Helen standing on the pavement looking out for him. 'Must have gone inside,' he muttered.

Fifty yards short, he spotted a car pulling up outside the entrance. A man jumped out and opened the rear passenger door. A woman emerged from the entrance. He realised she was supporting someone else. They disappeared into the car. Probably a drunk, he concluded.

Doors slammed, and the car pulled away, gathering speed towards him. The face pressed against the window did not notice him - but he recognised her - no doubt whatsoever - it was Helen.

'What the hell's going on?' he whispered, sensing serious trouble.

The waiter could not provide any details, only that the couple had taken the young lady to the hospital. 'She didn't seem so well.'

A surge of panic rose, dulling his ability to think. He shook his head as if to clear it. His old acquaintance, guilt, mingled with his troubled thoughts creating a profound sense of foreboding. His conscience told him whatever had happened would be down to him and his recent transgressions. Has she found out? *Someone's told her - and she's had some kind of turn - it must be something like that.*

Moments later, he stood outside again, looking up and down the High Street for a taxi - but there were none to be seen. Then he remembered the bus, the one that stopped at the *Crows Nest* and continued to the General Hospital in the next town. He ran to the bus stop and checked the timetable. A bus was due in ten minutes. He stood, sucking in air as he tried to regain his breath and control his shaking.

The journey seemed interminable. The bus crawled, stopping several times, its doors hissing open to disgorge the few passengers who shared the ride with him. It took an hour to reach its final stop opposite the hospital main entrance. Not waiting for the doors to open fully, he elbowed through them, prompting a shout of annoyance from the driver.

As he darted across the road, a van screeched to a braking halt to avoid hitting him. 'You Flamin' nutter!' yelled an angry voice.

Confused by the hospital signage, he stopped a nurse and explained through breathless gasps the circumstances. She pointed to a sign: "Casualty": 'Try there.'

Not waiting to thank her, he dashed down the corridor but reduced to a walking pace after careering into a bed containing a patient emerging from a side door, together with its paraphernalia of bottles and pipes. He muttered his apologies to the accompanying nurses and a doctor in a white coat, who glared at him.

The dim lights along the corridors, and the sickly antiseptic aroma pervading the atmosphere, reminded him of a previous occasion he visited a hospital where he had experienced a similar state of emotions. It was in Southampton, many years before. Like now, he felt crushing panic and confusion, and not a small measure of real fear.

'It's your mother, they found her this morning. You need to go to the General. Here's money for the bus. Go now! I hope to God you're not too late.'

Striding down the corridor, he realised the hidden memory of that fateful day when he said goodbye to his mother fuelled his current state of panic. Mrs Taylor must have known there would be scant chance of him finding his mother alive. He found out later, she had called the ambulance after discovering his mother lying on the kitchen floor, her head inside the gas oven. He was too late - his mother was dead by the time he reached the hospital. A nurse told him. He remembered the look on her face even now.

At last, he arrived in "Casualty." He surveyed the waiting room. No sign of Helen. Maybe she was in one of the side-wards, he thought. The receptionist could find no record of her visiting the department. He was frustrated and knew he was being sharp and rude. She told him to sit down for a moment while she made enquiries. A few minutes later, she beckoned to him.

'They've taken Miss Park to "Obstetrics." She pointed down the corridor. 'Take the turning at the end to the left - you'll see it right in front of you.'

As he walked, he tried to think what "obstetrics" might mean, having never heard the term before. The receptionist smiled at him as she gave directions as if no further explanation would be needed.

Helen was alone in the side room when he entered the ward, lying on top of the bed, her head propped up on pillows. She turned her head to look at him as he came in. Her eyes were filled with tears; her mascara had run leaving smudged tracks down her cheeks. He couldn't think of anything to say - he still didn't understand what had happened, but he sensed that words were unnecessary. He sat on the bed and pulled Helen towards him, cradling her in his arms.

'It's okay, I'm here now,' he whispered.

Through choking sobs, she told him her devastating news. A few minutes later a nurse entered and ushered him out of the door into the waiting area.

'I need to discuss a few women things with your young lady!' she boomed in a brisk, no-nonsense manner.

He sat smoking a cigarette and staring at the wall in front of him. The various scenes of the previous few days reappeared, coaxing feelings of deep regret and shame. Then his mind presented a clear image of Helen's face - a mask of abject misery. His vision became blurred, and he realised he was weeping. It was the first time he had succumbed to tears since his mother died fifteen years before.

***

Helen took comfort from Frank's attentiveness and his obvious concern for her. The hospital discharged her. 'Let nature take its course,' the business-like nurse advised her.

They said little as they waited for a taxi - at least not with words. As they drove back, he sat with his arm around her and she fell asleep on his shoulder, waking only when they pulled up outside her house.

The taxi's interior light was turned on. As Frank counted out the fare, she realised his eyes were reddened. *Has he been crying? No, that's not his style - he'll be tired, but he's clearly being affected by all this.*

He asked the driver to wait for him, and then helped her up the drive to the front door.

'I'll stay over if you want. I can sleep on the settee - just in case...', he said as she unlocked the door.

'Best not - Dad might suspect something's up if he found you. I don't want him to find out what's happened. There's no need - not now.'

He nodded then turned and pulled her to his chest in a close embrace. This made her cry again.

'Okay, I'll come around tomorrow,' he said, adding 'Make sure you get plenty of rest, alright?'

She went inside after a parting kiss.

He stared at the closed door for a few moments then turned and walked back to the cab. A glance at his watch - approaching ten-thirty. He calculated the time it would take to reach the pub next to his digs. Enough time for a couple before closing time. 'Christ, I need a drink after that!' he muttered.

Chapter 20

"THE SWAN"

Frank phoned at midday. Bob answered. 'Helen's still in bed, I'm afraid - seems to be under the weather. She looks rough, mind you. I would leave it for today - let her rest. She'll be much better tomorrow, I'm sure.'

This suited him. Not that he didn't want to see Helen - he did. However, having only emerged from his own bed a few minutes before he called - a result of emotional exhaustion combined with the fact he enjoyed a lock-in at the *Greyhound* which extended until three in the morning, he was in no fit state for a visit. He groaned when, soon after waking, he remembered the van still needed to be unloaded at the depot. The notion of a lunchtime beer - "hair of the dog" - evaporated. Maybe tonight, he thought.

***

On Sunday, upon waking, Helen had to rush to the bathroom where she retched for several minutes. With a groan, she crawled back under the covers and lay in bed for the rest of the morning drowsing fitfully.

Some hours later, the aroma of cooking roused her. She visualised the scene in the kitchen: her dad, having returned from his Sunday morning round of golf, would be preparing a late breakfast. He called it "Brunch," although he could never recall where he got the name from, she reminded herself.

There would be a pan of scrambled egg, which he would be whisking frantically, trying to prevent it from sticking. In typical form, he would talk to himself, reminding of this and that, rebuking himself for not turning the sausages over in time. This represented a traditional Sunday in the Park household.

She smiled - her mind conjured comforting images - a vision of home. Rolling on her side, she peered at the clock on her bedside table: 12.30. The movement stirred fresh feelings of sickness - not as bad as before but enough to quell the rumblings of hunger emerging in response to the smells from the kitchen wafting up the stairs.

'Something's not right - I shouldn't feel like this,' she whispered, deciding at that moment to make another appointment at the clinic. The thought of meeting with the sanctimonious Doctor Scott depressed her even more.

Helen slid out of bed, put on her dressing gown and walked downstairs. Her father was not alone: she could hear Frank's voice as well - and laughter. They both turned as she entered. Frank came over and hugged her.

'Need to clean my teeth,' she whispered, pecking him on the cheek.

He steered her to a chair at the breakfast table. 'Here we go!' said Bob, slipping a large plate of bacon, scrambled eggs, and some small fried potatoes and baked beans in front of her.

'Oh, my God, I can't eat all that!' she said - but the rumbling in her stomach suggested otherwise.

The two men loaded their plates up and joined her at the table. They appeared to be in the best of humour, she noted. When Bob got up to answer the doorbell, she whispered: 'Did you say anything - you know, about the ...'

He shook his head and smiled reassuringly.

'Sodding kids from next door again! Wanted their ball back,' Bob said with such indignation, Helen and Frank laughed in unison. 'They better not have kicked it into the greenhouse!' He got up and gazed out of the kitchen window to confirm his precious greenhouse remained intact.

'Dad's convinced next door's kids are waging a vendetta against him. They're just children. At least they asked for their ball back.'

'If they hit my flower beds, I'll give them their ball back on the end of my bloody garden fork!'

Dad must always have the last word, she thought, smiling.

'Bob's suggested a visit to the pub. A few drinks before coming back here for a late dinner would do us all good. I bought a chicken, and there's plenty of vegetables. It would be great for us to go out together.'

She noted the slight hesitancy in his voice - and guessed he was uncertain how she might react. He wanted to please her, to make her happy.

After a few moments, she nodded: 'What a nice idea. I think that would be wonderful!' She looked at them, noting they were both grinning at her. 'Which means I'll be cooking dinner,' she said.

Later, ensconced in a corner of the lounge bar in the *Swan*, a short walk from the house, she watched as Frank and her father engaged in deep, animated conversation. They were talking about the exhibition and its obvious success for Park Domestic Appliances. She was content to allow them to talk. They both actively sought her opinion at various points - but her mind wandered elsewhere.

Helen smiled as Frank talked. He seemed so passionate, emphatic, and confident as he challenged some of her dad's ideas, steering him towards his own. This is what I want, she assured herself: a strong, reliable man to build a family with. Her recent doubts about him and his level of commitment vanished: he had been so tender, caring and understanding since the awful trip to the hospital. Without his compassion, she doubted whether she would have been able to rise above the depths of misery and depression which threatened to engulf her.

Two martinis and lemonades helped to relax her - drowsiness made her eyes heavy. She glanced at her watch.

'I'm going to go back and put the dinner on. You've got a bit more time to sort the world out - but don't be too late back or I'll give your dinners to next door's kids!'

***

"Last Orders" was called at twenty past two. They squeezed into the bar area, the unspoken agreement having been made to 'fit just one more in.' Their talk had, by this point, moved away from the future of Parks and onto the wedding plans.

'You need to agree on a date. The church here will be booked up for every Saturday from April through to August, and you'll be disappointed if you don't get a wiggle on.'

'I know Bob, I need to sit down with Helen and talk this through. Have to be honest, though, I've left the planning so far to her - wedding planning's her department.'

'Okay, I'll keep my oar out, but...'

Bob was distracted by the barman, keen to satisfy the remaining customers before ringing the bell for "Time." Moments later, they were sat in companionable silence back at their table.

'Where are you spending Christmas?' Bob asked.

Frank had been studying the decorated tree in the corner and pondering this very question. Mrs Bunning had already advised him she would shut the guest house over the festive period as she did every year while she visited her sister in Plymouth.

'I haven't made any final plans yet.' He realised this must sound rather lame with the 25th December less than a week away.

'Why don't you come and spend it with us? You'd be more than welcome.' Bob paused, and then added: 'You can stay in the spare room.'

Frank grinned. 'Thanks, I would like that very much!'

'Right, that's settled then. Come on, drink up - we'd better get back otherwise those bloody snot-nosed kids from next door will be given our dinner!'

Chapter 21

"GREGORY'S INTERVIEW"

(Wednesday 16th December 1959)

'Mr Park was impressed - reckons you've got what it takes to do well. There's a lot for you to learn - but we both think you've got potential. Welcome to the firm, Gregory, or do you prefer Greg?'

Gregory stared back, his face projecting shock and disbelief. He had been about to climb on his bike and pedal away from the depot as fast as possible to distance himself from the scene of what he recalled as one of humiliation and failure - a lost opportunity. Frank seemed to sense he was trying to escape and placed both hands on the handlebars to block him.

'But I don't understand. I made a complete mess of the interview - Mr Park must think I'm an idiot - I couldn't...'

'You did well, Greg,' Frank said soothingly, 'A little nervous perhaps, but you did okay - honestly.'

Mr Armstrong's apparent perception of the event in no way matched Gregory's recollection of what happened. A series of humiliating vignettes played through his mind reminding him of his inadequacy, his inability to project so much as a hint of ability.

'Come on Greg, when you talked about the products, you showed as much knowledge as that of an experienced salesman. You really impressed Bob - I mean Mr Park.'

Gregory frowned, pondering this thought. Retrieved from where it lay smothered by more negative images in his mind, he remembered how he could recall details of the vacuum cleaners from the brochure he had poured over in preparation. He saw himself using his fingers to tick off the key features of each. A faint voice, familiar with its northern accent, spoke to him. 'You need to know the unique selling points, the yoo ess pees!'

To him, it was as if he had stepped into an alternative universe - his face projected profound doubt. Positive feedback did not sit comfortably with his self-perception.

It was as if Mr Armstrong could read his mind.

'Now look here, Greg, I'm not Mr Ramsay. I'll be showing you the ropes: you'll be my apprentice. We'll start with simple tasks and then build you up from there. If you make mistakes, you'll learn from them - no one will make things difficult for you. Give it a few months and you'll be fine. What do you say?'

Gregory nodded and smiled: guidance and encouragement were what he needed. Things were looking up and he experienced a small, rare tinge of confidence and optimism.

***

Frank watched as Gregory rode away. His fixed smile disappeared replaced with a frown. *Can I really make something of him? I hope so - for my sake if not for his - I've got a reputation to maintain.*

'Bloody hell, Frank - I can't believe you're serious! Can that kid even tie his shoelaces unaided?' Bob appeared at his shoulder, puffing on his pipe, his face a picture of concern tinged with a discernible tincture of amusement.

'He has potential, Bob - all he needs is guidance and encouragement. The poor kid's never had a break. He'll do well, I'm sure of it.'

Bob snorted, his disbelief clear.

'Alright - but he's on a trial basis. If he doesn't show promise inside a month, he's out - I can't afford to carry passengers. He's your responsibility. Don't let me down, Frank.'

They agreed that Gregory would start work in the first week of January, after the Christmas break.

Chapter 22

"UNEXPECTED NEWS"

'These things just happen – it's nature's way of saying you're not ready to have a baby - an unfortunate fact of life but, well, that's the nub of it, I'm afraid.'

Helen nodded - he wasn't telling her anything she hadn't already worked out for herself. As in her last meeting with Doctor Scott, she felt her eyes strangely drawn to his shiny bald head, a distraction she had created for herself as she couldn't look him directly in the eyes. Her recollection of his previous words, and the insinuations behind them, still played on her mind. She loathed him.

'Now, these spells of sickness you've been having over the weekend...'

'This morning as well,' she cut in.

'Really?'

She detected disinterest in his voice.

'When is your appointment at the hospital, you know, for your...'

'D & C,' she finished for him.

He coughed as though embarrassed. *Perhaps he's uncomfortable talking about woman's' problems.* This thought gave her the faintest hint of sadistic satisfaction.

'Indeed,' he said nodding, 'a D & C.'

'A week Wednesday.' She was looking him in the eyes now, triumphant at the thought of his potential weakness.

He smiled and nodded – his expression showing he was not in the slightest bit perturbed now, which disappointed her. After making a brief note in her medical records, he lay down his pen and leaned back in the chair. He seemed relaxed and untroubled, she noted with some annoyance.

'I suspect your feelings are psychosomatic. Do you understand what that means?' The way he spoke made his question sound condescending and accusing.

She nodded, 'Yes, it's all in my head. Not real. That's what it means, isn't it?'

'Perhaps not as simple as that, but close enough. It would not be uncommon for a woman suffering a miscarriage to feel the symptoms of pregnancy after it has ended. Your mind is, in effect, tricking you into thinking you're still pregnant when, in fact, there is no baby - hence the effects, you are experiencing.'

'But I don't understand why I should be so sick?'

'It will pass. Now, if you'll excuse me, I've got ill patients to see.' He gathered up the notes on his desk, indicating the session was over.

***

An air of levity permeated the Park Domestic Appliances depot. It was Wednesday, the last day before the seasonal break. Tomorrow would be Christmas Eve. A gramophone hooked up to the TANNOY played carols which could be heard throughout the main building. Mr Park, the Managing Director, conducted his morning tour of the depot sporting a Santa hat and exuding uncharacteristic jollity. He was in a buoyant mood! Well, business was looking good, very good indeed!

The sales department had been inundated with fresh orders, requests for brochures and sample products - all because of the exhibition. Business was booming and the prospects for the coming year augured well.

As he toured the building, he spent time with each member of his staff, thanking them for their efforts and sharing his vision of a bright future for all. Mrs Whelan, the accounts clerk, followed him, carrying a tray of small brown envelopes containing weekly salaries, which she distributed as they walked. Every member of the Park workforce would open their pay packet to find the addition of a crisp brown ten-shilling note as a bonus.

While Mr Park spread festive cheer, Frank sat in his office with the door shut, staring blankly at the wall in front of him. It was a fortnight since his return from Birmingham and, after the trauma of that Friday evening, if not back to normal, life seemed at least back on track. He convinced himself his relationship with Helen, which teetered on the brink a couple of weeks ago, now appeared to be stronger than ever. But nothing could change the past, and his dalliance with Fleur troubled him. His brief indiscretion at the *Alhambra* now seemed trivial compared to his fling with that young lady.

His mind taunted him with reminders of what his intentions had been - before, that is, he was presented with the fact Helen was - no, had been - expecting his child. He recalled, not for the first time, the look on her face when he walked into the side ward where she lay, her eyes reflecting the deepest misery he had ever seen.

'I'm so sorry!' she had said.

Christ, why should she be apologising? He remembered thinking.

His guilt tempered his mood. He lit a cigarette and smoked for a while. But then he perked up. *Perhaps everything happens for a reason*, he mused. *After all, I now know I really do love her*. The thought cheered him. But a small voice in his head hissed: 'You're a shit, Frank!'

A knock at the door halted his reverie. The door opened - it was Hugh O'Driscoll.

'Young fella to see you.' Hugh stepped aside and ushered Gregory into the room.

Appearing distinctly ill at ease, Gregory stood in front of the desk as though uncertain what to do. Then he stepped forward.

'I just wanted to give you this as a small token of my gratitude.'

Frank detected a rehearsed speech and visualised Gregory's mother dictating to him what to say. He accepted the small amateurishly wrapped present and grinned.

'What's this then?'

'Oh, it's just a little something - nothing much. I'm grateful for what you did–saving my life and for - well, you know - getting me a job here. Anyway, got to run. See you in January.'

Gregory left the office only to appear moments later. 'Happy Christmas! Mr Armstrong!'

As the door swung shut, Frank tore off the wrapping paper and extracted the contents. He held the bright yellow coloured box up to the light. There was the logo "DINKY TOYS" and an image of an Austin Healey. He grinned with delight. The picture on the box depicted a white version. Mine's blue, but that doesn't matter, he thought. He opened the box and rolled out the car within. Out came a blue model, carefully repainted to match in exact detail the real one - his pride and joy, right down to the silver hub studs on the wheels. He stepped over to the window and surveyed his car below, then at the toy in his hand: a replica.

'Well, I never.' he muttered, grinning, touched by the clear effort Gregory had put into creating such a unique gift. He made a mental reminder to send a Christmas card with a note of thanks.

He noticed the time on his desk clock - nearly 10 o'clock. Helen's appointment at the hospital was at eleven. She insisted on going alone. 'I'll be fine, Frank, and you've got so much to do at work before the festive break. I'll get the bus in. I'll be home before you.'

He had little to do. His paperwork was complete, his in-tray empty. He needed to brief Alf in distribution about a delivery for the first week in January, but that wouldn't take long. He calculated he could be clear of the office, provided Bob agreed, by about 11 o'clock. It would take only thirty minutes to drive to the hospital. Small gestures add up, he told himself.

***

While Frank stood admiring his model Healey, Helen climbed onto the bus that would take her to the dreaded appointment. The nurse tried to assure her the procedure would be straight forward - but the thought of enduring it filled her with foreboding. On waking that morning, she had been sick again. The severity of her nausea, the cramping in her stomach, and the miserable retching, made Doctor Scott's suggestion they were probably psychosomatic hard to believe. A seed of worry grew in her mind. *Maybe I'm seriously ill - there must be a reason for this - I'm not imagining being so sick - this is real!*

The day before her appointment, unable to face work, she went to the library to see if one of the medical reference books could provide a clue why she felt the way she did. She returned home none the wiser, rebuking herself for showing all the signs of being a hypochondriac.

As she sat alone near the front of the bus, staring with little interest out of the window, she noticed a tingling sensation in her breasts. This is not right, she thought.

A memory of her childhood emerged suddenly. 'It's a phantom pregnancy,' the vet advised. The six-year-old Helen didn't understand - but she remembered how miserable Tess, her Collie, had looked with her swollen teats. Oh yes, and how protective she was towards her favourite toy: her imaginary pup.

It can't be, surely not! Some form of human phantom pregnancy? Despite herself, she smiled at the thought, wondering how Frank would react if she confided this notion to him.

Something's not right, though.

Her thoughts turned to Vee. She had told her about the miscarriage over a tearful phone call.

'Frank's been a brick - he's really helping me through this.'

'Good for him,' had been the notably offhand reply.

Vee was due home - she would arrive early evening. She found this thought comforting, distracting her momentarily from her worries. With Frank staying over, it'll be like a real family gathering. 'We're going to have a great Christmas,' she whispered, 'once I've sorted out what's happening to me.'

The bell rang - another passenger signalling he wanted the next stop. She glanced out of the window and saw the hospital.

***

Vee settled back into university life with ease. She caught up with her coursework and enjoyed the intellectual demands of her studies far more than she did previously. Her active, distracting social life no longer featured - a few drinks with her closest friends in local pubs seemed more enjoyable than the former intensity of the clubs and bars central to her previous beatnik lifestyle. In the three weeks leading up to the end of term, she settled back in and it was if she had never been away.

The term ended, and, like hundreds of other students, she headed home for the Christmas vacation. She sat in the buffet carriage enjoying a cup of coffee and a cigarette. As so often in the last few weeks, her mind filled with worries about Helen. News of the miscarriage created ambivalent emotions. She was sorry for her - but the thought of that man - she still could not bring herself to use his name - stirred less charitable thoughts.

So, he's being supportive. I wonder what his reaction would have been if she hadn't lost the baby? I bet he would have scarpered at the thought of being saddled with an unwanted child!

Another thought emerged.

I'm going to meet him now - again. How am I going to react? And what will he do when he realises that the girl he was pawing turns out to be his fiancée's sister?

The train slowed as it approached Crewe station. She pressed her nose to the window against which rain lashed. The outside world was obscured by horizontal rivulets of water. Not exactly festive, she thought. The prospect of seeing Helen and her dad again cheered her; she pushed the thought of "That Man" to the back of her mind.

***

Helen wished she had accepted Frank's offer to accompany her. As she sat waiting for her appointment in "Obstetrics", misery and loneliness sapped her soul. She sipped a cup of over-strong hospital tea while throwing furtive glances at the two women sharing the waiting room with her. Both heavily pregnant and looking, in Helen's view, smug and pleased with themselves, they chatted happily together. She guessed that, although strangers prior to this visit, the two women were naturally drawn to each other. It was so hard not to scowl at them. I'm not in their exclusive little club! she thought bitterly.

A voice called out a name from the doorway - one of the pregnant ladies raised herself with difficulty to her feet and shuffled towards the beckoning voice. The remaining expectant mother pulled a copy of "Woman's Own" from a shopping bag and leafed through it. Helen found it hard to suppress her feelings of resentment and jealousy.

'Miss Park?' It was the nurse who had looked after her on Friday evening. 'Come on through!' she boomed. Helen walked into the side-ward and sat in the chair offered to her.

'I really am dreading this, sorry - but I am...'

182

'That's perfectly normal. Try not to worry, though. The procedure's slightly uncomfortable, but it won't take long. We'll be able to do some checks, make sure nothing else untoward is going on. Now, I just need to ask you a few questions and then we can make a start.'

To her own ears, her responses sounded mechanical, almost monosyllabic. Apprehension fogged her mind, and it was only when the nurse put down the clipboard and invited her to undress behind the screen that she remembered there was more to tell.

'There's something else,' she began, 'I don't know whether this is linked to the miscarriage but...' She explained her nausea and the newer tingling sensation in her breasts. 'The doctor thinks it's probably psychosomatic - all in my mind and...'

'Utter balls!' the nurse muttered, shaking her head. 'He's got no idea what he's talking about! Okay, I think we should do a full examination and see what's going on here. Get yourself undressed behind the screen; you'll find a gown there - then onto the bed, please!' She was business-like again, which Helen found reassuring.

'I'll need to talk to the consultant before we do anything else - so sit tight for a few moments,' said the nurse, before leaving the room.

Helen changed into the hospital gown and sat on the bed, facing the door. Several minutes passed, and she fretted, convincing herself something was wrong - a result of the failed pregnancy.

At the point where her worry turned to overwhelming anxiety, the nurse reappeared accompanied by a severe-looking woman in a white coat. 'Helen, this is Mrs Groves, our resident expert in obstetrics,' she said smiling.

Soon, the anxiety dominating her thoughts vanished to be replaced instead with an excitement so intense, she wanted to dance around the room.

'But I can't be pregnant. I've had a miscarriage - you said so last Friday,' she looked at the nurse for confirmation.

The consultant smiled. 'I'm not saying you are, at least not definitely,' she said gently, 'I can't be sure at this stage - but you are showing all the signs. So, there's a chance you are. We can forget about a D & C - at least until we have the results of another pregnancy test. You see, what I'm thinking is there is a possibility you were expecting twins.' She paused then added, 'If that's the case, then you have miscarried one - but you're still carrying the other.'

'So, we need to carry out that test as soon as possible.' This was the nurse. 'I think we can get a result quickly if you could give me a wee sample now.' The consultant nodded in affirmation.

'We're trialling a new pregnancy test called hemagglutination inhibition testing. Quite a mouthful,' the doctor said laughing, 'but I know all about it because I'm leading the trial here. It's not fool-proof: it can give a false reading - so we can't rely on it. But, given the symptoms you've been experiencing, I think it might be worth a try. What do you think, Helen, would you like me to conduct the test?'

***

Helen was alone again in the now empty waiting room. Less than an hour ago, she had sat in the same seat, filled with negative emotions. Now her heart thudded with excitement, which she could not suppress despite the voice of caution whispering to her: 'Be prepared for disappointment.'

The door opened. She swung around, expecting to see the nurse or the consultant - but it was...

'Frank, I didn't think you...'

'Are you alright, darling?' he whispered, 'I couldn't let you do this on your own - I wanted to be with you.'

184

He knelt in front of her and held her face in his hands. She registered his quizzical expression and guessed the fact she appeared far from miserable didn't tally with what he had expected.

The double doors on the other side of the waiting room burst open and the consultant swept into the room with the nurse scuttling closely behind her - both were smiling.

'I think you'd better come through,' the nurse said nodding towards the side-ward in to which the Doctor Groves had disappeared.

'Stay here. I'll be able to explain everything when I come out.'

He stared at the door through which Helen entered. 'What's going on?' he muttered, puzzled.

A few minutes later, the door reopened, and Helen's head poked through. 'Frank!' She beckoned to him, 'Quick!'

Confused, knowing something was amiss but sensing this might not be bad news, he strode into the room. The white-coated doctor was sitting in a chair by the bed studying notes on a clipboard. She glanced up and smiled as he sat next to Helen.

'Well, do you want to tell him?'

Helen's words came out in a rush. 'I'm still pregnant, Frank. Or at least, we're pretty sure I am.' She looked at the consultant as though seeking support.

'Yes, it certainly looks that way. The test we've just done came back positive. Now, I must warn you it can never be certain. But...' she paused and smiled, 'the results of this new test have proven to be more reliable than with the older ones. Taking account of your other symptoms: the morning sickness and the tingling sensation in your breasts - they could be symptomatic of several other things - but your temperature is normal and therefore, I believe you may be pregnant with the surviving twin.'

***

They stopped off at a café on the High Street and celebrated their unexpected news with iced buns and a pot of tea. Helen was all smiles - her happiness was in marked contrast to the misery and apprehension the day had started with.

'But are you alright about this, Frank? Is this what you want? I mean, we didn't...'

'Of course, it is! Couldn't be happier. I can't wait to be a dad. We'll have a boy and...'

'Maybe. But look,' she grabbed his hand, 'nothing's definite yet - we need to wait for confirmation - and that won't be until after Christmas now. So, let's keep it to ourselves, at least for the time being. I don't think we should tempt fate.'

'Okay, makes sense.'

'Except for my sister. I do want to tell her - is that okay with you?'

'Of course - I know how close you are. You need to be able to talk about things - well, things you can't talk to me about.'

'I can talk to you about anything, Frank. You're going to be such a good husband - and a dad too!'

'Talking of Vee,' Helen glanced at her watch. 'She's due in at ten past six. Dad will pick her up, but I should go with him. Can you drop me off at home?'

***

Ten minutes later, Frank pulled up outside the house. He leaned over and put his arm around Helen, drawing her to him. 'Everything's going to be fine now,' he whispered. She nodded and smiled. 'Let's keep our fingers crossed, eh?'

He watched as she disappeared into the house, then he drove back towards the office where he felt duty-bound to show his face before shutting time at 5 o'clock. As he drove, thoughts rushed through his mind, which he attempted to rationalise.

'What's happened is done now. It's time to move on.' He said this out loud to the reflection of his eyes in the rear-view mirror. 'Things are looking up again!'

Inevitably, recollections of his recent behaviour returned - but this time, instead of being wracked with guilt, he decided to put his indiscretions behind him and to stop punishing himself. He convinced himself his transgressions had made his relationship with Helen much stronger. Now he knew she was the right one.

It's time I accept this and settle down. I've got an intelligent, attractive woman who wants to marry me - and, all being well, we'll have a son. I'm going to have a family - and, if I play my cards right, my future's looking bright - very bright indeed! Oh yes, things are definitely looking up!

Chapter 23

"CONFRONTATION"

(Wednesday 23rd December)
'Sorry to drop this on you, Frank. Sod's Law, I'm afraid! I'd only just sent the drivers home, as they'd completed all the pre-Christmas deliveries - then this one came in. They're open in Guildford on Boxing Day, and they want to showcase the new model.'

Frank groaned. He checked the time: almost four pm.

'Okay. No problem, Bob. Can you let Helen know I might be late back and tell her you're to blame and not me?'

Bob grinned. 'I will, Frank. If you get a move on, you should be back in Fairfield by Six. The van's loaded up ready.'

He caught the keys Bob threw to him and headed out to the car park where the van and its load waited. As he pulled out onto the main road heading south, he reminded himself that fortune had smiled upon him and, with that in mind, he would not allow an unexpected inconvenience to dampen his good mood. He lit a cigarette and inhaled, relishing the calming effect and realising this was his first smoke since leaving the office that morning for the hospital.

Stopped in a queue at traffic lights, he scanned the cab and tutted with annoyance at the debris littering the passenger seat and spilling onto the floor. As he made a mental note to talk to Bill, the Distribution Manager, who was responsible for the Park's vans, about the need to ensure a clean image for the firm, he spotted a transistor radio buried under a pile of work-related detritus. 'I wonder?' he muttered, picking it up and rolling the bevelled power switch on the side until it clicked. A hiss of static. A small adjustment of the tuning bezel and the "BBC Light Radio" crackled into life'. He recognised the voice of Bob Miller introducing "Parade of the Pops." Frank grinned - his journey would have musical accompaniment.

The traffic crawled along the road leading northwards and became denser the further he travelled. He knew all the alternative routes but decided it would be pointless to attempt a diversion during rush-hour. At least we're moving, he thought.

The outward journey took two hours, by which time the grey of the day had turned to dusk.

'Where the hell have you been? I was expecting you over an hour ago.'

The unseasonal greeting from the shop-owner almost provoked a retaliatory response in the same vein from him; instead, he decided his new elevated role of Operations Director demanded he must maintain a professional front.

He delivered the three "Superlux" vacuum cleaners, even carrying each of them inside the shop for the owner, who continued to moan.

'Have a great Christmas!' Frank said cheerfully, climbing back into the van. As he drove away, he muttered a less charitable seasonal message - this made him feel better.

The traffic exiting Guildford to the south crept along nose to tail - a sea of red rear-lights spread ahead of him. At 7 o'clock, he turned onto the A3, which would take him most of the way towards Fairfield. As he surveyed the road in front, he noted that, although not as heavy as that in the city, the traffic still crawled.

'Oh well, no point in fretting - can't do anything about it. That first pint will go down well, anyway.'

As time passed, and still no sign of the road freeing up, his patience waned, and became more acute when movement slowed yet further, eventually grinding to a halt. He had been looking forward to the visit to the pub. It was a "ticket only" event, the tickets free to the regulars of the *Swan*. The landlord would provide an array of refreshments to sustain the festive drinkers through the evening. He realised that having skipped lunch, he was now ravenous. Static brake lights of the car a few feet in front told him he was well and truly stuck.

'Bollocks!' he exclaimed. The thoughts of food made him even more frustrated. Helen will save me some sandwiches, he thought, consoling himself, and a couple of pork pies. Hope she remembers they're my favourite!

The traffic moved forward a few yards and stopped again. He slapped the steering wheel in frustration and swore.

The transistor radio was lying silently on the passenger seat; he had forgotten about it in his rush to get back on the road after dropping off his delivery. Glancing ahead and noting there was still no traffic movement, he turned it on, filling the cab with the hiss of static. He moved the aerial, searching for a signal. It faded in and out and then he found a pop music station.

When he looked up, he saw there was a large gap between his van and the car in front - the mass of traffic was moving at last. Putting the radio back onto the passenger seat, he slipped into first. Just as he did this, he felt a sudden juddering thump behind him, which thrust him forward in his seat, causing his nose to collide with the windscreen. As he fell back, the voice of Elvis was crooning 'It's now or never!' A warm trickle of blood ran down his face.

'It could only happen to me!' he groaned.

***

Vee tumbled from the train, struggling with her bags, full of festive cheer. She had spent the last leg of her journey from London in the company of a group of young sailors in the highest of spirits who, having completed their basic training at HMS Ganges, were returning home for Christmas leave. They had welcomed her into their party, which began in the *Wellesley Pub* on Waterloo Station. Laden with beer bottles and duty-free cigarettes the lads were determined to maintain the festivities all the way home to Portsmouth, the last stop.

Although loud and raucous, singing like seasoned matelots, they did not cause too much annoyance to their fellow passengers; it was Christmas after all! By the time the train pulled up in Fairfield, Vee had, what she would describe as a 'bit of a wobble on.'

'For heaven's sake eat a mouthful of these!'

Helen detected the waft of alcohol and stale tobacco. She emptied several Polo mints into Vee's outstretched palm. Seeing the smile vanish from her face, and not wanting to start off the holiday sounding like a nag, she added: 'Best not get on the wrong side of Dad before we've even got you home. He's waiting outside in the car.'

They hugged.

'I'm so sorry about the baby. Such rotten luck.'

Helen smiled - although desperate to impart the latest news, this wasn't the right place.

'Come on, Dad will be getting anxious - he's looking forward to a family gathering in the pub!'

***

They were sat on Helen's bed in her room ready to go out for the evening's entertainment. Bob was downstairs expecting Frank to appear at any moment.

'So, you're sure you are. Wow, Helen, that is such wonderful news! I can hardly believe it!'

'Well, the consultant said this new test can give false results, but she seemed to be pretty confident. I shouldn't be raising my hopes so high - not yet - but I can't help it. I just have this feeling - you know?'

'Let's keep our fingers crossed, eh?'

'Only you and Frank have any inkling of this. I want it to remain that way, at least until I find out for definite.'

'Come on you two. We'll not find a table if you don't move yourselves!' came a shout from the bottom of the stairs.

As they gathered in the hallway putting on hats and coats, Helen suggested she should stay behind and wait for Frank. 'And anyway, he might ring if there's a problem - and if no one's here, he could...'

'No,' said Bob, 'there will not be a problem. Let's leave a note for him. No point in you hanging on here. He might be late - in which case you'll miss a great night out. Frank will understand.'

Although not convinced, she agreed reluctantly.

***

They sat at a corner table in the pub. Vee looked around her trying hard to hide her distaste. To her, the atmosphere in the lounge bar was sedate, polite and downright boring. This would not be one of her venues of choice, even now the most hedonistic side of her social life lay in the past. She watched her dad's attempts to calm Helen's escalating concern due to Frank's lateness.

'He'll be caught in traffic - bound to be heavier tonight being the last working day before Christmas; everyone trying to drive home. Come on, stop worrying.'

Vee was also becoming increasingly agitated. Since returning to university, various iterations of the inevitable confrontation had played through her mind. None of these potential scenarios concluded with any sense of satisfaction for her. She tempered her desire to exact retribution for his blatant betrayal, with the sure knowledge this could only be achieved by hurting Helen.

How should I handle this? And how will he react when he sees me again?

Her glass of Guinness - a pint had been refused with a peremptory 'It's not lady like' - stood almost empty on the table. A few pints would help - and a couple of fags. But smoking in front of her dad was unthinkable.

'But, what's the point in you going home?' said her dad.

'He might be unwell - perhaps he's gone straight to bed - or...' Helen was clearly worried.

'For heaven's sake, he would have called the pub - or come over and told us. He's stuck on the road in heavy traffic, that's all.'

Vee detected an edge of irritation in her dad's voice and was inclined to agree with him. Helen needed to calm down, especially now she was, perhaps, pregnant.

Draining the remains of her drink, she stood. 'Dad?' she pointed at his pint glass, which was also empty. He nodded and held it out for her. Helen had barely touched her orange juice.

'Just Dad and me, then!'

Relieved to escape the confines of the table which had become claustrophobic, Vee prised her way towards the bar and, when she thought neither her dad nor Helen could see her, slipped through the side door into the courtyard at the rear of the pub. A couple of roll-ups beckoned.

***

'Look, I *have* to go back to the house. Frank might be there. Perhaps he's got a reason for not coming over, or maybe he's left a message for me.'

Bob sighed. 'Okay, I'll walk you over. I think you're worrying too much, but if it makes you feel better.'

Helen pulled on her coat. 'No, Dad - you stay here, talk to Vee. I'll come back over later - hopefully with Frank.'

She eased her way through the standing drinkers, edging towards the door.

***

After a few seconds, Frank regained his senses. As he fell back into the seat, he felt, then tasted warm blood trickling from his nose. He pulled a handkerchief from his pocket and pressed it to his nostrils to stem the flow. Not too bad, he thought - it doesn't feel broken.

The van door opened. 'You okay, mate?'

A man dressed in overalls leant through the gap, his face creased in concern.

'Yeh, I'm fine - I think. Nose smacked the steering wheel - a bit of a bleed but nothing serious. Was it you who rammed into me?'

'No. I was behind the one that piled into you and saw what happened. Two young blokes scarpered. They've probably been drinking and don't want to be around when the Police turn up.'

'Better see what the damage is,' said Frank. He slid out of his seat, holding the top of the door to steady himself.

They stood together and surveyed the scene behind the van. 'Bloody hell - what a mess,' said Frank.

'The car's a write off, I should think,' said the man in overalls. 'The front's caved in, the engine will be knackered. Your van doesn't seem too bad - back doors are pushed in, but it should be okay to drive.'

Steam hissed from under the crumpled bonnet of the Morris Minor. A queue of static headlights stretched behind.

'I don't want to hang around,' said Frank, 'I'm going to make a note of the registration. Would you mind being a witness?'

Frank was not the only one in a hurry it seemed. Dave, who turned out to be a car mechanic, was anxious to return home to his wife and kids.

'Give me a hand to push this wreck to the side of the road. I'll call the garage where I work once I'm home. They'll send a truck out and tow it away. I can let the Police know as well.'

As expected, the van remained in working order; the engine had merely stalled.

'Thank God, for small mercies!' Frank muttered.

He arrived back in Fairfield at half past nine and drove straight to the house rather than the depot. Only when he got through the front door and turned on the hall lights did he realise the extent of damage to his face. The image staring back at him from the mirror shocked him. Although the bleeding had stopped, a cut on the bridge of his nose made him resemble an unlucky prize-fighter, an impression intensified by the fact his shirt front was stained with blood.

He picked up the note with his name on it. 'Good!' he announced to the hallway, pleased they were safely in the pub and would not have to witness his sorry state before he could tidy himself up.

Fifteen minutes later, he inspected himself in the bathroom mirror. The plaster stuck horizontally across the bridge of his nose, which was swollen, gave him a thug-like appearance. He shrugged. At least I got here in one piece, and there's still plenty of drinking time. With this happy thought, he left the house and walked towards the *Swan,* savouring the prospect of the first pint of the day.

When he pulled open the front door to the pub, Helen, who was exiting at the same time, piled into him.

'Excuse me,' she said, not recognising him. He stopped her, his hand on her shoulders.

'Hang on - it's me.'

'Oh, my God, what's happened to you? Have you been in a fight? You look awful?'

He grinned and put his arms around her. 'Thanks, Helen. No, I haven't been fighting. I've been in an accident - a minor one!'

He registered the alarm on her face.

'Wasn't my fault - some idiot rammed into me. I smacked my nose on the steering wheel. Don't worry, it's not as bad as it looks. I'm okay – really, but I need a drink - desperately! Where's your dad? I'd better tell him about the van.'

'You poor thing,' she said, her voice full of concern, 'Dad's over there. He's seen us – there, he's waving. Go and sit down before you fall over. I'll get you a pint.'

Her eyes followed him as he manoeuvred himself through the crowded bar towards the table. Her father, she noted, stood up and prised himself through the groups of standing punters to reach him. She could see the deep concern on his face. He put an arm around Frank's shoulders and exchanged a few words before both edged back to the table and sat down.

After negotiated her way through the thickening crowd of drinkers around the bar, she found herself standing behind Vee, in the process of paying the barman.

'Can you get a pint of bitter for Frank?' she said, tapping her on the shoulder and squeezing a ten-shilling note into her hand. 'You'd better add a whiskey - oh, and another beer for Dad.'

As she turned her face towards her, she registered for the briefest of moments how Vee's eyes opened wide as if she had faced something shocking.

***

Much to Frank's relief, Bob appeared to be sanguine about the accident. 'As long as you're alright, that's the main thing. We can sort out the insurance details when we're back at work. Ah, here come the drinks at last. I guess you could do with one!'

Frank glanced up to see Helen standing next to a girl holding a tray of glasses. He recognised her in an instant - and knew from the glint in her eyes and a knowing smile, she remembered him too.

'Hello Frank, I've heard so much about you,' said the girl. 'I'm Vee, Helen's *sister*.'

He noticed the emphasis. She placed the tray on the table and thrust her hand out.

'Nice to meet you,' he replied, accepting her hand, giving it a small squeeze, and hoping his voice didn't betray the turmoil twisting his guts.

'Frank's been in the wars as you can see. He's not always so thug-like - he's normally quite suave looking.'

'Oh dear. You poor thing, Frank!' Vee said, sitting down and throwing him a sympathetic smile.

Her expression reflected concern - but he understood the unuttered message, her eyes conveyed: 'You and I have unfinished business.'

Drinks were passed around and they sat down at the table. Bob suggested they raise their glasses.

'Here's to a wonderful Christmas together!'

They all clinked glasses. Frank registered a small, but significant pause as Vee tapped her glass against his with an almost imperceptible touch.

'Welcome to the family, Frank,' she whispered.

'Yes, welcome indeed!' said Bob.

For the briefest of moments, his imaginings conjured a vision of a courtroom where he stood in the dock as the accused. Bob presided as the judge; Helen and Vee were his cheerful accusers. There was no "Defence."

He nodded and smiled, hoping his face did not give away recognition. Any moment now, he thought.

But nothing happened. The conversation resumed. Helen and Vee giggled, sharing a private joke perhaps. Bob talked about his plans for the firm in the New Year.

He cast a surreptitious glance at her, looking for a sign. Nothing.

'I'm going outside for some fresh air,' Vee said suddenly.

Helen laughed. 'You mean you're going for a smoke. It's alright - I'm sure Dad doesn't mind you lighting up in here - even if it is one of those awful roll-up jobs.'

'I'll just be a few minutes.'

He detected a hint of irritation in her voice. As she edged around the table, squeezing behind his chair, he felt her breath on his ear. 'Coming outside for a smoke, Frank?' she whispered.

He swung his head around - their eyes locked onto each other. 'We need to talk,' her eyes said.

Vee eased her way through the crowd towards the front door. He remained rooted to his chair. Suddenly she shot a look back - her eyes met his for a few seconds again as if to say, 'What are you waiting for?'

His heart pounded - instinct told him trouble was brewing; perhaps some kind of ultimatum:

'Go now, never come back, or I'll tell Helen everything,' he imagined her saying.

He whispered in Helen's ear. 'Forgot my bloody wallet - left it in the kitchen when I came in. Won't be long.'

He paused for a few moments at the door through which he had seen Vee exiting a few moments before. A flurry of thoughts rushed through his mind - images of the evening he had met her in the *Alhambra* - reminders of his guilt. He based his sense of foreboding on the belief that this girl could ruin everything.

A new emotion emerged: resentment. *I had no idea who she was, and if I had, I wouldn't have gone anywhere near her. In fact, I didn't want to be in that club in the first place! Anyway, what did I do? I kissed her - no, I responded to her kissing me. Was that such a crime?*

He opened the door and stepped outside into the car park. A heavy pall of drizzle fell - the air damp and clinging. She stood a few paces away from the entrance, huddled under the overhang of the roof. As he emerged from the doorway, she beckoned to him. He squeezed in beside her in the cramped space, conscious of how they huddled together and experienced a strange sensation of forced intimacy.

'I hope you've come for a smoke?' she said.

He pulled out his packet of cigarettes, extracted one and put it to his lips. He lit his cigarette; then realised she needed a light as well. He lit a match and cupped his hands to shield the flame. Another unexpected sense of intimacy when she leant into him to light her cigarette. They both smoked for a few moments and then as if on cue, spoke at the same time, talking over each other.

'Go on, you first,' she said.

'I really don't know what to say. Obviously, I had no idea you were her sister. What happened - well, it was a mistake and should never have happened. And if I'd...'

He took a drag on his cigarette and exhaled, staring down at his shoes.

A long period of silence followed. He glanced at her; she was looking at him with an intensity that made him embarrassed. A sense of powerlessness swept over him knowing she had full control of the confrontation. His resentment evaporated, replaced instead with resignation.

At last, she spoke.

'You and I will forget we've met before. My sister thinks you're a good man - the one for her. Helen's told me about the baby, and how pleased you are - so I'm guessing you're not going to shirk your responsibilities. No, be quiet.'

He had tried to interject.

'I'm not going to say anything. We're both going to forget what happened. But listen, if you ever hurt her, I'll make sure you suffer.'

Chapter 24

NEW YEAR – "NEW BEGINNINGS"

(January 1960)
Despite Bob's deep reservations, and Frank's concerns he might have overestimated their new employee's ability to cope, Gregory surprised them both my making tangible progress within a short space of time. Frank provided the promised guidance, spending an agreed amount of time with his apprentice every day, setting him tasks, checking clear understanding, observing where appropriate, and giving feedback emphasising what he did well rather than focusing on what might only confirm Gregory' feelings of worthlessness. Being responsible for someone else's performance provided a new experience and, to Frank's surprise, he found he not only enjoyed the responsibility, he was good at it.

'He's taken to it like a duck to water,' he whispered to Bob as they observed a role-play exercise where Gregory simulated briefing a franchise owner on the Park products. Bob confirmed Gregory's full-time employment status later that day.

The Christmas break seemed like a distant dream. The New Year marked a turning point in the history of Park Domestic Appliances. After the success of the exhibition in December, Bob ended the door-to-door sales regime and focused his business instead on trading wholesale. He decided also to open three franchises, one of which would be in Southampton, another in Winchester, and the third in Guildford. The area salesmen in Winchester and Guildford were transferred to franchise manager roles. The salesman to whom Frank had handed over his patch to in Southampton, freeing him to come up to Head Office, proved to be a disappointment and had been dismissed after a few weeks. It was now necessary to recruit a manager capable of taking on the Southampton franchise. Bob asked him to find a suitable man for the role.

Helen helped him create the advertisement for the job which they posted in Southampton's *Daily Echo*. The response had been positive, and he was preparing to interview the first of five well qualified and experienced applicants that afternoon.

***

Frank sat at his desk, reading through the applications, making occasional notes to prepare for the first candidate, frowning in concentration. Every now and again he stopped and looked up at the ceiling, distracted and wearing a smile as though remembering something particularly pleasing. If anyone were watching him, they might well conclude: here sits a contented man.

The brief crisis that might have derailed his plans was now over. His love life, and therefore his career, remained safe and back on course. He lit a cigarette, took a slurp of his coffee and grimaced because it was cold - forgotten due to his focus on the task at hand. A deep drag - he leant back in his seat and blew smoke in the air. As so often when smoking alone, he drifted into a daydream.

In his mind, he relived the moments when he and Vee prised their way back into the lounge after their conversation outside. Once again, he experienced an enormous sense of relief - the crisis averted. They had returned to the table as if nothing untoward had happened.

'Been breaking the ice with Frank over a fag,' he heard her say to Helen, who smiled as if in approval at this attempt at relationship-building.

He recalled how he remained on edge for much of the evening. What if Vee drank too much and sounded off? He had made a determined effort to appear relaxed. A few more drinks helped. The pub stayed open much later than the legal closing time. They walked back arm in arm, all, apart from Helen, drunk.

They sat in the living room. Vee went over to the gramophone and sifted through her dad's 78's, sighed and returned to her seat.

'Bloody hell, nothing worth playing there,' she whispered.

Bob suggested a nightcap and produced a bottle of malt. 'Been saving this for a special occasion.'

Helen declined and retired to bed but not before she fired a warning glance at him: 'Don't stay up too long drinking,' the look said.

Soon after Helen's exit, Bob muttered an almost indecipherable 'Good night,' having drunk half of his shot of whiskey. Frank was left alone with Vee to finish what remained in the bottle. His fiancée's sister, he noted, possessed remarkable stamina, and could hold her booze!

At his desk, Frank grinned, remembering how, much later, Vee poured what she referred to as an ABF for herself and him. 'Absolute Bloody Final,' she explained.

They chatted as if keen to get to know each other. Not once did she mention or even hint at the recent "crisis." After pouring yet another ABF, she held up her glass as if to propose a toast, which she drained in a single gulp followed by a belch then a hiccup.

'Gosh, a couple of more things and I'll have done the lot,' she said giggling. 'Right, I'm off to bed now.' She lurched towards the door of the lounge where she stopped and stared back at him.

'Make Helen happy, Frank - she deserves it.'

***

Never had he experienced such a sense of domestic contentment as he did during that Christmas holiday. The niggling doubt that lingered after his talk with Vee vanished after a few days. She meant what she said: they would forget what happened. As each day passed, he felt more and more a part of the Park family.

There were several visits to the *Swan*, sometimes all together, but mostly with Helen. On Christmas Eve, Frank and Vee visited a pub in town, just the two of them, which proved to be a key point in their early relationship.

Earlier, they had been with Helen on Fairfield High Street doing last minute shopping before the stores shut - the usual odds and ends considered so essential at the time but often not used. They were waiting at the bus stop when Helen said: 'Bugger - we've forgotten salad cream!' He remembered how the mention of the condiment made him laugh because of the distant memory evoked. It was the week of the Queen's Coronation, and his mother wanted to make "Coronation Chicken," the recipe used at the event published in the papers. He saw again the wizened face of Winnie at the corner shop. 'No, ain't got no mayonnaise. Got this stuff, though,' she said, brandishing a bottle of Heinz Salad Cream. 'Rots yer socks, mind you,' she had added.

The bus was drawing in. 'I'll get it. Go home and put your feet up - you must be exhausted. I'll catch the next one,' he said. Helen protested but relented.

'I'll come with you – run low on baccy,' said Vee, grabbing his arm.

The supermarket on the high street, the one he opened several weeks ago in his capacity as "local hero," provided both salad cream and Vee's tobacco. An hour remained before the next bus, and it had started to rain. He suggested a visit to a café for a cup of tea and a fag.

'Tea! Flipping heck, it's Christmas. Let's have a proper drink!'

She grabbed his arm, adding: 'I know a brilliant little back-street boozer where they don't worry too much about the licensing law. Out of sight, out of mind - so the Police aren't bothered about it.'

It was open. Although their visit to the pub was brief, it cemented their new relationship. She seemed keen to find out about Frank's past; not in a prying way, but one that showed genuine interest. In return, he asked her about university and her interests. By the time they left, a sound basis of friendship had been established.

***

Frank studied the DINKY car version of his Healey, which sat on his desk in a small model display case. He stooped and examined the miniature car at eye level, admiring the detail Gregory had captured with his paintbrush - a remarkable representation of his treasured car. The trill of the telephone interrupted his thoughts. He grabbed the receiver, thinking it would be Reception advising him the first of the interviewees had arrived.

'Frank!' The edge of excitement in her voice was unmistakable. 'Frank, we're going to have to bring the wedding forward. I'm pregnant! Frank, it's been confirmed. Frank, are you there?'

'Yes, I'm here. Wow, that's fantastic news!' When he put the phone down, he punched the air and paced around the room, unable to sit down.

***

He moved back to Mrs Bunning's guest house after the Christmas break. Bob protested: 'Stay, you're part of the family now - and there's plenty of room.'

Unbeknown to Bob, it was Helen's suggestion he move out. 'It doesn't seem right somehow, living under the same roof when we're not married yet. And, apart from that,' she added, 'it's too tempting, you know...?'

He understood perfectly what she meant. Helen had rebuffed several amorous advances by him much to his frustration. However, the prospect of regaining his independence, albeit for a short period, presented as most welcoming.

A few days later, she phoned again. 'I've just been for my check up and everything's fine.' She paused and then added, 'I told Dad and...'

'Oh Christ,' he muttered, his heart lurching.

'No, he's okay with it - happy even. But be careful what you say - he can be a bit funny sometimes.'

Five minutes later a knock on the door announced Bob's arrival. When he entered, his face suggested the meeting would be uncomfortable. He looked grim and angry. But it was an act. Suddenly, his face creased into a warm smile and he shook Frank's hand in a firm grip.

'I guess congratulations are in order,' he said. 'But I think you'd better get a move on with organising that wedding!'

***

Two churches served the Parish of Fairfield. The one at the end of the High Street was new, built on the site of a previous church destroyed by incendiary bombs in the War. The second church, "Saint Giles," perched on a cliff promontory on the coast road leading out of town. This was where Bob married his wife, Jane, in 1928.

'I want us to be married in the same place as Mum and Dad,' Helen announced. He agreed, not having any view on the subject.

An initial enquiry proved disappointing - the church was booked right up to and through the summer months. Nonetheless, they made an appointment with Reverend Lee, the Vicar of Saint Giles, to see what he might arrange.

Neither Helen nor Frank were church-goers. The last time he visited a religious establishment was to attend his mother's funeral at Southampton Crematorium. Helen had not been to church since Sunday School. Religion, it seemed, had passed them by.

'I feel such a fraud - why should the vicar help when we've never been to one of his services?' said Helen.

Reverend Lee, or Matt as he preferred to be called, appeared to be relaxed about the issue of church attendance. 'God will never shut his door on anyone,' he advised. Then, as though realising he sounded pompous, he made an amusing comment that made them both laugh.

'It just so happens that I have a cancellation: the last Saturday in April. How does that suit?'

***

Frank faced a quandary: he did not have a Best Man. Joe, his friend since their army days together in West Germany, wrote a brief letter in response to his own requesting he might consider taking on the role.

'Sorry mate. I'll be driving a lorry around the Continent in April. But, I hope it goes well and — I think you're mad getting married so young!'

Frank didn't have a close circle of friends - the people he engaged with professionally and socially were acquaintances. Joe was different - his one enduring friend; they had been through much together, and, as his mate told him when they last met, he represented the obvious, in fact, the only choice.

After explaining the problem to Helen, he realised that, although disappointed, he was also relieved. His imagination played out various scenes at the wedding involving Joe. Each scene made him wince.

The Best Man's speech would doubtless embarrass him and others on the day. Joe, he reminded himself, lacked subtlety and would not know when a line had been crossed into unacceptable territory. Reference to or even the hint of some of the escapades they shared in Germany would raise eyebrows. He pictured the look of shock on his new father-in-law's face, and the accusing looks he would receive from Helen. His mind created a vision of Joe's drink-fuelled antics as the day progressed. More nightmare than celebration - Joe's imagined behaviour could be depicted in a Hogarth print. No, he told himself, the fact he can't make it is a blessing. *But who the hell's going to be my Best Man?*

Helen suggested Gregory. Frank dismissed the suggestion with a snort.

'Gregory's my apprentice, not my mate. And, apart from that, he'll never be up to the task.'

'But why not?' she challenged. 'You've said yourself he's made excellent progress. You said he's got... what were your words? Oh yes, you said he's got hidden talent. If you gave him clear instructions on what he's supposed to do, I'm sure he'll do a fab job. Anyway, who else are you going to get?'

He thought about his relationship with Gregory or Greg as he preferred to be known. His young charge had become a friend, but not in the conventional sense - more an elder brother, little brother relationship. Greg, he sensed, looked up to him and listened to his instruction and advice. But could he cope with the challenges facing a Best Man? Perhaps? No, he can - with some guidance. Let's face it, he's a far safer bet than Joe would have been!

Gregory accepted straight away. The delight on his face was evident - but his smile turned to a worried frown. 'I haven't got a clue what to do!' he admitted.

The following day, Frank handed him a book.

'Here you go, Greg,' he said. 'Read and digest this. Any questions, just ask.'

He smiled whenever he saw Gregory on his break in the days leading up to the wedding. His head would be buried in his copy of "Best Man - Everything you need to know," and, having armed himself with a notebook, he made copious notes. He realised his protégé would memorise every required detail of his duties, true to form.

Later, they prepared the Best Man's speech together at Gregory's request. He provided him with some amusing but innocuous stories about himself to include. It became obvious his trainee Best Man was determined to do a good job.

***

Frank's stag party turned out to be a mild and turgid affair which lacked, in his view, most of the essential requirements of such events, fun being chief among these. Bob announced he would organise the night's festivities. 'No point in leaving it to Gregory - he won't have a clue,' he said.

An hour into the evening and Frank wished he had insisted on allowing his Best Man to fulfil his duties - even someone with little experience of a man's world, which described Gregory, would surely have organised a more enjoyable event than that arranged by his future father-in-law.

Bob invited - or perhaps coerced - several male colleagues from the depot to attend. They visited three pubs along the High Street.

'We'd best stick to halves - we need to pace ourselves,' Bob said - more a command than a suggestion. A few of the group tried to enter the spirit of the stag. They made ribald comments and told risqué jokes, perhaps helped by the fact they had already spent an hour drinking before the main party began. Bob countered these with annoyed looks and occasional rebukes.

'Let's calm it down a little, shall we? There're other people about. We don't need language like that.' Similar comments set the tone for the evening. By the third pub, Bob insisted they all sit down around a table.

'Nice to take the weight off your feet,' he announced.

Frank groaned as the conversation turned to shop. Soon after, the party started to disperse. One by one, individuals bade polite farewells, clapping him on the back, wishing him well. By half past ten, only he, Bob, Gregory and Hugh, the Irish Production Manager remained.

'I'd better be off, then,' Hugh said, much to Frank's disappointment. At least his Irish colleague could be relied upon to provide amusement. Just before he left, Hugh whispered to him so only he could hear: 'Sorry, mate, can't stand any more of this, it's like a fecking board meeting!'

'Yeh,' he replied, 'to be honest, I've had more fun in a coma!'

Later, emboldened by the few beers he had put away, he led Bob and Gregory to the pub Vee introduced him to on Christmas Eve. Bound to be a lock-in there, he told himself, noting he was nowhere near the state of cheerful drunkenness he should be at by this late stage of the evening. *Bloody hell, some stag run this is turning out to be!* Maybe there'll be a skiffle group or folk singer, he thought to himself, hoping that would be the case so he wouldn't need to make too much effort talking to Bob.

An hour later, he surveyed the scene. The bar was empty apart from the barman - who seemed happy to stay open as long as drinks were being bought - Bob, Gregory and himself. Bob's chin nodded above his chest as he dozed in his seat, a pint of ale untouched on the table in front of him. Gregory emptied the last of his beer and placed the glass on the table with visible relief.

'But I don't drink,' he had said when Frank thrust the beer into his hand an hour before.

'Another one, Greg? That one went down quick!'

'Thanks, but best not, I might fall off my bike if I have another.'

He frowned, wondering where the bike featured in the evening's events. Gregory seemed to read his thoughts.

'Left it at the office. I need to pick it up then ride home. In fact, Frank, I should go - it'll take me a while to walk to the depot. And, Mum doesn't like me staying out too late,' he added, looking sheepish.

'Don't worry, Greg, you go. I'll finish my pint and get the old boy here home.'

He stared into his half-empty pint, alone with his thoughts. The landlord, clearly bored, had turned on a transistor radio. Frank recognised the *Everly Brothers'* "Cathy's Clown," Helen's current favourite number. He smiled when he reminded himself how much he hated that song - but could never admit this to her.

Bob had fallen asleep, slumped in his chair and was snoring. With no sign of the landlord wanting to close the bar, Frank drained his glass and bought another beer. Ten minutes later he bought another.

Soon after, having downed his drink, he stared blearily at the table top in front of Bob. 'No point in wasting it,' he advised himself in a whisper, replacing Bob's full pint with his now empty pint pot.

Frank leant back in the chair, his eyes heavy. In a semi-doze, he created in his mind an alternative night out, one where he didn't have a wedding hanging over him.

***

The Reeperbahn thronged with revellers, many of them drunk. The usual mix of British and American servicemen filled the streets with sightseers of various denominations, all drawn to the hedonistic attractions on offer. An atmosphere of alcohol-fuelled revelry pervaded the bars and clubs. All around, an almost tangible frisson of sexual anticipation filled the air.

They downed their first drink when late afternoon began to turn into twilight. Several drinking dens followed. Joe always took the lead, at least until he became incapable, which he did without fail. During the evening, they careered in and out of familiar haunts, where they were well known, but not always welcome.

They presented as an unlikely pair: Joe, heavily built with a sense of humour and a big heart, but with a low flash point when drunk; Frank, medium height, stocky, but not imposing; always good-natured and even-tempered - the perfect foil for his friend. And, unlike his mate, he possessed an inbuilt mechanism that told him when danger lurked. Despite their differences, they were close friends and took care of each other.

Joe, for some unfathomable reason given his bulk, always became drunk far quicker than Frank. When this happened, following a well-defined pattern of behaviour, he would do one of three things, although which one of these he followed remained unpredictable. Sometimes he would become belligerent and objectionable - a frequent outcome of a prolonged drinking session. This created by far the most difficult situation to deal with. His volatile temper, easily riled, caused them to be ejected from several venues. On some occasions, he might disappear without warning. This often involved the solicitations of one or more of the girls who worked the bars and clubs. When he did this, he would return to the barracks alone having forgotten about Frank, who would not know where he had gone. The third possible outcome, and the preferable situation, saw him drifting off into a heavy, drunken slumber. In this malleable state, it was relatively easy to coax him into a taxi where he would always fall asleep again.

It was Frank's idea to visit the *Club Flamingo*, a favourite of theirs. Sitting at the bar, he surveyed the scene playing out around him. Joe, although well past the point where he had full control of his faculties, appeared to be in good humour: he muttered to himself and wore an inane grin.

The cavernous bar brimmed with revellers, most of them servicemen and all in various states of inebriation; the atmosphere was not unfriendly but to him, it seemed charged, edgy - ready to change moods in an instant.

A girl danced in a cage elevated above the heads of the drinkers: He didn't recognise the music she gyrated to, but he registered the bored look on her face and the fact she was stark naked.

A tap on his shoulder. He turned his head around. 'Frank!' It was one of the girls who worked the club, who was well known to him. He cast his eyes around the room. Ange would be around somewhere - she and Claudia always worked together. There she was, whispering in Joe's ear, who, in typical fashion, lay face-down among the beer glasses asleep.

'Frank!'

He smiled, welcoming the physical contact.

'Frank!' Much louder this time. Claudia seemed to be shaking him as if to wake him from a trance.

'Wake up, Frank, for God's sake.'

He woke with a start - disorientated. 'What? What's up?'

Bob stood in front of him, a hand on each shoulder. 'Come on Frank, we'd better get you home,' he said.

Frank noted the disapproving tone in his voice and the hint of disappointment in his eyes.

Chapter 25

"THE WEDDING"

(Saturday 30th April 1960)

The Reverent Lee conducted the occasion with a light touch, raising ripples of laughter with his well-placed humour. Park Head Office employees filled the pews, delighted with the free half-day holiday granted to them on the proviso they attend the betrothal of the Boss's daughter. Everyone appeared happy and relaxed - all looking forward to the reception that would follow the wedding service.

The formalities completed, Frank walked Helen down the aisle. Her smile radiated happiness - his face self-consciousness. They passed through the front doors into a flurry of confetti - this was Vee and Gregory. The congregation followed them, spilling out into the early spring sunshine where they gathered in small huddles waiting to be told what to do next.

The photographer, a short, fussy man with a sense of humour only veneer deep, attempted to coax the guests into groups around the Bride and Groom. Gregory tried to help him, but Bob stepped in instead.

'Hells bloody bells! Right then, Park senior managers over here!'

After what seemed to be an interminable period, the group photographs were done. While Bob with the help of Gregory ushered the guests to waiting taxis, Helen and Frank slipped away. Helen had briefed the photographer she wanted a few photographs featuring just her and Frank; these would be in colour rather than the black and white ordered for the main set. She had chosen her spot for this, which they reached by negotiating winding stone steps meandering down from the graveyard.

**

'You know that wedding picture of my Mum and Dad? It was taken right here.'

They stood on the walled parapet with a telescope on a pedestal in the centre. The photographer took several pictures, most of them with the Bride and Groom standing so that the sea would be in the background.

Alone together, at last, she put her arm around his neck, pulled his face down to hers and kissed him.

'This place is magical - let's stay here a little while longer.'

'Yes, let's do that.' He smiled and walked over to the telescope pedestal and reached down behind the concrete base. 'Ah, well done Gregory,' he said. He held up a bottle of champagne and two glasses. 'Let's drink to us,' he said smiling.

'Frank, I'm pregnant - I shouldn't be drinking alcohol. But I suppose one won't hurt.'

They toasted each other, their arms linked as they attempted to offer their glasses to the other's lips, which ended in giggles and spillage. 'Oh, sod this!' he said laughing. He poured them both more champagne.

'To us!' he declared, holding his glass up.

'To us!'

He stood a few feet away from her and lit a cigarette, the first one as a married man. Then, leaning on the telescope, he looked out to sea. She saw he was smiling. Her mind captured the image - it was one she wanted to imprint on her mind, so the scene might be seen again in the future, and the same sense of complete contentment experienced again.

She smiled and stepped onto the base of the pedestal on which the telescope stood, her face now level with his. 'Thank you,' she whispered, kissing him on his cheek.

'What's the matter?' he said, his smile disappearing. He could see there were traces of tears in her eyes.

'I'm fine. No, really... It's just that...,' she paused and fixed him with an unwavering gaze.

With a twist of anxiety, he recalled his recent transgressions. Had she found out?

'You'll never leave me, will you?' This was more a statement than a question. Helen would not have been able to explain why the thought emerged at that precise moment. Later, she would recall, as though viewing a snapshot image, the shadow that crossed his face.

'No, of course not. We're forever, you and me. What's brought this on?' He looked away, as if unable to maintain eye contact. He frowned and bit his lip.

She was suddenly distracted. 'Oh,' she said, putting her hand on her stomach, 'Frank, she moved! I can feel her kicking!'

***

The reception took place in the *Prince of Wales*, the biggest hotel on the High Street. While the newlyweds were drinking their champagne on the cliff vantage point, the Best Man herded everyone into various waiting cars so, by the time the Bride and Groom arrived, the guests were sitting at their allocated tables.

Everybody stood and clapped as the Best Man ushered the happy couple to their places at the top table. Several, already loosened up with few "stiffeners," cheered and made ribald comments.

After the "Wedding Breakfast" came the speeches, which Frank dreaded.

The "Father of the Bride" speech provided a true reflection of Bob's personality: dry, matter of fact, and devoid of humour.

'And, finally, I would like to welcome Frank to the family - I'm sure he'll take his new responsibilities as a husband seriously.'

Some picked up on this as confirmation of what they suspected: the wedding must have been arranged at such short notice because Helen was expecting. Whispers and nudges - knowing smiles. They acknowledged his speech with mild, polite applause, no doubt relieved it was over.

As Frank rose to make his own speech, he sensed a need to lighten the mood in the room which appeared sombre and serious after Bob's litany. With his nervous anticipation dissipated, helped by several glasses of wine, he experienced a surge of confidence.

He delivered his words, chosen with care, rehearsed many times in his head and in front of a mirror so he could speak without referring to the notes lying on the table. He thanked Bob for his 'kind words' and then lifted the atmosphere with a joke which made everyone, even Bob, laugh.

Gregory blushed deep rouge when Frank praised him for his efforts as Best Man. He presented him with a hip flask, engraved with his name and the date of the wedding. 'You can fill it with your favourite tipple - orange juice,' he said.

'And doesn't she look fabulous?' He turned toward Vee, the only bridesmaid. She blew him a kiss and winked in response, which pleased him. He had taken Helen's advice about an appropriate gift and gave her a first edition of Jack Kerouac's "On the Road" which he bought in a second-hand bookshop. The smile on her face told him the suggestion had been spot on.

'And now to my lovely wife.'

Much cheering and shouted comments. Helen's smiled at his words that followed. She wiped tears from her eyes, but he could see how happy she was. He sat down to tumultuous applause and congratulated himself on a job well done.

The Best Man surprised everyone by delivering his speech with confidence and aplomb. Although Frank had helped him prepare it, he noted how Gregory included several amusing anecdotes of his own. The audience, buoyed by the Groom's humour, was in an appreciative mood now and responded with hoots of laughter and occasional good-natured heckling.

He knew how much his protégé dreaded having to stand and speak in front of so many people - an ordeal he had never faced before. A nagging worry Gregory might freeze or, as he sometimes did when under pressure, reach for his inhaler, proved groundless.

'The Bride and Groom!' chorused the guests in response to Gregory's toast. Frank smiled in pleasure, noting the pleased grin on Gregory's face when he sat down. He clapped him on the back.

'Well done, Greg, you did us proud,' he whispered. Gregory smiled, his pleasure tangible.

With the formalities over, the wedding party began. Everyone transferred to an adjoining hall where a small dance band awaited them. Once all the guests had exited the dining room, they followed. When they entered, thunderous applause and encouraging shouts greeted them.

'Come on,' said Helen leading him onto the floor accompanied by cheering and clapping. Frank flushed with embarrassment - but she guided him, and soon other couples joined them. He relaxed now the focus of attention was no longer on him.

Later, he stood at the bar with a group of his male workmates, including Gregory, who, although he didn't touch alcohol, acted as inebriated as everyone else. He wondered whether someone might have spiked his orange juice.

Helen was dancing with her father. 'Never seen Mr Park smile so much,' said Gregory, his face pink with perspiration, his voice louder than was necessary above the din of the music.

'Every inch, the proud Father of the Bride,' Frank agreed.

Helen was smiling. He wondered whether she was thinking about marriage to him, or about the child growing inside her - perhaps both? The wedding dress hid the small swelling in her belly. No one except Bob and Vee knew for sure - but he guessed that others suspected. So, what? They'll find out soon enough, he thought.

As he watched, her words repeated in his head. 'You'll never leave me, will you, Frank?' *Why had she asked me that?*

A few minutes later, Helen stood by his side, leaning into him. He put a protective arm around her shoulders.

'You're looking tired,' he whispered.

'Gosh, I am - but I'll be okay. Let's stay for another half an hour - I think I can manage that.'

The dance band retired to be replaced by a deejay, one of the van drivers from Parks, who had arranged a stack of his records. The music was loud but proved to be more popular than the band in persuading the guests to the floor.

He led Helen to a table where they sat, watching the dancers.

'Oh, my God, what is Gregory doing?' she said laughing.

Gregory was gyrating on the dance floor alone, his arms flailing in all directions, grinning.

'I reckon he's been on more that orange juice,' Frank replied. At this point, Gregory tripped over his feet and landed on his backside on the dance floor where he stayed, an inane smile fixed on his face.

Through the haze of cigarette smoke and gyrating and twisting couples, Frank caught glimpses of Vee. Many of the single men from the depot wanted to make her acquaintance, and he spotted her with several of them dancing during the party. Not for the first time in his life, he wished he had learned to dance.

He went to the bar and ordered a pint of ale for himself and a glass of water for Helen. When he sat down again, he spied Vee and the deejay head-to-head in discussion as she sifted through his stack of records. They seem to be getting on well together, he noted, feeling a jealous tug.

Helen rested her head on his shoulder. He glanced down at her with a stab of guilt.

'Frank,' she said yawning, 'I'm done in. Do you think we might get away with no one noticing? I'm not sure I could stand the fuss of having to say goodbye to everyone.'

He had booked a room in the hotel, a fact they kept secret from their guests, except for Bob, Greg, and Vee. The plan was to leave as though destined for somewhere else and return later, hoping they wouldn't be spotted. But now, the prospect of formal leave-taking seemed too much.

'Let's go up separately,' he suggested, 'If we're seen leaving together, they'll twig we're off. I'll be a couple of minutes behind you. I need to pick up the room key from reception.'

A few minutes later, having retrieved the key, he was relieved to find the lobby empty of guests as he made his way to the staircase leading to the bedrooms. He was half-way up the steps when he heard a familiar female voice. The area below was in shadows but, as he looked over the banister, he glimpsed Vee and the deejay. They spoke in hushed tones. She giggled and then looked up. He pulled

220

his head back hoping she hadn't seen him acting like a voyeur. But he couldn't stop himself from looking again a few moments later. He thought they'd gone, but then he saw them. Even from a distance, he sensed the passion in their embrace.

For the second time that day, he experienced the pangs of jealousy.

PART TWO

"THE CRACKS APPEAR"
(May 1963 – August 1964)

Chapter 26

"SCHOOL TEACHER"

(Friday 24th May 1963)

'So,' said the severe-looking lady in the tweed suit, 'Class 4A is all yours! They'll be fresh out of infant school, and like rabbits in the headlights. But, don't let them fool you - these kids can be absolute terrors, and if you show any weakness, they'll take full advantage of it!'

Taking off her horn-rimmed glasses and blinking, muttering, 'I can't get used to these bloody things,' the Head Mistress appeared less severe and more human. She surveyed the young women sitting in front of her and then nodded as if satisfied.

'You'll be fine, Miss Park. You will doubtless find it a little daunting at first. They can be little buggers sometimes - but I'm sure you'll cope. Your report from teacher training college, and from your placement - where was it again?'

'Manchester.'

Oh yes, Manchester - they were both excellent, so I don't expect you'll have too many problems. Just remember, my door is always open.'

The Headmistress stood and shook her hand. 'Best of British and all that,' she said.

'Thank you, Mrs Bishop - I won't let you down,' Vee said, seeing a vision of riotous, out-of-control youngsters.

***

Helen persuaded Vee to sever her ties with Manchester and move south. She graduated from university in the summer of 1961 with full honours: an "Upper-Second" in English Literature. Professor O'Donnell, her tutor, expressed disappointment. 'You should have got a "First,"' Vee - your dissertation was outstanding!' But for her, an "Upper-Second" represented an acceptable achievement, and it won her a place at the teacher training college.

She enjoyed her training, not least because the college she attended was in Manchester, a city which she thought of as home. The balance between work and socialising had shifted – although she still enjoyed an active social life, it was nowhere near the reckless hedonism of her early student days. Her transition to the role of teacher represented a watershed for her - she had grown up.

She completed her training with a placement at an inner-city junior school. Teaching children from working class and, most times, underprivileged backgrounds, created many challenges, which she overcame with an ease that surprised some of the other teachers. Towards the end of her time there, the Principal offered her a permanent position at the school - she was about to accept but Helen persuaded her otherwise. Her sister planted the seed during one of their frequent telephone conversations.

'Why don't you take up a teaching post nearer home?'

The thought of returning to Fairfield presented an instant vision of living with her father again with all its restrictions and strictures. 'I'm happy in Manchester, Helen. This is my home now and, anyway, they've offered me a fantastic job here.'

'But wouldn't it be fab if you could be here to see Peter growing up? You wouldn't need to live with Dad - God, I understand how you might think about that! No, you could rent a flat, or share a house with others. I could make enquiries for you. Come on, Vee, we all miss you. Peter is always asking where his Aunty is!'

It took much persuasion - but she began to warm to the idea. The thought of being able to see her nephew as often as she liked was appealing. Within a few days, Helen sent her details of a teaching post at a junior school in a small village not too far from Fairfield.

'You'll like it, Vee! And they're desperate to get a new teacher. You're everything they're looking for.'

Although reluctant to leave Manchester, Vee agreed to go for an interview for the teaching job. When she arrived, she fell in love with the school straight away. It presented in marked contrast to the post-war constructed, prefabricated school in the city. Whereas the inner-city school appeared stark and forbidding, Crofton Junior School, newly-built and surrounded by green playing fields, gave an immediate welcoming impression. Following her successful interview with three of the governors, and the Headmistress, she was taken on a tour of the building and grounds.

Helen met her outside, an expectant expression on her face. 'Well?'

'It's perfect! I know I'll love it here!'

They all went out for dinner that night to celebrate. Peter, who was too young to attend, became peevish because he would have to stay home with his babysitter but was mollified when his mum told him Aunty Vee was coming home to stay.

Vee returned to Manchester where she taught until the end of term before bidding a tearful farewell to the city she loved. Back in Fairfield, with several weeks of summer holiday ahead of her before the start of her new job, the problem of where to live needed resolving. With considerable reluctance, she accepted the offer to stay with her dad until she could find suitable lodgings nearer the school. However, contrary to her expectations of restrictions and rules, he seemed to have become far more relaxed and, as she would describe it, "laid back".

'You're a grown woman - you can come and go as you please. Just don't wake me up when you come in late - and don't hog the bathroom in the mornings,' he instructed.

225

It didn't take long for her to realise she was now occupying the significant gap left by Helen when she had moved out to set up home with Frank. Even though Helen lived only fifteen minutes away by car, and would visit regularly, he missed having company. Vee had always assumed Helen was his favourite daughter, an assumption based on the fact her sister had taken on such a supportive role for him when their mother died. Her own relationship with him always seemed remote, which didn't bother her overmuch. But now she spent more time with him, they became much closer.

When she found a place to live, a flat near to the school, she would reflect upon the weeks she spent with her dad. His attitude towards her had changed. He treated her as an adult, asked about her career as a teacher and, most of all, appeared happy in her company. They visited *The Swan*, where he introduced her to his friends and acquaintances with a notable hint of pride in his voice. She no longer saw him as a distant figure.

Chapter 27

"A DAY TO REMEMBER"

(Saturday 24th August 1963)
Frank sat in his deckchair smoking a cigarette with a contented smile. Every now and again, he laughed. Watching his son playing always amused and fascinated him.

Peter, absorbed in his game, didn't realise he was being observed. His plastic soldiers, a mix of blue-clad "Yankees" and green World War Two counterparts, fought side-by-side defending the wooden fort from the onslaught of apaches. The attackers were not faring well as many of them lay dead, strewn across the lawn. He supplied sound effects as each of them was picked off. At last, they were all killed, most in graphic and ghastly fashion. In Peter's world, the Indians were never permitted to win.

'Peter, tea time. Come in and wash your hands!'

Helen leaned on the back of Frank's deckchair and kissed him on the top of his head. 'What a lovely day!' she said. He nodded in agreement. They had spent the day in Portsmouth and Southsea, a last-minute decision made in the morning when they woke to glorious August sunshine, perfect for a family day out.

With strong misgivings, he had allowed her to drive.

'And we got back in one piece. Well done, Helen!'

She flicked a tea towel at him in mock annoyance. It was the first time she had driven beyond the outskirts of Fairfield since passing her driving test, and their first real outing in the new Morris Traveller recently bought to supplement the Healey as a family car. It had been with a certain amount of trepidation he placed Peter in the car seat that morning.

'Perhaps it might be better if I drove, Helen. The A27 will be busy - and there are lots of traffic lights - it'll be stop-start all the way.'

He worried about Helen's driving ability, even though she passed her test first time. She met his suggestion with a withering look, requiring no words to convey meaning.

Arriving in Portsmouth mid-morning without mishap, they parked up at Southsea Common and headed for Clarence Pier and *Billy Manning's* amusement park, where they spent most of the morning. Peter was rapt with pleasure, his senses in overload with the noise, the flashing colours and the smell of fried onions and candyfloss. Apparently fearless, he experienced several rides, each more daring than the previous. Helen allowed Frank to accompany him on most while she watched, but she joined in when they went on the dodgems, taking a car for herself, while he and Peter sat in another. She shrieked with laughter when she rammed into the back of their car; he laughed, knowing she was making a point.

They took lunch sitting on a concrete step leading from the promenade to the beach. Helen and Frank ate fish and chips in a newspaper; Peter a battered sausage, which he tackled by nibbling the batter off first before demolishing the middle. A passer-by took their photograph with Helen's Kodak Instamatic.

They stopped off at Debenhams before driving home. Helen wanted to visit the Homes and Furnishings department. By this point, Peter had become irritable, so Frank suggested he take him to look at the toys. They met up again, as agreed, for a cup of tea in the in-store restaurant. By then, Peter had regained his usual sunny mood. He gazed in wonder at the box of "Yankee" soldiers, each in various poses behind their plastic window.

'You spoil him, Frank,' Helen rebuked, 'You could have saved it for his birthday next week.'

Peter ripped open the box on the drive home, eager to get acquainted with his new friends. These were the blue uniformed soldiers who teamed up with their green-clad comrades to win the inevitable victory over the Red Indians later that afternoon.

While Helen went indoors to supervise the ritual of Peter's tea time, Frank gathered up the plastic adversaries and put then inside the fort. As he stooped to extract a concealed apache from a flowerbed, he saw Bob's Austin Consul pull up outside. He watched as his father-in-law climbed out of the car, opened the front gate and walked up the path towards him.

'Hello Bob, we weren't expecting you. Is everything okay?'

'Of course, everything's okay. I just thought I'd pop 'round and see that grandson of mine. And, I was hoping you might have a bottle of Guinness cooling in your refrigerator,' he said, parking himself in the deck chair next to his. 'Anyway, "What's My Line?" is on at six, and, as my TV's on the blink, I rather hoped you wouldn't mind me watching it on your set.'

As if as an after-thought, he added: 'You and Helen could go out for an hour - give you some space and allow me some time with my Grandson.'

'I like the sound of that, Bob - that's really good of you. I'd better tell her to get her glad rags on, and I'll fetch you that Guinness.'

Frank smiled - a relaxing hour in the *Crows Nest* sounded appealing. Peter meant everything to him, but he welcomed the opportunity to spend time alone with Helen.

Peter was finishing his beans on toast when he entered the kitchen, laden with the wooden fort and the detritus of the game.

'Your dad's here. He's offered to babysit for us, so we can go out for an hour. Thought we could go to the pub. It should be warm enough to sit outside and watch the sun go down. What do you think?'

'What a fab idea - we haven't been out together for weeks.'

Peter disappeared out of the back door as soon as his plate was empty, snatching a handful of plastic figurines to feature in a new game.

'He's tired: I'll get him off to bed before we go out. You'd better bring him in soon.'

Looking out of the kitchen window, he noticed Bob had settled himself in a deck chair and was watching Peter playing with his miniature companions. He puffed on a pipe and wore an amused expression as he witnessed the enactment of Peter's imagination. Frank grinned and extracted a bottle of Guinness from the fridge.

***

Later that evening, they sat at their favourite table in the pub garden, right up against the wall which overlooked the cliff below, watching the sun slowly descend in the cloudless sky.

'A perfect end to a wonderful day,' she whispered, leaning into him. He put his arm around her and gave her shoulder a gentle squeeze.

'You're so right,' he said, adding: 'couldn't be better!'

They stayed like that for some time until the sun was well below the horizon and they both shivered. 'Come on Mrs Armstrong - I think it's about time I took you home and warmed you up.'

'That sounds like a very nice idea.'

In the car park, he sidled around to the passenger's side and opened the door for her. 'Such a gentleman,' she said laughing.

Just as he inserted the keys into the ignition, she leant over and whispered in his ear: 'I hope we can always stay this happy.'

As he flashed the engine, he turned to her. 'We will, Helen, I'll make sure we do.'

Chapter 28

"THE LETTER"

(Monday 26th August)

Helen studied him as he made a small adjustment to his tie. His fastidiousness amused and fascinated her: a part of his attraction - a subtle hint of his dependability and apparent determination to create a positive image. He smiled at her from his reflection in the mirror, knowing she was watching him.

'Right then, I'm off!' He grabbed his brief case, walked over and kissed her. 'See you later, darling!'

Peter was contentedly mashing egg soldiers into his mouth. Frank waved to him, hoping he wouldn't insist on being kissed.

'Behave yourself or there'll be big trouble!' he said with mock sternness.

He was rewarded with an eggy grin – even though he was only three, Peter seemed to understand irony.

'Don't forget to pick up a bottle of wine for tonight, Frank.'

He groaned. 'Oh, God! I'd forgotten about that. Don't suppose there's any chance you can find an excuse not to go?'

'Oh, come on, it won't be that bad. Just a couple of hours and we'll be able to escape to the pub.'

Helen acknowledged privately she was downplaying the probable tedium of the soirée. She was dreading the evening as much as him. Nick and Eve, their neighbours, having recently returned from a caravan holiday in the Lake District, were keen to show off their snaps.

'It'll be a Kodachrome endurance test!' he muttered darkly.

Helen's mind presented her with a preview of the evening. She imagined herself with a fixed smile on her face, feigning interest as Nick related holiday details; Eve twittering away in the background; Frank looking thoroughly bored and apparently not caring if anyone noticed.

'You're right, it will be awful, but we're going and that's that! I've booked the babysitter. And, anyway, they would be hurt if we backed out.'

He shrugged, his face conveying the clear message Eve and Nicks' feelings didn't matter to him. She saw he was about to argue, but then he seemed to change his mind. He grinned: 'We could always ask the babysitter to phone with a problem - that way, we'll escape and be able to go somewhere, just you and me!'

She gave him one of her looks requiring no words to convey meaning. Receiving the message, he shrugged in resignation. 'Just a thought,' he offered.

As he turned to leave, plucking his trilby from the hat stand by the front door, the letterbox rattled, and post fell on the door mat. He knelt and picked up a handful of mail.

'On the side table,' he said, nodding to the letters he dropped there.

If she could see his face, she would have seen a shadow cross it as he slipped one envelope into his jacket pocket.

'Don't be late!' she shouted at him as he opened the front door. He raised his hat to her in a mock salute, closing the door behind him.

***

After Frank left for work, and the challenge of getting Peter to complete his breakfast without spreading a large proportion of it over the table had been overcome, there followed a brief but satisfying interlude, allowing time for peace and reflection before starting the daily domestic tasks. Pouring a cup of tea, Helen thought how routine her life seemed now: a predictable pattern of activities that for some women might seem mundane and boring. As she watched her son rummaging in his toy box, she smiled with contentment.

Life was - well, how could it possibly be better? One of her current favourite songs came on the wireless playing in the living room. She went in quickly to turn it up before returning to the chair at the kitchen table. The words to Kathy Kirby's "Dance On" made her smile, and she hummed along with her.

As she cast her eyes around the kitchen, and through the open door leading to the combined dining and living room, she noted the oddments of domesticity: appliances, implements, furniture, ornaments - all were bought outright, not on hire purchase. Her father loaned them the money for the deposit on the house where they moved after Peter was born. Frank's salary covered the mortgage and the bills, and they would soon be able to pay her father back for the loan.

The house, a former coastguard cottage, stood on the coast road leading to the *Crows Nest*, their local pub. A front garden afforded a view over the top of the cliffs to the sea beyond. On a clear night, they could see the lights of ships far away in the distance.

Watching Peter playing made her smile - it always did. He had organised a game for himself involving toy cars and his plastic soldiers, which made sense to him but would be unfathomable to anyone else. His vocabulary remained limited: he seemed to have grasped about twenty words, including a reasonable attempt at Mummy (Umma) and Dad (Da). To Helen's annoyance, he could articulate very clearly Frank's favourite expletive, 'bugger,' used a little too frequently within his earshot.

Frank had been overjoyed when the daughter Helen believed in turned out to be a boy. He doted on his son, spending every spare moment playing with him.

'I don't know who the biggest child is, Peter or you!' she said on more than one occasion with contrived exasperation. But his connection with their son made her exceedingly happy - it completed their union, made them whole and permanent - a family. No longer did she feel occasional nagging doubt about Frank's commitment: he was now husband and father, and he seemed to be content in both roles.

His career at Parks developed at a pace. Now her father's deputy, a trusted "right hand-man," he was being groomed to take over as General Manager for when her father retired, which was not too far away, a fact confirmed over Sunday Dinner just a week ago. She smiled at the prospect. Although not overly interested in the trappings of status, she felt proud of Frank and his achievements.

Sipping her tea, savouring the moment of satisfying reflection, she considered her own level of contentment. For her, life focused on the home, on raising their son and being a good wife for Frank. She had relinquished her role at Parks, so she could look after Peter. Being a mother and a wife - now that was the pinnacle of happiness and fulfilment.

'Yes: life is just wonderful!' she informed herself with a smile.

***

Frank hoped Helen hadn't seen his expression when he spotted the envelope, the one he slipped into his jacket pocket. The sudden jolt of fear that hit him when seeing the wording on the front would have registered clearly on his face. As he sat in the driver's seat of the Healey, he wanted to take it out, tear it open and read the contents straight away - but Helen might be watching through the kitchen window and would no doubt wonder what he was doing.

He drove along the coast road towards town. Once the house was far behind him, he fished in his pocket and laid the envelope on the passenger seat. His eyes were drawn constantly to it, focusing on the words – "Personal and Confidential," and three addresses, two of which were crossed out with "RE-DIRECTED" written above them. There was his current address, etched in neat capital letters. The two scored through addresses were his former digs in Southampton and Mrs Bunning's guest house in Fairfield. He registered the first as a woman's handwriting. The epithet "Private and Confidential," underlined at the top of the envelope, could only mean trouble, he thought.

'Sod it!' he muttered, pulling into a lay-by. As soon as he wrenched the handbrake on, he grabbed the envelope and ripped it open, extracting the single folded sheet of blue vellum paper inside. As he read the letter, he realised his worst fears.

The letter, brief and neatly written in a woman's hand, contained a clear message: Fleur wanted him to contact her. The tone of the letter, although friendly, included hints of accusation: 'You said you'd stay in touch, but I haven't heard from you!' Through her words, he could also hear pleading: 'I would love to talk to you again, catch up. Please call me. Frank!!! Here's my number...'

Fleur gave her address in Birmingham, and a telephone number, which was underlined three times. When he read the last part of it, a cold hand squeezed his heart: *Frank, we spent two wonderful nights together. I know we were only meant to be friends, but you were so tender, so loving.*

He imagined what would have happened had he not retrieved it from the post. A vision of Helen appeared - a suspicious look on her face, opening the envelope addressed to him, reading the damning contents. Stuffing it back into his jacket pocket, he thought desperately. What if she wrote to him again, assuming she hadn't done so already? The thought of another letter arriving, in the same way, made his heart lurch. 'Stay calm - you can sort this out,' he whispered.

Later that day, he diverted from his normal route home. He parked the Healey in the car park of the *Golden Lion*, the pub opposite the shell of Ramsay's Autos. As he walked to the nearby telephone box, he noted with distracted interest the garage was now a pile of rubble.

He looked at his watch: a quarter past six. Fleur would most likely be at home now having returned from the department store in which she worked in Birmingham town centre. Entering the phone box, which smelled predictably of stale tobacco with a faint hint of urine, he dialled her number. It was answered on the third ring. He pushed in some coins.

'Hello?' said a female voice.

'Fleur?'

'No, it's Jen, Fleur's not home yet. Can I take a message?'

'What time do you think she'll be in?' he said, hoping his voice sounded friendly and nonchalant.

'She's normally home by about six thirty. Do you want me to ask her to call you? By the way, who is it? Can I say who called?'

He detected a strong element of female curiosity.

'I'll try again later,' he said hurriedly, ignoring her question. Before she could interject, he put the phone down.

'Bugger,' he muttered - the delay meant he would be cutting it fine and may be late home. He looked at the *Golden Lion* - the pub door beckoned him. A few moments later, he sat at the bar, a pint of bitter in front of him. With the gift of prescience, he would have known, he was sitting in the same spot "Alf" Ramsay had been on the night before he died.

237

Back in the phone box, he tried the number again. It was answered straight away by a familiar voice.

'Hello Fleur, I...,' he began. Unsure how to start the conversation, he hesitated - although he knew what message he should convey: *Please, no further contact; let's both carry on with our own lives without each other.*

She gave a small scream of delight. 'I thought it would be you. Oh, Frank, how lovely to hear from you! How are you? Why didn't you write? You said you would and...!'

Her words came out in a rush. His heart sank - this would be more difficult than expected. He lit a cigarette, inhaling deeply, then exhaling, filling the phone box with smoke. She finally stopped speaking and seemed to wait for him to say something.

He had spent most of the day in a state of distraction, rehearsing what he would say. His message would be clear - friendly but to the point: there must be no further contact. What happened nearly three years ago should be forgotten. He was married now, with a son and responsibilities.

But this conversation did not happen.

Later, as he drove home, he re-played what was actually said and cursed himself for his weakness and betrayal. He would not have been able to explain why he said what he did. Perhaps, he couldn't bring himself to upset her - she sounded so pleased he made contact. Harder to articulate, but a significant factor was the rekindling of deeper, primeval stirrings. Hearing her voice prompted intense images of hidden, forbidden pleasures.

He told her it would be best if she did not write to him, explaining he moved about a lot, so it would take too long for her letters to reach him. He expected a protestation, but none came. There was no point in giving her a telephone number either, for the same reason, he explained. He detected a slight hesitancy in her tacit acceptance of this, but he promised to call her regularly, just to catch up on things.

If she thought, he was being disingenuous - and hiding a few significant details - she did not challenge. His instinct told him that, if she knew the truth about his current circumstances, she would not have minded overmuch. More important for her was the renewal of their relationship. When she suggested they might meet, he detected a hint of pleading in her voice.

'That would be great - in fact, it just so happens I may be up your way quite often. I'll call as soon as I know for definite.'

The words tumbled out without consideration of consequence. As he drove home, he realised two immediate facts: first, he had opened a door marked danger; second, he felt compelled to enter it.

I'm due to go up to the Midlands, he reminded himself. This would be a regular occurrence now Parks had established franchises in Solihull and Birmingham. There would be many opportunities to meet with her. Driving home, his mind presented images of Helen and Peter. Waves of guilt swept over him.

As he passed a phone box on the coast road, he considered stopping, calling Fleur back and telling her the truth. 'I'm happily married with a son.' The image of the phone box receded in the rear-view mirror - the opportunity lost.

He arrived home to find Helen dressed and ready to go out.

'Where on earth have you been, Frank? We were due at Nick and Eves' half an hour ago! And, where's the wine I asked you to get?'

'I had a quick one with the lads from distribution. I couldn't let them down, they've done such a good job, I promised I'd buy them a round. It's just, well, you know how it is - it went on longer than I thought it would.'

Registering her look, which suggested that this would be discussed in more depth later, he groaned. Returning to the bar after the phone call with Fleur, just to steady his nerves, had been a very bad move.

Chapter 29

"SCHOOL"

(September 1963)
The first day of term arrived and Vee was terrified. Her experience of teaching in an inner-city school presented more challenges than those she would face in the more sedate setting of Crofton Juniors. But, in Salford, she had been under close supervision, guided by a more experienced teacher, always on hand to help if circumstances required it. Despite the Head Mistress's encouraging words during their meeting the day before, she felt exposed and vulnerable.

The reflection looking back at her in the hall mirror would be unrecognisable to the student version of herself. Her former beatnik image had been consigned to the past. Instead, she adopted a new professional appearance, one with which she was not entirely comfortable. She wore a two-piece suit; the skirt a couple of inches above her knees, the jacket short and boxy with over-sized plastic buttons. Gone the bright red lipstick - her makeup presented a more modest and demure visage.

'Bloody hell, what a state!' she muttered.

'Rubbish, you look fantastic! Very Jackie Kennedy, but without the hat! Come on, girl - let's go - your class awaits you!'

This was Carrie, her housemate and fellow teacher, a veteran, in Vee's eyes, with a year's experience at the school.

***

A few days before the start of term, Carrie helped her choose the outfits, which involved a day out in

Portsmouth. They had taken the train instead of driving. After a visit to Debenhams to get Vee "rigged out," as Carrie called the ordeal of finding suitable attire for her new friend, they walked to Old Portsmouth and visited several of the pubs there. At shutting time, they piled out of the door giggling and drunk.

They spent the afternoon sobering up on Southsea beach, soaking up the warm September sunshine. Both fell asleep and didn't wake until early evening. At this point, Vee realised two things: first, they were sunburnt, and second, the shopping bags with her new clothes were nowhere to be seen.

'Oh bollocks - we must have left them in the pub,' announced Carrie, who burst out laughing, clearly finding the situation highly amusing.

A frantic dash back to the *Dolphin*, the last pub they had visited earlier, followed, coinciding with early evening opening. Fortunately, the landlord had rescued the bags, anticipating their return. It seemed only polite to stay for a drink or two, which turned into a prolonged session. They caught the last train home with only minutes to spare.

***

Despite her initial worries, Vee settled quickly into the school routine. The class of eight-year-olds, contrary to her expectations, turned out to be easy to manage.

'You just wait; they'll soon start playing you up!' Carrie advised.

However, three weeks into the job without mishap, her confidence grew.

Every morning, having taken the register, she led her class in single file into the assembly hall. Her charges stood in an obedient line at the front, facing the stage, while the more senior classes filed in and formed lines behind them. She would join the other teachers, sitting on chairs looking inwards, parallel with their respective charges, ready to issue any corrective action if required to maintain discipline, which never seemed necessary.

Mrs Bishop, the Head Mistress, would glide into the hall at exactly 9 o'clock, all tweed and brogues with a faint whiff of Chanel perfume. Ascending the stage with a briskness that belied her age, she would stand and face the rows of up-turned faces and, after a brief pause during which she appeared to survey everyone in the room, she would announce 'Good morning children!'

'Good morning, Mrs Bishop,' the serried ranks would reply in high-voiced unison.

The hymn of the day followed - the discordant harmony of childish singing muffled by the strident, enthusiastic playing of the piano by Mrs Iltman. The Head Mistress then led the recitation of the Lord's Prayer. By half past nine, the children would be back in their classrooms ready for the first of the day's lessons.

***

When Vee started her studies at Manchester University, thoughts of a possible future career never crossed her mind. Later, though, her tutor, Professor O'Donnell, suggested teaching might be a worthwhile, fulfilling vocation for her. She was doubtful at first but the idea of being a teacher began to appeal. Despite an initial crisis of confidence, she thrived during her training. Following teacher training college, a placement at an inner-city school in Salford enabled her to apply theory into practice. By this point, she knew teaching would be her life-time profession.

Vee's placement provided a sound basis upon which to build her career. During her sojourn there, she experienced more challenges in dealing with pupils than many teachers would experience in a lifetime - and she coped well. In comparison with Salford, Crofton Junior School was, as she would describe it, a doddle. The children behaved well and were compliant, respectful of authority and, apparently, carried no domestic problems into the arena.

Each day followed the same comfortable routine: registration; the assembly, and then lessons. The first lesson of the day involved a ritualistic chanting of the times-table, moving slowly up the scale as the age-old formulae became embedded in the minds of the youngsters. By her second week of teaching, the class could cover their four-times table with confidence. Vee experienced a glow of achievement. Nearly all her class were confident in reading, most progressing from "Janet and John" to the literary delights of Enid Blyton.

One boy, Anthony, however, lagged a long way behind the other children. While the rest of the class immersed themselves in their favourite books, or other distractions during reading time, Vee would spend time with him coaching and encouraging. Much to her delight, he responded well to her tutoring and made real progress.

Apart from being confident in her practical abilities, she found teaching allowed her to be herself - her personality fitted that of an effective teacher: she did not have to adopt a different persona to gain acceptance in her role. Her confidence grew.

Each day, although following a similar, predictable pattern, still offered new and unexpected pleasures: such as teaching Anthony to read. The environment, an ambience of innocence, the smell of wax crayons, floor polish and the pervasive aroma of cooking, evoked comfortable feelings of both belonging and purpose.

Chapter 30

"CARRIE"

Carrie's previous flatmate was the teacher, whose departure provided the vacancy into which Vee stepped. They hit it off straight away.

The flat occupied the ground floor of an Edwardian house on the coast road, almost five miles further on from where Helen, Frank, and Peter lived, and a short drive to the school. Each had their own bedroom but shared a living room, bathroom, and kitchen.

Vee's bedroom provided a haven - her private space. She never felt pressure to spend evenings with her flatmate in the living room watching the television they rented although they often did. They agreed at the outset they both needed to be alone sometimes, and this must never cause offence to the other.

They both enjoyed nights out. During the weekdays, they stayed in, taking turns to cook dinner, and sharing a bottle, sometimes two. Having spent a gap year in Rome, Carrie had developed a love of Italian cuisine and wine - she introduced Vee to both.

When Friday evening arrived, they would go out. Carrie introduced Vee to her social circuit: an eclectic mix of teachers and other professionals, including Royal Naval officers based in Portsmouth.

A nearby yacht marina provided a varied and active environment, and this was where they spent most Friday and Saturday evenings. The many pubs and bars were full of what Carrie described as 'a better class of people.'

'The hoi polloi goes to the city for kicks - people like us come here!' she explained.

Vee loved the atmosphere in the various venues her friend led her into. They would visit one or two traditional fishermen's pubs; then more lively haunts with perhaps a jazz group playing, making it difficult to talk, although this didn't matter: communication passed without words.

Every Friday and Saturday evening followed a similar itinerary. The hub of their social activity, and always the last venue they visited, was a club, a converted grain storage building, which its regular patrons called the GX. When Vee asked what GX stood for, Carrie laughed. 'It's supposed to stand for "Grain Exchange" but most people think of it as the "Groin Exchange" - you'll soon see why!'

Carrie was a club member of the GX and persuaded Vee to join. 'Ensures we get in, and saves us queuing,' she advised. Vee considered the sum of thirty shillings for an annual membership of the club a sound investment. She looked forward to her visits, knowing she could enjoy herself in the knowledge Sunday would allow time to recover before returning to school on Monday morning.

The club was small, accessed by a narrow, winding staircase from street level on which non-members queued hoping to gain extra drinking time after the pubs shut. A bar provided a cramped area for drinkers to congregate in sociable groups. A tiny dance floor would fill, and a low beam overhead often caught out the unwary.

As regular visitors, they became well known. Many of the friends and acquaintances they encountered in the various venues they visited earlier in the evening would appear. The atmosphere was always friendly and good-natured - the clientele were young, professional people, most of them single, although Vee suspected some of the men might be married, despite the absence of a wedding ring.

On one occasion, a man, who reminded her of Frank, offered to buy them both a drink. It was clear from the way he directed his conversation to Carrie that she was his target. Not wanting to cramp her friend's style, she was about to excuse herself when she noticed the man's wedding finger, devoid of a ring but showing a tell-tale white line. This sparked a flash of anger at the deception and she decided to stay and make mischief. The man glared at her as she made a point of smiling with a knowing expression, looking down at where his wedding band should have been and then back at his face again. Her meaning was clear - it didn't take long for him to realise this. He became flustered and embarrassed. After finishing his drink with obvious haste, he walked away.

'He's married, Carrie.'

'Yes, I know. I can't believe they think we won't notice. They always try it! Oh, don't look so shocked, Vee! It doesn't bother me. It's their problem, not mine. They're the ones who must live with the consequences, not me. I'm just having fun.'

Although Vee didn't dwell on the issue, she found Carrie's attitude difficult to reconcile with her own values. There was much to her friend that lay hidden, and she realised, although they shared much in common, some aspects of Carrie's character were at odds with her own way of thinking. Little by little, she learned more about her flat mate.

One evening, fuelled by several glasses of wine, Carrie volunteered the fact she recently ended a long-term relationship, one that nearly ended in marriage.

'Caught them at it *in flagrante*.' She laughed as she related the story. 'His face was a picture! Anyway, after that, I decided there would be no more meaningful relationships for me - I've learned my lesson. I'm living for the moment - and if that means breaking a few taboos, then so be it.'

Vee could see the hurt behind the mask because she had also been hurt but in a different way. She had never been in a serious relationship, at least not one that lasted for more than a few weeks. There was her brief but torrid affair with Jonny - but that never meant anything. Her attitude to casual relationships - she had been in several at university and at teacher training college - was that they should remain that: casual. On more than one occasion, the other partner in her intended "no ties" affair had pushed for a more permanent arrangement; when this happened, she would always end the liaison.

'Helen and I are opposites when it came to relationships with men,' she imparted to Carrie during another of the regular wine-fuelled heart-to-hearts. 'I'm sure Helen was a virgin before she met Frank. In fact, I can't recall any other men before him.'

Carrie rolled her eyes in disbelief and incomprehension when she heard this.

'Gosh, I can't think of anything worse than being stuck with one man. There's a whole sea full of them out there - why stick only to one?'

'I agree,' Vee replied.

Although happy her sister seemed to have found love and happiness in marriage and motherhood, the thought of being in a similar arrangement presented as anathema for her. There would be plenty of time later for marriage and children; in the meantime, like Carrie, she intended to live life to the full.

Vee came to realise that, although she and Carrie shared a similar view of men and relationships, in that that they should be plentiful and non-committal, they differed on one fundamental point: their attitude to married men. For Vee, married men were off the menu. She despised men who tried to conceal their marital status in the hope of a new conquest. But in Carrie's opinion, if a married man was prepared to be unfaithful this could be justified on the basis of some underlying reason, something that somehow mitigated the actions of the man.

'What about the man's poor wife?' Vee protested.

'What about her? She's probably the reason he needs to find his kicks elsewhere.'

Vee was very unhappy with Carrie's attitude - but rather than allow their fundamental disagreement to mar their relationship, she didn't push the debate.

***

Carrie owned a brand-new Hillman Imp, a twenty-first birthday present from her parents. Vee had been touched but also fearful when Carrie offered to teach her to drive, visualising various dents and scratches to the otherwise spotless, immaculate car. But her friend insisted, waving away her protestations.

'You'll pick it up in no time, you're a quick learner!'

They rigged "Learner" plates, and every weekday, Vee would drive the car to and from school. To her surprise, having mastered the intricacies of the clutch, accelerator, and gear coordination, she developed her skill and confidence. Within a matter of weeks, she took her driving test which she passed the first time.

Carrie found Vee's preference for roll-up cigarettes amusing: 'Very exotic darling; so urban!' She preferred Rothmans, but she did, on occasion, roll her own cigarettes, although these were, she explained, a 'special sort of roll-up.'

Vee recognised a spliff - plenty of students smoked them at university, and the cafes, and bars that went with her beatnik scene. Jonny had smoked them occasionally, but despite his exhortations and accusations she was 'square,' she had stuck to the more conventional type.

But, after a particularly satisfying evening meal, which Carrie cooked, and well into the second bottle of Barolo wine, Vee finally succumbed to the lure of cannabis.

Chapter 31

"A FLEETING IMAGE"

(Monday 11th November 1963)

Monday evening followed an established pattern: they cooked and ate supper together while swapping stories of their weekend exploits. Carrie talked at length about her renewed relationship with a naval officer who, having spent several months at sea, during which time she had forgotten about him, re-emerged into her life. Vee, usually inquisitive about her friend's love life, said little.

'I have an inkling he's married, but...,'

This caused Vee to raise her eyebrows in apparent shock at this flagrant attitude to infidelity - but, other than that, she only half-listened.

'You seem down, Vee, what's up? You've barely said a word.'

'Sorry - I am listening - but - well, something happened over the weekend, and it's been on my mind, eating away. I think you'd better open that second bottle and I'll tell you - at least I'll try to explain.'

Vee explained she went to the Marina on Saturday intending to meet the usual crowd of friends they socialised with in the various venues.

'It was just like any other weekend night there. We met up at the *Corner House* where we spent an hour. Then someone, can't remember who, said a trad jazz band was playing in the *Plume and Feathers*, so we went there next. That's where this strange thing happened. I'm not sure how to describe the sensation - a sudden onset of anxiety perhaps - almost a panic attack. But the point is, I can't think of the cause. One minute everything seemed - well - normal, the next, I became overcome with fear.'

She took a drag on her roll-up and blew smoke up towards the ceiling.

'I stood outside smoking, a few minutes after this feeling came over me, trying to calm down and work out what spooked me. I just couldn't think of anything specific – but, and this is what I can't explain, I felt threatened. I know it sounds weird - you must think I'm being silly but...'

'Did you smoke any of this stuff?' said Carrie holding up her spliff. 'Cannabis can bring on feelings of paranoia– or at least some people say. Perhaps...'

'No,' Vee cut in. 'I only smoked roll-ups. But I could sense something was not right.'

The expression on Carrie's face showed she still didn't understand.

'Let's go through your evening step-by-step from the moment you stepped into the pub. Can you remember anything unusual, strange at any point - something you might not have registered at the time?'

Vee stared ahead of her as if thinking hard. 'The band - they were good but very loud. Wall-to-wall people - everybody squeezed in together - and it was so hot and uncomfortable. I remember coming over dizzy and sick.'

She paused as if in thought. 'That's right, I wanted to go outside. I needed fresh air.'

'So, the anxiety hadn't kicked in at this point?'

'No - but it did soon after.'

'Try this - it might help you recall something,' said Carrie, passing over her joint.

Vee took a drag and held in the smoke, enjoying the calming effect, so much more effective than normal tobacco. She took another intake of aromatic smoke and then handed the joint back.

'I said nothing to anyone - I wanted to go outside for a minute or two, you know, to clear my head.'

She thought hard, conscious Carrie was watching her. In her mind, she was back in the *Plume and Feathers*, this time without the cacophony of noise from the jazz band - only images. The scene in the pub played frame by frame. The cannabis it seemed helped to add clarity. She saw the door: her escape from the claustrophobia. The exit is beyond the main bar area, crowded with drinkers. Desperate to reach the exit, she finds progress slow because bodies are packed so close together they impede her movement.

In front of her, she sees the back of a broad shouldered, stocky individual with a bald head. She reaches out and taps him on the shoulder. He turns, a grin on his face - she notices several gold teeth. He leans back, his arm raised. She ducks underneath. In his hand is a glass of spirit - she is careful not to nudge his sleeve in case any spilled. He makes some amusing remark - his lips move. She nods her thanks.

Just for a moment, her eyes glance towards the bar area over his shoulder. A momentary scene so quick, she couldn't assimilate the detail or comprehend the significance - but the image was etched into her sub-conscious. That's when the intense anxiety began.

'What is it, Vee?' Carrie sounded concerned. 'What's the matter? You look terrified.'

Vee said nothing - it was as though her friend was not there. The image prints on her mind like a snapshot. His back is to the bar, so he is facing towards her. He is wearing a black jacket, like a reefer. On his head is a black hat - a beanie? Dark glasses hide his eyes - but she imagines the piercing gaze behind the lenses. He has a beard - not as full and unkempt as she remembered it - now it is neatly trimmed. On his face is the slight, knowing smile that once attracted her. Or had she imagined that?

'Oh, my God!' she whispered. 'He's come looking for me.'

'Who has?'

'Jonny,' she replied.

Carrie looked perplexed. 'Who's, Jonny?'

After a large shot of brandy and a few drags on a fresh joint, she had calmed down enough to tell Carrie the story of the man who had attempted to dominate her life.

'He wrote twice from prison. He used my hall of residence address, and the letters were forwarded to my home address in Fairfield. I returned both, unopened. He never tried to contact me again - I hoped he'd given up - forgotten about me.'

'But you said you didn't register you had seen this man, Jonny. Only your sub-conscience registered him, at least that's what you seem to be saying. So, are you sure you did see him? Sorry, Vee, but it doesn't make sense. Surely, if you had seen this character, even for just a split second, you would have known straight away who he was - wouldn't you?'

Vee tried to study the image in her mind again. But it was less sharp now. Carrie's words had planted a promising seed of doubt.

'Perhaps I imagined the whole thing. You could be right, Carrie - I hope you are, anyway.'

She found this thought assuring to some extent - but the nagging fear would not go away entirely.

Chapter 32

"A DISASTROUS SUNDAY DINNER"

(Sunday 17th November 1963)
By the following Sunday, the fear that threatened to dominate Vee's thoughts had reduced to a level where she could, for most of the time, bury it somewhere in the recesses of her mind. A family gathering at the Armstrongs' - a term she used to acknowledge their domesticity - provided a distraction.

She sat on the carpet of the living room with Peter. They were watching one of his current favourite television programmes, "Wagon Trains." As usual, he spread his many miniature Cowboys and Indians around him together with some newly acquired plastic wagons to match those he watched in black and white on the TV screen. She ignored the discomfort of sitting on the floor - as a teacher she was used to coming down to the level of a child, and anyway, being with her only nephew more than compensated.

Raised voices from the kitchen caused her to turn her head and stare at the closed door, a frown replacing the smile she wore a moment ago. Something's happened, and it sounds like Frank's in the wrong, she thought.

The banging of a cupboard door startled her. Then his voice: 'Oh for God's sake, calm down. I thought I'd explained all this!'

The seeds of discontent emerged from almost the moment she arrived earlier that afternoon. The good-natured banter that usually accompanied her visits remained absent - instead, there was what she might describe as an "atmosphere." She turned back and looked at Peter and, seeing he had also been distracted by the sound of marital discord and as a consequence wore a troubled expression, ruffled his hair.

'Come on, if you're not careful, the Indians will win, and we can't have that, can we?'

Absorbed back into his game, in seconds he regained his normal happy composure.

***

'Don't you want to be with us? Why do you want to be away all the time?'

'But I'm not away all the time - only when I have to be. And I must be in the Midlands tomorrow. There are two new franchises to visit - I've got to make sure everything's okay. For heaven's sake, I'll be away for one night - maybe two at the most and I...'

Helen slammed the cupboard door where she had been searching unsuccessfully for a box of OXO cubes, and turned to face him, her eyes blazing fury.

'You don't need to stay away for one night let alone two!' she shouted. 'And, for that matter, I don't see why you can't sort everything out that has to be done by telephone. Apart from that, you hired a perfectly capable area sales manager who can do whatever's necessary. You're supposed to be in Head Office working with Dad.'

'Oh, for God's sake, calm down - you're blowing this all out of proportion.'

Frank realised he was shouting as well and threw a glance towards the closed door leading to the sitting room where Vee and Peter were. He turned to her and held up his hands in a placatory gesture.

'Look,' he said, his voice softer now, 'I know you want me here all the time - but it's simply not possible now. I do need to go up tomorrow. The area sales manager is new - he's still on probation - and I'm not convinced he's fully up to the job yet. But, after this week, hopefully, I won't have to be away so much.'

'Dad says you're being over-cautious. You've been up once so they should be able to manage on their own now. He agrees with me.'

He detected a triumphant tone, which irritated him. The knowledge she went behind his back and discussed what he considered his business with her father, annoyed him.

'Your dad knows as well as I do that opening a new franchise is a risky undertaking - they will always need hand-holding during the first few weeks and...'

'We'll see, won't we!' she snapped, indicating she would have the last word on the subject.

He was on the verge of retaliating with a rejoinder - something like 'Being apart seems to me like a very good idea when you behave like a spoilt daddy's girl who's not got her own way!' but he stopped himself - instinct told him to leave the kitchen instead. As he stepped into the sitting room, he saw the frown of concern on Vee's face - he guessed she had heard much of the argument. He shrugged, smiled at Peter, and then headed towards the back door.

Heaving on his old army greatcoat he always left on a hook by the door, he exited into the cold air. Helen insisted he smoke outside - it had been hard to accept this dictate at first, but he now welcomed the opportunity to be alone with his thoughts. It would be his first cigarette since lunchtime, and he needed one now.

As he smoked, he dissected his argument with her. She was right - he acknowledged this irrefutable truth - he did not need to spend two days in the Midlands. The two new Park franchises, one in Solihull and the other in Walsall, had been open for nearly a month. Both were performing well, with capable and enthusiastic managers in charge. The area manager proved to be a sound choice - he recruited him personally and had been impressed with his progress.

'The Midland operation is all systems go. I think you're being over-cautious going up there to check on them again,' Bob advised him at their weekly operations meeting.

'I need to be absolutely certain they know what they're doing. Invest time right at the beginning and less chance we'll be sorting out a bloody mess later.'

Staring at the tip of his glowing cigarette, he felt strong pangs of guilt. His reason for going up to the Midlands could not be justified on the grounds of business need - he knew that. He was being drawn like a moth to the flame, knowing guilty pleasures awaited him.

Laughter filtered through the small gap in the door which he had left ajar. Vee appeared to be pretending to remonstrate with Peter. He imagined the scene in the living room: his son taking childish pleasure in provoking a reaction from Vee - she would be chasing him in circles around the settee. The vision was one of such happy domesticity that, for a few moments, he considered cancelling his plans for the forthcoming week. He had all but decided to go back inside and tell Helen she was right: going to the Midlands was not necessary, he was just trying to the best he could for Parks. They would be reconciled - all back to normal again.

But the flame flickered into life again. He knew he would go - his case was already packed. Guilty thoughts were replaced with anticipation and erotic yearning that he could not extinguish. Despite accusing stabs of guilt, he thought about his recent visit to the Midlands, and his meetings with Fleur: the evenings of easy conversation and laughter; and the nights of passion.

***

Frank appeared subdued and morose for the rest of the day. The roast beef was over-cooked and wooden; the vegetables, in contrast, under-cooked. Her dad described them "al dente" - 'Just the way they should be.' No one agreed with him judging by the amount of food lying untouched on their plates. Dinner was a disaster. Vee understood why.

She did her best to generate conversation but failed to raise the mood. Her dad, who arrived after the argument in the kitchen, met her eyes at one point and raised his eyebrows in a "God this is painful" expression. Peter picked up on the atmosphere and was unusually quiet and unhappy-looking.

Earlier, while Frank stood outside smoking and simmering following the row, Vee had entered the kitchen where she found Helen crying. Having overheard most of the heated exchange, she understood the reasons for the impasse.

'He doesn't need to go up there. It's just sheer pig-headedness on his part - he won't listen to reason.'

'But, he's only doing his job. He...'

Her attempt at conciliation failed. Helen made it clear she would not change her view of the situation and refused Vee's offer to help with the dinner.

Vee had returned to the living room and resumed her position at floor level with Peter, but she cast frequent glances towards the closed kitchen door behind which cupboard doors banged. Even the distraction of the game could not raise her mood. She tried to console herself with the thought disagreements were a part - perhaps a healthy and essential feature of matrimony. But, Helen and Frank fell out frequently over trivial matters. *I will never get married - not ever - not if that's what marriage is all about!*

Helen collected the plates after the ordeal of the main course. She scraped the huge quantity of leftovers into the bowl which still contained much of the under-cooked vegetables.

'Sorry, it was all so horrible!' she said, which was met with protests suggesting otherwise. But they all privately acknowledged the dinner had been awful.

Frank got up and tried to help Helen tidy the table.

'No, Frank, why don't you go outside and smoke - like you always do?'

'Well, I'm going to make a move, I'm afraid - need an early night - lots on in the depot tomorrow,' said Bob, thrusting his pipe in his pocket and throwing a meaningful look towards Vee.

Picking up on the cue, Vee interjected, 'Oh, why don't I come with you? Save Frank having to drop me off later.' She realised she must have sounded desperate to get away and smiled at Helen in what she hoped would be interpreted as a non-verbal message of apology and understanding.

'I think they've got a few things to sort out,' she whispered to her dad as they went into the hallway to pick up the coats.

'I think you're right!'

Twenty minutes later, Bob stopped the car outside her flat. Just as she was about to climb out of the car, he grunted: 'Hang on a second - forgot to give you this. Arrived a few days ago, addressed to you.'

He pulled out a crumpled envelope from his jacket pocket.

'Thanks, Dad - see you soon,' she said, cramming it into her handbag and brushing his cheek with a kiss. A few minutes later, with the door to her flat shut behind her, she lit a roll-up and inhaled deeply, relishing the calming effect after such a horrible day. There was a half-full bottle of red on the kitchen table - she spent a few moments fighting the temptation to have a large glass.

'Sod it,' she announced to the room, 'one won't hurt - and I bloody well need it!' She sat at the table sipping her wine. 'Oh yes,' she muttered, remembering the envelope.

Probably some circular, or rubbish from the university - who else would write to me at my home address? she wondered, retrieving it from her bag.

The briefest of glances told her who had written to her. The untidy scrawled handwriting was instantly recognisable - she had seen that script twice before. With a small scream, she dropped the envelope as if it had suddenly become red hot. There was no doubt who the author of the letter was. The image of the dark-haired man in the reefer jacket flashed into her mind just as it did with the mind-enhancing help of cannabis.

The shaking started immediately, her breathing coming in short gasps as the panic attack took grip. Her hand knocked over the wine glass, which rolled off the table and onto the floor where it shattered.

She remembered the tin of ready-rolled spliffs, Carrie kept in the kitchen cupboard. Only when she had smoked one and lit another did her shaking begin to subside.

Chapter 33

"INTEREST WANES"

When Frank left home early on Monday morning, Helen stayed in bed and didn't bother saying goodbye to him. In fact, after the ruined Sunday dinner, they barely spoke. It was clear she would not back down.

Having booked himself into a hotel in the city centre which would be his headquarters for the week, he visited both Park franchises in a show of professional interest. He wanted to report back to Bob daily, which, he thought, would provide legitimacy and justification for his time away from the office. He hoped his father-in-law might convey the positive message to Helen.

In the evening, he returned to his hotel and telephoned Helen from the telephone booth in the lobby. As expected, the conversation was brief.

'Oh, you're staying up there for another night, are you? Well, don't bother ringing me again.' She cut him off in mid-sentence by putting the phone down.

'For Christ's sake!' he slammed the receiver back into the cradle.

Returning to his room, he washed and changed. Within half an hour of his unsatisfactory call home, he was sitting in the pub across the road from his hotel, a pint of bitter in front of him and a cigarette in his hand. His thoughts turned from the home to the prospect of meeting Fleur again - this made him feel better.

He didn't phone Helen on Tuesday evening. He couldn't face another angry exchange with her. As well as this, he felt guilty and wondered if, perhaps, Helen might detect this in his voice.

On Wednesday, he did phone home and was surprised when she spoke to him in a way that showed she might have thawed a little. He wondered whether Bob might have spoken up for him. Hearing a more familiar friendly tone to her voice stirred his feelings of guilt. He had now spent two nights with Fleur, both at his hotel where, with a nod and a wink, and the proffering of a ten-shilling note to the hall porter, he smuggled her into his room. Sex with her was good - but by this point, she had begun to irritate him.

***

After being in Fleur's company for a few hours, he realised he was rapidly losing interest in her. The more time they spent together, the less he felt attracted to her, and the more he questioned his foolishness at renewing their relationship. He acknowledged his feelings for her were based solely on his carnal urges and nothing else. *Let's face it, I don't even like her*, he reasoned with himself.

Their easy-going conversations now seemed shallow and meaningless. Her apparent joie de vivre, that had amused him at first, now presented as banal and silly. Behind the veneer, he detected a childish petulance and immaturity. Her conversation included nothing of any substance or originality. He came to realise, they shared little in common. Her current fascination for the *Beatles* provided a clear example of their difference. As an ardent fan, the "Fab Four" meant everything to her. She talked endlessly about them, and he would listen with feigned interest. Having recently attended a *Beatles* concert at the London Palladium with her housemate Jen, she believed if he went to a gig with her, he too would become a fan.

'They're playing in Wimbledon, London in December. We're all going down in a coach from work. Please say you'll go, Frank - pleeeeze!'

She used the epithet "fab" a great deal to describe anything that made her happy. To him, this sounded contrived, a pathetic attempt to be "with it," another term she peppered her prattling with. She teased him for being "square," based on the fact he always wore a jacket and tie and kept his hair neatly trimmed in a slick "short back and sides." He laughed off her attempts to persuade him to be more relaxed in his attire.

He saw the child behind the woman's body. At twenty-three, she was the same age as Vee - but their level of maturity was markedly different. Vee possessed clear intelligence and was lively, witty, and genuinely funny. Fleur, in contrast, although not dim-witted, would never compete on intellect. Her interests were narrow, focusing entirely, or so it seemed, on pop music, fashion, and the latest scandals as covered in the tabloid press, the contents of which she appeared to believe without question.

**

Fleur invited him to her flat in Nuneaton. 'I want to cook you a meal. I can make a lovely Lasagne - got the recipe from "Woman's Own." It would be so nice to be like a couple!'

It was Wednesday, early evening. Looking at his watch, Frank considered cancelling. He thought desperately for an excuse to decline the invitation, but she had been insistent.

'Time to put an end to this relationship,' he told himself as he climbed into his Healey and headed into the suburbs of Birmingham towards her flat. Smoking a cigarette as he drove, he drew comparisons in his mind between the clandestine life he was living and the life he had created for himself with his wife and son.

'I'm being a bloody fool!' he muttered.

**

'Excuse me, sir!'

Frank shot an irritated glance at the old man behind the reception, waving a small note in his hand.

'Your wife. She called several times during the night. Says it's urgent. She wants you to phone as soon as you can.'

He noted the hint of a knowing grin on the elderly man's face. His heart thudded when the implications hit him. It must be an emergency! Was it Peter? Has he been in an accident? Then the next thought sprung in to his head.

'When did she call? I mean, when did she phone last?'

'Three-thirty this morning, sir. I had to tell her I couldn't find you, I'm afraid. Sorry if...' He raised his eyebrows in a knowing expression.

There was a phone booth in the lobby - but the open dome of sound proofing would offer no protection from the prying ears of the receptionist, who hovered nearby. He stepped outside instead and ran to the phone box a few yards along the road. Before picking up the receiver, he tried to control his breathing, at the same time thinking desperately how he might explain his absence from the hotel. His call was answered straight away.

'Helen?'

'No, it's Vee - we've been waiting for you to call. Helen's at the hospital with him now. You need to talk to her. Have you got a pen? I'll give you the number.'

'Yes, yes - I've got one. Now, slow down can you? What's happened? Is it Peter?'

'No...,' she paused. He heard a faint sob.

'Dad's had a heart attack. They say he's seriously ill. You've got to come home. Helen's been frantic, trying to contact you! Where on earth have you been?'

He could hear the emotion in her voice. A brief vision of his exploits the previous night flashed through his mind as if to taunt him. Ignoring her question, he asked her to tell him the number to ring. He jotted it down.

'Come as soon as you can. I'm going there now. He's in Casualty.'

'Look, there's no point in me wasting time calling the hospital. I'm going to get on the road. Can you let Helen know I'm on my way? I should be back in a couple of hours, providing the traffic's not too heavy. Oh, and Vee,' he winced, 'tell Helen I love her, will you?'

Within a quarter of an hour, he had checked out of the hotel and was heading out of Birmingham. With his mind in turmoil, it took considerable effort to calm down enough to think. He needed to devise a credible explanation covering where he'd been overnight. It didn't take long for him to plan a story.

As he drove, thoughts of his betrayal came back - small visions, soundless clips presented to him as evidence. 'I am a complete and utter shit!' he told himself.

***

He ran through the main entrance of the hospital, looking frantically for signs showing the direction towards "Casualty." A sudden flashback reminded him of a similar panicked dash through the same hospital only two years previously.

He spotted Vee first. She looked up when he entered, offering no greeting, just an accusatory stare which he registered straight away.

'Helen's with Dad now. He's sleeping, but they think he's stable. You'd better go through.' She pointed towards a pair of swing doors with opaque glass windows. He nodded, breathing deeply, a combination of exertion and near panic.

Helen sat next to the bed. Bob was asleep, an oxygen mask on his face and several tubes dangled from a metal frame and into his arm.

After a few moments, she spoke. 'Where have you been, Frank?' Her words were spoken in a flat monotone, laden with meaning.

'How is he?' he asked lamely.

She glanced at her father, then back at him. He noticed her eyes appeared swollen and red - she had been crying.

'Where were you, Frank? The hotel said you hadn't been there all night. Please don't lie to me.' Again, her voice was flat, almost a whisper.

'Look, I can explain,' he said, hoping his voice sounded confident and devoid of guilt. The lies poured from his mouth.

Chapter 34

"I WANT YOU BACK"

'Go home, you're done in - you've been here for ages. You need to sleep.'

'Vee's right, Helen - no point in you staying. He'll be out for hours. I'll bring you back this evening - your dad might be awake by then, no doubt wondering what all the fuss is about.'

Helen seemed to ponder this then nodded slowly. 'Are you going to stay a little longer, Vee - just in case he wakes up?'

'Of course, I will. I'll call you at home later. Go home and sort things out with Frank.'

Although Vee whispered, he heard her words as he hovered by the door. They've been talking about me while I was fetching the tea, he told himself. Helen hadn't probed the explanation he concocted for his overnight absence from the hotel, and he was confident his story would stand up to scrutiny. But something about the look she gave him suggested she had not been entirely convinced.

They drove home in silence. He sensed the tension knowing there would be more words, maybe not straight away but later. As he pulled the car up outside the house, he glanced at her; she was staring ahead, her expression blank.

'You'd better fetch Peter - Eve and Nick are looking after him,' she snapped suddenly.

'Okay, let's get you inside and then I'll pick him up.'

He realised with a start he'd given no thought to the whereabouts of his son. She'll have noticed - another addition to the argument to follow, he thought.

'I can see myself in. Just bring Peter home.'

***

Vee watched the slow, rhythmic breathing assisted by the machine hooked up to her father. He appeared peaceful, she thought. Although the oxygen mask had been removed, he remained attached to the electronic apparatus - an "ECG" the nurse explained. The machine emitted a steady beep which she understood signalled a regular heartbeat.

'He'll wake up soon, and when he does, he might seem a little confused, so we need to keep an eye on him for a while,' the nurse advised.

Even the very strong tea bought from the hospital canteen could not stave off the effects of drowsiness. She put the cup down and allowed herself to drop into a semi-doze. But her restful slumber didn't last for more than a few minutes. She woke with a jolt, disorientated and fearful without knowing why. Then, she remembered the letter.

Reaching into her handbag, she pulled out the crumpled envelope that had dominated her thoughts since her father gave it to her on Sunday. She examined the untidy capital letters, the black ink smudged, her name written at the top. Above her name the statement "DELIVERED BY HAND" - no stamp and no postmark to identify the source. *How did he find my address? He must have got it from the university.*

'Bastard,' she whispered, a flush of anger erupting. She sensed a clear intention to display control, and to dominate.

His imagined words taunted her. 'I've tracked you down. I have been to your home, seen where you live. I will come again.'

Her imagination presented the image of the now hated Jonny walking up the driveway to her dad's house, and then stopping, surveying the door and windows with

268

interest, wondering whether she might be inside somewhere.

Pulling out the folded sheet of vellum, she read the single statement again.

"I want you back." No other words - neither salutation nor signature.

Carrie seemed bemused when she showed her the letter at school on Monday morning.

'This makes absolutely no sense, Vee. You were only with this man for what, three months or so? He made a nuisance of himself when you ditched him, but then he got himself put away in prison. He wrote to you before, didn't he? You said you sent the letters back unopened.'

'That's right – I thought he would have got the message - but it seems not. He's come back to make my life a misery - to scare me - perhaps worse. I feel so threatened! It *was* him at the Marina, I knew it!'

'But, as he's got your address - your dad's that is - surely he...'

'I know - why doesn't he simply wait for me? For all he knows, I might still live at home. The bastard's playing with me like a cat with a mouse - he would do that - wanting to terrify me - his way of getting revenge because I rejected him.'

'He's stalking you! You mustn't let him get away with that. Report him to the Police – they'll do something about it!'

'They wouldn't be interested – no doubt they'd accuse me of being neurotic.'

The sound of a groan jerked her out of the angry reverie. He was stirring. She reached across and took his hand. His eyes were open wide, and he stared at her.

'It's alright, Dad - you're in hospital. You had a bit of a turn, but you're okay. Everything's going to be fine.'

She was relieved to see a nurse entering the room.

'Dad's woken up - he's fretting.'

269

The hospital routine went into motion. The nurse checked his pulse and assured Vee all was well. He tried to talk, his voice croaky and incoherent. The nurse coaxed him to put back on the oxygen mask, which he did without protest.

The nurse turned to her. 'Take a break. I'll need to call the doctor, so he can carry out some routine checks. I'm sure everything will be fine. Go on!' she said, pushing her gently towards the door.

Vee felt relieved to be free of the hospital room, which she found too warm and claustrophobic. The thought of a cup of tea and a sandwich was appealing. She realised she had eaten nothing all day and now it was almost 5 o'clock in the afternoon. Before setting off towards the canteen, she cast her eyes around for a phone booth, conscious Helen would welcome an update now their father had woken up.

Thinking of Helen prompted thoughts about Frank. There had been an edge to his voice in the phone call earlier that morning, and she saw something in the way he had looked at her. Was it guilt? Fear? Something is not right, her instinct told her. But maybe there's a hidden side to him, she thought. On the face of it, he acted like a devoted father and husband. But something else lurked in the background, secret things - another life, perhaps? She shook her head as if to extinguish thoughts of a possible dark side to him. Then she frowned, realising that the notion Frank might hide a different character, one that appealed to the baser side of her own imagining, excited her.

Chapter 35

"THE VOYAGER"

(Friday 15th November 1963)
The passage through the Dover Straits and up into the North Sea proved to be particularly uncomfortable - the coaster made slow progress as it corkscrewed erratically through the north-easterly gale. Entering the calm of the North Sea Canal came as a huge relief for everyone on board. The small ship gradually came back to life. The crew emerged from the shelter of the interior with its fug and all-pervading smell of diesel and cigarette smoke to brave the freezing cold November air on the upper deck.

A small group huddled in the bow of the ship, smoking and chatting - no doubt planning a debauched run ashore in the fleshpots of Amsterdam, thought Captain Ericson sourly as he surveyed the deck below from the shelter of the bridge.

'What's that chap's name - the tall one standing on his own?' he asked, waving the end of his pipe to indicate a solitary figure on the fo'c'sle standing at a distance from the main huddle of crew members.

The helmsman raised himself from his seat to look out of the bridge window. 'No idea, I'm afraid. He keeps himself to himself. Joined in Southampton a few weeks ago. Been on a couple of trips now. Horse brought him on - reckons he's a good hand.'

'Horse! He wouldn't know a good hand if one came and smacked him on the arse!' the Captain replied, chuckling at his own joke.

He remembered when the Chief Officer hired Horse, the strange, stocky individual with a bald head and an intriguing name, as a deckhand. It quickly became common knowledge the new addition to the crew was no stranger to the inside of a prison and had served several sentences for theft and fraud offences. It came to light, soon after his arrival on board, he'd just been released from his latest stretch. This discovery nearly led to his instant dismissal.

'He's not the only one who's done time,' the Chief Officer had pointed out.

The Captain recalled his warning to his Second-in-Command: 'On your head, be it!' Since then, Horse had been on several of the brief voyages across the North Sea to Amsterdam, Rotterdam, and Keel. In the view of the Chief Officer, he proved to be a competent and reliable worker.

'So, is he?'

'Is he what, skipper?'

'A good hand?'

'There haven't been any complaints, at least not that I'm aware of. He's a funny bugger, though!'

'Why's that?'

'Very quiet - he only talks to Horse. You can barely get a word out of him, although he's polite enough. He's always got his head stuck in some book - you know, highbrow stuff that no one else would read.' He paused before adding, 'I have to be honest; he gives me the creeps! Doesn't strike me as the sort of bloke you'd want to hang about with.'

Captain Ericson studied the figure of the tall man, who, at that moment, turned and stared up at the bridge as if he sensed he was being discussed.

'Strange looking fellow, isn't he?' said the helmsman.

'Indeed, he is,' the Captain replied, gaining an immediate impression of darkness. Although many of the crew dressed in dark clothes, this man was clad entirely in black as if it were a statement. His face, black-bearded and bracketed by the upturned collar of a black refer jacket; his head topped with a black beanie hat, a few strands of black hair blowing crazily in the wind whipping across the deck - everything about him was black. Even from a distance, the man's eyes glinted dark and intense behind plastic rimmed glasses; his face expressionless as he stared back. *But was there a hint of a smile on his face?*

***

Jonny sensed he was being studied. As he looked up at the bridge, he saw the Captain's face looking directly at him from behind the murky window. The fact he should be of interest pleased him - this confirmed his conviction he differed from the others. He looked back - just a hint of defiance, but also amusement.

Being the centre of attention was his social metier, an underpinning need. His yearning to be listened to and acknowledged had been suppressed during his years inside where he deemed a much lower profile to be necessary. His instinct warned him that standing out from the crowd might break the unwritten rules of prison etiquette and, more to the point, it would have attracted attention from some of the more dangerous personalities with whom he shared his incarceration. As a prisoner with brains, he enjoyed a certain amount of notoriety. He was labelled an "intellectual" a pejorative term at first but, over time, his superior intelligence seemed to give him status: "The Professor," he became known as, a man who carried an aura of mystery.

He cast a glance at the small group of his fellow crew members gathered in the bow of the ship. I'm not like them, he reminded himself. These men hold no interest or significance for me. He observed them with disdain, noting how they seemed to bond easily with each other. One of them was relating an amusing story; he overheard occasional words, many of a bawdy, ribald nature. They all laughed. He didn't.

I have nothing in common with men such as these, he assured himself. In a different social milieu, where he felt safe, and where his audience might be considered intellectually capable of understanding, he would, given the chance, espouse with enthusiasm his view of politics and the world-order. But the views he articulated, apparently underpinned with a belief in egalitarianism and ridding the world of the "ruling classes," didn't tally with the low opinion he held of his fellow man. The only men he really admired were philosophers, who spoke to him beyond the grave in the books he read, and whose words he repeated. Being considered as an oddity, a loner, suited him. Not for him the typical sailors' bars and brothels in the company of his social inferiors.

***

'Dash us a fag, Jonny.'

The stocky, bald individual grinned up at him, displaying displaced and discoloured teeth, interspersed with gold ones, which appeared strangely incongruous.

He disguised his instinctive repugnance for Horse behind a contrived indulgent smile, as though humouring an adolescent of inferior intellectual capacity. But although he secretly loathed his companion, Jonny acknowledged Horse had protected him during their time together in prison where they had shared a cell. He knew he had depended on him in the uncertain and potentially dangerous environment. Horse, he realised, was quick-witted and understood how prison worked. Without him, he would have found himself on the wrong side of the unofficial prison management system: a target for "special treatment." Horse taught him how to avoid unnecessary attention: what he should not do, and what he should do, to stay reasonably safe.

Jonny recognised his acquaintance possessed a unique form of intelligence, one based on cunning and knowledge of the criminal world. His skills had been learned, it seemed, during a lifetime carving an existence through petty crime. He learned how, during the post-war period of austerity and rationing, Horse enjoyed a comfortable living from black market racketeering of scarce goods. From there, he had branched into bootlegging alcohol and, just before his latest prison sentence, he had diversified further into the expanding trade of drugs, primarily cannabis and amphetamines.

Although Jonny sensed he was accepted as the superior in their strange relationship, he, in turn, acknowledged the fact he had become an apprentice to his wily companion. Horse, for whom respect, and acknowledgement of any kind was an unknown experience, was only too willing to teach him. Having been released before Jonny, he had used his wide range of contacts to secure his own employment as a deckhand on the "Voyager," and he arranged for Jonny to join as well on his release three months later.

'So, what happens when we get alongside?' Jonny asked, reaching into his pocket for his cigarettes and a Zippo lighter.

'I have to make a phone call first - find out where the meet will be. I'll let you know. Make sure I can find you though - don't go wandering off on your own.'

He noticed Horse was looking at the group of men gathered in the bow.

'Keep clear of them, Jonny,' he said, 'Don't want any of them tagging along with us.'

Not much chance of that, he thought to himself, it's not as if any of them are likely to want my company, nor me theirs.

"Harbour stations!" barked from the broadcast system, prompting purposeful movement from the men dotted around the upper deck, who moved to their positions to man the various hawsers and lines.

Horse nodded to Jonny 'See you later,' he said, flicking his cigarette butt over the side.

***

Jonny reclined on his bunk staring at the wooden base of the one above him less than two feet away from his nose. A copy of "The Condition of the Working Class in England" by Friedrich Engels lay open, face down on his bed; his right hand rested on it as if drawing comfort from its physical presence. In his other hand dangled a cigarette upon which he drew languidly, ignoring the lengthening tip of ash, which dropped intermittently onto the counterpane.

In such moments of solitude, rare in the confines of the mess-deck, he disappeared into his innermost thoughts without the interruption and distraction of those with whom he shared the cramped living space. He glanced at the photograph pinned to the small cork-faced board bolted to the bulkhead next to his head. The other seven bunk spaces on the mess deck were personalised with pictorial reminders of a life beyond the sea. Most displayed pictures of families, wives, and girlfriends, real and imaginary. Jonny's featured a solitary picture. The black-and-white photograph of the girl was crumpled now. It had been with him during his two years in prison, hidden away in a pocket for much of the time until much later when he felt bold enough to display it next to his bed in his cell.

He raised his fingers from the spine of the book, put his middle three fingertips to his lips and then pressed them to the face that grinned out from the photograph. He smiled back. 'Soon, Vee - not long now,' he whispered.

Lighting a fresh cigarette from the stub of the one burnt almost down to his nicotine-stained fingers, his thoughts focusing on her, the memory of whom, he could not extinguish. By closing his eyes, he could concentrate on the series of reflections from their shared time. His mind synthesised scenes of happiness from the reality.

Although not a religious man - he held no belief in divinity - he remained convinced she should be with him as some form of divine right. When he last laid eyes on her three years ago, peering down at him from the window of her bedroom, he sensed fear. Remembering the scene, he rationalised now that her terror was not of him but of the faceless and nameless beings who conspired against him. These others, who he called "Them," presented a threat. They resented and envied him for his intellect and his convictions. He convinced himself Vee understood this. She was in the thrall of his enemies - their shared enemies. Because of "Them," she could not show her true feelings for him.

He wrote to her twice while in prison. Both had been sent back–more evidence, he concluded, of a conspiracy by "Them," aimed at preventing her from seeing him. Those behind this vendetta against him - "Them" - remained an enigma, faceless beings who, he decided, represented the hated "Establishment" and "Authority." He could not articulate or visualise, even in his inner-most thoughts, the identity of the conspirators - but he believed in their existence.

***

Finding her home address proved relatively easy: a phone call to the Students Matriculation Office in the university's administrative offices yielded that little gem of information, facilitated by the most basic of ruses: an urgent need to communicate news about an employment opportunity. A small victory, he congratulated himself, against the forces of "Them."

He smiled as he recalled how patient he had been, meticulous in his planning, avoiding the temptation to attempt immediate contact - such a clumsy approach

277

would surely have attracted the attention of his enemies, who would have found a way to upset his plans.

Having signed on as a deckhand on the "Voyager," berthed in Southampton Docks, he checked in to a Seaman's Mission. From the railway station, Fairfield was only two stops further east, less than twenty minutes away, the perfect base from where to make covert visits and make plans for his next move.

Feelings of triumph turned to disappointment and frustration. He had made several close passes by her house, noting a saloon car on the driveway. Each time he would stand outside, staying just long enough to make a careful study of the windows and the front door, hoping to catch a glimpse of her, to confirm she lived there.

He timed his visits to coincide with the possibility she might be one of the commuter crowd, leaving home to join the mass of humanity heading to the towns and cities. From a bus shelter opposite the house, he would look up and down the road as commuters returned in the early evening, looking tired and care-worn. On one occasion, the front door of the house opened, and a middle-aged man stepped out, making towards the car - her father, he concluded. But of Vee, there was no sign.

Two weeks of every month spent at sea provided plenty of time to think about his next move. Finally, he wrote a letter and posted it through the doorway of her house. No stamp or postmark - his enemies would have tracked him down had he been foolish enough to provide clues as to his whereabouts.

Horse accompanied him to Fairfield on the occasion he posted the envelope through the door. He left him at the pub down the road from her house, not wanting him to know what he was doing. It had been as if the presence of his uncouth, uncultured, but necessary companion might somehow sully the sanctity of his enterprise.

It had been a massive stroke of luck when he agreed, although with reluctance, to travel onwards to the Marina with Horse, who was keen to establish himself and his illicit trade in drugs there. Later, he was glad to have been persuaded.

'You'll see, Jonny! The place is full of young'uns looking for a thrill. There's plenty of room for another trader, and that's me, with you as my assistant.'

He had watched as Horse plied his trade in various bars recommended to him by other traders, who didn't seem to resent a new stall being laid out on their patch. There were enough eager customers to go around. Despite his negative feelings towards him, he could not help but admire the way Horse recognised a likely group of punters, and then inveigled himself into their midst with a welcoming grin on his face, gaining their trust in a few minutes. But, he reminded himself, Horse possessed what they wanted. These people would buy from the Devil if he was selling the weed and pills these pathetic people craved. He was not averse to cannabis himself - he enjoyed the sensation of release it gave him, and how it helped to clarify his thoughts. But Jonny convinced himself his own need for the drug was spiritual and pure, a means of enabling his mind to reach even higher levels of attainment. These people, prepared to accept Horse into their midst, were parasites looking for a recreational buzz - for them, the drug represented a fashion, a way of looking "hip".

Jonny had been leaning against the bar smoking, watching and feeling bored when he was distracted by a movement a few feet in front of him. He had just registered it was a girl trying to weave her way through the crowd of people, which included the small group thronged around Horse, when he realised with a start, she bore a startling resemblance to Vee. He leant forward to get a better view. The girl who looked like her ducked down to get

279

underneath the arm Horse raised to let her past. He noted how she smiled in acknowledgement.

For just a second or two, she glanced in his direction. For a moment he thought she had seen and recognised him. Then she was gone, sliding through the crowd towards the door.

'It was her!' he whispered, remembering the scene as he lay on his bunk. 'Yes, it was her,' he agreed with himself.

He had considered shouldering his way outside, to chase after her - but then a voice of calm and reasoning spoke to him: 'You've found her - she will come back here - you know she will. There will be plenty of time to plan your next move. Be patient! Don't give "Them" an opportunity to stop you.'

Thoughts of "Them," troubled him - they were always there in the background of his mind as if seeking entry, wanting to control him. Sometimes they seemed to gain power - and at such times, he sensed they were most dangerous and might break down his mental defences. This was happening now, and he needed help to combat "Them."

He heaved himself off his bunk and slid down to the deck. He pulled a key from under his mattress and opened his locker where hidden inside a hollowed-out book, lay the tin. As he slipped this into his pocket, he experienced the familiar thrill of anticipation.

Chapter 36

PROMOTION

(Sunday 1st December 1963)

The storm passed, at least the worst part - but an uneasy peace followed. To his great relief, Helen did not question the tale he concocted to explain his absence from the hotel. He congratulated himself on the realism of his alibi, which included a hint of wrongdoing on his part to add plausibility.

'Lee, the manager of the Walsall branch, phoned me,' he explained, 'He was in a state - problems with his wife - said he wanted my advice. I agreed to meet for a drink with him in his local and, well, we drank a lot and I didn't think it safe to drive back to the hotel - so I crashed at his place. He didn't have a phone otherwise I would have called you. Look, Helen, I feel terrible about this - the one night you needed to contact me and, well..., I'm so sorry.'

She appeared to be convinced by the emotion and sincerity he included in his apology - and that seemed to be the end of the matter, or so he thought, thinking perhaps her father's recovery had softened her stance. However, although she didn't press him for more detail as a way of testing his story, he couldn't help wondering if she might be harbouring some suspicion.

A phone call to Lee, as soon as escaped from the watchful eye of Helen, ensured his story would be secure. Best to be on the safe side, he advised himself. Helen might telephone to check my story.

As the days passed, he noticed a difference in Helen and the way she behaved towards him. He detected a look in her eyes when she regarded him, one not there before. Although he tried to convince himself he was imagining it, he wondered if she had not been entirely convinced by his story. The germ of doubt grew, and he became worried. The implications of his latest transgression being discovered were too awful to contemplate.

Perhaps this is the final "wake-up" call, he concluded. Regular reminders of just how much he had put at risk presented to him, stirring feelings of anger at himself, his selfishness and stupidity.

How could I do this to her? Helen's not only a good wife and mother, she's intelligent, articulate and, let's face it, a fine-looking woman - Mum would have called her a 'catch'. And Peter - any father would be proud of him! What was I thinking when I risked my family for that girl?

A few days later, sixty miles to the north, Fleur stared in incomprehension at the letter bearing a Southampton postmark received that morning. She read the words, noting no return address had been included for her to respond to. The message was clear and to the point: Frank was 'calling it a day.' He offered neither reason nor apology.

'Why?' she whispered before bursting into tears. When she calmed down sufficiently to think, she tried to identify why he should dump her. He didn't seem unhappy when they had been together a few days ago. She played every moment of the last few hours they had spent in her flat, analysing details, searching her memory for clues, but couldn't find any reasons that might justify his cold rejection.

She looked again at the short message as if it might contain hidden meaning she had missed. The briefness of the letter, and its practical "straight to the point" tone, combined with the fact she had been given no opportunity to respond, made it all the crueller. She was devastated.

***

'So, Frank, you're going to step up and take on more management responsibility. Reckon you're up to it?'

Bob had been discharged from hospital the previous day and was beginning his convalescence. He sat in his dressing gown, a pipe unlit in his hand, looking much better now, although he was far from full recovery. Frank noted for the first time how his father-in-law seemed old and tired.

'Of course, he is! Aren't you, Frank? And I can help. You can leave everything to us and don't worry. We'll keep you in the loop about what's going on, but you must relax - take things easy like the doctor told you.'

He noticed the brief but meaningful glance from Helen, interpreting its meaning correctly: 'Say nothing to contradict me!'

Not as if I've got much choice, he thought bitterly. Why does she feel the need to speak on my behalf? For Christ's sake, who wears the trousers around here? And what does she know about the business now we've expanded into franchise management? She hasn't had anything to do with Parks since Peter was born.

He kept his bitterness internal - but we will discuss this more at an appropriate time, he assured himself. Adopting what he hoped was a "can-do" expression, he grinned. 'Don't worry about a thing, Bob, we've got a fab team at Parks and I'm sure we can manage just fine.'

He hoped Helen picked up on the fact he hadn't acknowledged her and the role she intended to play in managing the business.

Bob nodded and smiled, raising himself from his chair and extending his hand across the coffee table towards him. Frank lifted himself awkwardly from the soft depths of the settee on which he had been sitting with Helen, to grasp his hand.

'You're a good man, Frank, I know I can trust you. Helen's offered to lead the marketing effort.'

She nodded, an eager expression on her face.

'Helen's got a flair for this sort of thing,' he continued, 'so, Parks will be led by a husband and wife team!'

'That's right, Dad, leave it with us - you don't need to worry about a thing.'

Again, he noted a meaningful expression, this one saying, 'It's all agreed.'

'You'll find your salary increased by a significant margin. You deserve a leg up - you've done wonders for Parks.'

He wondered whether she might say something like, 'There's no need for that, Frank was just doing his job.' But as soon as the thought emerged, he crushed it. What's got into me? he thought, why would she want to belittle me in that way?

The thought of taking on significantly more management responsibility worried him. However, the prospect of an enhanced pay packet put this into perspective: he began to see the positive aspects of moving up.

Helen brought the familial business planning meeting to an end, insisting her father lie down and rest. A few minutes later, they were returning home in the Morris. Helen insisted she would drive.

'Well, it looks like we're going to be busy!' He offered this as a way of prompting discussion - perhaps an argument, which he would have welcomed.

He glanced at her - she appeared to be considering his comment. He saw her nod as if to herself. 'We are,' she said. After a pause, she added, 'We will have to think about who will cover your role. We might need to bring someone in. I can't think of anyone in the company who has the right level of experience.'

'What do you mean?' he muttered, frowning. 'I can do the ops job and manage the business.' Seeing Helen was about to object, he added, 'particularly as you're going to be spending more time in the office.'

'No. I'm afraid your days of gallivanting around the country are over. You'll be needed at the depot on a full-time basis now.'

She turned her head and fixed him with a stare for a few moments before looking back at the road ahead. Although momentary, her face radiated meaning. For a few moments, he wondered whether Helen could see inside his soul.

Chapter 37

"SPEED"

(Saturday 7th December 1963)
Several weeks passed since Vee last visited the Marina. During this time, the image of Jonny watching her appeared in her mind like a malevolent presence, a reminder he might lurk somewhere in the background ready to pounce and exert his influence on her - this made her favourite social arena appear threatening and dangerous. If not for the letter, she might have convinced herself she made a mistake – a mere trick of the mind. But he was not a figment of her imagination - his brief message confirmed that fact.

His letter - just one sentence - terrified her, awakening fears almost forgotten - and these dominated for some time. But, as time passed without incident, she rationalised her thoughts and questioned what frightened her so much about him. After all, she reasoned, he showed no violence towards me when we were together. He grabbed at me after I dumped him - when he wouldn't accept I wanted him out of my life–but real violence? Why should I be afraid of him now? He's playing stupid games, that's all.

A new emotion emerged: anger. How dare he try to scare me! What gave him the right to invade my space and make me miserable? The angrier she became, the more her fear subsided.

When she recalled the circumstances precipitating the end of their relationship, her face would break into a smile. The remembered image of him with blood-stained tissues clamped to his nose, and his attempts to justify himself presented as pathetic and comical. But the memories of the weeks following this incident: the hounding, his persistent harassment, the feeling of being trapped causing her to run away to Fairfield - well - there was nothing funny about that. He behaved erratically, bizarrely even. What hidden depths lay buried in that warped mind?

'Bastard!' she muttered every time she thought about him. Her heart lifted, though, when she realised her fear had all but disappeared. The thought he might try to accost her presented as almost welcoming because now she wanted to hit back.

The possibility he might be mentally damaged, perhaps mad, occurred to her. That first letter he sent whilst he was in prison – that would have been a year after he began his sentence at Strangeways - suggested a deranged mind. She remembered the jumbled ramblings covering several pages, making little sense - a clear sign he may not be right in the head. It was if he were incapable of acknowledging the unshakeable fact their relationship was dead.

The second letter arrived almost a year later, forwarded from her university halls of residence to the teacher training college. This time, she decided not to open it, sending it back instead with her name crossed out and "not known at this address" replacing it. No further letters arrived after this, and she concluded he'd finally got the message.

But then the hand-delivered note appeared, and her old fears returned - at least for a while - until anger took over.

It was now three weeks since she received this latest communication, and nothing had happened: no more attempts at contact and no sightings of him. She wondered if he had faded away once more.

'I reckon he's given up,' said Carrie. 'Perhaps he just wanted to scare you - his way of getting some kind of revenge. I mean, what can he do? He didn't give you an address or a telephone number to contact him - why? Because he knew you wouldn't respond. He's well gone - you should stop worrying about him.'

Vee sensed Carrie's suggestion was based more on frustration at having their active social life being interrupted, most importantly that aspect of it focusing on the Marina.

'You can't go on living in fear like this. Surely, he would have made some kind of contact by now if he was determined to get to you?'

'Oh, I don't think I'm scared - not now. I was frightened until recently, probably jumping at shadows thinking he might be watching me, or he could appear out of nowhere and...'

'Don't you think he would have done that by now if that was his intention? And what if he did, you know, try to confront you? You said he's never been violent to you. I know you found him intimidating, but he's never actually harmed you. He sounds like a pathetic creep who's got a strange idea in his head you'll take him back. If he appears, and I don't suppose for one moment he will, just tell him to go to hell!'

Vee nodded. These thoughts mirrored her own. Carrie handed her the joint she was smoking. She took a deep drag and paused before exhaling. Then, with a smile on her face: 'Come on - it's Friday night - let's get a taxi and go to the Marina.'

'Now you're talking!' Carrie replied.

***

Vee woke up not knowing where she was or how she got there. She lay in an unfamiliar bed in a strange room - and, glancing down at the tousled head on the pillow next to hers, realised she had no idea of his identity. Disorientated and panicking, she lifted the candlewick counterpane and gazed at her body - naked from the waist up.

'Oh, my God!' she whispered, studying the man's head and trying desperately to remember who he might be and

- did they? She laid her head, which throbbed painfully making her dizzy, back down on the pillow. How the hell did I get here? In gradual stages, the events of the previous evening and night came back to her.

Their taxi arrived at the Marina too late for them to visit the bars they always included in their itinerary. The "GX" beckoned like an old friend. By-passing the queue on the stairs, using their status as full members, they ensconced themselves at their favourite table near to the dance floor.

'Talk of Jonny is banned,' Carrie declared.

'I'll drink to that,' replied Vee eagerly. For the first time in weeks, she felt relaxed able to enjoy herself

The club filled, and various friends and acquaintances arrived. A party atmosphere developed. A smartly dressed young man they had not seen before, who introduced himself as James, was celebrating his birthday and seemed determined to ensure everybody, whoever they might be, friend, acquaintance, or stranger, celebrated it with him.

'Champagne Charlie,' muttered Carrie; 'He's got more money than sense!'

James was lavish in his generosity, placing an enormous amount of cash behind the bar which friends and strangers alike took advantage of. Carrie and Vee accepted a drink out of politeness, knowing the affable man was being taken for a mug. Their inhibitions crumbled later when he arrived at their table bearing a magnum of champagne, which he insisted on sharing with them. By this point, they were both cheerfully drunk and took little persuading.

'Bring a bottle, or two, or three!' James shouted when the music finished, the lights turned back on and the club started to clear. A steady stream of people in varying degrees of drunkenness followed him out of the GX and along the main road through the Marina leading to his house, a short distance away. "Sidney House," the grand title of his abode, was an imposing Georgian town house with three floors, which appeared to be familiar to many of his party guests, who quickly made themselves at home.

The living room of the house, on the first floor, filled with people, noise and cigarette smoke. Selections from James' record collection added to the cacophony making it difficult to talk except through shouting.

Vee felt at home in the crowd, even though she lost Carrie in the melee of people leaving the club. She spectated with amusement as an exotic looking woman with wild hair, wearing a kaftan and several loops of colourful beads around her neck danced on her own in the corner of the room. She appeared in and out as the crowd in the room obscured the view; Vee was mesmerised by her apparent lack of self-consciousness.

'High as a kite!' said a voice at her shoulder. She swung around. James stood grinning at her, holding a bottle of white wine in one hand and red in the other.

'That's Gina – she's in her own little world,' he yelled to make himself heard above the noise. 'What a hoot!'

'She seems very happy!' shouted Vee.

'And believe it or not, she doesn't drink! Not a drop!' He laughed as if registering her unarticulated question: 'Speed - does weird things to you!' he explained.

'I think I'll stick to the alcohol and an occasional joint,' Vee replied with a frown. She looked at James, beckoning him to stoop down so she could shout in his ear; as if concerned she might be overheard. 'Don't suppose you've got any smokes - you know, of the whacky type?'

'I'm afraid not - never touch it myself - I like to stay in control. But, see that rather imposing looking chap over there?'

Vee followed the direction of James' gaze, which he confirmed with a nod of his head.

'Goes by the name of "Horse," apparently - God knows why. Strange character but harmless enough - and he's a

290

walking bazaar of alternative tobacco and other interesting products if you take my drift?' He nodded towards Gina, who, having ceased her rhythmic gyrations now swayed gently from side to side as she looked upwards at the ceiling with her eyes closed as if in a trance.

James moved away with his bottles, the perfect host, leaving her alone again. She edged across to the group surrounding Horse, observing the scene.

Horse presented as a strange looking character: short but stockily built. Dressed incongruously in an old army greatcoat, despite the stifling warmth of the living room, he seemed out of place among the fashionably attired younger people at the party. His face wore a permanent grin which revealed several gold teeth. His eyes sparkled with merriment. He was telling a joke, or an amusing story - the small group around him appeared enthralled. As one, they burst out laughing, and he smiled, nodding as if satisfied that he had done a good job at entertaining his personal guests.

He took a half step back, obviously aware of her approaching presence and, as though gatekeeper to the group he held in thrall around him, allowed her to enter. Turning to her, he grinned, his metal teeth glinting in the light from the chandelier under which they stood.

For a moment, she experienced a sudden sense of déjà vu.

'So, what did you do?' one of the group asked. Everyone leaned forward as though anxious not to miss a word. Horse laughed with a hint of irony in the tone. 'Well now - that would be telling, wouldn't it?' he replied.

At that moment, they all became distracted by a sudden roar of cheering from the corner of the room, the one in which Gina danced in her private, drug-fuelled world. As though oblivious to the sizeable audience gathered around her, she had peeled off her Kaftan and now gyrated wearing only her knickers. To accompanying cheers of the men and a few women around her, the girl slipped off the last vestige of her dignity. There was a sudden flash of light: a camera, then a surge of movement. James and a girl grabbed the gyrating woman by her elbow and draped a dressing gown over her shoulders. The crowd parted as the rescuers led her out of the room. Vee was pleased to note several sheepish looks from the witnesses to the scene.

The rest of the group who had been gathered around Horse dispersed, leaving her alone with him. With her inhibitions dulled through alcohol, she was at ease in the close company of this strange exotic individual who, she noted, stood only marginally taller than her, although he made up for his lack of stature by his broadness. It would be a mistake to get on the wrong side of him, she concluded.

'Far out!' he muttered in her ear. The words sounded contrived, used for effect, it seemed to her, coming from a man who was evidently not from the same generation as those who might use the expression. She guessed he must be in his late 'thirties, perhaps older - in marked contrast in age and looks to the rest of the guests.

'Poor girl' she offered as a reply, noting he was grinning at her as if she had said something amusing.

'Been on the happy pills,' he said, his tone suggesting he knew what type they might be.

'Apparently so,' she replied, wishing she could remember what James had called those pills, so she might impress with her knowledge. She found it hard not to stare at his teeth, which although ghastly, fascinating her at the same time.

'So, what can I do for you, young lady?'

Vee had never bought drugs - her supply of cannabis was always provided by Carrie. Suddenly she was at a loss and uncertain how to proceed.

'Weed, pills - I'm a walking sweetie shop for the happy stuff!' She detected a faint West Country drawl in his voice. He looked at her and then smiled in a disarming way. 'Never done this before, have you?'

'No, I'm a complete virgin to this game.' She was ready to excuse herself, sure he would attempt to take advantage of her lack of experience.

'Here,' he said, leaning in towards her, 'try one of these. You only need one, though, as it's your first time.' He gripped her left hand and pressed what felt like a small sachet into it. He closed her fingers around it.

She was completely out of her depth, uncertain of what she was supposed to do. 'How much do I pay? I've only got...'

He cut in before she could finish: 'You can have this on the house: my treat!' He nodded at her as if to say, 'We're agreed then,' and moved away, disappearing into the crowd.

She opened her palm and peeked furtively at the small twist of waxed paper resting on it. Closing her hand again to hide it, she edged through the throng of people in the living room, looking for space where she might examine the contents of the sachet. Despite the alcohol that had lowered her inhibitions, there remained a well-honed instinct for self-preservation. She was on the verge of letting the small packet drop to the floor as if it had become red hot. However, balanced against common-sense was an urge towards reckless abandonment - she might have described this as a spirit of adventure - others complete foolishness.

Inside the paper nestled two small orange coloured pills. Locked in a bathroom, she had, after much deliberation, and several sips of her drink tried one. She held it momentarily on the tip of her tongue before taking a large gulp of wine and then sat on the edge of the bath waiting to see what the effects would be. After a few minutes, she sighed with disappointment. Apart from being moderately drunk, no more than before swallowing the pill, there appeared to be no other reaction.

Someone banged on the door 'Are you going to be long?' shouted a female voice. 'Please hurry - I'm desperate!'

She stood, experiencing immediate dizziness. 'Only the booze,' she muttered. The other pill was still nesting in its paper wrapping in her palm. 'Oh well, what difference does it make?' She hastily swallowed it. The girl burst through the door as soon as Vee unlocked it.

'Time to party!' announced Vee to the empty landing.

***

Vague, kaleidoscopic memories of what happened the rest of that night would emerge in random order over the coming days. She would recall a sensation of euphoria and confidence - her inhibitions dulled. Smiling faces appeared in and out of vision, nodding, murmuring encouragement. Sometimes they laughed - and she laughed with them - but she couldn't remember what was so funny.

The images appearing in her mind had no logical order, no sequence: they became prominent and then disappeared. And it was not just a visual memory - she could recall the all-pervading smell of cigarette smoke, and then the intrusion of another aroma: cannabis. At some point in the evening, she had vague recollections of sitting on the carpet in a small circle of people. For some reason or other, they were all topless.

Several flashes of light lit up the scene during the night - a camera, perhaps? She remembered the earlier flash when Gina had been performing her ritualistic dance - but there were others.

Like an accusing finger, the memory of being violently sick prodded her, reminding her of the punishment for her excesses. A vision of the toilet bowl - the remembered warm dampness against her cheek where she had laid it on the wooden seat as she retched miserably. This presented as the final shameful recollection she could summon of the evening - it was all blank after that.

Most worrying for her in the days that followed was the fact that other brief and incoherent images would appear - she didn't know if she'd imagined these or if they reflected reality. But in the background of her mind prodded fingers of shame.

What did I do? Why am I getting anxious about what I simply can't remember?

'You were fine,' James assured her, 'you were having fun. You'd certainly stacked a bit of booze away, and you smoked a lot of weed. I put you to bed - with Georgia's help. She suggested I stay with you to make sure you were okay. Hope you don't mind but I did get in next to you - kept my clothes on, though, as you can see. Good party, wasn't it?' he said grinning.

***

Horse witnessed most of the various scenes that merged and appeared randomly in Vee's memories; in fact, quite a few more than she would ever remember.

It always surprised him how easily he could inveigle himself into the social milieu of people with whom he shared nothing whatsoever in common. Of course, being fêted as a purveyor of recreational drugs often provided an unequivocal entry pass to parties such as the one he attended that night.

The Marina proved to be an excellent source of revenue - a haven for what Jonny called the "Intelligentsia:" young professionals with money to spend and a penchant for the latest quick fixes. Unlike his strange friend, who despised people like these, he considered them as a client base to be nurtured and taken advantage of. He realised he liked the people with whom he mixed, particularly those who were now regular customers. Voyages to Amsterdam, Rotterdam, and Antwerp ensured he always held a steady supply of merchandise - and his time away restocking made his punters all the hungrier when he returned.

The party at "Sidney House" - he made a point of noting the address for future reference - proved to be a great success for him. He had been loitering outside the Three Crowns, smoking a cigarette, congratulating himself on a successful evening of trade around the pubs and bars when he heard, then spotted the approaching crowd. Seeing many were clutching bottles, and most were drunk, he guessed an "on-on" party was in the offing.

He gained entry with ease, mingling with the throng of drunken revellers careering down the road. Using his wit and strangely alluring charm, the group accepted him willingly. By the time they reached Sidney House, he was one of them, despite how different he looked.

Once inside, where the party geared up to full swing, he started trading. He completed his first deal in minutes. The woman, who later entertained with her drug-fuelled hypnotic moves, proved to be desperate for amphetamines.

He became aware of the smart looking young man dressed in blazer and slacks, clearly, the host, hovering nearby as the exchange took place. Horse grinned at him, conveying, 'everything's in order - don't you go worrying yourself.' A brief shadow of doubt clouded the young man's face, then he nodded as if acknowledging his unspoken message and sidled away, a bottle of wine in each hand.

It was at the earlier stages of the party when the small dark-haired girl appeared in his peripheral vision. By this point, comfortably at home and thoroughly enjoying himself, he had been entertaining his new friends with a rich array of real and fictional stories, risqué and amusing in equal measure. He congratulated himself on his ability to draw in potential customers and become accepted despite his incongruity amongst these people. He guessed immediately that the girl would be a novice punter, and he adopted his technique of offering a free sample to hook her as a regular customer. The distraction of the lone dancer in the corner of the room, by this point almost naked, provided the opportunity to break from the group he had been entertaining and to focus on his new prospect. He noted the look of disdain when he commented on the spectacle that attracted everyone's attention - but he saw something else in her eyes, a look now so familiar to him: hunger.

Later that night, he witnessed clear evidence the girl had taken one of the pills. He suspected she may have consumed both, judging by her outrageous behaviour. At one point, she lurched into him and, as though realising who he was, grinned up at him, her eyes wide and pupils dilated. She shouted something incomprehensible, barely audible above the cacophony of noise - then she kissed him on his lips before releasing her grip on his greatcoat and careering away back into the crowd. Perhaps an hour after this incident, the numbers of revellers in the living room started to diminish as some of the party goers decided to call it a night; this left the hard core, all drunk, stoned, or both. The only sober ones, he noted, were himself and the host who appeared to enjoy giving out alcohol more than he did imbibing it.

Surveying the scene in the living room, he could not help indulging in a sense of satisfaction. He sold more drugs in just a few hours than during several visits to the pubs in the Marina. The results of his efforts played out in front of him. He found the strange antics he witnessed fascinating and took pleasure in the knowledge he had contributed to the entertainment. With a mixture of fascination and amusement, tinged with a certain degree of disbelief, he studied what they did.

He was drawn to the dark-haired girl - the novice. She behaved as though she were in her own private world, aware of those around her, but oblivious to the effect she was creating - an exhibitionist seemingly devoid of self-consciousness. At one point, he studied her with interest as she joined a small group sat in a circle, cross-legged, all topless, male and female, passing a joint from one to the other. He noted the crazy intensity of the group as each person took it and inhaled the smoke, cheering and clapping as the individual exhaled. The dark-haired girl, he noted, removed her top and bra as well, although with a little help from her neighbours on either side of her: a man and a woman.

The house owner, James - Horse had learned the young man's name by this point - had relinquished his role as attentive host and was now downing glasses of wine. He noted that, despite his apparent eagerness to catch up with his guests and get drunk, he remained detached from the antics occurring in his living room while watching everything with clear fascination, like a voyeur.

Someone produced a camera with a flash gun and spent several minutes taking pictures, including the topless circle in the centre of the room, who posed with flagrant eagerness for him. He watched with interest, noting it was an expensive Leica, and became especially interested when he observed the owner putting it down on a window sill behind a curtain, secreting it, no doubt, for retrieval later.

When he left Sidney House, most of the remaining guests had found space for themselves to pass out, either individually, in pairs or in small huddles. Horse retrieved the Leica from its hiding place and slipped it into his pocket. 'That'll fetch a few quid,' he told himself with a satisfied smile on his face. The thought occurred to him as he walked swiftly away from the house that he might have the film in the camera developed; he had no idea why other than to satisfy a mischievous curiosity.

Chapter 38

"A CHANCE DISCOVERY"

(Saturday 7th December 1963)
Jonny declined Horse's invitation to accompany him to the Marina. Although tempted by the possibility of spotting Vee again with the chance of confronting her - his instinct told him, even if the opportunity arose, such a direct approach would achieve nothing. He could not think of any way of getting her alone - there would be too many people and the inevitable likelihood of interference. Instead, he remained in Fairfield.

Frustration and simmering anger at his inability to meet her prompted decisive action - but he had no idea what form this should take. He wandered disconsolately down the main street, his chin buried into the upturned collar of his reefer jacket, a woollen hat hiding his black hair. The voices in his head debated, unable to agree how to guide him. A lone voice suggested the only option would be to go back to the house where he left his message. But what if she doesn't live there anymore? Perhaps her family had moved away.

Nagging doubts taunted him. He wondered whether his letter ever reached her? A vision of a puzzled recipient slipping his letter into a dustbin made him angry and depressed.

But I saw her!

'Yes,' the voice of doubt in is head responded, 'but that doesn't mean she still lives in this town, does it? What if she was visiting a friend when you spotted her? She might live a long way from here now, in which case your chances of tracking her down are few and far between.'

He listened to a more strident voice and nodded. *Yes, that seems to be the most sensible - no, the only course of action.* The thought she might have read his message and discarded it slipped into his mind. He dismissed the notion straight away - his words were far too profound to have been ignored. He stopped, pretending to show interest in a shop window while he gathered his thoughts. The single voice appeared to win the debate - so now a stratagem needed to be devised, decisions made about what he would try to achieve, and how. The voices resumed their chatter, confusing him.

His frustration rose again. He studied the images in his mind, trying to make sense of them, listening to the confused voices in his head, unable to discern any clear message. It took a few moments before the real world emerged once more - and when it did, and his eyes focused again, he gasped in shock and surprise. She stared out at him from behind the shop window. It was a black-and-white image - one of several depicting what seemed to be an auspicious occasion involving many children - she was one of a small number of adults.

With his heart pounding wildly, wondering if this might be nothing more than a cruel but intense daydream, he tried to make sense of the scene. A glance at the sign above the shop window announced the fact the premises belonged to the "Fairfield Herald." Looking again at the collection of images, he understood these were press photographs taken at a local school. A few lines of neat italic script on a card explained that Sergeant Major Phillip Slocombe, Royal Marines (Retired), a former pupil, had visited to mark Remembrance Day. The veteran soldier grinned from his wheelchair, his chest full of medals. She stood behind him, clearly his chaperone for the occasion.

Jonny smiled with delight. 'This is real,' he whispered, 'a gift for my patience and effort.' "Crofton County Junior School," he read. She must be a teacher, he realised with a triumphant grin. The voices in his head chattered excitedly, planning his next move for him. He listened to them and nodded in acknowledgement when they counselled him this was fortuitous.

But he knew this was not merely a case of luck. This was pre-ordained: a clear sign he and the object of his desire would be together.

'What must I do now?' he whispered to the voices.

'Be patient,' they seemed to agree – 'something will guide you.'

Chapter 39

"THE ROW"

(Monday 9th December 1963)
Gregory hesitated - he had been about to knock on the office door and turn the polished brass knob in anticipation of a cheery 'Enter!' With his monthly sales results exceeding his target, and the fact he had passed his driving test that morning, his mood was buoyant. Frank would be so pleased on both counts of success, and Gregory was eager to tell him his news.

With his knuckle about to knock on the opaque glass window, raised voices from behind the door stopped him. It didn't take long for him to realise a major disagreement was playing out between Frank and Helen. He heard Frank's voice but couldn't make out what he said. Helen's voice, though, was loud and shrill - her words clear. After a few moments, he decided against knocking and, with his mood dampened, he walked away.

***

What started as a mild disagreement turned into a full-blown row. To Frank, it sounded like they were returning to a now worn out argument. Although he still visited franchises, these visits were much less frequent than they had been, and when he made them, he usually avoided overnight stays.

But that's not enough for Helen, apparently. It's like she wants to control my every movement!

'I said I would see him. It's been months since my last visit and he's got one or two things he needs to discuss.'

'But I thought we'd agreed, you don't need to make these visits any more. Let him come to you here at Head Office. You don't ...'

'No, I have to go because I'm supposed to spend time with his team, inspect the books and make sure everything is okay.'

'But there's no need for you to stay overnight, is there?' This sounded more like a statement than a question.

'Well, actually, there is.'

From this point, the disagreement escalated, drawing not only upon various aspects of his professional relationship with her at Parks, but also his failings as a husband and father. She was taking advantage of their argument as an opportunity to lambaste him about what she considered his many shortcomings on both counts. She raised a whole new range of fallibilities, which he considered unjustified. Using her fingers to count off each one, something she often did when rebuking him, which he found infuriating, she presented her case. At the point where Gregory retreated, she had been at "Number 3," this being the amount of time he spent in various local hostelries drinking.

'We've talked about this,' he interjected in what he hoped sounded a reasonable tone. Open retaliation, he knew, would backfire.

'I've got to spend time with the teams - the distribution boys, the drivers, the franchise managers - when they come to Fairfield, that is. That's what a good manager does. I find out what they're thinking, what's going on in their areas of work, whether they're happy or not - things like that...'

'Yes,' she cut in, 'but you don't need to be out just about every other night of the week - and you certainly don't have to drink as much as you do. You smell like a brewery when you come home - and you're driving a car - that's idiotic, Frank. If you got pulled over by the Police or, or...' she warmed to her theme, determined to ram her point firmly home 'you were to knock someone down when you're drunk...'

'For heaven's sake, Helen, stop talking rubbish! For a start, I'm not out every other night at all - more like one or two nights a week at most. And I don't think a couple of pints of beer will have much effect on me.'

In a recess of his mind, where his more rational thoughts were hidden, he acknowledged Helen's version of reality was much closer to the truth than his own. Recently, at her insistence, he submitted to a medical during which he admitted drinking what he considered a reasonable amount of beer, wine, and whiskey. He remembered the look the doctor fixed on him before saying: 'I'm guessing I can double that - patients are often conservative with the truth when it comes to alcohol. If that is the case, you are heading for trouble. Cut back on your drinking, young man, before you do yourself permanent damage!'

He would never admit this to Helen - but he had already decided to reduce his intake of alcohol. In the meantime, her nagging served simply to annoy him. It was as if she needed to exert control over every aspect of his life.

'You used to be home in time to play with Peter or read to him - but now you're falling through the front door with hardly time to say goodnight to him. How do you think he feels having a father who...?'

'Okay, I get the message. I'll cut back on the after-work pub visits with the lads and...'

'Yes, you will, Frank - your family must be more important than spending time with people you barely know.'

Off she goes again - must have the last say - can't even see where I'm prepared to give ground. The urge to retaliate with words expressing his frustration was strong, but he stopped himself. An angry period of silence followed. He sensed Helen's eyes boring into him, challenging a rejoinder.

'Nothing to say for yourself, Frank? Cat got your tongue?' she said, with a caustic edge to her voice.

He felt a surge of intense anger that almost resulted in a snarled response, which he stopped before the words escaped from his mouth. Instead, he raised his hands in a placating way - or was it defeat?

'What do you want me to say? What do you want me to do?'

He allowed a brief pause, giving her a chance to respond. When she didn't, he added in what he knew made him sound like a child: 'Whatever I do is bound to be wrong.'

She ignored his petulance.

'If you don't know the answer to that, Frank, then I suggest you do some hard thinking and work it out!'

The telephone on his desk rang. 'I'd better answer that,' he said, hoping this might end the argument. His heart sank when the familiar Brummie accent belonging to the franchise manager who he planned to visit - the one sparking the row, boomed down the line. He pressed the receiver to his ear to blank the man's voice, which Helen might hear.

'Come on Frank, stay over for the night. You can always crash in my spare room. I know a great little boozer at the end of the road where they always do lock-ins.'

'Sorry, Neil, no can do. I've a meeting at Head Office in the morning, so I'll need to get back. Maybe some other time.'

When he put the receiver down, he looked at Helen as if to say, 'You've got what you wanted, I'm not going to stay over - are you happy now?'

'So, you're still going, are you?' Her eyes blazed with anger.

'Yes, I have to. I'll be there and back in a day and then, when I get back, perhaps we could...'

But she didn't let him finish his sentence, in which he was going to suggest they go out for a meal together - instead, she turned on her heel and marched out of his office, slamming the door so hard it shook in the frame.

He stared at the door for several moments, frustration twisting to anger at what he considered Helen's unreasonableness and unwillingness to acknowledge when he had given way to her. It took ten minutes and the calming effects of two cigarettes to bring his mood back down to a level where he could rationalise his thoughts.

She was right about the overnight stays - these were mostly not necessary. Nor did he need the cover of business trips to disguise extra-marital dalliances - there weren't any. After the near-miss with Fleur, he had decided to clean up his act. What he would never admit to Helen - and found it hard to acknowledge even to himself - was that he missed the freedom he enjoyed before he was married.

Chapter 40

"POST HIGH REGRET"

(Monday 9th December)

Vee was surprised and annoyed at Carrie's reaction when, after several glasses of wine, she felt able to recount the story of her drug-fuelled night at James' party.

'Oh, my God, I wish I'd seen you!' said Carrie, laughing.

'Well, I'm glad you find it so amusing - but I certainly don't. It was a ghastly experience - and I'm worried I've done permanent damage to myself - and, and...., well, my reputation will be in tatters! What must people think of me? I mean, look at the way I behaved in front of them - I was practically naked!'

Carrie, who had adopted a concerned expression as she listened to her worries, seemed unable to stop herself from laughing again at this point. Then, faced with Vee's unwavering glare, she became serious again.

'Okay, so what did these pills look like?'

Vee explained what she could remember.

'That's Speed,' said Carrie in a tone suggesting she possessed an intimate awareness of the drug. 'Sounds like you took a heavy dose. It can cause some pretty strange effects and, from what you're saying, you experienced a few of them.'

'Have you ever tried it?'

'Oh God, yes, loads of times,' said Carrie laughing. 'In fact, many varieties of amphetamines and barbiturates. I suppose that makes me an aficionado on mind-bending drugs.'

'But why would you want to take stuff like that if it does such awful things to you like it did to me?'

'Doesn't always happen like that. The mistake you made was to take two pills at once. If you'd waited a while after taking the first pill, you wouldn't have needed the second. Speed doesn't kick in straight away - unless you mainline.'

Seeing Vee's quizzical look, she added, 'Inject it directly into your blood stream.'

Vee shuddered at the thought. 'So, without realising, I took an overdose. How could I be so stupid? I might've died!'

'Well, you didn't. But you need to be careful,' Carrie said, adopting a serious tone. 'Cannabis is one thing - I mean, you're safe with "Weed" - but these pills going around now - you have no idea what's in them, nor what they might do to you. I'm not saying don't try one every now and again - but make sure you know what you're taking. And never buy from strangers - you should only use a supplier you trust. Who was this Horse guy? Strange name for a man - he sounds very dodgy!'

Vee shook her head, unable to comprehend the depths of foolishness into which she had allowed herself to plunge.

'Come on, cheer up - there's no harm done and, if you think about it, this has been a valuable lesson for you, one which might save your life in the future. Put this down to experience. I shouldn't think for one moment you've caused any lasting damage to yourself - just your pride! Those people at the Marina - they won't give a damn; I mean, sounds like most of them were off their faces, anyway. And, I think some good might come of this because you seem to have forgotten all about this Jonny fellow.'

'You know what, you're absolutely right, I had put him out of my mind.'

Vee smiled, the realisation cheering her. 'I haven't thought about him at all since that night. It's as if I had never seen him, nor received his awful letter.'

Chapter 41

"THE PACKAGE"

(Saturday 28th December)

The caretaker watched as the dark clad figure walked past him towards the lift. As usual, there was no acknowledgement or even eye contact. The man's chin, as always, remained hidden, buried in the upturned collar of his reefer jacket. Most of the other tenants at the Seaman's Mission would attempt some form of greeting but not this man. Never in the six months since he rented his room did he offer so much as a grunt.

He appeared to be a complete loner, although Tony, who shared the caretaker's duties on the other shift, mentioned he had seen the "Dark One," as they called him, in the company of Horse, another of their residents. He cared little that the character did not stop to talk to him: he didn't seem like the type to share banter with. But he remained curious because something about the man stood out as unique compared with the hundreds of itinerant seamen he encountered since starting work at the Mission after his own career at sea. It was not only the man's foreboding appearance - he looked distinctive in an almost theatrical way - something else attracted attention. He gave off an aura - a black one.

'He looks bloody evil!' Tony said once. True: something about this man suggested his soul might be as dark as the visual image he projected.

***

Had Jonny known what the caretakers thought of him he would not have cared, not one iota. How others saw and judged him didn't bother him - their views were of no consequence. Confident in his innate superiority borne of a unique intellect and worldly knowledge, he lived on an elevated plane to the inferior beings living on the periphery of his world.

He possessed none of the trappings of success that might have been expected of one educated privately, with a university degree, and some claims to postgraduate study. In fact, an observer might note he appeared to live on the cusp of poverty. His life presented as an endless routine where he spent brief periods at sea on a grimy coaster, earning a basic deckhand's wage, and approximately equal time ashore where he roamed as if with no purpose.

But he didn't think his life was mundane - nor did he feel lonely - far from it! He was never alone. His head carried voices that talked to him - encouraged, advised, sometimes cajoled - but always there. Often, they disagreed and would argue with each other - when this happened, he felt confused and frustrated. But today, they spoke in unison and harmony, guiding him to what he knew would be a new dawn. His patience had paid off at last, and the "Guides" were pleased.

***

Earlier that day, Horse was sitting at his usual table in the *Shipwright's Arms*, his favourite dockside pub, sipping the first of what he anticipated would be several pints of ale.

'Right, then,' he muttered, placing his glass down, reaching in to his greatcoat pocket and pulling out a thickly packed brown envelope, 'let's see what we've got here.'

He had extracted the film from the Leica, stolen from the house at the Marina, before disposing of the camera for a tidy sum in this same pub. For several days, it lay secured and forgotten in its metal container in the pocket of his coat only to be re-discovered when delving into his

312

pockets for change. He thought about the practicalities of having it developed. If he took it to a chemist, surely there would be a danger the images might attract suspicion - after all, the happenings of that night were not exactly legal - and he guessed he might feature in a few of the photographs himself. But his curiosity stopped him from discarding the film. Then he remembered an acquaintance: a chemist's assistant and a regular customer, with a penchant for amphetamines. Fair game to ask a favour from.

He was glad he had not thrown the film away - the results fascinated him. With a grin on his face, he sifted through the images, amused at the antics captured. Then Jonny walked in and sat opposite him, his face unsmiling as usual. 'So, what's so funny?' his strange friend asked.

'Just told me' self a joke,' he replied, his instinct telling him his mate would not be as tickled by the pictures as he was. In fact, he reminded himself, Jonny didn't possess a sense of humour.

'Let me see them,' he said in a voice conveying a hint of interest. Horse shrugged and handed the stack across the table.

He studied Jonny's face as he looked at the photos and was surprised to note the normal, almost expressionless visage, break into an uncharacteristic delighted smile. He leafed through, pausing to study one or two which appeared to interest him more before quickly flipping through the pile until he once again became completely absorbed and entranced in an image.

After several minutes, during which Horse collected another pint from the bar, not bothering to buy Jonny a drink, and returned to his seat, Jonny had placed the photographs back in the envelope. 'I need these,' he said, thrusting the package in his jacket pocket. He got up without another word and left. Horse stared after him, his mouth agape in bewilderment.

'You're most welcome, mate!' he muttered.

***

As he walked past the caretaker, the voices in Jonny's head were chattering gleefully as if they had just been given some stupendously exciting news. As the cage door of the lift clattered shut, Jonny smiled indulgently. He rarely smiled, but his excitement matched that of the internal voices. He reached into the pocket of his reefer jacket and pinched the package laying there between his fingers, feeling the contents within as if to assure himself that it existed and was not the figment of his imagination.

His hands were shaking with excitement and he fumbled with his door key as he tried to insert it in the lock. After a furtive glance each way along the corridor as if anxious someone might guess what was in his pocket and try to steal his prize from him, he entered his room, closing the door behind him and locking it, attaching the security chain just to be sure. He sat on the wooden stool next to his unmade bed and took out the envelope. The voices in his head chattered excitedly, and he smiled. Let them celebrate, he thought. We've been given a wonderful gift, one that will open doors!

He extracted the wad of photographs and, spreading them out in a wide fan across his bed, surveyed them with a smile of intense satisfaction on his face. Then, to the accompaniment of encouraging voices, he selected several of the snaps which he placed in a neat pile, each photograph sharing a common feature.

Chapter 42

"DESECRATION"

(Monday 6th January 1964)
The first day of term arrived after what seemed an interminable period of absence. Vee decided to cycle to school, a decision based on a New Year's Resolution promising a healthier lifestyle. Wrapped up against the freezing cold morning, she breathed in the crisp air deeply as if convinced every breath she took would help cleanse her body of the poisons she had imbibed and inhaled over the previous few weeks. In the future, drugs would be off the menu, she decided - apart from an occasional joint - that would still be okay.

As she walked into the warmth of the school building, everything felt right - the familiar aromas and sights enveloped her like a comforting blanket, welcoming her to a haven where she belonged, and felt in full control. The Marina and the party were a distant dream, an aberration, a brief period of madness now to be forgotten.

She entered the staff room, where she intended to make a cup of tea, which would be a perfect start to the day. The room was empty except for Mr Roberts, the school caretaker, busy stuffing the pigeonholes with letters and circulars. They exchanged customary 'Happy New Year's,' and she offered to make him a hot drink. He declined politely.

'Boiler's playing up again; I'll need to go and find out what's going on before the damned thing packs in altogether. We can't have the children sitting around all day in their hats and coats!'

'Anything for me?' she asked, noticing at the same time the water urn had not been turned on. She grimaced, knowing it would be at least twenty minutes before the water was hot enough to make a pot of tea. Momentarily distracted, she turned to see Mr Roberts holding a brown envelope.

'Only this one. I picked it up when I came in. No stamp or address - just your name.' He held the envelope out for her to take.

'Are you okay, Miss Park? Looks like you've seen a ghost!'

She recognised the scrawl in which her name had been written. Her eyes met those of the caretaker. 'I don't want it, Mr Roberts, please take it away!'

'Okay, look, I'll leave it on the table for you,' he said uncertainly; then, with a shrug, he nodded at her as if to say, 'I've done my job,' turned and left the room.

She forced herself to examine the envelope, which, she noted, appeared to be thicker than might be expected for a normal letter - more like a package. Her sense of foreboding grew.

Although the envelope repelled her, she forced her hand to pluck it from the table. Her finger, as if controlled by a separate power, slipped inside a gap in the flap not completely stuck down. She registered a stack of photographs and, after a brief hesitation, pulled them out.

Before examining them, instinct told her they would be pictures of her. The knowledge her privacy should be invaded in this way by him filled her with anger. But when she looked at the first of the images anger turned to blind panic. Her hand shook so much, she found it difficult to focus on the likeness of herself grinning back at her.

Her heart jolted as she absorbed in an instant the damning details. In the picture, the features of the face were blurred, seen through a haze of smoke which plumed from her pursed lips. The unmistakable shape of a spliff dangled from her fingers. 'It's me,' she muttered, noting her image was naked from the waist up.

'Oh Christ!' she murmured as fear gripped her.

The sound of the door being opened startled her. She stifled a sob and stuffed the photographs back into the envelope, ramming it into her handbag, hoping the person entering had not noticed.

'Ah, Miss Park!' boomed the voice of the Head Mistress. 'Welcome back! Oh, and a Happy New Year. Please let everyone know there'll be a brief staff meeting at a quarter to nine.'

Vee nodded, not trusting herself to speak, knowing she was being studied and her face must show signs of the turmoil overwhelming her.

'Miss Park, are you alright? You seem a little, hum, distressed.'

'Oh, I'm fine, really, Mrs Bishop.' She struggled to find something to say - anything to divert attention away from her and prevent the inevitable probing - her emotions teetered on fragility and she could not cope with that. With a sinking heart, she felt the prick of tears.

At this moment, Mr Puckering, the oldest teacher in the school, and by far the most eccentric, entered the staff room with his customary boisterousness.

'Good morning one and all! Here we go again! Another bumper, fun packed term of boundless frolics with our little darlings!'

She picked up her handbag with its incriminating evidence and left the staffroom. Walking towards her classroom, she glanced at her watch: half past eight: fifteen minutes to pull herself together before the staff meeting. Taking deep breaths to calm her nerves, her state of near panic subsided. 'I need time to think,' she told herself.

The classroom presented an immediate impression of orderliness. A waft of polish hung in the air, together with a whiff of fresh paint from the decorating completed during the Christmas holidays. This represented a sanctuary: her personal space. The familiar smells made

317

her smile, although her heart pounded. She knew within a few hours the room would exude its usual odours of wax crayons and children. Placing her handbag on her desk, which looked unusually tidy, she surveyed the room taking in the neat clusters of desks with chairs upturned on top of them, the polished parquet floor, the walls bare - but they would soon to be filled with the earnestly completed artwork of the eight-year-olds, who would make the room come alive. This represented normality: her space.

She sat at her desk deep in thought. Her handbag lay open - the brown envelope with its hateful contents lying on top of the detritus within. *How did he get hold of the pictures? He wasn't at the party. But could someone have been stalking me on his behalf?* The image of the strange, exotically ugly Horse appeared in her mind. *What does he want from me? What's he trying to achieve from this? He didn't leave a note - no clue. None of this makes any sense!*

Despite her repulsion, she plucked out the envelope and half pulled the small pile of photographs from within before pushing them back again with a shudder. It was as though the presence of the images defiled the sanctity and purity of the room. Dropping the package back into her handbag, a burning sense of shame combined with uncertainty and fear swept over her.

Later that morning in the classroom now filled with children, she couldn't quite push nagging anxiety to the back of her mind. The rhythmic chant of her class grappling with the time's table provided a welcome distraction. She chalked the tables on the blackboard, filling the space with numbers. Having reached the sevens, the progress slowed, and she had to coax the final few correct responses from her young charges.

'Come on girls and boys, what are seven sevens? Seven sevens are...' She mouthed forty-nine and was pleased that Anthony, apparently the slowest witted of the children, picked up on her cue. 'Forty-nine!' he yelled, leaping almost out of his seat in enthusiasm. Several minutes later, she had completed the "sevens." The final correct response, given in triumphant unison by most of the class, was captured on the board just as the bell for first play time rang.

'Off you go!' she shouted, ushering the children towards the door leading onto the playground. 'Don't run!' she yelled at a small group of boisterous boys, eager to escape the confines of the classroom for twenty minutes of football.

With the room now empty, troubling thoughts returned. Going to the staff room, which would normally have been a welcome, temporary break and a chance to catch up with her colleagues, did not appeal. Her face, she was sure, would betray the fact her nerves were jangling - it would be so difficult to hide her anxiety. Instead, she prepared for the next lesson.

Whereas some teachers relied upon their ability to plan "on the hoof," Vee had made for herself carefully constructed lesson plans, which she kept filed in a ring binder in her desk at the front of the class. Intending to refer to this folder, she opened the drawer where it was stored in readiness. There it was - but sitting on it was a note, written in the jagged but legible scrawl she recognised straight away.

'He's been here! He's been in my school - in my classroom!'

The urge to slam the drawer shut felt strong. But then a new emotion burned through the numbing sense of fear: anger. Snatching the folded paper, she flipped it open. Her hand was steady now, an unexpected aura of calm enveloped her in a welcoming embrace.

'Fuck him,' she muttered as she started to read.

My Dearest Vee,

I am saddened to see how low you have sunk since you betrayed me. You have reached the depths of depravity. How much lower can you get? And you - a teacher! What would those innocent children think if they knew you to be a drug addict and a sex maniac? And what would the school authorities think? What would they do if they found out you are not fit to oversee minors? Destroy the pictures if you wish. I would if I were you: they are disgusting! But I have copies, Vee. I need to save you from yourself, you know that. I am the only person who can.

The note finished with an illegible signature, presumably Jonny's. Below it a Post Script which finally gave her an idea in which direction her nightmare would go. There was a telephone number - she noted it was local. The brief message commanded her to ring at 8 o'clock that night.

Panic returned, but her anger did not recede. She saw a sudden vision of Mrs Bishop opening an envelope in her office, emptying copies of the photographs. The implications seemed too unbearable to contemplate. She experienced fury and hatred so intense, it made her want to hit out. Take deep breaths and calm down, she advised herself. Give yourself time to think this through. There must be some way of getting rid of him.

She placed the note in her handbag with the envelope and forced herself to push the issue to the back of her mind. Opening the folder with the lesson plans, she flipped through to the page she needed. Walking with it to the blackboard, she reached for the board duster intending to erase the time's table that filled it. She stopped, deciding to save the workings for a brief consolidation period later in the morning. The blackboard was mounted on horizontal runners, which split into two halves so that one side or other could be slid across to reveal a fresh board beneath. She did exactly that, planning to fill it with words prompted from her lesson plan. But when the underneath was revealed it was not empty.

If Vee hadn't experienced such an intense explosion of shock and revulsion, she might have admired the handicraft displayed on the board. The cartoon characters were expertly drawn. The image of her; and it was most definitely her, was sitting on a desk - hers judging by the fact there was a blackboard just behind it. The picture included the childrens' desks facing the teacher's, and these were occupied by children wearing expressions of shock and incredulity. The reason for this was clear: her caricature was topless, just like her image in the photograph - and dangling from the fingers of one hand there was an over-sized joint from which smoke billowed.

Chapter 43

"THE FIX"

'Please don't make such a fuss, darling! I'm sure you'll make lots of new friends and...'

The fashionably dressed young women appeared to be struggling to find something to say. But her impatience was evident, and she did not try to disguise the fact - she wanted to be somewhere else. Standing near the platform edge, she stared intently up the line toward the tunnel entrance through which the locomotive would appear, glancing at her wristwatch before studying him with an expression that might be interpreted as distaste.

The memory was being seen from the perspective of a young boy of eight years old, but with the knowing and understanding of an adult. Although the scene on the railway platform occurred twenty years ago, he saw the details and experienced the same emotions as his younger self. There would be an expensive saloon car waiting outside the station with its engine running - the grown-up version of himself knew this. He imagined the man sitting in the driver's seat: suave, debonair - slicked back hair like a matinee idol - his mother's latest lover, the one who, she hoped, might open doors and land her a role in a motion picture.

The man had driven them both to the railway station. The little boy huddled alone in the cavernous space at the back of the expensive car; his mother in the front. She talked to the man, who said little. The adult Jonny remembered how, now and then, the man's eyes, reflected in the rear-view mirror, met his. Those eyes conveyed a clear message, he recalled with clarity and understanding - 'Say nothing,' the eyes said, 'or I will make you suffer.'

The boy version understood this man used his mother - and he had been used too.

On the platform, the adult Jonny studied his mother through his boy's eyes. She suddenly appeared happier and smiled at him.

'Here's it comes! At last! Now, pick up your things. Come along, it'll be here in a couple of minutes.'

He stared down at his battered canvass suitcase. One of the protective leather corner pieces was missing, he noted. Next to his case lay a tennis racket, its head encased in a wooden frame. As instructed, he picked them up and glanced at his mother's face.

'Well, goodbye darling. Write when you get a moment.'

She leant down and brushed the top of his head with the briefest of kisses. The waft of her perfume so intense and cloying - he could, with little effort, smell the aroma again after all these years. Then it was gone. She walked rapidly away, her patent leather heals clacking towards the platform exit. Not once did she look back. He recalled the image of the green door shutting behind her.

Left alone, he waited for the train to arrive.

The adult Jonny experienced a resurgence of boyish tears as he remembered feelings of desolation and abandonment. The urge to jump onto the track as, after halting for several minutes, the train approached the station platform, had been strong. But he recalled how logic advised him it was moving too slow to ensure finality. The sense of desperation was as intensive now as for the eight-year-old version of himself. The hated prep school waited with the bullying, ritual humiliations, and the irrefutable authority of tyrants who reigned under the title of teacher.

***

(Monday 6ᵗʰ January 1964)

The single-storey cottage remained unheated except for a meagre fire he had lit in the front room, now burned down to a few embers having been neglected for some time. Intent and focused on his task, he seemed oblivious to the cold. Perhaps the candle burning in the centre of the kitchen table at which he sat provided all the warmth he needed.

He hunched forward, staring with apparent fascination at the blackened spoon which he held over the flickering flame, in the bowl of which a solid, white crystalline substance had almost melted, the final lumps gradually absorbed into the yellow liquid goo that bubbled like spittle. After a few minutes, he decided it was ready and removed it from the heat, taking great care not to spill any of the precious contents. A glance at the table revealed a metal syringe, practically an antique with its finger rings and long plunger. A short hypodermic needle projected from the end - in contrast to the dull metallic body, shining and new, fresh from its plastic package.

Ready now, he picked up the casing and dipped the needle into the molten liquid. With practiced care, he levered upwards, watching the liquid being sucked up into the barrel. This task complete, he lay it down on a small towel spread on the table.

He rose from his chair, took off his reefer jacket allowing it to drop to the floor. The grimy shirt he wore had been white once but was now an uncertain shade of grey with several missing buttons. He pushed the left sleeve up towards his shoulder with ease.

As always when he was ready to shoot-up, a surge of excitement and anticipation made him impatient to begin. But he understood the need to wait a few minutes: the liquid in the syringe was too hot - it needed to cool several degrees before it could be used. He touched the barrel a few times as if that gesture might encourage the fluid to lose heat faster. His breaths came in urgent gasps, he was on the verge of hyperventilating in his eagerness to start. The voices in his head were chattering with excitement, their combined mutterings incomprehensible but they were pleased with the thought of what would happen. A final touch - it was ready at last!

He tied the ligature to his left bicep, which he tightened and then placed an end between his teeth, maintaining the pressure. His right hand now free, he reached down and took the syringe, holding it with needle upwards. He pushed in the plunger a little way to release any air bubbles. The veins in his upturned forearm were bulging; he studied the scene for a few moments, deciding upon the best place to insert the needle, noting the myriad of scabs and pin pricks that sign-posted previous encounters. He picked the spot: a vein in a patch of skin yet untouched. With a sharp intake of breath, he inserted the hypodermic and with studied care pushed down the plunger, releasing the liquid into his arm.

Chapter 44

"BLACKMAIL"

(Monday 6ᵗʰ January 1964 – 5pm)

She dialled the number at the exact time dictated in Jonny's note. It answered on the third ring with a click, but no acknowledgement. She couldn't push the sixpence into the slot at first - the coin box must be full, she concluded with dismay. But forcing her thumb on the rim of the coin, it shot in only to fall through into the refund tray. The line went dead. 'Shit!'

It took several deep breaths for her to calm down before dialling again. A click - the receiver picked up at the other end and she willed a new coin to drop safely into the box.

'Hello?' Her voice quavered despite her determination not to show fear. A hiss of static but no response. 'Hello?' she said again, 'is anybody...'

'It's been such a long time.' His voice, although barely above a whisper, was instantly recognisable

She couldn't speak - but he didn't seem to expect a response.

'We need to meet, *Vee* – we've so much to talk about, wouldn't you agree?' His voice now louder but a flat monotone. 'Would you like that?'

His use of her name with exaggerated emphasis filled her with dread. The images from the incriminating photographs flashed through her mind. For a moment, she imagined him planting those scenes there like a sorcerer.

She considered pleading with him but realised this would be a waste of time. He held all the cards and was in control. What could she do but go along with what he wanted?

'Yes,' she whispered. Part of her wanted to hit back and not give in to him. She tried to gain some ground.

'Look, I'm guessing you're in Fairfield, Jonny. Why don't we meet in town? There's a nice quiet pub off the main street, like one of those Irish pubs in Salford. Why don't we...?'

'No,' he cut in. Silence again - more static. The pips sounded. She fished in her pocket for another sixpence and pressed it with great care into the coin slot. When the line opened again, she heard him speak She cut in, breathlessly, 'Sorry, I needed to put in more money. I didn't hear what you said.'

A pause, then he spoke again, his voice a monotone but with a hint of irritability as he explained what he wanted.

'Do you know where it is?'

'Yes, I do. But why not...?'

'You'll be there. Tomorrow at 4 o'clock.' A pause before he added, 'Alone.'

'But I'll still be at school! Can't we meet a little later?'

'Tomorrow at four.' The phone line went dead.

She put the receiver back onto its cradle with some difficulty because her hand shook so much. Something in his voice suggested he posed more than the threat of blackmail. He had described a cottage off the coastal path, a half mile beyond the *Crows Nest*. She knew where it was although she thought it was derelict. Then she remembered Carrie commenting that it was occasionally rented out for the summer months: 'Artists, writers, people like that,' she had said.

I must go - what choice do I have?

***

(Tuesday 7ᵗʰ January 1964)

Frank looked up in surprise when Vee appeared in his office at 10 o'clock in the morning. He could not recall ever having seen her at the depot - something was wrong, his instinct told him when he noticed the anxious look on her face.

He expected her to ask where Helen was - but no, she wanted to speak to him.

'Frank, I need your advice. Can you spare me a few minutes?'

'You'd better sit down - you look, if you don't mind me saying, terrible!' he said, ushering her into a chair and pushing the office door shut.

'Do you mind if I...?' She took out her tin of roll-ups.

'Try one of these.' He slipped a packet of Rothmans across the desk. She took one and nodded.

'Thanks. Don't suppose you've got any whiskey in that drawer of yours? No, only joking - no really!'

He had stood and made to go over to the side cabinet where he hid his emergency supply of liquor. 'Things that bad, then?' he asked, sitting down again. He leant over the desk and lit the cigarette for her.

She nodded and smiled weakly. 'I'm in big trouble, Frank, and I'm not...' Tears welled in her eyes. She took a deep drag and blew a plume of smoke towards the ceiling.

'Do you want to tell me what's going on? I can see it's difficult, but I might be able to help. A problem shared and all that.'

She seemed to gather herself. 'I have told nobody about this - you're the only one I can talk to about what's happened. I can't trust anyone, not even Helen. There's too much at stake - and if someone were to react in the wrong way, I would be in deep shit.'

'Blood hell, that sounds serious. Are you sure you want to tell me about this?'

She was silent for several moments, her eyes looking ahead, staring fixedly at the wall.

'Look, Frank, I'm going to tell you something. Well...,' she hesitated, her voice tremulous. 'Well, a few things about me,' she paused as if trying to find the right words;

then she continued, 'and what I've done that I need to tell you in the strictest confidence. I want no one else to know - especially Helen. Can I trust you, Frank?'

'Of course, you can! Whatever you say will remain between us, I promise. Now, tell me what's wrong.'

It took almost an hour, and four cigarettes, to tell her story. She remained calm although he detected it would take little for her to become emotional. He listened without interrupting. When she hesitated, he encouraged her to continue. Her true emotions only revealed themselves when she came to an end, the point where she pulled out the incriminating photographs, which she handed over to him. She watched his face as he flicked through them.

He examined the pictures with mixed feelings, aware she was watching him intently, no doubt looking for a hint of what he might be thinking. The images of his sister-in-law topless and stoned interested him from several perspectives. He tried hard not to smile at the apparent absurdity of the scenes captured in the black and white stills. Wondering if she could read his face, he realised with a twinge of guilt, he found some of what he saw titillating. But most of all, the threat behind the photographs stirred anger in him, and a determination to protect her.

'I feel so ashamed, Frank. That's not me. Well, yes, it is me, but that's not how I would want to behave. I'd no idea what I was taking when I swallowed those pills. I was drunk, you know, not thinking and...'

'Stop, stop,' he whispered. 'I understand. Now let me think for a moment - let's sort this out.'

***

After the phone call with Jonny, a familiar sense of uncontrollable panic had returned. On returning to her flat, she drank two glasses of wine in quick succession, and

329

smoked a spliff - only then did the turmoil calm enough to allow coherent thought.

When she told Frank, he was the only one she could talk to about her problem, this had not been true. Carrie would have been her first and probably only confidante - but she was away having wangled two days holiday to spend with her naval officer boyfriend.

On waking that morning, having decided on her course of action, she rang the school and, for the first time in her short career as a teacher, called in sick: 'Think I may have gone down with a touch of flu - I'm so sorry, but I don't think I'm up to coming in today.'

Frank shared her dark story now - she found this heartening, glad she confided in him rather than Carrie, who would have advised her to go straight to the police. How wonderful it would be to do just that, she thought. But, that would expose her. The photographs would no doubt be exhibited in court - she shuddered at the thought of the public humiliation - and losing the job she loved. Frank understood her predicament and wanted to help her. The thought she no longer needed to battle Jonny on her own created a massive surge of relief.

Chapter 45

"THE LAST TRIP"

Tuesday 7th January (early afternoon)

He stared blankly at the empty tin of baked beans in front of him, its lid peeled back and a spoon handle sticking out. Then, as though suddenly remembering he had to do something, he pulled out his watch from his jacket pocket, its strap long broke, and forced his eyes to focus on the time.

Two hours before the meeting with her, he noted. Time to prepare.

With painful slowness, he rose from the kitchen table. His body ached, and a sudden wave of nausea hit causing him to groan. He lurched over to the sink and retched over the unwashed crockery and pans. After running the tap until the water cleared, he filled a glass and drank, which made his stomach heave again. He glanced back at the table, his eyes focusing on the two plastic bags containing the last few grams of brown crystals. A hubbub of encouraging voices chattered in his head - his "Guides" needed a fix as much as he did. But no, not yet: that would come later - preparations must be made first. Everything must be just so.

He stared down at the sink, filled with plates, saucepans, and cutlery, now spattered with the undigested contents of his stomach. His vision dimmed - he could not discern detail, only the blurred outlines of the detritus. His nostrils were assaulted by a combination of gas, old cooking, stale cigarette smoke and the tang of vomit - but his awareness remained dull.

If he had been capable of coherent thought, he might have registered his body no longer functioned in any way that might be considered as normal. He might also have associated the constant aches plaguing his body, and the intense waves of sickness threatening to overwhelm him, with the poison he injected into his blood stream.

He was a recent convert to heroin. Before, despite being a regular user of Cannabis, he always baulked at the thought of mainlining. Horse had suggested he try it.

'If you're careful, it's as safe as houses!' Horse advised, 'And much easier to get hold of than LSD.'

Jonny had experimented with LSD but not by injecting. Weed was no longer enough to satisfy his needs - his body needed a more intense high, and he had been persuaded to try something different. But the problem remained: the drug he craved was difficult to buy and prohibitively expensive.

Horse supplied him free of charge his first supply of brown heroin and the necessary equipment to administer it: a metal syringe and several hypodermic needles together with detailed written directions supported with diagrams showing how the drug should be prepared and used.

The first time he tried the new route to a high might easily have been his last. He followed the instructions with great care, preparing a small amount of the substance as recommended for a novice. The effects of his first experiment proved to be anything but pleasurable as he experienced a foretaste of the pain and nausea overwhelming him now. He had been violently sick, his suffering lasting for several hours before subsiding at last. But he persisted in his new adventure, heeding the advice that his body reacted in a negative way because it needed to adapt to how the narcotic worked. Subsequent uses proved more successful and, in no time at all, he was an addict.

After his initiation to the drug, Horse sold him regular batches. But he was away at sea when Jonny made his plans to move up to Fairfield. This caused intense frustration. He knew of the risks involved in using drugs from an unknown pusher, but his cravings grew too strong to ignore. The seaman's holdall he threw into the back of the grey, battered old Morris van borrowed from Horse, contained packets of brown chemical, sufficient, he calculated, to last for several days.

Despite the waves of pain that threatened to envelope him, he drove his body to respond. Every physical movement caused intense discomfort, varying from a dull ache in the joints of his arms to sudden stomach cramps that engulfed him, paralysing until each wave passed, providing a brief respite until the next spasm hit. It took considerable willpower to move – he walked with small, shuffling steps, his body stooped as though fearing standing erect might intensify his agony.

He shuffled into the hallway, unlocked the front door and pushed it open a few inches, an effort requiring a huge amount of concentration. This done, he trudged back to the kitchen and sat down at the table.

After a few moments of rest, he tried to gather and make sense of his confused thoughts. Disorientated, he panicked, realising he couldn't recall the details of his plan. The voices in his head soothed him and gave him direction. Still moving with painful sluggishness, but with a clear task to focus on, he stared at the length of rope coiled on a work surface and remembered why it was there. He fumbled in his pocket and found the small glass bottle, which he took out and placed in front of him. Again, confusion took hold, and a small twinge of panic erupted. But after a few moments of frantic thought, he understood what he needed to do. He smiled grimly, reached into his jacket pocket and pulled out the ball of cotton wadding, which he placed next to the bottle.

He checked the time again, staring at the hands on the face drifting in and out of focus, finally registering half past three. With great difficulty, he forced himself to think through the details of his plan. Something was missing, and he couldn't think what it might be. He studied the grey barrel lying next to the spoon and the candle. Then he remembered.

From an inner pocket of his reefer jacket, he pulled out a polythene bag, which he opened, extracting the two items from it: a plastic plunger and a hypodermic needle, and placed these next to the metal syringe. The sight of the larger antiquated version lying next to the smaller, more modern-looking one made him smile. He reached over and rolled them, so they lay as though conjoined.

'Soon, Vee - won't be long now and we'll be together again,' he whispered.

As always when starting the ritual of preparing to inject, he shivered with a thrill of anticipation. The excited chattering in his head irritated him - he shushed them like he might over-excited children spoiling his concentration. His eyes fixed on the bowl of the spoon, and he wondered whether he should charge both syringes from one batch. Would there be enough? He measured out two quantities of the heroin, which now lay in separate bags on the table, one much fuller than the other. He picked up the bag with the smaller quantity and opened it - his hand shook. The part of his brain still capable of coherent thought told him to prepare each dosage separately.

He lit the candle with a Zippo lighter and then held the spoon over the flame, watching with fascination as the melting process began. After a few minutes, the contents melted. He picked up the plastic barrel, his mind focused now as he concentrated on the task. Although he found it difficult to control the shaking of his hand, he drew up all the liquid. The heat radiated through the casing. He attached the hypodermic and, pointing the needle upwards, depressed the plunger a fraction, releasing the air. A few tiny droplets sprayed out. He lay it down and picked up the larger bag of crystals. The mutterings rose to a crescendo again. He smiled indulgently. 'My turn now,' he whispered.

Several minutes later, both doses were ready. He checked the time again: it was ten to four. His body shivered, not from the cold dankness of the cottage, but from desperation to feel the release from pain the drug would provide. He groaned as yet another cramping pain attacked together with the resurgence of nausea that had subsided while he was concentrating on his preparations. 'I've got to have it!' he told himself.

It had not been his intention to indulge before she arrived. Symbolically, it had been important they both inject at the same time; it was to have been a gesture of their renewed togetherness. The "Guides" split into two camps: the first advised patience: 'You must follow the prescribed steps.' Another reasoned he wouldn't be capable of carrying out what he planned to do without help. The second camp won.

Able to concentrate for a few seconds, he calculated there was just enough time to take his fix and position himself in readiness for Vee's arrival. 'But what if she's early?' a lone voice asked. 'She will be on time,' another voice insisted.

He shrugged off his reefer jacket, which fell to the floor. His heart raced as he waited for the barrel of the syringe to cool down. Again, he could sense the excited anticipation of the beings behind the vocalising in his head. Ready at last, he held the ligature between his teeth and pulled it taut. He had chosen the spot on his left forearm. He positioned the needle, and then inserted it, pushing down the plunger.

The calming feelings he usually experienced when the heroin surged into his blood stream were missing - in fact, the sensation that enveloped his body was very different. Instead of feeling at peace with his surroundings,

335

overwhelming panic took hold. His heart thumped at a quickening pace as though trying to burst from his chest, and his arms and legs shook uncontrollably. He moaned, his skin burning as if he had been plunged into hot liquid. His breathing became constricted and difficult, accentuating his terror. He slid off the kitchen table to the cold grimy floor linoleum, clawing at his neck. His body convulsed, and he screamed although no sound left his mouth. The voices in his head were roaring and shrieking in fear.

Chapter 46

"THE COTTAGE"

(Tuesday 7th January 1964 – late afternoon)
The light was already fading when Frank drove the Healey into the car park of the Crows Nest. He applied the handbrake and turned to her.

'You don't need to do this on your own, you know. I'll come with you - we'll confront him together. I promise he'll never bother you again once I've finished with the bastard!'

She considered this for a moment. The temptation was strong and compelling - to hand over the responsibility for action to someone else - to be released from the awful anticipation of having to act alone. Perhaps it would do the trick - after all, Jonny possessed the attributes of a coward - he would surely be intimidated by Frank. But a sense of reality told her this would only be a short-term solution. He would still have the photographs, and no amount of threat of, or actual violence would prevent him from using them against her. She shook her head. 'Let's stay with the plan. I'm not afraid of him - not anymore.'

This was not entirely true, she acknowledged to herself - Jonny did frighten her, very much so.

'He's obsessed with me. If I can find out what he's thinking, what he wants, I reckon I'll be able to reason with him - persuade him to give me all the photos.'

'Okay, your call. You know him, I don't. I'll be right outside - so if you think you're in danger, you've only got to scream out. Don't take any risks. If in doubt, yell.'

She nodded. 'Come on, we need to move - it's twenty to four already.' Her voice sounded breezy and confident, in marked contrast to the nerves sparking within. With the meeting near, her sense of foreboding strengthened, and she knew, very soon, this would turn to terror. As they got out of the car and headed across the car park towards the gate leading onto the coastal path, she grabbed hold of Frank's hand. He squeezed hers in return.

Within a few minutes, the grey shape of the building emerged from behind the trees. A light, faint and almost indiscernible, suggested life inside. A few yards further, they came to the entry track leading to the cottage door. They stopped.

'Right,' he whispered, 'five to four. Okay, let's wait for a moment - you don't want to arrive early, he might think you're keen to meet him.'

He grinned at her and she realised he might be enjoying the adventure.

'There's plenty of cover - I'll be able to get close to the front door. Don't forget, if you're in any doubt, scream out as loud as you can - I'll be in there like a flash. Ready? Right oh, I'll be behind you out of sight.'

He put his arm around her shoulders and squeezed. 'Go on,' he whispered, 'I won't allow anything to happen to you.' With that, he slipped into the tree shadows and vanished, leaving her alone.

She stood still for a few moments, conscious her nerve would fail her soon if she did not act. The temptation to turn around and run back to the safety of the car park presented itself. But something sparked inside her, igniting her resolve to see this through.

'This ends now!' she whispered.

With tentative steps, she walked a few paces along the entry track and then stopped and observed the cottage. Jonny might be watching her from one of the windows either side of the door of the single storey building. The thought made her shiver. The walls were enveloped in the shadows cast by the trees; they presented as dark, damp-looking and threatening. She spotted a grey van parked around the corner. Further confirmation someone was inside - her heart jumped at the thought. Taking several deep breaths to steady her nerves, she made her approach. Evening twilight was turning to night; the shadows merged with the approaching darkness. She noted for the first time there was no hint of a breeze. Glancing up at the tree tops, the leafless branches standing out in contrast to the steel grey sky, she could see no movement. Stopping again, she listened intently. Nothing. The silence felt unnatural and precipitated her nerves. For a few moments, she forgot Frank was nearby.

Only when within touching distance did she realise the door was ajar. She paused, contemplating knocking, and then pushed the door with the point of her knuckle as if the surface might be contaminated. She held her breath and stepped inside.

'Hello?' she whispered to the silence. Looking in front of her down the narrow hallway, she detected a faint glimmer of light emanating from an open door. As her eyes adjusted to the gloom, she realised the room ahead was a kitchen - a large steel stove took shape, covered in saucepans.

'Hello? Jonny?' A little louder now. She shivered - it was cold - perhaps colder even than outside - but just as silent. Then she noticed the smell: an intense, pungent aroma that comprised of cigarette smoke, stale cooking, damp, and something else - an overpowering stench of sickness.

As if in a trance, she felt herself being drawn towards the kitchen door, knowing, whatever might happen, her torment would end here. As she stood in the doorway, immobile and paralysed, she registered in a few brief moments the details within. A stub of a candle drew her gaze, standing in a cracked saucer on an ancient grime-topped table, its flame flickering unsteadily, the source of the light she had detected. A spoon, grey and blackened lay alongside the candle and next to that a plastic hypodermic syringe on a grubby piece of cloth.

Had she not spotted the body on the floor behind the table, she might have registered the small brown medicine bottle and the wad of cotton padding lying together. It was Jonny, it had to be, but she stepped a little nearer, needing to know for sure.

He lay on his back, his eyes gaping open, staring upwards at the ceiling. His mouth yawned wide as though locked in a soundless scream, his tongue protruding slightly. A trickle of blood dribbled down his cheek and through his beard, dripping onto the filthy floor, forming a sticky-looking pool. She took in the metal, antique-looking hypodermic dangling from his bare arm where the wrist met his elbow - the needle stuck into his skin, which looked sallow and withered.

She tried to call out for Frank, but nothing emerged from her mouth other than a squeak. It was as though she were in a dream, some form of detached reality. Her terror remained - but different now. It was not fear of him that overwhelmed her but more an inability to comprehend the scene in front of her. As she stared at Jonny's body, knowing for sure he was dead, the image of the small plastic syringe lying on the table behind her appeared in her mind and she realised at that point what Jonny had intended for her.

A movement behind her snapped her from her reverie and she swung around. Frank grabbed hold of her and held her close. 'You're okay, I've got you,' he whispered.

After a few moments, he became business-like. 'Better let me have a look.' He took a step into the room. 'I'm guessing that's Jonny,' he muttered.

***

When Frank stepped into the kitchen, he understood immediately the meaning of what he saw. As a young soldier, a frequent visitor to the seedier side of Hamburg, he had witnessed the world of drugs and recognised the accoutrements of the drug user. He guessed what had happened.

He pulled her gently to one side, knelt next to the body and examined the face of the man who had caused such anguish. 'Seems very much dead to me,' he said dispassionately. 'Best be sure, though.'

He placed his ear next to Jonny's mouth and listened. 'He's not breathing,' he said after a few moments. Then he picked up the arm in which the hypodermic dangled. 'Look at these,' he said, pointing to the many puncture marks. 'He's injected himself dozens of times!'

Holding his breath, he pinched the bony wrist and placed a finger against Jonny's neck. He glanced back at her. She was staring down at him, her face registering no emotion.

'He is dead, isn't he?' she whispered.

He nodded. 'No sign of a pulse. I reckon he overdosed on whatever shit was in that syringe.'

Looking back at Jonny's face, he shook his head, surprised to feel a wave of pity.

'How could anyone get this low?' he whispered.

With a sad shake of his head, he stepped back to where she stood by the kitchen table.

'You okay?' He placed a hand on each of her shoulders.

She nodded. He held her close and hugged her. 'He won't be bothering you anymore. It's all over now.'

She pulled back. 'Is it? How can it be over?' She sounded angry. 'If we call the police, they'll want to know my connection with him, and it'll all come out. He's won - he'll destroy me even though he's dead!'

Uncertain what to say, he turned around and surveyed the body. Then, he spotted the package jutting out of a pocket of the jacket. He knelt and pulled it out. 'Bingo!' he muttered, noting the wedge of photographs inside. He pinched a few of them out and flicked through them. The images were duplicates of the ones Vee showed him that morning, together with many more. Also, in the package were several strips of photographic transparencies. He placed the contents back and handed it to Vee who had been watching him. 'I think you'd better take care of these,' he said.

She gaped at the envelope in her hand as if not comprehending what they represented. 'Frank, what are we going to do? Shouldn't we call the Police?'

'You haven't touched anything, have you?'

She shook her head.

'Are you sure?'

'I didn't go any further than you. Why? What are you thinking?'

'You're going to have to trust me. You want this all to end, don't you?' He gripped her shoulders and fixed her with an unstaring gaze.

'Do you trust me? Do you want me to finish this once and for all?'

She nodded. 'Make it go away, Frank.'

'Okay. Go back out the front, wait there for me - and don't come back in whatever you do.'

She seemed hesitant but after a moment's contemplation she turned and walked out, leaving him alone. He waited until he guessed she was clear of the building - then, with great care, he carried out his plan.

***

He found her standing smoking at the end of the track leading from the cottage to the coastal path. She stared back at him with an expectant expression as he approached.

'Is it done?'

'It's done,' he echoed in response. 'Right, we'd better shift. If we meet anyone, act as normal as you can.'

They walked back towards the pub. After a few yards, she slipped her arm through his and pressed in tightly next to him. Neither talked.

As they approached the gate leading to the car park, a sudden whoomph followed by a much louder bang caused them both to crouch down involuntarily. They turned around to see an orange pulsing light emanating from the trees from the direction of where the cottage stood.

He stared into her eyes, which were wide, questioning. 'Everything's okay now,' he said, shaking his head, 'Let's try to forget this ever happened.'

They drove in silence. He glanced at Vee and saw she was staring ahead, her face blank and showing no emotion. Probably in shock, he thought.

Christ, what have I done?

The brief scene when he was alone in the cottage played through his mind as it would many times in the coming weeks. First, the candle appeared with its yellow, flickering flame. Then the ancient, greasy stove is in front of him and he sees his fingers opening each of the four regulator knobs in turn, and then the one that controlled the flow of gas to the oven.

Chapter 47

"SHOCK"

(Tuesday 7th January – early evening)

Helen gave him a strange look when, returning to the house with a muttered greeting, he walked over to the drinks cabinet in the living room and poured himself a generous measure of Courvoisier.

'Bad day,' he said. 'I'm going out for a smoke. Won't be long.'

Standing outside, leaning against the wall, his drink placed on a small garden table, he fished in his coat pocket and pulled out a crumpled packet of cigarettes together with a zippo lighter. His hands shook, and it took several attempts to light the cigarette. He took a deep drag and exhaled quickly, then followed this with a gulp of brandy. He winced as the fiery liquid passed his throat and entered his stomach but welcomed the immediate calming effect it provided. Leaning back against the wall, huddled into the greatcoat, he thought through the events of the last few hours.

Vee said nothing as he drove her home, he recalled. When he glanced at her, her face betrayed no emotion. She appeared to be deep in thought.

He suggested they might stop off at a pub on the way, but she shook her head.

'I think I need to go home.'

Earlier, when he stopped outside her flat, he detected a brief hesitation from her as if reluctant to part with him. She continued to stare ahead as though transfixed, and then she turned, crooked her arm around his neck and pulled him towards her. It was the briefest of kisses but seemed to suggest a need for intimacy.

'Thank you, Frank. Thank you for helping me.'

He watched as she ran up the pathway to her front door and disappeared inside.

As he leant against the wall smoking, he calculated it must have been less than an hour since they walked away from the cottage. The remembered images remained sharp, the implications yet undistorted by the passage of time. But doubts about what he had done started to trouble him.

With his cigarette down to the filter, he lit another from the burning tip. His thoughts confused, he tried to piece together his rationale for creating the explosion that must have destroyed the building and everything, including the body, inside it. Fear and guilt combined to trouble him. His fear was based on the realisation that, should the barest scrap of evidence be found in what remained of the cottage be linked to him, he could be accused of murder. There would be no proof to suggest Jonny was already dead when he started what would be his funeral pyre.

Why did I do it? Why did I not just walk away with her?

His feelings of guilt, he concluded, were borne of the knowledge his actions may have been fuelled by bravado. Taking another gulp of the brandy, he tried to remember what went through his mind when he ushered Vee to leave the cottage and he enacted his spur of the moment plan.

Was I trying to impress her? No, I wanted to destroy any chance of her being implicated in Jonny's death. Yes, we'd got the photos - but there could have been something else that might lead the Police to her. There was too much at stake to just leave everything in place.

'I didn't have a choice!' he muttered, knowing he was trying to convince himself.

His thoughts turned back to Vee and how she reacted after they left the cottage, and then after the explosion. *Did she guess what I'd done?* He recalled how she stared at him, her eyes wide open as soon as the initial horror passed. But she said nothing, not at that point nor later when he drove her home. She was in shock - probably still is - after all, it's not every day you see a dead body, and the circumstances of Jonny's death were disturbing.

He recalled the details in the kitchen: the grimy table and the candle - the instruments of the drug addict - the syringes; dirty spoon; the ligature. He shuddered remembering the overpowering smell of degradation and hopelessness. Vee had been on intimate terms with that man once. *She must be in a mess right now. I must talk to her - I need to know what she's thinking - get closure on this.*

The brandy and cigarettes had calmed his nerves a little. Draining the last of the drink, he leaned his back against the wall, shutting his eyes for a few moments. He pictured her face again and, with a sudden pinch of guilt, he realised the events over the last few hours had rekindled his latent yearning for her, feelings he had convinced himself were long buried. There was something else: perhaps I'm mistaken, he thought, but I'm beginning to sense the attraction may not be one-sided.

A thought grew and took shape in his mind, compelling him to action. He ground out his cigarette and re-entered the house, slipping off his greatcoat, which fell to the floor. Grabbing his car keys, he walked to the front door and, seeing Helen in his peripheral vision, scrabbled for an excuse.

'I think I've left the office unlocked - won't be long. Can't risk a break in.' He knew this sounded lame and might be questioned later - but he slipped out before she could protest.

In less than a minute, he was driving towards Vee's flat.

***

Vee shut the front door behind her and leant with her back against it, looking blankly ahead of her into the darkness. The hallway was illuminated for a few moments

346

by the sweep of car headlights - Frank, she guessed, turning around to head back home.

With the sound of the car engine fading into the night, a sense of loneliness enveloped her. Sliding to the floor, she sat with her back pressed against the door. Her breathing became rapid as suppressed panic emerged. She fumbled in her coat pocket, searching for the tin of roll-ups. Finding it, she struggled to prise off the lid because her hands were shaking. The top flipped off, spilling the contents to the floor. Picking up a roll-up, she secured it in her lips and, after several attempts, lit it.

Having finished her smoke, and feeling a little calmer now, she stood and walked a little unsteadily into the kitchen. The sight of familiar objects had a calming effect. But she still needed a stronger sedative. A tin of Quality Street hidden at the back of the larder provided what she craved - this was where Carrie kept her supply of cannabis. She found three ready-rolled joints. Taking all three, she sat at the kitchen table where an open and almost full bottle of red wine promised to help lift her spirits.

With a joint lit and a glass charged, she pieced together her recollections and feelings about what happened at the cottage. After a few minutes, the combined effects of cannabis and alcohol enabled her to examine the details of the remembered scenes in the kitchen with calm detachment. The filth, the squalor - the fact Jonny was dead and likely died a horrible death - these thoughts did not trouble her. But then she recalled the small plastic syringe lying on the table in its cloth bed - so clinical - clean-looking in contrast to everything else in that squalid kitchen. This image troubled her. She knew the contents of that hypodermic were intended for her. A vision of Jonny's face flashed into her mind, locked in a silent scream, the antiquated syringe case dangling from his arm.

If I had arrived sooner, I would be on that filthy floor next to him, dead or dying by the time Frank found me.

Then she remembered the small brown bottle and the wad of cotton padding - Chloroform. I would never have had the chance to yell out.

Despite the comforting effects of the cannabis and wine, the shaking would not stop. Remembered images flitted in and out of focus: the grimy kitchen; the ravaged face of her tormenter; the clutter of drug paraphernalia – and those two syringes, one surely intended for her. She recalled the expression on Frank's face immediately after the explosion and tried to interpret meaning from it. What did he say? Oh yes: 'Everything's okay now. Let's try and forget this ever happened.'

She understood he had caused it - knowing he would want to destroy any evidence linking Jonny to her. He has taken an enormous risk - the police might find out what he did - and then what would happen to him? 'Oh God, Frank, why did I involve you?' she whispered.

At that moment, there was a loud knocking at the door. Her heart leapt as her befuddled mind imagined a group of uniformed policemen standing outside. She rose, grabbing the back of the seat to steady herself before lurching into the hallway.

Chapter 48

"THE INVESTIGATION"

(Wednesday 8th January 1964)

From the outside, the cottage appeared derelict rather than devastated. The walls remained intact and the front door, blackened with soot, still clung to its frame. Square holes where the windows had been stared out like darkened, empty eyes. But the roof provided a sign of the destruction inside: the charred timbers still maintained a semblance of shape and symmetry, but the tiles were gone, leaving the building open to the elements.

Detective Inspector Lester nodded in acknowledgement of the salute from the Constable guarding the approach to the cottage.

'Have Forensics arrived yet?'

'They're inside now, sir.'

'Okay, let's see what we've got.'

The bespectacled inspector turned to his companion, a cheerless Detective Constable called McIntyre sent over from Portsmouth CID to assist in the investigation, a move justified by the fact the Fire Brigade, arriving at the scene when the fire had all but burnt itself out, reported a body had been found inside.

Although the open roof had allowed most of the post-fire smoke and fumes to escape, the air remained acrid, causing them to cough and their eyes to water as soon as they went through the front door. Three forensic team officers crouched among the debris in the kitchen area - the nearest one stood and turned as they walked into the hallway.

'Hello Rod,' he said, 'thought you'd be down sooner or later. Be careful, there's a lot of crap on the floor we've yet to sift through - don't want to disturb anything with your size elevens! We're just finishing. Look, do you mind if we step outside - this isn't doing my asthma any good.'

As they stepped into the fresh air, Simon Kemp, the Chief Forensics Officer took several deep breaths. 'What a bloody mess!'

DI Lester nodded. 'Must have been difficult for the Fire Brigade to access the site. The lane leading down is barely wide enough to get a car down let alone a tender!'

'I understand they got down to the level bit,' said Simon, pointing to a ridge above the cottage. 'They were able to direct their hoses from there down onto the building, which accounts for most of the missing roof.'

'Any idea how the fire started?'

'Not really. Hard to be sure given the extent of destruction. But they think the seat of the fire was almost certainly the kitchen, probably caused by a gas leak. The chap inside might have lit a cigarette - maybe he turned on a light; that's all it would take to cause an explosion.'

'What about the body? Any clues as to his identity?'

'Not much to go on, I'm afraid - it's so badly burned. The only way of identifying him - we're assuming a "him" due to the size - is possibly through dental records. But we've nowhere to start: nothing survived. We thought we'd struck gold when we found the remains of his wallet lying on the floor under the body. Unfortunately, it was empty apart from part of a photo which is so damaged, we can't make out any details. But that van over there might provide a clue.'

The van lay partially hidden in the trees to the side of the house, its paintwork ravaged by the fire, and its windows shattered.

'Check that out will you, McIntyre. I don't suppose the number plates survived, but there should be a serial number inside the engine housing.'

The morose DC grunted and walked towards the van at the same time as a man emerged from the front door and beckoned.

'Think you might want to see this, Simon.'

'It was hidden under a layer of soot,' he said, using a fountain pen to hold up a metal syringe by one of the loops on its plunger, 'I found a spoon as well, and what looks like a candle base. There may be other stuff lying among the debris, but I'd say our John Doe here liked his drugs.'

***

Later that day, DI Lester sat at his desk, reviewing the events of what, he concluded, proved to be a frustrating day. The burnt-out van offered a ray of hope. DC McIntyre reported that the rear registration plate remained undamaged by the fire. But disappointment followed when, after waiting for a considerable amount of time for the vehicle to be identified thus providing a clue to the owner, it transpired that it had been stolen several months before. The true owner explained he had not bothered to report the theft. 'It needed to be scrapped anyway,' he offered unhelpfully.

DC McIntyre entered the office looking even glummer than usual. 'You were right, Guv, the letting agency on the High Street rented out the cottage.'

'And? Who did they let the property to?'

'Apparently, they don't know. Unbelievable, isn't it? They told me the booking was made over the phone; they never took a name. He paid in advance by postal order.'

'So, are you telling me that no one from the letting agency met the man who rented the cottage? Surely he must have collected the key from them.'

DC McIntyre shook his head. 'They kept it under a rock by the front door - so he obviously let himself in, and no, you're right, no one can provide a description of him.'

Alone in his office, the DI took a gulp of whiskey from the bottle he stowed in his desk drawer. He turned on the lamp and, carefully holding the damaged photograph salvaged from the man's wallet, he moved it backwards and forwards under the bulb. Only half of the black-and-white picture remained, and that offered little in the way of detail. The dominant feature was the image of what appeared to be a girl wearing a beret. He reached into the desk drawer and pulled out a large magnifying glass. The expanded picture provided nothing more. A scorch mark obliterated the area where the face would be, although the hair, a distinctive dark bob, survived. Then he noticed a hand on the girl's left shoulder belonging to whoever had stood on the destroyed side of the photograph. Turning it over and examining it with the magnifying glass, his heart leapt when he made out faded blue printed writing. He squinted at the lettering, trying to read the smudged print. Holding it at an angle under the desk light, he found he could decipher the words. He scribbled in his notebook: "30th May 1959 – Manchester."

Frowning, he muttered, 'It's a clue, but not much of one.' He reached for the whiskey bottle and poured himself another drink.

Chapter 49

"WHERE'S JONNY?"

(Monday 27th January 1964)

'No idea mate, none whatsoever. He didn't say where he's going - never does. And anyway, I'm not his keeper!'

The manager of the Seaman's Mission stared at Horse doubtfully, as if suspicious he might be hiding something.

'Well, if you do see him, tell him he owes a month's rent. And, what's more,' he added darkly, 'I shall be contacting the Police. I'm not going to be made a fool of by anyone, especially by an ...,' he was about to add, 'itinerant sailor,' but thought better of it when he met Horse's glowering gaze.

'Like I said, I don't know where he is - and he isn't my problem,' muttered Horse, adopting an aggressive tone.

The manager sighed, defeated. 'Okay, but keep an eye out for him, will you? By the way, I'll be clearing out his room today, and I won't be storing anything he's left. If you want to hold onto his gear, I couldn't care less - I'll only be putting it in the bin.'

'Yeh, I'll do that. Give me the key to his room - I'll clear it out for you.'

Horse's offer had nothing to do with altruism - the thought of someone discovering narcotics somewhere in Jonny's room appeared in his mind, a prospect that might well lead eventually to his door. He caught the key thrown to him from behind the safety of the reception desk by the manager.

'Make sure you return it!' he said with bad grace.

He didn't find drugs in the room - in fact, he found nothing at all, the room stood empty, completely cleared as though Jonny had never been there.

***

Later that day, Horse sat at his usual table, alone in a dingy dockside pub overlooking the wharf on which the "Wanderer" was berthed. He would be joining the ship later that night. In the morning, the ship would set sail, this time to Rotterdam.

As always on the night before sailing, he found himself lost in glum retrospection. Only a hefty intake of alcohol would prevent a descent into the pits of gloom. Other crew members might be sad at leaving loved ones behind, but this never created an issue for Horse as he had no one. But the prospect of being thrown around in the North Sea in a winter gale, particularly for someone who suffered from chronic seasickness, was not a happy one.

He stared at his pint pot and shivered. The pub was empty except for a cheerless landlord who ignored him, and the soulless atmosphere sapped his soul as much as the chill of the unheated room.

As so often when alone like this, he reflected on his life and what it meant. Nothing, he concluded - it means nothing. The thought of spending the next ten days in the company of men who treated him as an oddity added to his gloom. Although possessing a quick wit and, in other circumstances, an ability to build relationships, when at sea he adopted a different persona. Onboard the ship, he maintained an aloof profile, rationalising this on the grounds he wanted no one to know his business. And the trips to Holland provided the source of his lucrative alternative trade: the drugs he touted around the Marina. On the ship, he knew he was held in low regard by everyone.

At the Marina, though - well, that's a different matter, isn't it? Those young toffs like me cos I'm funny and interesting - and I've got what they need.

'I'm a business man - a professional - I'm not just a fucking deckhand,' he muttered, as though defending himself to an invisible critic. 'They like me - they think I'm okay.' He flashed a glance at the barman, who continued to ignore him.

His effort at self-encouragement worked, and he cheered slightly. *I built a great business there - saw the opportunity and made it work.* Smiling now, he took another gulp of his pint.

But his buoyant mood didn't last. Later, having reached his capacity with beer, and drinking rum instead, depression overwhelmed him. His thoughts had turned to Jonny, his absent friend - or at least the nearest approximation to a friend.

'Funny bloke - downright weird in fact,' he said out loud, no longer caring if the barman heard him. 'I took care of him. He would never have survived Strangeways if it hadn't been for me. They would have pulled him apart - what, him with his pampered upbringing, his education - his funny ideas that no one could understand.'

He glanced at the barman who was staring at him. 'I kept him safe!' he said as if to explain.

He shook his head, an inane grin on his face. Silent now, he considered the notion of how much he had helped Jonny.

Gave him the drugs he needed - discount price an' all. But did he ever thank me? No! Ungrateful bastard! The times I had to listen to him talking total shit! Not exactly thrilling company, was he? Couldn't have much of a laugh and a joke with him - no sense of humour.

'In fact, maybe he's not actually human!' He said this out loud and burst out laughing.

'I think you've had enough, mate. You should get on your way.'

He looked blearily toward the barman's voice - 'Little longer,' he slurred.

He's gone, probably for good. Horse contemplated this notion for a few moments and then, raising the glass of rum, untouched since he bought it twenty minutes ago, toasted the vision of Jonny he imagined sitting opposite him.

'Here's to you, mate, wherever you are!' He drained the glass, and then sat back with a heavy sigh.

The barman shook his head at the scene of the stocky, bald man, who had tears streaming down his face.

Chapter 50

"RESENTMENT"

(Thursday 9th July 1964 – early morning)
'Make sure you take calamine lotion in case he gets sun-burned. Please don't let him stay out in the sun too long - he burns very easily. Oh, and don't let him near the water if he's just eaten.'

Frank sighed, trying hard to hide his irritation at Helen's unhappy knack of making him feel inadequate as a father. A verbal retaliation formed in his head: 'I have looked after my son before! I'm not a complete idiot, despite what you seem to think!' But he thought better of it. A petty argument with her would only heighten an already raised level of resentment.

With considerable effort, for Peter's sake rather than hers, he mustered a hint of enthusiasm. 'He'll be fine. We're going to have a great day, aren't we?'

Peter nodded emphatically. 'Swimming!' he said. His face changed in an instant from a smiling countenance to a frown; then he hurtled out of the living room. It always amused Frank how his son appeared to think at a hundred miles an hour. Judging by the sound of rapidly pounding feet on the stairs, he guessed he had forgotten something, probably one or more of his newest plastic figurines, his chosen companions for the day. Cowboys and Indians had recently been usurped by miniature recreations of the latest TV series characters to fire his imagination, these from his current favourite TV show, "Fireball XL5."

Less than a minute later, Peter burst back into the room, a fist full of plastic figures, which Frank recognised from the box set, a recent birthday present from his Aunty Vee.

He stuffed these into his duffle bag, and stood with an expectant expression, ready for the off.

'Toilet! Go on, we won't be stopping on the way.' Peter frowned, then grinned and raced out of the room again.

'Look, Frank, I know you're not happy - but I told you why I need to do this on my own. I'm not excluding you...'

'But, you are!' he replied, unable to stop himself from hitting back.

'No, I'm not,' Helen said in a tone suggesting she was doing her best to be patient. 'As I explained, I must work alone on this, because...'

'Oh, just leave it. You know what I think about all this. We should be working together on the marketing plans.'

He looked at her, wanting to see acknowledgement. Instead, he was met with a defiant stare.

'I've got ideas as well, you know,' he said, realising immediately he sound plaintive, hating the thought this made him sound weak.

Her face changed, and she smiled in a conciliatory way - but to him, he saw condescension.

'I know you have ideas, and some of them are good, and I will include them. It's just..., well, I need to work on my own. Enjoy a day with Peter. Some father-son time will do you both a power of good. I'll cook a nice dinner for us tonight - and we can discuss all the details over a bottle of wine. How does that sound?'

'Patronising!' But this was an unarticulated thought. Instead, he grunted. Further argument was saved by the interruption of the telephone ringing in the hall. Helen walked out to answer it leaving him alone, glowering in resentment as he thought about Helen's growing presence and influence at Parks.

She spent much more time at the office than she used to and was becoming increasingly assertive, wanting to change things. 'The company needs to grow and prosper,' she argued at the Board meeting a week ago, 'and that means new strategies, new directions.' Although broadly in agreement with this notion, he could not help thinking she was undermining him. After all, it was he who had been entrusted by Bob with the management of the business, not her. But of late, it appeared she considered herself to be of a higher status in terms of decision making than him. This rankled.

The reappearance of Peter snapped him out of his resentful reverie.

'Won't be long - we'll get going in a minute. Now then, let's have a look in that bag of yours.' He emptied the contents and extracted, without Peter noticing, several figures. Swimming trunks, a towel, Calamine Lotion, and a smaller team of plastic companions were re-packed.

They were ready to go. 'Come on, Helen, hurry it up,' he muttered irritably, cocking his ear towards the door and listening. He guessed she was speaking to Vee, which was confirmed a few moments later when Helen re-entered the room.

'Vee wants to go with you. She's at a loose end. I said you'd pick her up in about fifteen minutes. She'll be waiting outside.'

Helen shot him a glance as if expecting to be challenged. 'If that's alright with you?' she added.

He shrugged, conveying a message that said: 'You've already invited her, so I'm hardly likely to tell her she's not welcome.' In his mind, however, there was a very different reaction to the news that Vee would share their day, this one positive and welcoming, and not a notion he would want Helen to know of.

'Right then, young man, are we ready? Yes? Let's go, then. Say goodbye to your Mum.'

***

Helen did not plan to go in to the office until later that morning, intending instead to spend time at home where she could think without interruption. A new marketing strategy for Parks had been formulating in her head for some weeks but so far it remained unstructured, a series of loosely related ideas that needed to be thought through and joined in some form of meaningful pattern. Only once this had been done could she go to the office where she would meet with Hugh O'Driscoll, and a newly appointed Head of Sales, Kirk Boyle, the latter poached from a rival organisation and who, in her view, offered some exciting and innovative ideas, which she intended to tap into.

Hearing the car engine start up, she realised Frank was driving their new Singer Gazelle rather than the Healey. She assumed he would use the two-seater which Peter loved, especially with the hood down. But with Vee now going, he would need the bigger car.

'Oh bugger!' she muttered, guessing he'd taken the keys with him. She rushed to the front door and ran down the garden path to the road. The Singer was disappearing in the distance. She swore under her breath, not relishing the prospect of relying on the buses to take her to the depot later.

'Sod you, Frank - I bet you did that on purpose.'

When she closed the door behind her and stepped back into the hall, she saw the keys to the Healey hanging on a hook where she remembered, he always left them.

'Sorry, Frank,' she murmured, 'I should learn to trust you, shouldn't I?'

Sitting at the kitchen table, a mug of tea in front of her, she was not up to starting work yet. A combination of guilt and doubt nagged. Frank was clearly unhappy about her decision to create the marketing plan for Parks without his direct input. She guessed he did not believe his suggestions would be considered. But the problem remained: his ideas involved maintenance of the status quo. In her view, he was overly cautious about taking steps into unknown territory. She and others in the firm believed that radical change was essential for the future prosperity of the company. It was time to move forward.

She tried hard to separate her work and personal life. But even though she and Frank agreed never to let their respective roles at Parks affect their marriage, they clashed frequently, most often due to their professional differences.

During the lulls between their arguments, on the occasions when they could both talk rationally and without anger, they conceded they should not treat their home as an extension of the office. But it would not be long before another altercation started. Disagreements that should have stayed in the boardroom, or at least been saved for an appropriate time, often reignited in the kitchen or over the dinner table. She recalled the last significant disagreement, which caused her to storm out of a restaurant leaving him, red-faced, inside. That was our wedding anniversary, she reminded herself.

Their arguments usually erupted for the same underlying reason: one major difference in opinion neither could reconcile nor find a compromise on. He was ambitious and wanted Parks to grow. But in her view, he lacked vision. His enduring mantra was always 'more of the same.' He did not see the benefits of diversifying the product base. For him, success lay in evolving and improving the company's range of vacuum cleaner products.

'We should focus on what we're good at, not waste our assets by delving into new areas we have no experience of dealing with.'

But she remained convinced growth, and the very survival of the company, relied upon broadening the product-base. 'White goods are the future for Parks,' she argued. In her opinion, the firm could take on the production of a range of domestic products. 'The market's crying out for them. Open your eyes, Frank - you can read it in the magazines - watch the telly adverts! We could start with, say, twin tub washing machines and then expand further into refrigerators, then, perhaps, electric cookers.'

Despite her enthusiasm, she remained sensitive to his intransigence. He was firmly against her ideas for change and stated this, 'for the record,' at their last senior management meeting. It rankled Helen that the other Board members, all appointed by either her father or Frank, always took his side, at least formally. However, she felt heartened when both Hugh O'Driscoll, and Kirk Boyle approached her outside the meeting and expressed an interest in her ideas. Time for a palace revolution, she told herself. Things would change at Parks whether Frank liked it or not!

She stared at her mug of tea, untouched and going cold.

'But work's not the real issue, though, is it? Something is wrong with our marriage.'

Uttering her thoughts aloud brought the unhappiness, previously buried deep inside her, to the surface. She cried for several minutes. At last, her tears spent, she tried to rationalise what was troubling her.

Work served as a distraction. True, now Peter attended nursery school, she had more time to devote to Parks - but all the same, the energy she showed, the way she threw herself into work - all this provided a way of shielding herself from the nagging worry and doubts that might overwhelm her if she were forced to think about them too much. Something was wrong, her instinct told her. He seemed so distant these days, and his affection for her had cooled. They argued constantly, mostly about work. But lately, arguments would spark out of nowhere, escalating quickly into full blown rows.

Frank was without doubt different now. It was the small things, little details that might seem trivial, irrelevant even - but to her, they held huge significance. Before, he had been attentive: a true gentleman in a way that people might consider as old fashioned. She smiled, remembering how he would always insist on opening the car door for her. That charming idiosyncrasy had long gone. He used to bring me flowers, she reminded herself with a sad smile - not in acknowledgement of any occasion but as he would say: 'Because I love you.' There had not been flowers for some time.

Sometimes, she wondered if he was truly committed to her and to domesticity. Although he no longer stayed days away on business - she had won that battle - he still spent, in her view, far too much time in the pub. She did not believe him when he insisted this was necessary in his role as a manager. Sometimes, she wondered whether he was going to the pub after work on his own. The thought he preferred being inside a bar rather than being at home hurt her deeply.

There was something else though. Whereas before, they had been easy in each other's company - sharing their thoughts - he appeared so distant now. And, perhaps more worrying, he had become secretive. Often, he would leave the house with no explanation, returning sometimes much later. When asked where he had been, he would always have an excuse - plausible - but true?

The notion he might be having an affair had occurred to her - but the thought was so unpalatable, she would do her best to convince herself she was being silly. He would never be unfaithful to me - would he? She tried to dismiss her suspicion. This is a stressful time - for us both, with Dad stepping down and us having to give so much to Parks. But the nagging thoughts would not go away. Something is going on.

***

Vee turned her head to look at Peter, who was engrossed in his game of space adventure on the back seat of the car. He had been accompanying his game with the first few lines of the theme tune to the TV series from which his toy figures derived. 'I wish I was a spaceman, the fastest guy alive; I'd fly you round the universe in Fireball XL 5,' which he repeated tirelessly, until Frank, laughing with exasperation, asked him to 'Put a sock in it!' Peter frowned, evidently irritated by his dad's interruption to his game. Vee smiled fondly at him.

'Are you looking forward to the seaside? Your dad says we can go to the arcade and spend some of his pennies! Would you like that?'

Peter appeared to contemplate this for a few moments. 'I want to go swimming,' he said, his voice tone suggesting a reminder rather than a request.

'Oh, I think we can manage that, can't we Frank.'

He glanced at her and nodded. 'We'll go to the Lido in the afternoon - he'll like that.' She looked back at Peter and noted how his face changed to a broad smile.

'He can't actually swim, though,' Frank whispered.

'Yes, I can!' Peter announced indignantly.

'Alright son, we'll all swim in the pool together, okay?' said Frank laughing.

Although only a few miles as the crow flies from Fairfield to Lee-on-Solent, the roads were busy; many other families, it seemed, had decided to take advantage of the glorious August weather to visit the coast, and so progress was slow. The car crawled along the A27, the windows wound down in a futile attempt to stay cool.

'How's Helen?' Vee asked.

'Busy creating a bright new future for Parks.' He paused before adding, with a strong hint of bitterness, which she detected: 'Apparently, with no need for my input.'

'Oh,' she replied uncertainly. Vee knew the outline of Helen's ambitions for Parks; her sister had explained her plans with considerable enthusiasm over lunch at a café on the High Street. Helen had seemed excited. Vee remembered also how Frank featured in the conversation. Helen said nothing derogatory about him - but she suggested he was a problem in that he did not welcome significant change. She recalled being on the verge of responding with an indignant defence on his behalf but checked herself just in time.

If only Helen knew what's been going on right under her nose. Not for the first time, Vee experienced a sense of crushing guilt. *This can't go on - it's wrong. What have I done?*

She glanced at Frank - he appeared to be lost in thought, no doubt simmering with resentment. His irritability, if unchecked, would spoil the day.

'Come on Frank, Helen knows how valuable you are to Parks. She wouldn't change anything without your agreement - you do know that, don't you?'

'Perhaps,' he replied thoughtfully. 'But, I'm feeling more and more ignored when it comes to the business.' He sighed before adding, 'and in just about everything else if I'm honest.'

She reached across and put her hand on top of his, resting on the gear stick.

'It'll get better, I'm sure. You're just going through a bad patch.'

He shoved the stick into first and edged the car forward. She removed her hand sensing she might have irritated him but not knowing why. The car gathered momentum - they were on their way again.

'Let's just have a great day,' he said suddenly. 'Whatever the future holds, we can worry about that tomorrow, eh?'

He reached his hand over and patted her knee; his eyes met hers and a sense of understanding passing between them in that briefest of moments. She smiled and nodded, believing a crisis had been allayed, at least for the time being.

'I think I would much rather be spending the day with you than being holed up in an airless office talking clap trap.'

'Frank!' Vee shot a glance at Peter in the back seat. 'Little ears,' she whispered.

Chapter 51

"THE LEAD"

If one dominant trait might describe Detective Inspector Rod Lester, it would be dogged determination. Seven months passed since the fire at the cottage and, so far, the identity of the body, charred beyond recognition, had still not been established. Where others in his profession might accept this as simply another sorry manifestation of the drug culture sweeping the country, he remained determined to tie up the loose ends and establish the name of the victim.

His workload since January had been intensive, and he almost forgot about the cottage fire and the body. The publication of the Coroner's report coincided with an unusual lull in activity, which allowed him to re-focus on the case.

"Death by misadventure," concluded the Coroner; but the investigation suggested suicide although this could not be proven. The paraphernalia found at the scene supported the notion of an addict. Close inspection of the remains of the oven suggested the cause of the fire had been a gas explosion. The investigators discovered all the supply switches fully opened. Deliberate? Most likely, in the Inspector's opinion - why else would they be left open? The smallest spark would have triggered an explosion. Perhaps the man did this himself - an act of suicide. But there were many other possible reasons why the build-up of gas ignited: a cigarette being lit maybe, or even a light switch being thrown - the result, a devastating fireball, and a sad demise of a wasted life.

The case was closed and therefore he did not need to worry about it. But he did - and now he had time to focus, he refused to give up. The lack of a name bothered him: it seemed untidy, and he hated loose ends. The only possible clue remained the incomplete photograph found at the scene, now lying on his desk.

His discovery of the blue lettering, a photographer's stamp bearing the words "30th May 1959 - Manchester," lay forgotten in his drawer. This, he mused, presented at best a tenuous lead but a lead nonetheless. He made several phone calls to Manchester CID. His northern colleagues, uncooperative at first, finally produced a list and contact details of professional photographers active around the city in the late 'fifties. Having made copies of the photograph, front and back, and sent these to each of the addresses provided, he received a phone call.

'It looks like one of ours,' the northern-accented voice informed him, 'Taken at the University, the one on Oxford Road. We were hired to take photographs at the garden parties. All the faculties would hold one at the end of the Summer Term.'

'Do you know which one held a party on 30th May 1959?' The Inspector's heart raced with excitement.

'Could be one of several,' said the voice. 'You'll need to speak to the university - they'll probably be able to help you out.'

He contacted the University Registry and established that three faculties hosted parties on the day in question. The clerk helpfully provided contact details for each. With an invigorated sense of purpose, he followed up without delay. The next day, he took the train up to Manchester, armed with the fragment of photograph.

'Impossible to say without a face - many girls sported that hairdo at the time - it was the "in look" amongst certain elements of the student community.' This was the response of the first faculty he visited, the gist of this message to be repeated when he called upon the second.

He admitted to himself, he was clutching at straws with just the scrap of an old photograph to go on.

Someone with less determination and stamina might have given up at this point. Fortunately, he persisted. His final encounter at the university changed everything. Professor O'Donnell, Head of English Literature, studied the image. Expecting a non-committal response to echo those he had heard previously; the Inspector did not register immediately what the Professor said.

'Sorry, can you say that again; I didn't quite catch that.'

'It's the beret and the hair - I remember both - very distinctive.'

The Professor waved his pipe as if to add emphasis to his words.

'A bright girl. Awarded a "Two-One" in her Finals. Had a few problems, though, earlier in her time here. Got herself into a bit of bother with some chap who was pursuing her, I recall - but that was sorted out.'

'Can you tell me the girl's name?'

'Oh yes, of course - Virginia Park. A lovely girl - went on to be a teacher, I believe. Prefers to be called Vee.'

'Do you have any idea who might have been in the missing part of the picture? Or the name of the man who you said was bothering her?' His instinct told him they were the one and same. He found it hard to contain his excitement.

'Unfortunately, not, I'm afraid. I never met him, and Miss Park never mentioned his name to me. I just know she came near to giving up her degree studies because of him. Can I ask, by the way, what this is all about? I mean, she is alright, isn't she?'

DI Lester explained the circumstances behind the enquiry.

'It would be helpful if I could speak to this Miss Park - Vee. She's not in any trouble - but if she can tell me about the photo - who the missing person is, it might help us establish his identity.'

The Professor made a phone call to the University Registry. 'Yes, they've still got her details,' he said a few minutes later, his hand over the receiver. 'But, of course, she might not be living there now.' He jotted on a piece of notepaper and handed it over.

When he read the address, he found it hard not to show his excitement.

'That has been most helpful. Thank you so much for your help.'

***

(Thursday 9th July 1964 – late morning)

The next morning, he called at the address in Fairfield. The middle-aged man who answered the door confirmed he was Miss Park's father. Mr Park's face turned ashen when he was shown the warrant card. He sighed with relief when he was assured his daughter was not in any trouble.

'There's just a chance she might be able to help me identify a person of interest,' the Inspector explained, leaving out the small detail about that person being dead.

He drove to the address given to him but was disappointed to find she was not at home. After waiting for almost an hour he gave up, determined to try again first thing in the morning.

Chapter 52

"THE LIDO"

(Thursday 9th July 1964 - afternoon)

A precipitous ridge of copper pennies balanced precariously on the lip of the shelf behind the smudged glass screen. Peter glanced up and then back again at the coins: his goal. Frank delved into his pocket and pulled out three more.

'Last ones, Peter, and that's your lot! I think those pennies are glued down!'

Vee lifted Peter up, so he could reach the coin slot. He pushed in the first penny. The moving bar nudged it against the collective mass, which moved forward almost imperceptibly, the barest fraction of an inch. The second attempt landed on top of the bar. They groaned in unison.

'You have to wait until it moves back,' said Frank, almost as engrossed as his son.

'I'll tell you when, Peter,' said Vee, guiding his eager hand up to the brass slot. 'Not yet! Not yet! Now!'

The coin dropped on the shelf and the bar met it squarely, moving it forward to meet the seemingly fixed phalanx of coins. A pause, and then, like the side of a cliff collapsing into the sea, a wedge of copper fell into the tray beneath with a satisfying metal crash, to be followed moments later when the bar returned, with another pile of coins.

'I won, Peter yelled!'

They cheered.

'That'll pay for lunch!' said Frank.

'Don't be so mean!' said Vee, 'that's Peter's winnings!'

***

They lunched - a fantastically greasy affair - at the Wimpy on the High Street. Peter, having devoured an enormous plate of sausage, beans and chips and most of an improbably huge Strawberry Sundae, was eager to resume the day's entertainment.

'You can't go swimming 'til your dinner goes down,' said Frank, reaching for his cigarettes. Peter frowned but, as always, never complained - he searched instead for a new distraction. Slipping from his chair, he walked over to a tank of orange squash, the liquid contents of which was being propelled by a rotor with plastic oranges positioned at the end of each of the three blades.

Lighting two cigarettes, Frank handed one to Vee and then leant back in his seat, taking a deep drag. He sighed contentedly.

'I could stay here all afternoon and, to be honest, I'm not sure if I can move after that lunch!'

They smoked and watched Peter.

'What is going through that boy's mind?' said Frank laughing.

'Well, I'm guessing something like an orange space craft spinning through the Universe,' she replied in a serious voice. She looked at him and burst out laughing when he raised his eyebrows.

'We'd better get moving soon - we promised to take him to the lido, and I have an inkling the pool will be pretty busy this afternoon.' She called to Peter, still engrossed by the rotating "spacecraft."

'Come on Steve Zodiac, we've got to go.'

Peter frowned, then selected a figurine from the three he held in his fist. 'This is Steve Zodiac - I'm Peter,' he said wisely.

Her assessment turned out to be correct - they joined a long queue several yards short of the entrance. Frank groaned, anticipating a long wait in the stifling afternoon heat.

'Perhaps we should go to the beach instead,' he suggested - but Peter's disappointed expression precluded this - he was determined to experience a swimming pool.

'It shouldn't take too long,' said Vee, placatingly. 'There - look - lots of people are leaving - they'll be off for their lunch.'

A group of young men gathered together in the line ahead of them, sailors from the Naval Air Station just up the road, Frank guessed, judging by their short hair, the smattering of tattoos and the language they used, filled with ribald remarks. They were in high spirits, possibly helped by a visit to one or two local hostelries for a liquid lunch, he thought. One of them cradled a crate of beer bottles. They passed a football from one to the other - a game of static rugby, which was, in his view, getting out of hand. When the ball hit one of the sailors in the face, the unfortunate recipient swore loudly, prompting Frank to intervene.

'Tone it down a bit will you lads, there are women and children about, they don't need to hear that.'

They all apologised and appeared to be on the verge of engaging in friendly conversation and, he guessed, some flirting with Vee when the queue moved forward. In a few minutes, they squeezed into the lido past the gate attendant.

Frank and Peter squeezed through the door of the small, crowded changing room where they hurriedly changed into swimming trunks. Frank placed their clothes in the holdall brought for the purpose, and they edged their way towards the exit to meet Vee.

The young sailors they encountered at the entrance were in the changing room, their exuberance by no means diminished. They were ready to leave except for one of them, who seemed to have mislaid some item or other, and was busy searching the vicinity of the changing room for it accompanied by humorous, but unhelpful comments from his mates.

The ball was being passed around again. One of the sailors spotted Peter and tossed the ball to him gently, much to his delight. He caught it and immediately threw it back to the nearest young man in the group who promptly dropped it with exaggerated clumsiness. They all cheered - Peter joined in, entering the spirit of light-hearted fun.

'Smashing kid,' said one of the group.

Frank nodded proudly, ruffling Peter's hair. 'The best.'

'Got it!' shouted the young man, holding up a bottle opener.

'You tosser!' yelled another, who immediately shot a glance at Frank as if expecting a rebuke. They all left the changing room, jostling each other and exchanging insults.

'Was I good at catching the ball?' asked Peter as they emerged into the bright light outside.

'Yes, well done! Now, where's your Aunty Vee?'

'There she is - over there!' shouted Peter, pointing.

'Where? I can't see her.'

'There she is!'

Frank spotted her some distance away, jumping up and down and waving energetically, trying to catch their attention.

The lido was packed with people, and almost all the pool side areas were filled with bathers making the most of the gloriously sunny day as if this might be their only opportunity in the unpredictable summer months. It took some time for them to ease their way through the crowds but at last, they reached her. Vee laid out her towel - he added his and Peter's - their territory established. The sailors claimed a patch of ground nearby. The beers distributed, one of the group raised his bottle in their direction, grinning broadly. Frank acknowledged him with a brief thumbs up and then ignored him.

'Try to keep Peter in the shade,' said Vee, 'He'll burn to a crisp if he stays in the sun too long!'

'God, you sound just like Helen!' he said, smiling.

Peter pointed impatiently at the pool, tantalised by the apparent blueness of the water, its linear lines and the shouts of excitement emanating from it.

'We'll go for a swim soon, the pool's a bit busy now, and you've only just had your lunch,' said Frank, lighting a cigarette.

Uncomplaining as always, Peter sat on his towel and started a game with his plastic, space suited figurines.

***

Frank lay on his back and appeared to be studying the almost cloudless sky. He seemed contented, Vee thought, a rare mood of late when he tended to be moody and withdrawn.

The pervading holiday atmosphere was infectious. She closed her eyes, leaning back on her hands, her face turned up, enjoying the welcome warmth of the sun. It was easy to shut out the noise of shouts and laughter, chatter and general hubbub around the pool. The smell of cigarette smoke mixed with sea air, and the distinctive chemical-like waft from the ice cream kiosk overlooking their spot, created a holiday ambience.

Opening her eyes, she noticed Frank was asleep, his chest rising and falling accompanied by rhythmic snoring. She leant back and amused herself, watching Peter play, an activity he never tired of. His ability to create an absorbing game with the minimum of resources, and with no adult guidance, fascinated her.

Lighting a cigarette, she repositioned herself on her towel, wondering how Frank could fall so easily asleep on the hard concrete. A few feet away, a family group was sitting - mum and dad, she guessed, and two young children - a boy and girl, both a little older than Peter. She studied them for a few moments, thinking how happy they appeared to be.

The scene brought back memories of her childhood when her mother was still alive. She thought of the photograph: the two sisters sitting on the beach with their mum. Dad took that picture. We were happy then.

She glanced at Frank - still asleep and snoring - and then Peter, absorbed in his game. 'Oh God - what have I done?' she murmured.

Seven months had passed since the explosion and fire that consumed her Nemesis and ignited her affair with Frank. It started that night. He left her flat very late. She never asked him how he explained this to Helen, but he clearly managed to talk his way out of trouble somehow.

It should have ended there, she thought - a moment of reckless, thoughtless madness that should never have occurred. But it happened - and worse than that we - *I* let it carry on.

So far, she rationalised her behaviour as a strange aberration, a manifestation brought on by the surreal circumstances of that terrible night. Am I fooling myself, she thought - hadn't there always been something between us? Little clues that an affair might be imminent?

Several factors were not in doubt. First, never had she experienced such an intensity of self-loathing. Infidelity is bad enough, she thought, but to carry on with my sister's husband - how could I have allowed that to happen? Second, although presenting a normal front to everyone, she lived in a constant state of anxiety. Helen might find out about the affair - after all, Frank has been so moody lately, perhaps he might let his guard down? She was also worried her association with the cottage and the incineration of Jonny's body would be discovered, and she would be held to account. Frank assured her she couldn't be in any way linked to the fire.

'The police didn't identify the body - you read that in the paper. They've probably closed the case by now. We've nothing to worry about - not anymore.'

Several days after the event, Frank admitted he deliberately caused the explosion. She was aghast - more at hearing his confession than the confirmation of what she already concluded for herself. 'Why did you do it? Why didn't you just leave things as they were for the Police to discover? After all, we had the photos,' she asked him. He explained how he wanted to destroy any possible evidence linking Jonny to her. She accepted his rationale - but her anxiety remained unabated.

Only she and Frank knew what happened that late afternoon; even though a part of her yearned to share her thoughts with her closest friend, Carrie. But instinct told her this would be a mistake - so she kept the incident at the cottage and her affair with him to herself.

As she sat on her towel watching Peter playing, she realised there were tears in her eyes and turned away from him swiftly in case he spotted them. Somewhere in the background, a transistor radio was belting out Dusty Springfield's "I just don't know what to do with myself". As she listened to the words, her misery intensified.

The door in her mind, behind which lay her darkest thoughts, was now fully open. Where previously she had suppressed her feelings of guilt by burying them, now they emerged as though to taunt her. Scenes depicting the depths of her deceit presented themselves - several trysts played out. Then an older memory intruded. She recalled the first time she met him - when she had no idea what he meant to Helen. Then she remembered how she reacted to Carrie's flagrant disregard for the sanctity of marriage. I am a total hypocrite! she informed herself - and what I'm doing is far worse than simply having an affair with a married man.

My God, the risks we've been taking - all that sneaky subterfuge! She thought about the several calls she had made to his direct line at the office. They had agreed on a code to cover eventualities such as Helen being in earshot, or the fact Carrie would be away for the night thus allowing a safe assignation at her flat.

The memory of their most recent tryst caused her to flush with guilt and shame. That had been only two weeks ago. They had spent two consecutive nights together when Frank contrived a business trip to the Midlands. 'A teacher training course,' she announced to Helen in case she might wonder where *she* was. After every meeting, her conscience told her she must end what could only ever be a doomed affair. I was too weak to finish it, though, wasn't I?

She glanced at Frank. How can he sleep like that as though he didn't have a care in the world? But he's as much to blame as me - maybe more so. When she tried to press him on how he felt and why he was betraying Helen, he said little apart from hinting he was not happy.

Perhaps it was the awakened awareness she was not alone with her guilt that enabled her to shut the door in her mind. Needing his presence, she shook his shoulder. He grunted.

'Wake up, Frank! Peter needs a swim.'

He emerged reluctantly from his slumber and yawned.

'Do you think it'll be alright to leave the bags here? Our money - oh, and the car keys are in there,' she asked.

'Give me a moment.' He walked the few paces to the ice-cream kiosk behind their spot and talked to the woman behind the counter. In a few moments, he returned.

'The lady will keep an eye on the gear for us,' he said, nodding towards the kiosk and the smiling ice-cream vendor, who waved back in acknowledgement.

Threading their way slowly through the mass of people thronged around the swimming pool, they finally reached the shallow end.

'Flipping heck, it's bloody freezing!' said Frank as he climbed in to the water.

'Oh, stop being such a pansy,' she said laughing before diving beneath the water and emerging seconds later on the other side. Peter stood uncertainly with the water up to his shoulders. She swam up to him and took his hands in hers.

'Kick your legs behind you - I'll hold you up - don't worry.'

Frank spectated, wallowing up to his neck in the water. He smiled as Vee made several unsuccessful attempts to get Peter to lift both his feet from the firm safety of the pool bottom. Her patience and encouragement paid off, and soon he was kicking his legs. After twenty minutes he was moving his arms and legs in a passable display of doggy paddling, while she kept him afloat with her hands supporting him under his stomach. Frank positioned himself a few feet in front of him.

'Come on, you can do it! That's right, keep it going!'

At a nod from Vee, Frank held his arms out and she let go of Peter, who floundered across the short distance while she shrieked her encouragement behind him.

'Well done, you did it, you swam!' said Frank. Peter looked to be on the verge of tears.

'I think that'll do for the swimming lesson today,' said Vee.

Peter smiled, happy again now that the prospect of further terrifying challenges had been removed.

Frank seized the opportunity to escape the cold water. 'Getting a bit chilly in here - and crowded. Come on you two, let's go back and dry off. We can get an ice cream then - what do you say to that?'

'Bloody hell, it's freezing,' muttered Frank. He had always hated being cold, which might be the reason he had never learned to swim, a fact he was too embarrassed to share with Vee.

They exited the pool and walked carefully along the edge towards their spot. The centre area was dominated by the sailors with the ball - they were engaged in a boisterous game, which appeared to have little in the way of rules.

Having threaded their way back through the crowds, they reached their towels. Vee lay down. Peter retrieved his plastic spacemen from the towel where he left them. Frank went to the ice-cream kiosk.

'He's a lovely little boy - you're so lucky,' said the woman to whom he spoke earlier.

Frank grinned. 'He's a good kid. I think he deserves an extra-large ice-cream.'

When he returned to their spot, he found two of the sailors talking to Vee, who was sat on her towel smiling sweetly at them. Peter, he saw, was holding their ball, a delighted smile on his face.

'I don't think so but thanks all the same. Anyway, I think we all need a rest for a while and here are our ice creams.' She looked at him expectantly. 'Rescue me!' her eyes said.

'Maybe later then,' the taller one of the sailors said, taking the hint. He gestured to Peter to pass the ball back, which he did, none too accurately, causing the young man to dive like a goal keeper to catch it. They walked away, chatting animatedly to each other.

'I think those sailors have taken a shine to you,' Frank muttered.

'Nice lads,' she replied, smiling at him, detecting a hint of jealousy. 'Don't worry, I'm not tempted.' She shot a glance at Peter, her eyes wide in the realisation that the young ears might have interpreted what she had just said. But Peter was oblivious, his attention drawn instead to the clamorous noise from the sailors in the pool, demanding the return of the ball, which was duly delivered creating a tumult of boisterous activity as they fought for possession.

'Never mind them, here's your ice-cream. Come on, sit down, Peter, and eat it before it melts,' said Frank.

Peter sat down dutifully on his towel and focused on the melting mess gripped in his fist. But in a few moments, he was once again absorbed with watching the melee in the pool. Frank followed his gaze, wondering what it was that fascinated him. The party had grown, he noted, the sailors having been joined by a group of girls. He had a moment of reflective nostalgia, reliving the life of a young soldier: the camaraderie, the excitement, the thrill of the "pull."

After a few minutes, Peter finished his ice-cream and Vee attempted to clean his face with a handkerchief, which caused him to grimace. Frank smiled, remembering how he had hated being "spit washed."

'Can we swim again now? Can we, Dad?' Peter gazed eagerly towards the pool, apparently having forgotten his previous terror.

'We'll go in later if there's time - it's a bit crowded now.'

The look of disappointment on Peter's face was enough to make him feel guilty. Frank was enjoying the warmth of the sun that had re-emerged from behind the clouds, and the thought of immersing himself in the cold water again seemed far from attractive. He thought rapidly, not prepared to change his mind, but not wanting Peter to be unhappy.

'Listen, if you're careful and stay away from the edge, you can go and watch the game. Would you like that?'

'Are you sure that'll be okay, Frank?' Vee added with an edge of uncertainty in her voice.

'He'll be fine, won't you, Peter. You'll be careful, yes? You're not to go into the pool without either me or your Auntie Vee - you understand, don't you?'

Peter nodded, smiling happily. He held up one of his plastic figurines, his intention clear: he wanted company on his adventure.

'Off you go and remember what I said!' Frank said, waving his hand in a shooing motion.

Peter adopted an earnest "trust me" look and then weaved his way through the throng of people towards the pool.

'Don't worry, Vee – look, we can see him from here. If one of us is watching him all the time, he won't come to any harm. A bit of independence will do him good.' He smiled and patted her hand reassuringly.

***

When Peter reached his chosen viewing position near to the pool side, he looked back towards where his dad and Auntie Vee sat. He waved, and they waved back. His confidence grew and, feeling reassured, he turned around and watched in fascination the splashing mayhem. After a few moments, he sat down, safely away from the edge. He cast another look back and was assured when they both waved to him. He smiled.

***

'Are you sure he'll be alright?' asked Vee anxiously, 'There's a lot of people around.'

Frank shielded his eyes from the sun and stared towards where Peter was sitting.

'He'll be fine - don't worry. He's well back from the pool. We'll fetch him in five minutes or so - maybe give him a quick splash, then we better make tracks - try to beat the traffic going back.'

He glanced at her and saw she was watching Peter intently. Placing his arm around her he drew her in to him. She shivered, despite the heat of the afternoon sun. He reached around for his sports jacket and draped it over her shoulders.

'I'm not really cold - I'm just...,' she sounded tearful.

'What is it Vee?' he whispered, instinct telling him what the problem was, and wondering how he would deal with it.

'Oh, everything: you, me - Helen. I'm sorry, this is all getting too much. I feel like I'm losing control, and most of all, I'm so sad that I've...' she sobbed, her words lost. With a clear sense of prescience, he guessed what she was trying to explain.

'I understand - I know it can't be easy for you.' He held her tight as she cried.

'Everything's going to be okay,' he whispered soothingly, unable to think of anything else to say and knowing he sounded inadequate. He kissed the top of her head which was pressed firmly against his chest.

***

Business at the ice-cream kiosk had been brisk and relentless. For the first time that day, Nicky was free of customers and able to have a cigarette and some quiet contemplation while engaged in her favourite occupation: people watching. Her gaze focused on the young couple sitting in front of her.

He seems to be a lovely man - fine looking as well. Lucky lady! And such a lovely little boy - I wonder where he is?

She smiled at the scene. They were cuddled together, their backs towards her. His arm round her shoulders, which were draped in his jacket - so protective - so considerate! Then he leant down and kissed her - this evoked a memory of a time for her now long gone. It was so heart-warming to see a couple so obviously in love, she thought - but it made her sad as well.

After a few moments, she turned away, feeling a little guilty - but realising also she was jealous. 'Me and Reg used to be like that,' she muttered, 'but not anymore.'

***

'Are you alright now?' He squeezed her shoulders. She sniffed and reached into her bag, pulling out a tissue and dabbing her eyes.

'I'm fine - no, really, I'm okay now.'

He had been holding her closely to his chest; she eased herself free and leant back on her hands, looking up at the sky.

'We've got to end this, you understand that, don't you? This is wrong - we should never have started it - never let it get this far. It's my fault, I'm sorry.'

He said nothing. She glanced at him, noting how he seemed to ponder her words.

'Right oh,' he said, as though nothing had happened, 'let's fetch Peter. I think we should make a move. We don't want to be caught in the traffic.'

She nodded and stood shakily, her legs stiff with cramp.

'I'm going to change,' she said, gathering up her towel and sun cream and stuffing them into her bag. 'Why don't you take all your stuff and pick Peter up on the way to the changing room. I'll meet you at the gate when you're both ready.'

He nodded. 'Okay, no problem.'

He paused and glanced at her. 'We can talk about this later - once we've had a chance to think.'

She did not answer - her attention had been drawn to the pool area near to where Peter had been sitting a few minutes before. There was clamorous noise: shouting, splashing. Several more people had joined the ball-game, and it appeared chaotic and out of control.

'Where's Peter?' she whispered - then shouted, 'Where is he, Frank, he's not there!'

He swung around and stared. 'Oh Christ!' he whispered.

***

Peter had been fascinated by the riotous activity playing out before him in the water. The reckless antics of the men he recognised made him laugh - they were now joined by several others, all engaged in a game that seemed to involve little purpose other than to claim possession of the ball which appeared in and out of the splashing scrum. A throng of bodies surged towards the edge where he sat, causing a wave to wash over his feet. He shuffled backwards. Suddenly, the ball was rolling across the ground. It stopped next to him.

'Here! Here!' shouted several voices from the writhing mass in the water.

Hesitation caused him to glance back to the spot where his dad and Auntie Vee sat. They seemed to be deep in close conversation and weren't looking in his direction. He frowned, uncertain, not wanting to do something he might get in trouble for but compelled to please his new friends as well. His mind made up, he stood quickly, stooped, grabbed the ball, took a few steps towards the pool edge and launched it as high as he could into the air.

The wind was knocked out of him as the larger boy who was running along the edge cannoned into him, knocking him headlong into the water. Lost in the confusion in the midst of bodies all fighting for possession of the ball, he gasped at the shock of the cold water. He went under - panic engulfed him - he thrashed helplessly, desperate for air, unable to reach the surface. A foot kicked him in the stomach forcing an involuntary intake of water. No one saw what happened.

***

Frank stood on the spot where Peter had been sitting - he stared frantically around, his heart pounding wildly.

Vee joined him. 'Peter! Peter!' she screamed, gazing this way and that into the crowd of bodies in the pool. No one heard her above the yelling and splashing. The ball was thrown to the other side, and the scrum followed it.

With the area nearest to her now clear, she spotted the plastic figurine floating on top of the water, recognising it as Steve Zodiac, Peter's favourite. Then, as the ripples of the water subsided, a pink form took shape, wedged underneath the handrail bordering the edge of the pool.

Chapter 53

"CONSEQUENCES"

(Thursday 9th July – late afternoon)
The realisation something terrible had happened spread through the lido like a forest fire. Now that most understood there had been a terrible accident, eyes were drawn to the scene at the poolside.

The riotous game that amused and annoyed in equal measure had stopped abruptly. A little boy lay prostrate on the concrete edge of the pool. The woman (his mother?) finally stopped screaming and hovered over him while a young man administered what many knew as the "kiss of life." Standing a little way back, as though not quite connected with the scene, stood another man (the boy's father?) who seemed in a state of high agitation.

Vee knelt next to the sailor who seemed to know what to do. She wanted to help but didn't know how. 'Breathe - please breathe, Peter,' she whispered.

The determined lifesaver refused to give up and, after most of the many onlookers believed all was lost, a small but audible pop of air emerged from Peter's mouth, followed by a gasp and sudden deluge of water. The sailor rolled him on to his side.

'He's breathing - at least I think he is,' he announced grimly.

The group of young men who, only a short time before, were enjoying the effects of beer, sunshine, and frivolity, sobered up fast. One of them had called an ambulance; the others tried to help by keeping bystanders back and ensuring a clear path to the scene for the medics in expectation of their imminent arrival.

The holiday atmosphere that earlier permeated every corner of the lido vanished. A general understanding was generated as details of what happened passed from group to group in hushed whispers. All eyes focused on the scene by the side of the pool as if watching an open-air theatre production, the stage being occupied by the immobile body of a little boy and, what all believed to be, his distraught parents, who were now kneeling by his body.

An ambulance arrived eventually having fought its way through the late afternoon traffic.

***

Peter, breathing but unconscious, was transferred to the ambulance. Frank travelled with him in the back and Vee followed behind in the Singer.

She tried to keep the ambulance in sight as it weaved in and out of the traffic, but the blue flashing light gradually disappeared into the distance. Her mind in turmoil, she found it almost impossible to concentrate on her driving and, after narrowly avoiding ploughing into the back of a lorry stopped at one of the many traffic lights along the route, she had to pull over to the side to gather herself. But instead of becoming calmer, she sobbed uncontrollably, resting her head on the top of the steering wheel, oblivious to the curious and concerned looks of the pedestrians who passed by.

After several minutes, she looked up in response to tapping on the car window. It was a policeman. She wound the window down and explained what had happened and that she was desperate to reach the hospital. He offered to sit with her as she drove, suggesting a shortcut that would avoid the heavy commuter traffic - she accepted gratefully.

The look on Frank's face when she joined him several minutes later in the waiting area convinced her the worst had happened.

'They put an oxygen mask on him - but they couldn't get him to come around. Vee, they wouldn't tell me anything. I felt completely useless. Oh, Christ, what am I going to tell Helen?'

***

With her head pressed into her hands, she watched him through splayed fingers. He paced up and down, stopping intermittently in front of the shut doors through which the hospital orderlies and nurses had plunged through some thirty minutes previously with the trolley on which Peter lay. Smoking furiously, one cigarette after another, his face ashen, his eyes glistening and staring - it was as if he'd shut down and plunged into his own private world of misery, oblivious to everything other than what might be happening somewhere beyond those doors.

'Frank,' she whispered, 'you need to call Helen - tell her what's happened.'

He shook his head - she could see he was on the verge of tears. 'I can't - please Vee, can you ring her? I don't want to leave here in case - well, you know...'

Her heart sank at the prospect of breaking the news to her sister. But clearly, he couldn't find the inner strength to do it. She left him to his pacing and went in search of a phone box.

With no answer from the home number, she rang the depot. There was no response from her office so she re-dialled and connected with Reception.

'Helen's been in a meeting all afternoon and says she mustn't be disturbed,' announced the receptionist.

'Tell her it's an emergency,' Vee snapped back, 'and please tell her to hurry - I'm in a phone box and I'll run out of money if she's not quick!'

After what seemed to be an interminably long period, she heard Helen's voice, breathless as though she'd been running.

With all the strength she could muster, Vee forced herself to stay calm. She conveyed the message that Peter was seriously ill and he was in an emergency ward at the Queen Alexandra's Hospital in Portsmouth. Helen appeared to be strangely collected in her response - not what she had expected. 'I'm on my way - I'll be there as soon as I can,' she said before ringing off.

When Vee returned to the waiting area, she noted that Frank was now seated, his head held face down in cupped hands.

'She's on her way. Any news?'

He stared at her, his face conveying nervous exhaustion. 'Nothing,' he said.

She squeezed his hand. 'He's in good hands - the best.' The words sounded trite to her, and she doubted they offered any comfort to him.

Her thoughts turned to Helen. She would be on her way now, battling through the early evening rush hour traffic. She'll be desperately worried. This thought opened the gates in her mind and released the self-accusation eager to announce its presence.

Did I cause this? Am I to blame? If I hadn't been having a "crisis," at least one of us might have been watching Peter.

Shame joined guilt as the scenes of the afternoon played through her mind. Once again, she saw herself buried in Frank's chest - both distracted. Just a few seconds - but that's all it took. Why couldn't I have kept my mouth shut? It didn't need to come out then - I should have waited for a more appropriate time. Oh God, is this some form of divine punishment?

***

They sat in silence, each lost in their own thoughts. An hour passed.

'What am I going to tell Helen?' Frank muttered suddenly. 'How am I going to explain I let Peter wander off on his own?'

'It was an accident - just one of those things.'

As soon as the words left her mouth, Vee sensed how hollow her response must seem to him. They both knew why and how they had neglected Peter. She glanced at him, and he stared back at her. Did she see accusation in his eyes?

Pulling her hand away from his, she stared at the wall in front of her on which hung a framed poster depicting a smiling father holding a new born baby. The image blurred as her eyes filled with tears. She leant forward and cupped her face in her hands and then stood abruptly.

'I need some air,' she whispered. Moments later, she was almost running down the corridor towards the entrance, desperate to escape the confines of the hospital and the unbearable claustrophobic anxiety prevailing in the waiting room.

With her eyes fixed on her target: the exit doors ahead of her, she strode right past Helen without noticing.

'Vee - stop!'

Only when Helen grabbed her arm and pulled her to a halt did she register her presence. Her heart jolted - she turned and took a sharp intake of breath. In the first few moments of seeing and recognition, the reality of the situation hit her. Helen stared at her questioningly, her eyes wide with fright as though expecting to be told awful news.

Vee opened and closed her mouth - unable to formulate words. But inside her head, a storm raged - an eruption of thoughts all emphasising the extent of her betrayal and the cataclysmic consequences.

'What's happened? Please tell me! Where is he? Where's Frank?'

'I'm so sorry Helen, it's...' She was about to say, 'all my fault,' but the words were extinguished before being uttered.

'They're with him now - the doctors, I mean. Frank's waiting for news. It was an accident, Helen, it shouldn't have...'

Emotion overwhelmed her, and she couldn't say anything else. Helen grabbed her and heaved her into a close embrace.

'Come on,' she whispered, 'take me to him - I want to see my son.'

They walked back up the hospital corridor along which only minutes before, Vee had been making her escape. The thought of returning to the waiting room horrified her but she understood there was no choice.

The room was empty, except for an old woman who stared at them with mild curiosity when they came in through the swing doors.

'Are you looking for the man what was 'ere?' asked the woman, her eyes bright - perhaps sensing a drama in the offing.

'Yes, we are. Do you know where he went?' Vee said, her heart pounding, feeling an overwhelming sense of foreboding - guessing Frank had been summoned.

'They went in there,' said the old woman, nodding her head at one of the side rooms leading off the waiting room. The door had a "Do not disturb" sign on it.

'Come on, Vee, I've got to know what's happened. I need you with me - please!' Helen grabbed her hand and made a determined move towards the door.

'No. No! Helen, I can't - really, I...'

Vee snatched her hand away. Panic caused her to be far more abrupt than she intended. Helen stared at her, nodded and let go of her hand.

'You and Frank need to do this together - not with me.'

Helen nodded again, her face displaying acceptance but not understanding. She walked to the door, opened it and disappeared inside.

Chapter 54

"RUNNING AWAY"

(Thursday 9th July – early evening)

For the second time in less than an hour, the urge to escape, to distance herself from the point of crisis, seemed too powerful to resist. Vee retraced her steps to the hospital entrance and emerged into the fading light of the day.

With no idea where she was going, or for what purpose other than to get away, she meandered aimlessly. After a few minutes, she spotted a bus station terminal and headed towards it, her pace quickening when she sighted a green double-decker with Southampton showing on its destination board. It was pulling away. She sprinted, launched herself at the steel pole in the open door in the rear corner and jumped onto the platform. Her clumsy entrance, observed with amusement by passengers sitting in the seat overlooking the door, resulted in her slipping to the floor.

'Few too many,' whispered one wag a little too loudly. 'Fuck off!' muttered Vee with uncharacteristic venom, picking herself up and plunging into an empty seat. Her own eyes stared back at her from the steel handrail in front - the eyes were accusing.

'Fares, please!'

The conductor stood next to her, steadying himself on the corner of her seat as the bus lurched into the traffic exiting Portsmouth.

'Fairfield. Single.'

Normally polite, she silently rebuked herself for being discourteous. 'Please,' she added.

'Have to drop you at Ashcroft. We don't go through Fairfield. You should've waited for the Number Fourteen. Not to worry, though - a bit of a hike down to the coast road, but it's a pleasant enough evening. Don't suppose you'll find that too difficult, a fit looking young lady like you. That will be one and nine.'

She sniffed in acknowledgement and paid two shillings without looking at the conductor. He wound the handle on the metal machine he carried around his neck, ripped off the disgorged ticket and handed it to her. Then he rummaged in the leather satchel and gave her change before moving on unsteadily down the central aisle of the bus. She stared at his back, jealous momentarily at his apparent lack of concerns or cares, before returning to her own world of anguish, conscious she was running away, and ashamed of her cowardice.

***

'I gather he was under the water for a few moments?' The doctor fixed him with a level, unblinking gaze. Frank sensed the accusation.

'Maybe - well, I'm not sure - could have been longer because...'

'Oh, my God, Frank!' Helen gaped at him, her eyes raised in incomprehension.

'I'm guessing, he can't swim?'

'No - no he can't. He was watching some lads playing a ball game. I thought he'd be safe - but something happened. I think someone must have knocked him into the pool - I don't know.'

'But you should never have allowed him anywhere near the water on his own.' Her voice became raised. 'He's four years old for Christ's sake? What were you thinking? How....' Her voice broke into a sob and she shot him a look so full of venom, he took a step back.

'We were watching him - he wasn't far away. I don't know - I think something distracted us for a few seconds and...'

'It doesn't take long for someone to drown - especially if they can't swim. I'm afraid you should prepare yourselves for the worst. There may be brain damage – impossible to say yet. He's in a coma and on a ventilator to help him breathe. I'm sorry, I can't give you better news.'

'How bad? I mean how much damage do you think there could be?' Helen whispered, on the verge of tears.

'We'll need to do some tests - we won't know until we get the results.' The doctor paused. 'If his brain was starved of oxygen, even for a brief period, there is a possibility he may never wake.' He eyed them both in turn, nodding to emphasise the gravity of his meaning. 'I must warn you of that,' he added.

Helen took a sharp, audible intake of breath. Frank put his arm around her and squeezed her in. She pulled away as though his touch was poisonous

'Anyway, I'll leave you with Nurse Ellis, here - she'll go through some details with you about what happens next. He got up, making to go, and then paused as if gathering his thoughts. 'Your son's in the best hands here, please be assured of that. We'll do everything we can to help him.'

'Thank you,' she murmured. Frank said nothing - he stared at a point on the floor between his feet.

The nurse spent several minutes with them; neither listened to what she said, both were immersed in their own private thoughts.

'So, if you would just sign your authorisation as parents here.' She handed over a clipboard and a biro. Helen signed.

'Can I see him?'

Frank noted the emphasis on the "I," sensing a barrier being built between them, which would exclude him.

'Yes, of course - I would imagine that would be fine. Just give me a few moments to check what's going on.' The nurse left the room.

They sat in silence. Although only inches apart, they may as well have been sitting on separate sides of the hospital. A few minutes passed during which it appeared obvious Helen could not bring herself to talk to him. The nurse returned. 'If you'd like to follow me.'

Neither was prepared for the scene in the small room in which their son lay. Peter was obscured by a nurse, who was busy adjusting various knobs and switches on the equipment. A mass of wires and pipes trailed down to the bed. She turned when they came through the door and smiled, a sad smile, filled with sympathy and understanding. Neither took comfort from it.

Making a final adjustment to the equipment, the nurse stood aside revealing Peter, his face almost covered by a green rubber mask, pumping in oxygen from the machine that emitted a rhythmic 'thunk, thunk' to accompany the artificial breathing.

'Why don't you sit down here?' said the nurse to Helen, indicating a chair next to Peter's head. Frank could see her hands were shaking as she fumbled for Peter's hand. She could only hold his fingertips because his arm appeared to be encased in wires and tubes.

'It's a heart monitor; and we've also put him on a drip, to keep him hydrated,' the nurse explained.

Helen whispered something to Peter, which Frank could not make out. He stood at the foot of the bed helpless and excluded - again. Suddenly, she rose and brushed past, causing him to step back. She said nothing - her face locked in a mask of pure anguish, or was it fury?

The door swung shut leaving him alone with the nurse and his son. He sat in the chair she had vacated and, like she did, he grasped the tips of Peter's fingers. His eyes were closed, he noticed, and he appeared peaceful.

'Is he going to be okay?' he asked, dreading the response.

'We're doing everything we can for him We'll be monitoring him closely. Look, I'm sorry - I know you're worried - but I can't tell you anything further at this stage.'

She must have dealt with situations such as these many times before, he concluded. No offering of false hopes. He stayed for almost half an hour sitting, staring unseeing at the polished floor tiles.

'The best thing you can do is take your wife home. Come back in the morning - you'll feel better after some rest.' The nurse placed her hand on his shoulder; he had forgotten she was in the room.

He nodded. 'Hang in there, son,' he murmured. Standing, he made to leave but then stopped. Fishing in his jacket pocket, he pulled out three plastic figurines. He stood them up on a small metal shelf jutting from the machinery next to Peter's head.

'Your friends will watch over you,' he whispered.

***

He found her sitting in the hospital chapel in a central pew, her head bowed as if in prayer. It surprised him to find her here - she was not religious, at least not in the traditional regular church attendee sense. Uncertain what to do, he stood immobile watching, wanting to join her but sure he would not be welcome. After a few minutes, she turned and fired an accusing stare at him. Perhaps she had sensed his presence, or more likely felt the sudden draught when he opened the door.

Holding out his hands in a placatory gesture, he said, 'I come in peace,' regretting straight away the slight hint of humour.

She turned her head away again and stared towards the front of the chapel where there was a stained-glass window depicting the Virgin Mary cradling a swaddled baby Jesus.

He approached silently and, without knowing why, sat in the pew behind her. After a brief hesitation, he placed his hand on her shoulder, giving it a gentle squeeze. The rebuff, he expected, didn't happen - she did not pull away. He fumbled in his mind for something to say in the sure knowledge whatever emerged from his mouth would be inadequate. Finally, he said, 'I'm so sorry - I wish I could turn the clock back, but...'

'Don't!' Her voice conveyed a warning. He removed his hand and hung his head.

'I know you're sorry. But being sorry isn't going to help Peter, is it?'

In different circumstances, he might have retaliated. Their arguments often followed the pattern where an attempt at pacification by him was met with a rebuff. Instead, he put his hand back on her shoulder and said nothing, wishing she might respond with just the smallest sign of affection.

'If...,' she started to speak, but seemed to find it hard to utter the words formed in her mind. 'If,' she began again, 'we lose our son because of your negligence, I will never, ever forgive you!' With that, she stood, shrugging off his arm, causing his wrist to drop and thud on the back of the pew.

'Come on Helen, you're exhausted. Let's go home. We can come back first thing in the...'

'You can go home!' she snapped, 'I'm going nowhere, not while my son is lying there fighting for his life. You go, Frank. We don't need you here and,' she paused and then looked at him, 'I don't want you with me.'

***

He emerged from the hospital entrance into the dark of the early evening in an almost hypnotic state of numbness. After the stifling heat of the hospital, it felt cold. He turned up the collar of his sports jacket and reached into the pocket. 'Sod it!' Vee forgot to give him the keys.

With a heavy sigh, he realised he would have to hunt down Helen again and coax her into giving him the ones for the Healey. What in normal circumstances would be a simple transaction was likely to be problematic. He swore softly and re-entered the hospital.

As he approached the ward, he sensed something was wrong. From several yards along the corridor, he could hear Helen's voice, shouting, hysterical. Quickening his step, he entered to see her being held back by a nurse as she tried to reach the closed door to the inner room.

'Let them do their job. You'll be in the way. There's nothing you can do!' He detected an edge of panic in the nurse's voice.

'Out of the way, please!' A white-coated doctor and a medic pushed past him. They ignored Helen and disappeared into the room. A brief blur of activity could be seen before the door swung shut again.

Helen's hysterical energy vanished when she became aware of him. She collapsed into his arms, sobbing.

He coaxed her into a chair. She clung to him tightly when he sat down next to her and then put her head on his chest. He stroked her hair.

'What's happened?' he asked a nurse hovering nearby.

'I can't really say for sure,' she stuttered. 'I mean, I can't give you any details. The crash team was called - that's the two who just came in. They'll be doing everything they can. Please try not to...'

He guessed that she was about to add 'worry.' She smiled weakly. 'Why don't I make you both a nice cup of tea?' she said.

'Please,' he replied, nodding, guessing she was a student nurse, and feeling sorry for her, understanding how she would want to escape from the tense atmosphere over which she had no control or true comprehension.

'His heart's stopped. He's going to die!'

He looked down at the top of her head, unable to think of anything to say. At that moment, the door opened, and the white-coated doctor emerged. Helen made to rise.

'Sit down, sit down.' The doctor pulled a chair over and sat in front of them. 'We got him back, I'm happy to say.'

'Oh, thank God!' She began to cry again. The doctor waited patiently until she calmed a little and then took both of her hands in his.

'You've got a tough little boy there. He's hanging on. We will be watching him all the time in case his ticker plays up again.'

The young nurse reappeared carrying two cups and saucers. Her eyes were wide open, frightened looking, uncertain how to decipher the scene she had walked into.

'Perfect - a cup of tea. Come on, Mrs Armstrong, you will be no use to your son if you keel over from dehydration. Now then, I'm guessing you're going to want to stay. How about if we ask Nurse Ellis here to find you an empty side room with a bed in it? You look done in, the pair of you!'

Frank took both cups and handed one to Helen, relieved she accepted it.

'Will you wake me - I mean if something happens?' she whispered. He noted she appeared a little brighter, as though she had stood on the edge of the abyss and could now take a step back.

At Frank's request, they were allowed into the room to see Peter for a few minutes. The rhythmic thudding of the life support machine that presented so alien before now invited hope. They left, together this time.

Nurse Ellis found them a side room which contained a narrow hospital bed and a chair. It was stifling. Helen lay on the bed and stared blankly at the ceiling.

'Where did Vee go?' she asked.

'I've no idea. I think everything became too much for her and she went home. Must have, or she would have come and found us, wouldn't she?'

'Can you try to call her? She'll be sick with worry. Oh, and can you ring Dad? He knows nothing about what's happened, and he needs to know.'

In less than a minute, she fell asleep. He perched on the edge of the bed and, despite the growing discomfort, felt unable to move. Her hand rested on his own - the intimacy and implied affection was tenuous and fragile, but he wanted to maintain it for as long as possible. In seconds, she slipped into a deep sleep. After several minutes, he lowered himself gently into the seat next to the bed where he watched her, his exhaustion gradually overcoming him, his eyes becoming heavy. Then, he remembered he was supposed to contact Vee and Bob. Rising quietly, he left the room in search of a phone box.

He rang Vee's number first. No answer. Guessing she had gone to her dad's, he tried him next. After a few rings, the familiar formality of Bob's voice said: 'Fairfield 2359?' Bob's cheerful tone suggested he knew nothing. He responded with friendly surprise, not the frantic series of questions that would have followed if he knew what happened.

'Vee? No - haven't heard from her.'

After Frank explained the situation, Bob wanted to drive to the hospital straight away. It took several minutes to persuade him to delay until the morning. As he walked back to the side room, he was troubled by thoughts of Vee. She left earlier with no warning a few hours ago.

Where was she? And what state was she in?

Chapter 55

"ANGUISH"

(Thursday 9th July 1964 – late evening)
The moon emerged from behind a cloud, throwing a finger of silvery light across the sea below before being obscured again. A gentle breeze wafted across the top of the cliff picking up a small fragment of paper from the litter bin next to the bench and blowing it across the grass verge bordering the fence line marking the edge. Having sat down only a few minutes ago after walking for some time, it did not take long for the coolness of the night to have an effect.

At just after midnight, Helen was asleep on a hospital bed, Frank was trying to make himself comfortable in a chair next to her, and Vee sat shivering on a cliff top bench, contemplating the latest catastrophe to beset her.

Earlier, she had walked from the point where the bus dropped her off at the top of the hill leading down to the coast road. Despite the not inconsiderable distance, and the fatigue she should have been experiencing, a state of nervous energy drove her on. She stopped at an off license on the edge of Fairfield and bought a half bottle of vodka and a packet of cigarettes. By this time the sun had set, and twilight transformed to darkness.

Instead of walking towards her flat, she crossed the road and joined the coastal path which ran east and west. Her decision to head in a westerly direction was based on no definable logic. The easterly path would have taken her home, but the thought of being closed in was abhorrent. She needed to walk as if the physical act might reduce her intense anxiety.

The route took her past Helen and Frank's house, which remained in darkness. An elderly couple walking their dog passed her - the man greeted her with a brief 'Good evening' - she could not bring herself to reply.

After an hour of aimless exertion, she spotted a bench, positioned at a small prominence overlooking the cliff edge. She stopped to rest, and then remembered the vodka, unopened, in her handbag.

It failed to help - at least not at first. Her thoughts tortured her with relentless reminders of her guilt. Taking a larger gulp, hoping this might quicken the dulling of her pain, caused her to gag and choke. With eyes streaming, she screwed the lid back onto the bottle and dropped it back into her handbag.

She lit another cigarette, leaned back into the bench and stared out to sea. It was a beautiful evening - the moon, almost full, cast a swathe of light across the calm expanse of water stretching out before her. But her sight was turned inwards to her guilty, fearful thoughts.

'Why did I run away?' she muttered.

'Because I'm a coward,' she answered herself after a pause.

The image of Helen trying to pull her to the closed door appeared in her mind. She needed me, and I wouldn't help her. Her sense of panic returned as if she were back there again. What had been happening behind that door? Why was Frank called in?

'Because, Peter's dead,' she whispered, 'and I'm to blame.'

The vodka beckoned from the top of her open handbag. She reached for it, unscrewed the lid and took a gulp - and then another. Half an hour later, she stared through bleary eyes at the empty bottle in her hand. The pain had not diminished, and she wished she had bought a full one. She rose shakily to her feet and heaved it in an underarm motion towards the bin. It missed the target and shattered on the small area of concrete upon which the bench was fixed. Shivering with the cold, she looked left and right along the path, disorientated and uncertain. A momentary visitation of common-sense set her off in the right direction towards her flat.

***

(Friday 31st July 1964 – early morning)
Frank woke with a start and stared around, panicked at the unfamiliar surroundings. The memories of the day before came back in a rush. He groaned, a combination of discomfort and recollection. Glancing down at the bed, he noticed Helen was awake too. She was staring fearfully at the door to the room.

The door swung open and the doctor, who had saved Peter's life a few hours before, poked his head through the gap and then entered. He was smiling - this allayed an instant onset of panic.

'Your son's awake. He opened his eyes about ten minutes ago. I thought you would want to hear the good news.'

Helen slipped on the polished floor as she jumped off the bed. 'Is he okay? Can we see him?' She was reaching down for her shoes, struggling to pull them onto her feet.

The doctor signalled to her to sit down. Although he smiled, his voice soothing, something in his tone suggested that all might not be well.

'He became very agitated and distressed, so he's been sedated. He's much calmer now, but he's still being helped to breathe. I think you should both go and be with him. But...,' he looked meaningfully at Helen, 'I need you to stay calm for his sake. I'm hoping we can take him off the assisted breathing - but let's make him aware you're here, I think that'll help settle him down.'

A few minutes later, they followed the doctor through the door into the room where Peter lay. As they entered,

405

the familiar face of the nurse from the previous evening turned towards them from where she sat on the edge of the bed. She smiled. 'Look who's here,' she said.

The room appeared strangely silent. She moved a little to one side revealing Peter's face, fixed in an expectant expression. No longer concealed by the green breathing mask, his face still bore a red line where it had been. His face creased into a smile as soon as he spotted them.

The nurse stood, allowing Helen to replace her at the bedside. Frank couldn't speak. Helen, he saw, was crying softly and hugging Peter, who cried as well.

'The mask was upsetting him - he kept pulling it away from his face, so I guess you might say he decided he wanted to breathe for himself.'

The nurse addressed herself to the doctor, who nodded in agreement. They continued a whispered professional conversation. Frank overheard occasional words: 'not out of the woods yet' - 'keep him monitored' - 'a few days.'

'Daddy's here - look.' Helen had stopped crying and leant back to allow Peter to see him.

Peter smiled - and then he looked upwards and pointed to the metal apparatus next to his head.

A few moments later, three plastic spacemen - his guardian angels retrieved from the shelf were gripped in his hand. The trauma of the last twelve hours apparently forgotten - he was ready to play again.

***

The persistent ringing of the telephone woke her from a dreamless oblivion. For the briefest of moments, she felt disorientated - a combination of the alcohol in her body, and the sudden awareness she was in bed fully clothed. The shrill noise revived the sensation of intense anxiety the vodka had dulled. Glancing at the alarm clock next to her bed, she saw it was almost 11 o'clock; the daylight flooding through her bedroom window showed it was morning and not late in the evening.

The events of the previous day deluged back into her mind in a tidal wave of images and emotions. Memories re-engaged her sense of fear and foreboding, which she connected with the urgent sound. She knew the call would have something to do with the chain of events from which she had tried to escape. Answering it would open the door back into that world - the thought of this filled her with intense fear.

Sliding her feet onto the floor, she groaned, partly from the pain that every movement created, but also from the realisation that, whoever was on the other end of the line, would not go away. Slowly and carefully, she stepped out of her bedroom and into the hallway.

She paused at the table on which the phone lay, reluctant to pick up the handset but knowing she must. Her hand was about to snatch up the receiver when the ringing stopped. 'Damn!' Even though this came out as a whisper, her head thudded in pain. She turned - the prospect of crawling back under the counterpane and escaping from reality presented as highly attractive.

The phone rang again just as she started to walk back to her bed. She turned and grabbed the receiver. 'Hello!' Her voice came out in an anguished squeak.

'Vee! It's Frank. Listen - everything's okay - well, sort of! Peter's going to be alright! At least they seem to think so. He's awake! We've spoken to him and he's talked to us. He wants to come home! Hello, are you there?'

Her sense of relief was so overwhelming she took several moments to gather her senses before she could speak. 'Oh, thank God!' she whispered at last.

'Listen - Helen's with your dad at his place. I'm here at the hospital.'

He spoke rapidly as though eager to talk. She sensed the release in his voice.

'They want to keep him in for a couple of days for observation; you know, to be on the safe side. Helen's going to pop by and pick you up if that's okay with you.'

'Yes, of course. Oh, Frank…'

Vee started a breathless explanation about why she disappeared without telling him.

'I couldn't stand it, Frank, I had to get away. I'm so sorry I left you, and,' she paused, 'Helen...?'

'Don't worry. It's not a problem - not now. Everything's going to be okay. Oh, buggeration! I'm out of coins, I'll...'

She heard the pips and then the phone went dead. The shaking began as soon as she put the receiver down. Walking into the kitchen, she considered smoking a joint - there were always several ready-made spliffs in Carrie's secret stash. But Helen would be here at any moment. Instead, she decided a cigarette and a mug of coffee would go some way to help calm her nerves which were jangling. A few minutes later, the whistle of the kettle announced the water had boiled. She was about to pour water on the Maxwell House coffee when the doorbell rang.

Chapter 56

"A POLICEMAN VISITS"

(Friday 31ˢᵗ July 1964 – late morning)
Detective Inspector Lester wondered whether he may have wasted his time again in a fruitless visit. There didn't seem to be any signs of life in the house. A rolled local newspaper wedged out of the letter-box, and there were two bottles of gold-top on the doorstep, each of which, he noted, was pierced with the tell-tale signs of blue tit incursions. The morning sunshine was intensifying, auguring another warm day; the milk will heat up nicely, he thought. He rang the bell.

Not expecting a response, he turned back to his car - but then he heard a click from the door. It opened to reveal a young woman in a dressing gown who, despite looking as if she might, as his Mother would describe it, have been dragged through a hedge backwards, was without a doubt pretty. The smile on her face changed abruptly. It seemed she had been expecting somebody but not him.

'Miss Park?'

She nodded, her face looking frightened now as if anticipating being served with bad news.

He reached into his pocket and pulled out a small black leather wallet which he flipped open and held up to her face.

'Detective Inspector Lester,' he said cheerfully, 'I was rather hoping you might help me with my enquiries. Do you mind if I come in?'

***

They were standing in the living room. He was eyeing her with an expectant expression. She stared back at him and then gathered herself.

'Won't you sit down?' she said, indicating a battered-looking armchair. 'The kettle has just boiled. Would you like a tea, coffee?'

'A cup of tea would be nice; white with two, thanks,' he replied.

After the brief period of relieved euphoria following Frank's call, she had now plunged straight back into the pool of anxiety. It had been tempting to demand the reason for the intrusion: why would the Police be interested in her? But a shadow of doubt emerged and warned her to be careful: something told her the policeman's visit had nothing to do with the events of yesterday. The still clear memories of the cottage, Jonny, and the fire played through her mind. As she stirred sugar into the mug of tea, she noticed her hand was shaking.

'Got to stay calm!' she whispered silently to herself, feeling the onset of panic. She re-entered the living room with a mug of tea.

As if to confirm her fears, the Inspector handed over a fragment of a photograph, the incomplete image instantly familiar to her.

'I've been reliably informed this lady is you.'

He held the damaged picture in the palm of his hand, his arm extended so she could examine it.

She nodded. 'Yes, I think that probably is me. It was a long time ago. My hair used to be like that and I always wore a beret. The university library's in the background - I mean Manchester University - where I studied for my degree.'

He smiled. 'Have a good look,' he said in an encouraging tone, 'Can you confirm that is you?'

She nodded. No point in denying the fact, she reasoned with herself - but her heart pounded. He nodded with a satisfied expression.

'Here's what looks like a man's arm over the girl's - your shoulders?' He pointed to the image. I need you to think carefully now.' He stared meaningfully at her, his smile gone.

'Do you know who this man is, Miss Park?'

***

(Friday 31ˢᵗ July 1964 – late afternoon at the hospital)

Frank inhaled deeply and then blew out smoke in a stream from his nostrils. He appeared to be thinking. Vee gazed at him wanting a response, perhaps a small thread of comfort.

'I think everything's okay,' he said finally, his head nodding as if agreeing with his own statement. 'So, all he asked you to do was state who the man in the picture was - in other words, Jonny.'

'Yes. But he really pressed me on whether I'd had any contact with him since university like he was trying to find out if I might have had something to do with his death.'

'Tell me again precisely what you told him,' he said, 'Try to remember every detail you can.'

'Well, I didn't tell him anything about the fact we were at the cottage. And I said nothing about the business at the school. No one knows - only you.'

He nodded, smiling encouragingly.

'Great! So, what did you tell him? What did you say about your contact with Jonny?'

'I said he sent me a letter asking me to meet him, and I told him he delivered it to Dad's address, and that *he* gave it to me. He pressed me on that, asked me whether I still had it - I told him I threw it out.' She paused, frowning. 'He spoke to Professor O'Donnell, my tutor at the

411

university. He told him about Jonny's harassment of me - the reason I almost packed in my degree. I just know he's putting two and two together.'

'But that's okay! As far as he's concerned, this bloke, off his rocker on drugs, was obsessed with you and moved to Fairfield to make contact.'

He paused, studying her face.

'All you've done is provided a probable identity to the body. There's no evidence suggesting you were being blackmailed - unless you told someone other than me - your friend for example.'

'No. I almost told Carrie, but I told you instead. I did tell her, I thought I spotted him at the Marina and how that frightened me. But nothing about what happened after then. Only you and I know about the blackmail. And I still don't understand how Jonny got hold of those photos!'

He grinned and reached to put his arms around her in an embrace. She rested her head on his chest for a few moments and then pulled away gently.

'I hope you're right. I desperately want this to go away now. But everything else...'

She looked at him steadily.

'It stops now. These last couple of days - well, they've been a warning and I won't chance fate again.'

Chapter 57

"RETRIBUTION"

(Wednesday 15th July 1964)

'Alright, Dad, calm down! The main thing is, Peter's okay now.'

With his face flushed and angry, her dad paced around his living room. Helen worried about his blood pressure.

'No, this is wrong,' he said, waving his pipe to add emphasis to his words. 'Peter nearly drowned for heaven's sake! Who was looking out for his safety? No - the more I hear about what happened, the more appalled I am about the complete lack of care in a public arena!'

'But,' protested Helen, 'ultimately the fault lies with us - I mean with Frank and Vee. Frank's admitted he gave Peter permission to go alone to the poolside and...'

'Bloody stupid thing to do! Completely irresponsible!'

'They were distracted. Frank said they got into a flap because they couldn't find the car keys. That's when it happened.'

'Yes, very foolish and downright careless. They shouldn't have let Peter out of their sight. But it still doesn't change the fact the lido management didn't post life guards. According to Frank, the pool was packed, perhaps overcrowded. The whole situation beggars belief! Completely unacceptable and no doubt illegal. I'll bloody sue them!'

'Can't we leave it, Dad? I'm just so relieved Peter survived and, so far as the doctors can tell, with no real damage. And we are not blameless. It's six of one and half a dozen of the other, and...'

He held up his hand - a familiar gesture, one signalling his decision was made.

'No! I'm going to speak to the company solicitor – I'm sure, he'll be able to make a case.'

She sighed, knowing further protest would be pointless. What she didn't know at this point was how her father's determination to seek retribution would change all their lives irrevocably.

***

(Thursday 23rd July 1964)

Fiona winced at the torrent of expletives emanating from behind the closed door. Although Mr Jermy used bad language freely, oblivious to the reactions of others, something was seriously amiss this morning.

Following the normal pattern of his tirades, he eventually went quiet. She glanced at the door, making a mental note to polish the brass plaque, which announced the office belonged to "Mr Richard Jermy, Cdr RN Rtd – Manager". Rising from her desk seat, she walked over and knocked. Hearing no answer, she opened the door and poked her head through the gap, adopting her well-practiced winning smile.

'Everything alright, Mr Jermy? Can I get you a cup of coffee? Sounds like you need one!'

He glanced up from where he sat behind his desk and waved a piece of paper at her, accompanied by a further stream of bad language.

'This could ruin us, right at the start of the summer season.'

Well used to his peremptory method of communication, which always required unravelling as it appeared to rely on the recipient having sensory perception, she walked over to his desk.

'Can I see?' she asked, knowing he trusted her wisdom as his personal assistant.

He handed the paper over. She sat in the chair opposite him and read, conscious of his eyes boring into her, although on this occasion not in the usual lustful way - he was obviously a very worried man.

The letter, bearing the official looking letterhead "Morgan & Hill Solicitors," and written in the pompous and convoluted language of the legal profession, was clear in its meaning and intent.

Fiona knew about the unfortunate incident involving the near drowning of a young boy at the lido. She had been working that day and witnessed events at a distance from her office on the first floor above the changing rooms overlooking the pool. As would be expected of her, she investigated the incident and concluded it was just an unfortunate accident. The boy had not been, as far as she could ascertain, under proper supervision by his parents. Although there were no life guards on duty, a sign on the lido wall next to the entry gate stated - for those who could be bothered to read it - *"Use of the pool is at swimmer's own risk,"* and *"Children under the age of 14 must be under the supervision of a responsible adult."*

She had telephoned the hospital the following morning and received the happy news that, although it had been 'touch and go,' the little boy had recovered.

Having read the words in the official letter twice to ensure her understanding, she handed it back to Mr Jermy. He stared at her expectantly.

Choosing her words carefully, she said, 'Do you think we were overcrowded as it suggests? That's a point we haven't taken account of. Maybe there's a by-law or other council mandate about lifeguard cover.'

She had always worried about the lack of properly defined processes and procedures and, in her view, the rather cavalier attitude with which Mr Jermy managed the

415

facility. He would describe his approach as 'managing by the seat of my arse!' He hated what he called 'petty bureaucracy, the stuff of pen pushers.'

'Full, yes! I would imagine every lido in the South of England would've been stuffed to the gunnels on that day - after all, the weather was perfect! Over-crowded? What exactly does that mean? We don't stipulate a fixed maximum capacity. We've never needed to bother with one before and, anyway... well, it would be impossible to know to a man how many visitors there are at any one point, it wouldn't be...'

His voice was raised, his face red with the perceived injustice of the accusation of negligence being made against him. He paused before adding, 'And how many accidents have there been in the three years since I've been Captain of this establishment?'

'None that might be considered serious,' she replied, adopting a soothing tone. 'Look, Mr Jermy - Richard, we need to build our defence - prove we were not to blame, or at least not to the extent suggested in the letter. Leave this with me - I'll try and work something out.'

***

The sky was grey and overcast, the air damp and clammy - not a good day for a lido visit. Only a handful of visitors were using the pool for exercise. Fiona sat with Nicky, the owner of the ice cream kiosk, at a small table in front of the closed shutters – there would be little prospect of customers on a day like this.

'They set up right there in front of me, a few feet away,' Nicky said, pointing. 'The little boy was with them. I remember they took him to the pool at one point. The man asked me to keep an eye on their gear. Such a lovely family. It was so sad what happened later! It really upset me.'

'Tell me about the parents - did they seem responsible? We're they attentive to the boy?'

'Well, yes - but...' Nicky hesitated. 'I mean, they didn't play with him or talk to him *all* the time. They both had a kip, I noticed. But the boy seemed happy enough- amusing himself and staying put, sitting on his towel.'

'Would you be able to say at what point the boy went off on his own?'

'Not precisely, no. I remember noticing he wasn't with them - but it didn't strike me as odd, not at the time. Only after - you know - when it happened, I...'

Fiona detected Nicky might be holding something back.

'Would you say the parents kept a close eye on him when the little boy was on his own at the poolside?'

Nicky appeared to ponder this, then shook her head. 'They can't have done,' she replied emphatically.

'Why not? What makes you so sure?'

'Because they only had eyes for each other at that point. They were all over one another, kissing and cuddling. I felt embarrassed. I'm not being a prude or anything, but this is a public place and, after what happened, I think they should have saved all that for a more appropriate time. The little boy almost drowned.'

Fiona turned her head and gazed up at the windows overlooking the pool; she guessed Mr Jermy might be watching but could not see him. If he was watching, he would have seen the triumphant smile on her face.

'Thanks, Nicky, you've been very helpful. Do you think you might pop by my office at some point today? I will need a written statement from you – just to confirm what you saw.'

Chapter 58

"REALISATION"

(Friday 31st July – late morning)
Helen drove directly from Park's depot in response to the brief, cryptic phone call from the company solicitor.

'There have been some developments. It would be better if we discuss the situation face-to-face.'

As she covered the short distance from Park's central office to "Morgan and Hills Solicitors" on the High Street, she had no idea how devastating the developments would be.

He greeted her with an oily smile, extending his hand to offer a damp handshake before indicating a seat.

'This letter,' he said, waving a piece of paper, 'has arrived from the lawyer representing the Lido's manager. It, err, does rather put a different spin on things.'

She stared at him uncomprehendingly. He gazed back at her, his eyes impassive and unblinking above the rim of his glasses perched on the end of his nose. She detected an almost imperceptible smile hovering on his lips the top of which, she noticed, was sprinkled with small beads of sweat, even though it was cool in the wood-panelled office. *Why did he not simply hand the letter over to me?* she wondered.

Instead, he read, throwing in 'blah blahs' to cover up the legal language and enabling him to get quickly to the key points, which, she suspected, he could not wait to convey.

She anticipated a denial of direct negligence; nothing a few clever words from a solicitor like Eugene Morgan might sort out. *This is just another excuse to bring me to* his office and charge his exorbitant rate for an unnecessary meeting, she told herself as he continued reading.

'It is acknowledged no lifeguards were on duty on the day in question; although it should be pointed out that all appropriate safety procedures, blah, blah. However...' he paused and uttered an 'ahem,' before delivering the devastating words that would change several lives irrevocably.

'... a key witness,' he continued in a monotone, 'Mrs Nicola Austin, who was managing an ice cream kiosk overlooking the position where Mr Armstrong and Miss Park and the boy, Peter Armstrong, had been occupying throughout the afternoon, reported that...'

Another 'ahem' followed. She glanced at him and registered a knowing look.

'... the couple appeared to be engrossed in each other and paid the boy little attention.'

And then the coup de grace.

'Mrs Austin reported seeing them locked in an embrace and kissing thus paying no heed to the boy. Furthermore, the witness stated that she could not see the boy at this point and it can only be surmised, therefore, he had been left unsupervised at the pool edge.'

'What?' she whispered. Her breathing became rapid and laboured.

'Would you like some water, Mrs Armstrong? I know this must be hard for you.'

She shook her head, struggling to get her breathing under control.

He continued, his voice measured, enunciating every word as though anxious nothing must be missed.

'An analysis of the timeline, based on the testimony of several witnesses, including Mrs Austin's, suggests the incident leading to the near drowning of Peter Armstrong occurred whilst Mr Armstrong and Miss Park were distracted and not providing adequate supervision to the minor and, therefore, blah, blah, we await blah, blah.'

She stared at a point on the wall behind the solicitor's head. At first bewildered and uncomprehending, his words hit with ferocious clarity. Unable to speak, she could see he was reading the letter to himself again, his half-rim spectacles perched on the end of his nose.

'We can fight this,' he said, 'if we...'

'Drop the case,' she cut in, her voice conveying certainty and finality.

'But we can still provide a strong argument, Mrs Armstrong. There is clear evidence the lido has a case to answer. The crowding issue could be argued, and...'

She laughed without a hint of amusement.

'Drop it. That's the end of the matter. Please do not discuss this with my father: I'll be talking to him myself.'

She rose from the chair abruptly, fixing him with a glare that challenged him to contradict her, and then strode out of his office. It was only when cocooned in the Healey in the car park, she allowed her pent-up emotion to overwhelm her. She cried uncontrollably for several minutes, and then sat blankly, staring ahead through the windscreen. Her thoughts, at first in turmoil, gradually took form and structure.

Could the witness have been mistaken? She wondered. 'No,' she said aloud. The testimony provided had been specific. Why would the woman lie or exaggerate?

Inevitably, she started to associate Frank's recent behaviour with what had allegedly occurred. There was no denying the fact he had become distant and secretive. She recalled his frequent absences, and her suspicions escalated as half-forgotten incidents re-emerged to be examined.

Her thoughts turned to Vee: hadn't she been unusually friendly with him? Was there something significant in the way they looked at each other?

'My own sister!' she spat the words.

***

(Friday 31st July 1964 – Midday)

If Frank had turned around, he would have seen the car speeding past and recognised it as the Healey. He would no doubt also have registered that it was being driven at a much faster rate than the normal, careful speed at which Helen drove. But he did not turn around.

He sat on a bench overlooking the play area in the newly opened recreational park, built on the bomb site at the bottom end of the high street, watching Peter playing on the roundabout.

The glorious summer heralded by the last few weeks had given way to unseasonal chill and dampness as September approached. He shivered. His mood, however, was not affected by the depressing weather. On the contrary, he could not remember how long it had been since he experienced anything that might be called contentment.

Lighting a cigarette, he leant back in his seat and blew out a cloud of smoke. He smiled as he watched Peter playing.

A sudden thought prodded him, and his smile vanished. 'Christ, I nearly lost him,' he whispered. His heart lurched at the thought. Remembered fear gradually subsided to be replaced by guilt, his frequent companion.

'Come on,' he muttered, reminded of his promise to himself that he must move on and put the past behind him. This thought made him feel better.

Peter's recovery seemed like a miraculous blessing - if he'd been taken away, all other concerns, including his doomed relationship with Vee, would have been pushed into the shadows. But with that storm passed, worry his affair might be discovered caused him several sleepless nights.

Contrary to his expectations, Helen did not press too hard about the events at the lido. He anticipated searching questions about how he and Vee managed to be so distracted that they neglected Peter. But she never challenged the story he concocted with Vee's connivance – how they'd lost the car keys and got into a panic. 'They were in my jacket pocket all the time!' he had added to inject realism to the lie.

The anger Helen displayed at the hospital never reappeared. During the days following the accident, with Peter removed successfully from the life support machine, he took turns with her at his bedside. Each day saw a marked improvement in Peter's condition which delighted them both. Perhaps there was no room left for recrimination and anger.

After five days, Peter was assessed to be out of danger and, according to the doctor, clear of any apparent side effects. His return home was a joyous occasion for the family. Frank recalled how, after persuading Peter to go to bed, he and Helen sat together watching television and sharing a bottle of wine - such contented intimacy had not featured in their relationship for several months.

He glanced at his watch. 'Five more minutes, Peter, then we need to go home!'

***

(Friday 31ˢᵗ July 1964 – late morning)

Vee put the phone back into its cradle and frowned. 'Is that it? Is it all over now?' she muttered. Inspector Lester's voice, flat and matter of fact, gave nothing away. He made it all sound so simple. 'Nothing to worry about,' he said, 'I just need a written statement from you. The body has now been formally identified. As I thought, he is your...' he seemed to hesitate before adding, 'your former boyfriend. I'm sorry, by the way - I don't know if you retained any feelings for him?'

422

'No. None.' she replied. 'It's been years since I felt anything for him.'

'Anyway, I need a statement from you to tie up the loose ends - it won't take long. I'll send a car over to you if you like.'

'No - that won't be necessary - there's a bus in about half an hour.'

She returned the kitchen where her mug of coffee stood cooling on the table and a roll-up, burned almost to the end, balanced precariously on the rim of the ashtray. The drink was tepid but, she decided, still drinkable. She perched on the edge of the table and lit another cigarette.

'I'm jumping at shadows.' The intake of tobacco smoke helped clarify her thoughts. 'I've got nothing to worry about - he wants a statement, that's all.'

Again, her words were whispered as though embarrassed someone might overhear her. But she needed to be convinced - assured there would be no hidden agenda, something to catch her out.

'I'm being paranoid!' she said, louder now, wanting to hear the reassurance of her own voice.

Intervals of acute anxiety were now a constant feature - and getting worse. She lived in a state of perpetual fear. Try as she might, she could not bury her guilt. This and self-loathing were making her life miserable. But added to this was the nagging thought that at any moment her crimes might be discovered - this made life almost unbearable.

She analysed her conversation with the Inspector, searching for hidden meaning, hints that things might not be as straight forward as she hoped.

In moments of rational thought, she would consider the reasons for her persistent state of unease. The incident at the lido merely presented as the latest in a series of misadventures - but the most profound in its effect. The unthinkable never happened - but the near-miss still gave her sleepless nights. In her frequent moments of reflection and introspection, she acknowledged that the last twelve months had been a nightmare.

But the blackmail that threatened the career she loved paled compared to the repercussions, real and imagined, of her affair with Frank. It may be over now - they both accepted this, and, for her part, she was relieved - but this did not take away the fact it happened.

Frank and Helen appeared to be reconciled - their obvious differences ironed out. He acted as if he didn't have a care in the world. She remembered how, at the Sunday lunch they all attended at her dad's house, he seemed relaxed and carefree. She remembered how this made her angry and resentful - it was as if, she thought, it is up to me to carry all the guilt and misery.

'All's well that ends well!' Her mind presented an image of him saying this and wanted to hit out at what she considered to be his unjustifiable smugness.

Every time the phone rang, her heart lurched. She imagined a new disaster, a threat of exposure. Her anxiety levels had reached such a painful peak, she contemplated making an appointment to see the doctor - perhaps he might prescribe something to help.

Her thoughts returned to the phone call received earlier that day from the Police Station. *Could it be so simple? Is that it? Just a brief statement and then the nightmare will be over? Surely not!*

***

Had Vee been able to read Inspector Lester's mind, she would have been far less anxious and suspicious. A tidy, meticulous man despite his shambolic appearance, he smiled in satisfaction the case had finally reached closure with an identification of the body at the burned-out cottage.

A long career had hardened him to death in its many guises. He felt nothing for the man who once lived in the ravaged shell of a body. That pathetic individual threw his own life away through weakness and foolishness. As he sat at his desk, the small scrap of a photograph now so familiar to him pinched between two fingers, he pondered what he found out about him.

With the probable identity provided by Miss Park, corroborated from dental records retained at Strangeways Prison in Manchester, the body was identified. From there, fragments of the man's life emerged. And what a sad and wasted life it had been, he thought.

The product of a union between a married naval officer and a wealthy divorcee, a once hopeful movie actress, the presence of a child was likely to have been an unwelcome intrusion. His mother packed him off to boarding school as soon as she could and had very little to do with him throughout his childhood.

Out of curiosity rather than necessity, the Inspector contacted the minor public school in which Jonathan had been exiled and was put in contact with the now retired headmaster.

'A loner - a strange boy not liked by his peers. They were repelled by his strangeness. I think he was bullied. But, he possessed a sharp intellect. He could have done well with a little application, but...'

'Dreadful, wayward woman! Absolutely no interest in anything but herself,' was the retired headmaster's response when asked about the mother. Another wasted, pointless life it transpired. Just like her unwanted, loveless son, she ended it by her own hand and was found drowned in a hotel room bath in Paris, the post-mortem revealing she had taken a cocktail of barbiturates. There had been no suicide note.

A glance at the clock on the wall told him Miss Park would arrive soon. He smiled, allowing himself a sense of satisfaction at a job well done - he hated loose ends and this one was now nicely tied up.

***

(Friday 31ˢᵗ July 1964 – 1pm)
Vee was reaching for her raincoat, hooked untidily on the coat stand when the sound of a car pulling up outside made her turn towards the front door. She recognised the throaty reverberation of the three-litre engine and frowned.

Didn't he agree to give me some space? Why would he be visiting me now?

She glanced nervously at the opaque glass of the door, expecting his silhouette to appear. Her paranoia kicked in again - is this more bad news?

'What does he want? Why can't he leave me alone?' She fumbled with the door latch and pulled it open.

'Helen?'

'You sound surprised - did you think it would be Frank?'

Something was very wrong. Helen's expression - was it repressed rage? Her eyes bore into her own - as if searching her soul.

'I think you've got something you need to tell me. We can do it here on the doorstep and you can share your sordid secret with your neighbours - or we can go inside - just the two of us. You can tell me all about you - and him.'

***

They were in the small living room. Vee stood with her back to the fire place; Helen leaned against the doorframe.

'Tell me. I'm not angry - I just want to know what's been going on? Tell me everything and maybe I'll be able to understand.'

The look on Helen's face suggested she did not need to be told anything at all - she knew already.

426

Vee's heart thumped - she trembled and gripped her hands together to stop them shaking. All the time, her sister stared at her with an odd smile. Had he told her? she wondered. Perhaps, he came clean as a way of moving forward. No, he wouldn't do that! But how has she found out?

'Did he start it? It's okay. You can tell me? Let's try and work this out.'

Helen spoke quietly and without emotion - almost kindly, which appeared so incongruous. 'Come on, I appreciate this must be difficult for you - but I have to hear the truth.'

She continued to fix her with that icy stare - her lips turned at the corners in what seemed now like a sad smile. Nothing in her voice or look projected anger - but there was an aura of knowing suggesting denial would be pointless.

A sudden overwhelming urge to be close to her sister again shattered whatever defences remained. Vee sobbed.

'I'm so sorry, I was...,' she stumbled forward from the fireplace with her arms out.

Helen took a step back, her hands outstretched in a halting gesture.

'No! Don't you come near me. I want nothing - nothing whatsoever...,'

Her gentle unemotional voice was replaced with one Vee had never heard before, '...to do with you again!' Her voice was raised now. 'How dare you!' she shrieked. 'I will never, ever forgive you!'

With that, Helen strode out of the flat, slamming the door so hard it shook in its frame. Seconds later, there was the screech of wheels spinning as the car sped away.

***

Peter sat cross-legged on the carpet in front of the TV set watching "Andy Pandy."

Frank studied him for a moment smiling, and then remembered he needed to monitor the progress of the fish fingers under the grill and the chip pan bubbling away on the top of the stove.

The phone rang. He hesitated, wondering whether he might risk leaving the pan on the gas ring; the chips were nowhere near cooked. Caution prevailed, and he removed it from the heat. He hurried into the hallway and picked up the receiver.

'Fairfield 24 ...'

'Frank, it's me!'

'Yes. Hi! What's wrong - are you...?'

Her voice sounded tremulous - she was crying, breathless - and clearly in a state of panic.

'Okay - look, Vee, calm down. Now, what's up?'

But he did not need to ask her to explain - his instinct told him immediately that bad news would follow.

'It's Helen - she's just left me. She knows everything - about you and me. She's on her way to you now!'

As if on cue, the unmistakable sound of the Healey heralded Helen's arrival. His heart lurched.

'Oh, Christ!' he muttered. He shot a glance towards the front door. For the briefest of moments, he considered exiting through the back door. A myriad of confused thoughts raced through his mind. He stared at the phone receiver in his hand before placing it back in the cradle.

The door rattled - the sound of a key being inserted, the click of the lock, and the cool draught as the door opened. She stood, framed in the open doorway but did not enter. Her eyes bore into his, and in those few moments, he saw anger, disbelief and hurt.

He wanted to say something - but he had no idea what.

'Helen – I...' he began. But the spell was broken by the smell of burning.

The diversion provided a momentary break from her accusing stare. He darted into the kitchen, pulled out the

428

smoking grill plan and tipped it and the blackened remnants of Peter's lunch into the sink.

He sensed her presence behind him and turned reluctantly to face her. She glared at him in a fixed stare before turning her head to the living room where Peter sat cross legged on the carpet engrossed in his TV programme, oblivious to the storm about to erupt a few feet away in the kitchen

'Go to your room, Peter,' she commanded.

Peter swivelled round and stared at them. He looked confused and surprised, then frightened - he must he must have seen something in his mother's face. Without a word, he jumped to his feet and dashed up the stairs. There was the sound of pounding feet followed by his bedroom door shutting with a bang.

Helen flung the car keys onto the kitchen table where they landed before skidding to the floor. She resumed her staring, which she maintained for several seconds before eventually breaking the silence.

'I know everything. No, shut up!'

He raised his hands in placation. She made a slapping motion towards them and he lowered them. Unable to meet the blazing anger in her eyes, he bowed his head and stared unseeing at the kitchen lino.

'How could you, Frank? I mean, having an affair is one thing,' She spat the words - then added in a more emphatic, measured tone, 'but with my sister?'

He continued to stare at the floor. A brief idea he might try denial was quashed as soon as it emerged. No point - she knew the truth, that was clear.

'Why, Frank? Wasn't I enough for you?'

Glancing up from his focus on the kitchen lino, he met her gaze, but only briefly. He made an inarticulate sound as if trying to find suitable words but sighed instead, unable to formulate anything coherent or meaningful.

'You've destroyed everything, Frank,' she said slowly, 'our marriage, our family, and your future. Why? How could you do that?' Her voice had become raised and he detected her apparently rehearsed stance beginning to crumble. He took a step towards her, his arms outstretched as if to hold her.

'Don't!' she shrieked, taking a step back, as though his touch might be poison. 'You will never come near me again, ever! You! You disgust me!'

She tugged at the ring on her finger, her face twisted in a mask of fury.

'I don't want this! Sell it - give it to that bitch if you want!'

She hurled the ring at him. It flew past his head and chinked against the window.

Although she stood an arm's length away from him, the invisible barrier between them prevented the physical contact he wanted. At that moment, he acknowledged the stark veracity of her words: beyond any shadow of a doubt he had indeed lost everything. Nothing he could say or do would help him. He did not trust himself to speak.

Feeling a desperate need to escape, he edged past her. She stepped back sharply, a grimace on her face as if physical contact with him might contaminate her. He walked the short distance to the back door, grabbed his cigarettes and lighter from the pocket of the army greatcoat hanging next to it, and slipped out of the back door.

The relentless drizzle soaked into his shirt, but he did not notice or care. When he tried to light a cigarette, his hands shook.

After twenty minutes of rambling, incoherent thoughts and three cigarettes, he re-entered the house. As he opened the back door and stepped into the hallway, there stood his old army suitcase on the hall rug at the foot of the stairs. The keys to the Healey had been placed on top of it together with a white envelope. With a deep sigh, he picked up the envelope, pulled out the note inside and read it.

He crumpled the paper in his hand and dropped it to the floor. As he stood staring blindly at his case, the words in the note played through his mind, and an understanding was realised: a dark era in his life was about to begin.

"We're finished. I am going to divorce you. I want you out of my house now and don't want you to come back."

Chapter 59

"AFTERMATH"

The phone cut off suddenly. Vee understood why, imagining the state of panic Frank must be in. She placed the receiver down and sunk to the ground, a wave of self-pity sweeping over her.

'Why now, after we'd ended it? It's so unfair!' she whispered.

After several minutes the tears dried up. More would follow for sure - but for now, numbness enveloped her. She rose unsteadily, staggered over to the kitchen table and sat down. After lighting a roll-up, she leant back in her seat and stared at the ceiling.

'He'll blame me - of course, he will,' she muttered bitterly, 'It will be me who started it - me who led him on.'

She spoke these words to the empty room, knowing as soon as she uttered them that Frank could never divert guilt away from himself. Helen would no doubt hold them equally to blame.

'Oh God, what am I going to do now?'

The enormity of her situation hit her with full force. She cried again.

***

(Friday 31st July 1964 – late afternoon)

Vee kept her appointment with Inspector Lester. With her nerves now painfully acute, she welcomed the distraction offered by the meeting with the policeman. On her journey into town, she forced herself to focus on what needed to be included in her statement. There would be plenty of time later to dwell upon the significance of the morning's events. But even the sure knowledge she might commit perjury, a fact that would, in normal circumstances, cause her considerable anxiety, could not compare with the intensity of what happened earlier.

Her misery and despair grew more intense by the minute. If the policeman accused her of aiding and abetting a serious crime, her confession would follow. Further trauma would make no difference to her now. With a small twinge of guilt, she realised the thought of making a full confession appealed, as this would implicate Frank, who would likely be punished more than her.

But there were no accusations. The appointment turned out to be straightforward. She was asked to provide a statement detailing her association with Jonny at university. The Inspector focused only briefly on the letters Jonny had written to her. He did not ask whether there had been any further communication. Later, Vee would acknowledge to herself she would have made no attempt to deny or distort the truth if asked directly.

'Just procedure,' he assured her, 'Your identification from the photograph enabled confirmation of his identity from dental records. You've been most helpful, Miss Park.'

The meeting at the police station lasted an hour. If the events of the morning had not occurred, she would be in a state of relieved elation at this point in the knowledge it was all finally over. But she felt nothing other than a sense of foreboding about what the future would now hold for her.

Her nervous tension grew. Instead of taking the bus, she walked back to her flat, despite the relentless drizzle filling the air. Only physical exertion, she thought, might dull her jangling nerves. She moved like an automaton, her mind in turmoil, her thoughts so intense, tiredness and discomfort seemed to make little difference. It took well over an hour to reach home, by which time she was drenched and no longer immune to the cold.

As Vee opened the door to her flat, she picked up a blue envelope with a chequered border bearing the motif "Air Mail." She recognised Carrie's handwriting. She sat at the kitchen table and ripped the letter open. A blank signed cheque dropped out together with a single sheet of flimsy paper. Having read the brief letter, she smiled and cried at the same time. Carrie wrote she had found herself a husband, a very rich French vineyard owner. She would not be returning. *"I sent my resignation to the school - teaching's not for me anyway - can't stand children!"* The cheque was to cover any outstanding rent due. *"Sorry to drop you in it with the flat, but you'll find another flatmate in no time."* At the bottom of the letter, Carrie added as a PS: *"You're welcome to the rest of my stash - although I bet there's none left!"*

Vee thought of the biscuit tin - she had smoked the last of the spliffs several days ago. 'God, I could do with one now!' she muttered.

Finding someone else to share the rent with would not be as easy as Carrie suggested. Paying double would not be possible. *I'll have to move out! But where will I live? I'm not likely to be welcome at Dad's - not after Helen tells him what I've done.* As the hopelessness and desperation of her situation became evident, she cried again.

Some vinegary tasting vin de pays provided a shred of comfort along with a cigarette. She had just poured a second glass when a loud knocking at the door jerked her from her inner contemplation.

She guessed with a lurch of her heart it might be Helen who, after a heart-to-heart with Frank, was back for round two with her. *Or maybe it's him - yes, that's more likely. Helen's kicked him out, and he's coming to chance his luck with me. Well, he can fuck off!*

The banging became more persistent and louder now. Rising a little unsteadily, she walked to the front door. Bound to be him, her fogged mind told her. The niggling doubts she may not possess the resolve to reject him worried her. With a heavy sigh, she pulled the door open. It wasn't Frank.

Moments later, Vee sat on the floor next to the door. She pressed her fingers to the still stinging corner of her mouth. A warm trickle of blood ran down her cheek where her father's signet ring had impacted.

'You are no longer my daughter!' were his final words as he left, slamming her front door behind him.

PART THREE

"DESCENT"
(August 1964 – June 1966)

Chapter 60

"BANISHED"

He stared for several moments at his battered suitcase, brown with worn leather corner pieces. Bizarrely, his mind conjured up a brief scene: the day he was issued with the case, together with various other items of kit confirming he now belonged to the British Army. The polished wooden counter; the expressionless Quarter Master's Assistant; the smell of mothballs and gun oil - all this came back to him in irrelevant detail. He even experienced again for a few moments a long-forgotten sensation of anxiety, and the faint itch of an overly short haircut: the rite of passage into the Military with its strange and unfamiliar rituals about to be learned in weeks of unmitigated misery.

His suitcase stood on the polished tiles of the empty hallway, alone like a coffin on its stand in front of the pulpit. This new image that appeared, replacing the remembered scene from 1950, told him his life as a family man with a loving wife and son was irrevocably over. He glanced up the stairs and listened - not a sound.

The note from Helen lay crumpled on the floor where he dropped it. Without knowing why, he bent and picked the paper up, smoothed out the creases and placed it next to the telephone. Moving slowly and methodically, he took his jacket and raincoat from the hat stand and retrieved his wallet from its usual place on the hall table.

As he exited, he paused and looked back into the house. He doubted he would ever see the inside again. He left, closing the door softly but with finality behind him.

***

Driving along the coast road, he had the vaguest idea of where to go, although he knew he wanted to distance himself from Fairfield. He slowed down as he approached Vee's flat, glancing towards her lounge window as if expecting to spot her looking out. The thought of stopping and calling on her crossed his mind. But something, perhaps instinct, told him to keep moving. After several minutes of introspective contemplation, he realised why he did not stop. An ill-formed thought, a germ of an idea, suggested there might be a chance Helen could be placated and their marriage salvaged. But if she found out he ran straight to his former mistress, there would never be a reconciliation.

Once planted, the seed grew and, ever the optimist, he focused his thoughts on the goal of winning back his family. He decided to head for Portsmouth, sufficient distance from Fairfield to provide space to think - but not too far.

***

His mother would have described the small hotel in Southsea as 'cheap and cheerful'. To Frank, it was ideally located as it provided walking access to a range of pubs and bars where he intended to plan what he might do next, aided by the calming effects of alcohol.

He stepped into the first pub at half-past five. Two hours later, he still sat at a corner table where he ensconced himself on arrival. Mick Jagger's voice emerged from a jukebox singing 'It's all over now.'

'I think he may be right,' Frank muttered.

The bar area filled with, he guessed from the snippets of conversation he overheard, sailors and marines. He watched them, envious of their easy familiarity and the fact they appeared cheerful and carefree. By 9 o'clock, the pub had filled. Still, he sat on his own - and by this time, after several pints, he was quietly intoxicated.

Staring blearily at the half-finished pint standing on a sodden beer mat in front of him, he acknowledged to himself he had no idea what he might do to save his marriage. Despite the dulling effects of alcohol, he could identify the many flaws in every notion that occurred to him. Oblivious to his surroundings, he became lost in his inner contemplation.

He did not register at first, the woman, sitting alone at the bar, observing him. As she came briefly into focus, he noted with distaste the garish red lipstick curving into what might have been a smile as their eyes met. Her image separated into two separate ones. He turned away, squeezing his eyes shut as if to extinguish the apparition. Struggling to focus, he held his hand out for his beer glass and picked it up, spilling some of the contents as he brought it up to his mouth. He almost toppled the glass when he placed it down again.

Gazing blearily at the copper top of the table ringed with stains, he felt his eyelids droop and, perhaps for just a few moments, he dozed. He woke with a start, momentarily disorientated, staring around him wildly. Then he realised he was no longer alone. The woman observing him earlier now sat squeezed next to him. He turned and stared at her drunkenly, registering the fact that despite his current inability to focus, she was much older than him. Her face, heavily covered in make-up, her lipstick a bright red gash across her lower face – not a pleasing vision. In fact, she was hideous, he thought. She smiled at him, displaying two rows of uneven and discoloured teeth.

'Buy me a drink, mate,' she said, the tone of her voice suggesting instant familiarity.

He saw her nod towards the bar and, after a few seconds, a barmaid stood next to the table. An exchange of words followed, and a few minutes later a pint of beer appeared. He stared at the sticky-looking concoction, decorated with a small paper umbrella, placed in front of his uninvited companion. The barmaid looked expectantly at him, and he stared blankly back at her before realising what she wanted. He reached into his jacket pocket and pulled out his wallet, spilling some small change onto the floor, which she picked up and dropped on the table. With some difficulty, he plucked out a ten-shilling note and handed it to her, nodding his thanks - despite his intoxication, he always took great care to be courteous.

Had he been less drunk, he might have noted he received no change. He placed his wallet on the table and turned to his new companion, smiling, and noting she had removed the shawl she wore over her shoulders, revealing a considerable amount of cleavage.

'Come on, mate, wake up. Time to go home! Come on now! Up you get!'

Frank woke for the second time that evening, disorientated and confused. The bar was empty, his erstwhile companion had vanished. A man, who he guessed was the landlord, was shaking him roughly.

He could not remember how he found his way back to the hotel.

***

(Saturday 1st August 1964)

Frank woke late in the morning, and within seconds, he recalled the events of the previous day, which twisted his guts. Various items of his clothing littered the floor where he had discarded them the night before. As always after a heavy drinking binge, he conducted an immediate mental inventory of what had occurred. Vague memories of a painted face - garish lipstick - a disguised older woman - flashed back. A horrifying thought! With a panicked jerk of his head, he shot a glance at the pillow next to his. 'Oh, thank God!' he exclaimed, for a few seconds, thinking he might see that red gash of a smile leering up at him.

Another thought occurred to him. He groaned as he swung out of bed, his head spinning, nearly toppling with dizziness as he stood. He picked up his jacket from the floor, slipped his fingers into the pocket where he always kept his wallet.

'Shit!'

He cast his eyes around the detritus hoping he might see it. But no - he resigned himself to the fact it had been lost or stolen, and he was now penniless.

Groaning in pain, his head spinning, causing waves of nausea, he managed to stand and walk unsteadily to the bathroom down the corridor. After taking a shower, he stood in front of the mirror and shaved, which helped a little to revive him.

His immediate thought as he pulled himself together was what he must do about his missing wallet. Perhaps I should go back to the pub - someone might have picked it up and given it to the bar for safe-keeping, he thought.

'Fat chance of that,' he announced to his image in the mirror. Images of the "Painted Lady," as he called her now, flashed through his mind - she would no doubt be congratulating herself on easy pickings.

A search through his trouser and jacket pockets gleaned a crumpled pound note, five shillings, and four pence. A café nearby offered a full English, which helped to ease him back into humanity. Having not eaten for over twenty-four hours, he had not realised how hungry he was. With a second mug of strong tea in front of him, he lit another cigarette and took stock of his situation. It did not look good.

With less than two pounds to draw upon, he could manage one more night at the hotel - but that would be with no form of sustenance. He groaned when he recalled his wallet had contained the best part of two weeks' salary.

He returned to his room dispirited, contemplating a return to bed. As he walked into his room, a thought hit him - a brief memory of the evening before when he dressed to go out. *Wasn't there a...? Yes, there it is!* He snatched the cheque book from under the pile of clothes in his suitcase. 'Yes!'

His discovery cheered him a little, and with this came the thought Helen must have been thinking, perhaps just a little, about his welfare. But then he remembered he had left it there himself following his last overnight stay, the one he spent with Vee in Birmingham. The reminder shattered most of his sudden joy.

He found a Midlands Bank where, after a phone call to the Fairfield branch and the production of a driving license, he could cash a cheque for fifty pounds, sufficient, he calculated, to keep him afloat for two, possibly three weeks. That would be time enough, he calculated, to sort himself out and make concrete steps towards repairing his marriage.

A visit to Woolworths where he bought another wallet was followed by an aimless meander through Southsea. By one o'clock his hangover by no means diminished, he heeded the imagined voice of his old friend, Joe, who advised him to 'get some hair of the dog.'

Chapter 61

"JOBLESS"

(Monday 3rd August 1964)
This was the first time Bob had been in his old office since standing down in favour of Frank. As he opened the door, he registered the fact his own name plaque had been removed and replaced with a gleaming brass plate with "Frank Armstrong - Managing Director" etched on it.

'Well, that can come down for a start!'

He frowned and sighed - 'To think things would come to this.'

The necessity of his return to work, at least temporarily until a full-time replacement could be found, was precipitated by the unexpected crisis that had exploded.

'Never thought I'd find myself back here,' he muttered. Fumbling in his pocket, he pulled out his pipe and sucked on the end. No tobacco - not after his heart attack - but he needed a comforter. The tumultuous events that changed their lives revisited his mind, and he winced at the memories.

It all started on Friday afternoon when Helen arrived at his door unexpectedly with a very unhappy looking Peter hovering uncertainly behind her. The look on her face signalled trouble, and he guessed immediately it would be something to do with Frank.

Peter had been sent into the garden to play so he would not have to hear the upsetting details. He recalled how calm Helen had been, strangely so, at least at first. But she had always been adept at hiding her true emotions - just like her mother. Only when she focused on Vee's role in the betrayal did her defences crumble. She cried uncontrollably for a minute or two before gathering herself again. In hindsight, he thought ruefully, this was where I should have held her - let her be a child again for a few minutes.

Standing in the centre of the office staring blankly at the desk, he experienced again the intense surge of anger that swept through him when he realised the extent of Vee's involvement. If she stood in front of me right now, he remembered thinking, well, God help her. But the instant remorse he felt after lashing out soon after made him flush with shame.

'It had to be done,' he whispered as if seeking reassurance from his own voice. 'She needed to be punished, otherwise...' He shook his head and looked at the floor, realising there were tears in his eyes.

Yesterday, Helen called round again. 'I'm going to take Peter away somewhere,' she told him, 'He's never been on a proper holiday and now's a good time. I think I'll take him to Butlins at Bognor - he'd like that.'

'That's exactly what I was thinking – get yourself away for a while – it'll do you both good. We can tell everyone you decided to take a family break - simply leave out the bit about it not including Frank. But look, Helen, I'm going back to work.'

'But Dad, your...'

'No. I'll be fine - I'm not going to let it kill me, so don't worry. In fact, I think it'll do me good – take my mind off things, you know? Anyway, you can leave everything with me. Get yourself and Peter away from this mess. I'll deal with the gossip.'

She agreed readily, and he guessed she was relieved he would manage everything for her. But then the faint, relieved smile on her face turned into a frown.

'But what about him? What if he turns up at the office? He might - actually, I'm sure he will.'

He registered she could not utter his name. 'I doubt he's got the gall to do that,' he replied with certainty. 'I would imagine he's simply buggered off with his tail between his legs.'

'But what if he does - come back, I mean?'

'He won't, but if he does, well, I'll sort him out,' he said grimly. But he knew he was uncertain himself as to what he might do in those circumstances.

She phoned him later Sunday afternoon to let him know she had managed to secure a last-minute booking for a fortnight. He was pleased - this took care of her and Peter.

'Look, Helen, I've had a thought. I'm going to confide in Kirk and Hugh. We can trust them - and we'll need their help in creating a story to explain why Frank isn't working here anymore. I'm sure Hugh will be able to come up with some believable blarney.'

'Okay, Dad, I'll leave that to you.'

There was a hint of hesitation in her voice - but he guessed she would be happy to let him handle the situation in his own way.

'I'll ring every day,' she said.

'No, you won't - forget about all this. Send me a postcard instead!'

***

As Bob sat at Frank's desk, he decided to put thoughts of Helen and Peter aside for the time-being. Two weeks away from Fairfield will do them the power of good - and everything will have settled down by the time they come back.

'Now then,' he said out loud to the empty room, 'let's sort this business out.'

He picked up the telephone and called reception. 'Please send Mr O'Driscoll and Mr Boyle to the MD's office.'

Half an hour later, the meeting was closing. 'Okay, we don't want any rumours. I'm here on a temporary basis, purely to give the family a chance to enjoy a well-earned holiday - got it?'

They nodded - 'Got it!' they replied in unison.

Just as they were rising to leave, they heard the distinctive noise of the familiar three-litre engine in the car park below. Bob strode to the window and looked down. The Healey was pulling up next to the space reserved for the Managing Director in which his own Consul was parked. He watched Frank emerge from the car, dressed in a suit as if for work. He stared upwards towards his office.

'Right!' Bob said stepping back from the window. 'Okay, you two, best leave this to me - it looks like there's going to be a confrontation here and I need to do this on my own. If you meet him coming in don't talk to him if you can help it. Act like nothing's happened.'

***

During the drive along the A27 from Portsmouth, Frank wondered whether he was doing the right thing by turning up at the office. Perhaps it's too soon - maybe I should have left it a few days.

'But I still work there - at least I think I do,' he announced to himself. His eyes stared back at him from the rear-view mirror - they reflected uncertainty and fear.

His decision to go to the depot had been made on Sunday evening as he smoked a post-dinner cigarette at his hotel in Southsea. He emptied the third bottle of Mackeson, the only beer the bar sold, into his glass and placed it back on the table.

'That's what I'm going to do!' he announced to the empty dining room. Instead of visiting a pub for a couple of "proper beers," which had been his plan, he got an early night in readiness for the morning.

The nearer he got to Fairfield, the more his determination and courage failed him. As he turned off the High Street onto the side road leading to the Parks depot and head office, he was tempted to turn around and head back to Portsmouth. But he forced himself to continue.

His heartbeat quickened as he steered into the car park. At 10 o'clock on a Monday morning, it was predictably full. He automatically headed for his reserved space. 'Bloody hell,' he said when he saw it was occupied. He groaned when he realised it was Bob's Consul.

Stepping out of the car, he surveyed the car park in search of the Singer. No sign of it. Not good, he thought. He glanced up towards his office window. A face appeared briefly before vanishing - he recognised Bob. With a groan, his courage threatening to fail him again, he dreaded the prospect of a confrontation.

Knowing if he hesitated, even for a second or two, he would turn around, get back into his car and drive away, he walked to the front door and entered.

'Morning Mr Armstrong,' said the uniformed Commissionaire with a polite salute.

Frank nodded in return and smiled, his mood lifted a little by the acknowledgement of his presence.

The office door was shut. About to knock, he stopped himself. *This is my office for Heaven's sake!* He paused and took a deep breath and then opened the door. Bob sat behind the desk, his eyes locking onto his own in an unblinking stare, his face unsmiling and unwelcoming.

'Morning, Bob!' Frank said breezily. But he could see straight away this would not be a friendly chat.

'I think you'd better sit down, Frank.' Bob nodded at the chair on the opposite side of the desk, not normally left in that position.

He sat and studied Bob's face. 'So, I guess you know,' he said, after a few moments of heavy silence.

'Yes, I do.' Bob fixed him with a piercing look. He said nothing for several seconds - just stared.

Frank looked at the model of the Healey that occupied pride of place on his desk - he did not feel able to look Bob directly in the eyes.

'Why Frank? Why did you do it? How could you betray your own family? What kind of man are you?'

No reply was expected, it seemed. He contemplated walking out, feeling a flash of anger. He thought but did not utter what went through his mind: 'Don't you lecture me, you condescending bastard!' Instead, he remained silent, knowing Bob wanted him to say something.

'You were given everything,' Bob's voice softened. 'I thought of you - treated you like a son.'

He looked up and noticed Bob had tears in his eyes.

'I knew you weren't perfect - Christ, who is? But I never thought you capable of sinking so low.'

'Look,' Frank began, sensing an opportunity to intercede. He had the vaguest idea of what he wanted or needed to say, but perhaps acknowledging he was in the wrong might move things in the right direction.

Bob held up his hand in a halting motion.

'You're finished Frank - I'm sorry. After what you did, there isn't anything left for you here. You're no longer required at Parks. I'm arranging for you to be replaced - and I think we can all do without your presence here. In other words, you're fired.'

He stood as if to signal the meeting was now over.

'You've been paid up to last week, so nothing is owed you. I'll give you exactly fifteen minutes to clear your desk here before I send up someone to escort you off site. Goodbye, Frank.'

Bob walked out of the office leaving the door to shut slowly behind him.

Ten minutes later Frank was walking down the stairs as if in a daze, carrying a small box which contained all he wanted to take away with him as he left Parks for the final time. There were only two items in it: the model of the Healey in its glass display case, and a small plastic box containing a brass medal with a fading yellow and green ribbon.

***

Gregory burst through the main door of the office building, his face pink with exertion. He was late for a meeting with Mr Boyle, his line manager.

'Just my luck to get a puncture today,' he shouted to Reg, the Commissionaire who sat behind his booth reading a newspaper. He turned and ran up the first flight of steps, a feat he could achieve with ease now his asthma seemed to have disappeared. As he turned the corner to the next run, he tumbled head-long into Frank, knocking the cardboard box he was carrying onto the floor.

'Oh, I'm so sorry, please excuse me!'

He bent down and picked up the box, which had dropped squarely onto a step without spilling its contents.

'Mum always said I was a clumsy oaf. Sorry about that.' He stood and handed the box to Frank.

Expecting a good-humoured rebuke for his clumsiness - or at least an acknowledgement of his presence - he was surprised when instead, Frank stared straight through him before brushing past and continuing his descent.

The strange, out of character behaviour troubled him all day. Later, before leaving for home, he stopped to chat with Reg, sharing with him his concerns.

'Something's up,' Gregory replied - 'that wasn't the Frank I know.'

'You don't know what's happened, then?'

'What?'

The Commissionaire told him.

Chapter 62

"VEE'S FAREWELL"

(Wednesday 26th August 1964)

She arrived at the airport very early having allowed plenty of time for her journey, imagining several scenarios that might lead her to be late for or miss her flight. But there were no train delays and, contrary to her expectations, London proved to be relatively easy to negotiate even with the encumbrance of a heavy suitcase. Although this was her first time in an airport, she found her way through the check in process without mishap.

Safely through departures, a cup of tea and a sandwich served as lunch in a small café. After this, she found her way to the gate waiting area, which was empty when she arrived. Despite the discomfort of the chair, exhausted by her journey, she fell promptly asleep.

The "TANNOY" crackled into life loudly, jolting her awake from a doze. *"British Eagle flight 217 to Singapore will shortly be boarding from Gate number 2."*

Her head shot up, her eyes wide and fearful, momentarily disorientated. Suspecting she might have made some form of strangled, startled noise, she flushed with embarrassment, realising the room had filled since she fell asleep. A quick glance around her revealed that no one appeared to be paying her any attention, and she relaxed a little although a nagging sense of foreboding still weighed heavily in the pit of her stomach. Opening her handbag, she pulled out a packet of cigarettes and a lighter. Her cigarette lit, she leant back and took in more detail of her fellow passengers who would share the eighteen-hour flight via Kuwait and Bombay to Singapore.

Now full awake, she surveyed her surroundings. In the row of chairs in front of her sat a young family: mum, dad, and two children, a girl, and a boy, about the same age as those from her class. This thought prompted a stab of longing and regret causing her eyes to well up with tears. She turned away quickly, hoping her sudden onset of emotion had not been noticed. A quick glance back and she registered the mum was looking at her with a concerned expression on her face. Please don't talk to me! Vee thought.

Anxious to avoid eye contact, she gazed around the room as if trying to locate someone familiar. Everywhere she looked, groups of people gathered: couples, some with children; clusters of men and women who, even though not in uniform, presented as Service people. A sense of excitement and adventure filled the air. People talked animatedly and with apparent easy informality. Vee felt excluded, isolated and alone.

Glancing back at the family in front of her, she was relieved to see both parents were now focused on calming down their children who had become fractious.

**

When, several hours previously, she slipped her key to the flat through the letter-box with a note of thanks to her landlord, a sense of finality and closure swept over her. This is it: I'm leaving Fairfield for good, she thought, struggling with her heavy suitcase towards the waiting taxi. She cried a little as they drove through the High Street, knowing she would never see the shops and pubs there again. The driver's eyes met hers from the rear-view mirror. 'You alright love?' he asked.

She nodded: 'Yes, I'm fine. At least I will be once I've gotten out of this dump!'

**

A month had passed since the day Helen confronted her, and her father disowned her with such ferocity. The morning after that terrible day, she woke with the decision formulated during yet another sleepless night: I need to get as far away from Fairfield as possible.

A return to Manchester, perhaps to the school where she taught during her placement year, appeared to be the obvious and ideal solution. But indecision delayed her, and the longer she did nothing, the more anxious and desperate she became.

It was an advertisement in the Times Education Supplement that offered her a way out. Within hours, she posted her application to be a teacher in the British Forces Overseas Teaching Service. A week before the start of the new term back at school, an official-looking brown envelope marked "On Her Majesty's Service" dropped through her letter-box. A few days after that, she travelled up to London for an interview. By the time she got back on the Portsmouth-bound train, she had been offered and had accepted a teaching position in Singapore.

Returning to her flat, she opened a bottle of red wine: a Barolo in honour of Carrie. She drank it dry and went to bed drunk, and vaguely happy for the first time in months.

Her flight tickets duly arrived along with a pile of administrative documentation, including details of her new role. In different circumstances, her sense of adventure would have kicked in and she would have been filled with excitement. The fact there was no one to share her news with hit hard.

As days passed, her impending departure to the Far East took on significance. She was escaping - running away from a situation she could not handle. No one would miss her, she convinced herself. This thought upset her hugely.

***

Vee was one of the last passengers to approach the gate. The maroon-uniformed woman at the departure desk handed back her passport and ticket.

'Have a pleasant flight!' she said, smiling.

Vee nodded briefly in acknowledgement, aware she was once again on the verge of tears. A bus waited at the end of a short corridor, already filled with passengers. In the distance, a Britannia aeroplane glistened wetly in the late summer rain.

Before stepping onto the bus, she turned and stared back into the departure lounge. She did not know why.

Chapter 63

"THE LABOUR EXCHANGE"

(Monday 24th August 1964)
Returning to the familiarity of Southampton seemed to be a logical move. Frank arrived three weeks ago, driving directly from the scene of his dismissal and banishment from the Park family.

The boarding house for business travellers stood near to the docks, an area familiar to him from his boyhood and his early years at Parks when Southampton had been his sales region. He favoured the dock-side pubs over the more salubrious venues in the city centre and, as he checked into the shabby residence, part of him already looked forward to renewing his acquaintance with some of the earthy drinking dens he used to frequent.

Within a matter of days, he became a regular at several of the pubs and, although he spoke to none of the other punters, preferring to drink alone, they appeared to accept him.

His bank account emptied, most of his money spent on beer, which he considered necessary to ease his misery. But drinking did not help. The more he drank, the more depressed he became - particularly in the mornings when he would wake with a hangover, feeling wretched and guilty at his weakness. Often neglecting to eat, spending his diminishing financial resources on drink instead, he found himself in a spiral of despair.

Then came a wake-up call.

He woke one day - as usual, hung over and miserable. As he struggled to dress, still dizzy with the effects of the previous evening's alcohol, he noticed his clothes no longer fitted him properly. His trousers hung off his hips, and he needed to tighten his belt by a couple of notches. He stared at himself in a mirror - an untidy looking, haggard and unkempt man gazed back. It was at this moment, he decided it was time to sort himself out - before it became too late.

That morning, he forced himself to eat breakfast: a proper meal in a greasy spoon where of late a coffee and cigarette had sufficed. Then, although with a distinct sense of shame, he walked to the local Labour Exchange where he signed on as "unemployed."

The official who interviewed him and took down his details appeared surprisingly encouraging.

'A man with your experience should have no problem finding another position. There are plenty of businesses in the area looking for salesmen,' he said.

'But, I was sacked - surely that will make getting another job pretty difficult?'

'Not necessarily,' the young man replied, 'You've got impressive sales experience. Believe me, I see so many hopeless cases coming in here, and you're clearly not one of them. Look, try contacting this one,' he said, writing down details, including a phone number and address, on a piece of paper and handing it to him.

'They're looking for sales managers, and I reckon this might be the job for you.' He looked at Frank and smiled. 'Go on, you might get lucky.'

Frank's mood when he left was significantly more positive than when he went in. Finding a telephone box, he rang the number on the piece of paper given to him. Five minutes later, he punched the air with joy. He had been invited to an interview the next day.

***

The following morning, Frank woke with a renewed sense of purpose and vigour - and for the first time in weeks without a hangover. Negative thoughts that tried to take hold - as they always did first thing in the morning - were quashed. This would mark, he assured himself, the first significant movement out of the mess I've found myself in.

Looking around his small, cramped room, which he kept scrupulously tidy - a habit ingrained in him from his army days - he smiled. This depressing dump is just a temporary residence, he told himself, just a place to crash while I build myself back up again.

Metcalf's, a small company trading in electronic components, was located in the northern outskirts of Southampton. Allowing plenty of time to negotiate the city centre traffic, he arrived at the gates of the main office building early. A small café across the road provided the opportunity to take breakfast and to have a couple of cigarettes to calm his nerves. By the time he entered the site, his confidence was as buoyant as it could be for a man facing imminent ruin.

'This is it!' he told himself, 'you're going to get this job!'

Less than fifteen minutes later, he was walking out of the yard back to his car. He got in and sat immobile, staring unseeingly out of the windscreen.

The interview - if it could be called that - had not gone well.

'As I said, Mr Armstrong, your previous employer, Mr Park, has refused to provide you with a reference. He would not say why, but I can only assume either your conduct, performance or both were not to his satisfaction. In fact, I'm guessing, he must have had a very serious reason to dismiss you. You didn't tell me you were sacked. If I'd been able to contact you last night, I would have advised you not to bother coming in at all because you would be wasting your time.'

When, the evening before, he called Metcalf's and spoke to the manager, he had not mentioned his dismissal

- instead, he suggested he had left to seek new opportunities. He realised, how foolish he had been not to realise contact would be made with Bob, who was hardly likely to provide a glowing reference.

He tried to argue, desperate when he saw the job on which his sights had been set was about to be whipped away from him. In his frustration, he raised his voice. At this point, he was ushered to the door.

'Will you escort Mr Armstrong off the site, please?'

The uniformed security guard had grasped him firmly by the elbow and frog-marched him to the exit gate.

Sitting in his car, he wept tears of shame.

Chapter 64

"NADIR"

(Sunday 30th August 1964)

His feet follow the path of their own accord - he does not understand where he is heading nor the purpose of his journey. It could be twilight, or maybe early dawn; he is not sure which. All around is gloom, rendering shapes indistinct and threatening. His progress is slow and plodding. He focuses his eyes on the track ahead of him, seeing only sand and stone but wary of bigger obstacles that might cause him to stumble and fall. A high solid obstacle runs the length of the path on his right side, parallel with his direction of movement. Without looking, he knows it will be dark grey and foreboding - a wall.

The journey continues - a relentless trudge with no apparent aim.

After some time, the route, straight so far, twists to the right, marked by what appears to be the end of the wall - except it is not an end but a corner. His feet follow automatically as if driven by an external force.

At this moment, he understands the purpose of his journey. They are ahead of him, walking in the same direction.

Hope surges through him and he shouts out to them, only no sound emits from his mouth. Panic grips as he struggles to comprehend why, although they are ambling with no indication of urgency and momentum, the distance between them seems to grow steadily. They are leaving him behind and seem unaware of his presence. He does not understand why - his anxiety escalates.

'Please turn back!' he shouts – but his voice is soundless.

He yells again, more forcefully this time - still no sound. Desperately, he urges his feet to move faster, but to no avail. He weeps in frustration.

Then, as though suddenly aware of his presence, she stops and turns. The boy holding her hand turns as well. He knows they recognise him. The woman kneels next to the boy and whispers something in his ear, glancing back towards him at the same time.

He calls again, beckoning them to come to him because, even though he is moving forward, he is not getting any closer.

The boy waves and smiles - but his smile vanishes to be replaced with a frown. The woman stands again, spinning the boy around by his shoulders, propelling him onwards in the direction they had been walking. She turns her head towards him, her eyes meeting his for a few moments. He can see and sense her sorrow. She turns away again with finality.

Frantic now, he pumps his arms as if this might encourage his feet to move faster, but they maintain their slow trudge, oblivious to his curses and exhortations.

Much further away now, their forms become distorted and indistinct.

A light, faint at first, appears in front of them and grows rapidly in intensity. Shielding his eyes from the glare, he makes out the frame of a huge doorway through which the light is shining. He understands instinctively once they walk through the opening, they will be gone forever. He screams, desperate to make them stop. Too late. Their shapes ripple as if consumed by flames. They vanish.

'No!' he shrieks. This time, he can shout.

***

The hammering on the wall next to his bed wakes him. 'Shut the fuck up!' someone shouts.

Frank stares with frightened eyes around the room, and then remembers where he is - and why. He shivers as he stretches down to the floor to retrieve the top covers of his bed kicked off during the night.

The dull ache in his head, the sour taste of stale alcohol and cigarettes, and the fact his clothes are scattered randomly around his room remind him he had been drunk, hammered when he climbed with great difficulty into his bed.

Brief recollections of a drinking binge around the dockside pubs flash through his mind. His vision is blurred, and he feels a continuous throbbing pain under his right eye. He winces as his fingers touch the swelling around the socket, the pain prompting a vague memory of an outraged female and large, red-faced dockyard worker - an altercation - a meaty fist. A follow-on scene flashes up - one in which he is face-down on a wet pavement - the sound of laughing behind him - the slamming of a door.

Although the details of his drunken humiliation, or at least some of them, emerge during the minutes following his awakening, his conscious mind has already forgotten the intensity of his dream - but the sense of desolation and loss remain.

A bright light is shining through the thin curtains of his room from outside - a lorry manoeuvring in the parking bay, he guesses. The light hurts his eyes - he turns his head away.

There is a framed photograph lying on the floor by his bed. He reaches over and picks it up, groaning as he notes the cracked glass - a vague memory of the frame falling to the hard floor as he staggered into it while attempting to undress. Unable to look at the picture, he places it down again. The image, though, appears in his mind in sharp relief. There they were: the three of them together.

For just a few moments, he is back there again, in Portsmouth on their day out with Helen and Peter. They had been a family then - happy, with a bright future.

'You destroyed all that!' his inner voice reminds him.

Chapter 65

"MOVING ON"

(Tuesday 8th September 1964)

Helen experienced a twinge of guilt when he glanced back and smiled. 'I've been giving him the "glad eye," and he knows!' the voice in her head whispered with a hint of mild disapproval. She turned away embarrassed, admonishing herself for being so obvious. With exaggerated concentration, she picked up a pen and scribbled notes on the pad in front of her.

Although focused on writing meaningless words, she sensed he was observing her. The compulsion to look up became too strong. Their eyes met, and he smiled at her.

'Well, everything appears to be in order. I mean, at least the figures add up and make sense. There are a few outstanding debts, nothing too serious. But you're going to have to write off the Carlton account - they've folded, and I don't think you should bother pursuing - it'll cost more in legal fees than any return you're likely to get and...'

'Thanks, Nigel, that's a great relief. I wondered whether he might, well, you know...'

She detected an immediate sense of understanding in his eyes. He nodded and smiled.

'This must be so difficult for you. Perhaps I should run this past your father? I mean, as I said, everything appears to be fine - nothing in the books to raise my suspicions - no funds being siphoned off, no secret payments. So, in a nutshell, he's done nothing wrong.'

'Other than screwing my sister!'

She regretted the retort as soon as the words left her lips. Since returning to work, she had maintained a calm

462

aloofness. She acknowledged her parting from Frank was now common knowledge and the subject of considerable speculation and gossip around the Head Office. The sordid details, however, remained a closely guarded secret - no one, other than her father, knew exactly what happened.

'I'm sorry - you didn't need that - you touched a nerve, I'm afraid. Please say nothing - I mean to anyone.'

'Hey, listen,' he said gently, 'none of my business. Your words are forgotten, so worry not.'

She gazed at him steadily as if appraising. Finally, she smiled and nodded.

'Thanks.'

Something in his eyes and the way he looked at her gave her the impression he could be trusted.

'Are you married, Nigel?' she asked before she could stop herself.

'I'm a widower,' he replied. 'My wife died two years ago - cancer.'

'Oh, I'm so sorry! I didn't mean to pry, I just...'

'I understand,' he said, handing a handkerchief to her.'

The still vivid memory of her mother's sudden demise, combined with the most recent devastation of the parting from Frank, forced a breach in her usual reserve. It took every ounce of self-control to stop her from breaking down in tears, but she could not hide her emotions completely, and she sensed he could tell.

'Come on, we've had a long day. Let's go for a well-earned drink,' he said gently.

His words were more a command than a request, and she was happy to obey.

***

The following morning, Helen was sat in the familiar surroundings of the solicitor's office. The meeting was not going well - the contentment created by a pleasant evening with her new man dissipated rapidly. Helen found herself glaring in open hostility at the bespectacled, balding man sitting opposite her, wishing she had followed her instinct and appointed someone other than the company solicitor to handle her divorce.

'If only it were that simple,' he said, pushing a packet of cigarettes towards her after extracting one for himself, which he lit.

She shook her head, hating him even more. He damn well knows I don't smoke, she thought.

He appeared to take her gesture as denial of the truth he was expounding.

'You've nothing but a verbal acknowledgement of guilt from your husband and your sister. Do you think they will both admit their adultery in writing?' He fixed her with a level stare and with what Helen interpreted as a knowing smile.

She stared back defiantly.

'They're both as guilty as sin!' She spat the words. 'How could they deny what they've done? And why would they? Surely, you can draft some kind of admission letter they just need to sign? I mean...'

'Of course - if that is your wish. Do you know their addresses? I understand your husband...'

'He's not my husband, he's a...' she cut in.

'I'm sorry, Helen, in the eyes of the Law, he's still your husband and will remain so until the divorce is finalised. In the meantime, you can consider yourself to be officially separated.'

He leant back in his expensive-looking leather seat behind his walnut desk and surveyed her across the top of his glasses.

'Have you thought this through?' he said in almost a whisper.

'What do you mean? Of course, I've thought it through! The man I considered to be my husband - the father of my child - has been having an affair with my own sister!'

464

Her voice was raised. With a huge effort, she forced herself to calm down, not wanting to break down in front of the solicitor against whom she held a strong antipathy.

'But divorce will always be a stigma. You must consider the facts. Yes, your husband is clearly the guilty party - he is to blame for the breakdown of your marriage. But be aware Mrs Armstrong...,' he adopted a softer tone, which to Helen merely made him sound patronising, '...the sordid facts of this case will enter the public domain and you will be judged as well.'

'What?' she shrieked, finally losing her self-control, 'Are you suggesting people might think I'm in some way to blame for this?'

'Some will think that way, you can be sure of that.'

Unable to respond in words, she drew a series of sharp, ragged breaths and glared, hoping he knew how much she hated him.

'You should think about the effect divorce proceedings might have on your son. Isn't he due to start school soon? Imagine how he would feel if other children...'

'Shut up!' she snapped. 'I've heard enough. This divorce is going ahead - and if you can't handle it, I'll find someone else who will.'

***

(Same day)

Frank glowered at the official sitting in front of him as if the inoffensive young man was the gatekeeper to his chances of recovery. But he understood the clerk was trying to help him. With some effort, he softened his face into a smile.

'You're right, I need to start again - build up my reputation. I managed it before, I can do it again.' He sat back in his chair and lit a cigarette.

'What sort of role do you have in mind?'

The young man, who he now knew as Trevor, was the same Labour Exchange official, who provided the contact details of the sales roles that raised his hopes, only for them to be dashed. Trevor showed a maturity and level-headedness belying his youth. Frank considered him as his trusted advisor and now the only friend he possessed.

'A club's about to open in the centre of town, and they're looking for bar staff.'

'Oh, for Christ's sake, you must be joking! Is that all I'm good for - bar work?'

'Now, hear me out, Frank. The club's quite big. It has a dance hall, a small restaurant, and a casino. And according to the owner, for the right man, this job offers the opportunity to move upwards.'

He took a drag on his cigarette and stared at the nicotine-stained ceiling as if seeking guidance, then sighed, exhaling a cloud of smoke.

'Okay, but I don't have any experience of working in a bar. And won't they ask for references?'

'I was speaking to the owner only yesterday. He said the experience of working a bar is not an essential requirement. He went on to say he was looking for staff that were confident in dealing with people. You came to mind straight away! I mentioned you as a possibility, and he seemed very impressed with your credentials. He's not going to bother with references.'

'Well, as you say, I need to start somewhere. Thanks, I owe you. What do I do next?'

'Here're his details and the address of the club. I'll call him and say you'll be in touch.'

He looked at the coloured flyer, Trevor slipped across the table to him.

'Strange name?'

'It is, isn't it? Why would someone call himself Horse?'

***

466

'It's too soon Nigel, I'm sorry but I...'

With the unhappy meeting with solicitor that morning still playing on her mind, Helen found it difficult to raise any enthusiasm.

Her relationship with Nigel had sparked and developed with a speed that surprised them both. She felt overwhelmed and a little fearful. Conscious she was still, at least in the eyes of the Law, married - and with the solicitor's warning she might be judged by others - she wondered whether they were moving a little too quickly.

They were sat in a pub, one she never visited with Frank, when Nigel suggested they should spend a weekend away together.

As though he had not heard her, he continued with enthusiasm.

'We can take the ferry from Portsmouth over to Saint Malo - drive around a bit, take in the sights, the restaurants - and I know a wonderful little hotel right on the seafront.'

Although she would not ask, the thought perhaps the same holiday had featured in his marriage troubled her. Why else would he mention it? Nigel, she noticed, never talked about his wife. His responses when asked about his marriage remained brief. Maybe he's protecting her memory, she wondered. This thought made her sad although she did not understand why.

He took her hand. 'It's okay, Helen, I can see you're not enthused. Maybe later, eh?' He smiled, breaking her negative chain of thoughts.

She nodded, glad a potential argument was diverted.

'It is, I'm afraid - too soon, I mean. It wouldn't be right. I have to think about Peter, and my dad, of course.'

As she said this, a recent conversation with her father appeared in her mind contradicting some of what she said.

'He seems like a pleasant enough bloke - if you think he's right for you, I don't see any reason why you shouldn't take up with him. I certainly won't stand in your way.'

Peter, however, was an issue. He had become withdrawn and moody, and even the distraction of nursery school did not help. A few days ago, she had been alarmed to receive a phone call from his teacher:

'He's distraught and we can't calm him down,' she advised.

Helen drove to the school and took him home where, upon arriving, he ran up to his room slamming the door behind him. He emerged much later, hungry and miserable.

Peter missed his father, that was clear, and he would ask her constantly where he had gone. Her responses to his questioning were vague - but she could not think of any safe way of telling him. 'He's gone away for a while,' she told him, hating herself for her dishonesty and inability to handle the situation.

'When will he come home?'

'I don't know darling, I have no idea, I'm afraid.'

***

'Are you alright, Helen?' I know this has been a hard day for you.'

She realised she had been staring vacantly ahead of her, for a few moments oblivious to Nigel as she pondered the challenge of dealing with Peter.

'Sorry, I was miles way.' She smiled sadly. 'It's all such a bloody mess! If only I could press a button and make it all go away - especially Frank. I feel like I'm the one being punished for something that was none of my doing. I need proof of his adultery apparently. If he's not prepared to provide a written confession, then I have to wait for at least three years before I can be finally rid of him. It's so unfair!'

Helen had already shared some of her concerns with Nigel. He seemed so understanding, she thought, and it was good to be able to trust someone and share some of her worries.

'I suspect he's been unfaithful before as well. I mean, if he could betray me with my sister, well...'

He listened, making occasional sympathetic noises.

'You, poor girl,' he said, 'he must be a complete fool to wreck his marriage like that.'

***

Later that day, Helen sat at the kitchen table sipping a mug of tea and contemplating her conversation with Nigel during which she had told him it was too early for them to go away together on holiday. Suddenly, she decided.

She went into the hall, picked up the phone and dialled Nigel's number. He answered after a few rings.

'Is it okay if I change my mind, I mean about going away together?'

'Absolutely!'

'But I don't want to go abroad. Perhaps we might go somewhere a little nearer? Maybe a place neither of us has visited before? Edinburgh is lovely toward Christmas, they say.'

'Edinburgh, it is then - we have a date!'

Chapter 66

"RAVELLES"

(Tuesday 22nd September - morning)
'You could at least pretend you're enjoying yourself - flipping 'eck, your face is like a well-smacked arse!'

'You try stripping off when it's bloody freezing! Can't you turn the heating up a bit?'

'It'll be warm enough when the room's full of punters. Go on, Lil, get dressed - but remember, keep a smile fixed on your clock - I want you to bring customers in, not scare them away?'

She pulled her mouth into an exaggerated expression of bliss, knelt and gathered up the items of clothing recently shed, scattered around her feet. Clutching the bundle to her chest, she jumped off the small stage and brushed past him and then stopped.

'Oo's he?' She jerked her chin towards the smartly dressed man, who gazed back at her with a mischievous grin.

'Oh, what, this man here?' Horse responded as if surprised she would want to know, 'Why, this is Frank. You'll be seeing a lot of this feller, so you better be nice to him! Now then, off you go - me and 'im have things to talk about!' This was accompanied by a smack on Lil's ample rump. She scowled and walked away towards the exit door, looking back over her shoulder at Frank, who grinned back at her. She winked in acknowledgement.

'I see what you mean, Horse. Are they all like that?'

'Not all - let's just say she's at the lower end. But she's alright, don't get me wrong, Lil's got potential - it just needs nurturing. Now, compare her with Yvonne - she was the one on before her. That girl's got the looks, and she enjoys stripping off - gets a kick out of it. The punters will love her! I bet she really knows how to play a crowd. There'll be enough money thrown onto the stage to keep her in fags for a week. Lil, well, she's got to sort herself out or I'll put her back behind the bar which I hired her for in the first place.'

Horse grinned. 'I want to make *Ravelles* the best nightclub in Southampton - the venue of choice for the discerning gentleman.' He paused than added, laughing: 'Took me ages to think of that! I've been advertising all around the city. There'll be loads interest, you wait and see! Plenty of the right sort of punters out there.'

Frank smiled. It was impossible not to be infected by Horse's enthusiasm. This was his second visit to the club in two days. Arriving for his arranged interview with the manager who called himself Horse, his expectations had been low as were his spirits. I'm at rock bottom, he thought when he stood outside looking up at the newly painted sign announcing the arrival of *Ravelles*.

The meeting was clearly unplanned and, contrary to his anticipation of being grilled on his experience and knowledge of bar work, it became clear that Horse had other ideas about his potential.

When he left the club on the first day, his mood had been markedly more positive than when he arrived. He was not offered the job of a barman - instead, Horse invited him to come back the next day.

'I need to do some thinking, Frank. You'd be wasted behind the bar - I think you might be more useful in other ways.'

'So, what is it that you want me to do?' Frank asked when he returned for his second appointment.

Horse clapped him on the back, his face cracked into a broad grin, displaying uneven rows of teeth, the gold ones glinting in the light. 'I want you to be my Number Two. You'll be my Deputy Manager!'

A few minutes later they sat in Horse's office. Frank smoked a cigarette; Horse puffed contentedly on a huge, fat cigar.

'There's a lot to be done before we open to the clientele. The decorating needs to be finished - you'll need to keep an eye on that - they're already saying there's more to be done than we thought. Robbing bastards! And there're more staff to be hired - kitchen, casino, a few other places.' He waved his hand as if it to indicate there was more, but with no need to go into the details now. 'You'll be my eyes and ears. I want you to manage the club on a day-to-day basis, making sure everything works, everybody does what's expected of them. Most importantly, I want you to make sure we're ready to be open on schedule - that's in December, a few weeks away, but time's flying.'

'You want me to manage everything?'

'Yes, more or less. I'll be busy behind the scenes - you know, marketing, stuff like that. Growing the business. I need to be sure the day-to-day running of the club is in good, safe hands - with someone I can trust. Keep the bar staff from robbing the till - if you catch them, you've got my permission to cut their hands off! Only joking Frank! So, are you in?'

Frank could barely restrain his excitement, but he was determined to maintain a professional front. 'Sounds great, but, obviously, we need to agree on the terms.'

'Oh, I think you'll like the pay. You work hard for me and I'll reward you well - and not just with money. You can stay in the flat upstairs - move out of those shitty digs you're in.'

His feelings of elation reached a crescendo - he raised himself from the chair and thrust his hand out.

'I'm in, Horse!'

'Welcome to *Ravelles*, Frank!' Horse grinned as they shook hands. 'You can start tomorrow!'

***

472

Horse glanced at the wall clock. It was one o'clock.

'Fuck it - the sun's over the yardarm somewhere in the World.'

He poured himself a generous measure of rum, his drink of choice, a vestige of his brief career at sea, now a distant memory. He lifted his glass and swirled the amber fluid.

'Things are looking up!' he said to the empty room before downing the fiery liquid. He fixed himself another shot, intending to imbibe this one more slowly as he finished his cigar.

Things were, indeed, looking up for Horse. Several sound business investments in recent months had yielded profitable returns. *Ravelles* was his newest and most ambitious venture.

He grinned when he recalled the night marking a change in his fortunes, which until that time had been little more than a struggle for survival. The party at *Sydney House* in the Marina had introduced him to a new circle of clients and enhanced his reputation. But most significantly, the host of the party, the affable, extremely wealthy and, as chance would have it, gullible and easily led James, proved to be ripe for nurturing - a complete mug. Horse became a frequent visitor to James' residence in the Marina where he would be made welcome due to his apparently limitless supply of recreational drugs, and because he presented as an interesting and exotic character, at ease in the company of the wealthy young man's educated, kick-seeking friends.

Soon after Jonny's disappearance, he came up with the idea of a fantastic business venture, one that would be certain to see a massive return on the necessary investment.

As he stubbed out the remains of the cigar and took a sip of rum, he grinned at the recollection of how simple it had been to dupe the idiot into parting with ten thousand pounds. James fell over himself in his eagerness to accept the offer of a partnership in the venture, even though, to add a modicum of authenticity to the story, Horse mentioned there may be some risks involved.

'Nothing ventured, nothing gained! Count me in! I'll draw out the money first thing tomorrow. You can come with me - my bank's in Fareham. I'll drop you at the station straight after that. Does that give you enough time to get up to Town? Perhaps I should come with you?'

Horse had conjured up the story of a business meeting in London where the deal would be conducted, requiring the down-payment.

'Probably best if I go alone. I know these people - they might be suspicious if someone they don't know turns up,' he advised.

James drove him to the bank where he withdrew the money, and then on to the railway station in Fareham. Thinking back to that day, Horse laughed at just how easy the plan materialised. There had been no meeting in London. The mug in smart trousers and a blazer waved to him as the train pulled away - he nodded back with a huge grin splitting his face, already planning on how he might invest his newfound wealth. Of course, the down-side was that he could never return to the Marina – but, like all ventures, that one had run its course – it was time to move on to better things.

An expansion in his drug dealing activities had been his priority, which would be supported by the club. He invested a proportion of the money in stock and started paying a small network of trusted associates to deal on his behalf. The business was flourishing.

His glass now empty, he was about to screw the cap back on the bottle when, as so often happened when alcohol kicked in, his mood changed abruptly from contentment to melancholy. He sighed and filled it again with a small amount of rum.

'To you, Jonny - I wish you'd stuck around to share this with me.'

Jonny's death had hit him hard. It was the Warden at the Seaman's Mission, who showed him the brief newspaper article. The dark-bearded face stared back at him with his familiar cynical scowl in a prison mug shot. The narrative accompanying the picture reflected the Coroner's verdict: 'misadventure – suspected suicide – drugs overdose'.

Remembering his reaction on reading this, Horse, now in a sombre mood, muttered to himself: 'My fault, he died, I got him onto the hard stuff.'

Another slug of rum revived his spirits. 'Oh well, no point in dwelling on the past,' he said out loud to the empty office. He looked at his watch and noted it was now too late to do any of the tasks he had planned for the afternoon. He did a quick inventory in his head of what needed to be done before the club could open to the public, the grand opening set for the first Saturday in November.

'Plenty of time and...'

He was addressing the room again.

'There's a deputy to run around for me now.'

His thoughts turned to Frank. He reached for the bottle. 'Last one.' He realised he was now drunk.

'Can I trust him?' he asked the clock on the wall. 'Best take it step-by-step - introduce him to the business and then later some of the...' He struggled to find appropriate words to describe "more unusual activities".

Chapter 67

"FRANK WRITES A LETTER"

(Tuesday 22ⁿᵈ September 1964 – midday)
'This is it - I'm on the way up again!'

Frank spoke aloud to himself as if to affirm the reality of his new circumstances. Sitting on his bed, its ancient mattress and bedsprings sinking under his weight, he reminded himself, again, 'One more night in this shit hole.'

With a smile on his face, he lay back and gazed at the nicotine-stained ceiling. For the first time in many weeks, he realised his almost forgotten state of optimism had returned. In this positive mood, the impossible might be achieved - and at this moment, winning back his family dominated his thoughts.

'First things first, I need a well-paid job - one that will give me back my self-respect. Well, I'm well on the way to sorting that out!' he announced to the ceiling with a triumphant smile.

'Next? What happens next?' He frowned, his mood dampened a little. There had been no form of communication between them since the fateful day when she packed his case and kicked him out. How long ago was it? Six weeks? Seven?

Reminding himself he was now on the move back up from the pits, he forced his positive spirits to return.

'Well, one of us has got to break the silence - and as I created this mess, it should be me.'

As he lay staring upwards, he pondered the scale of the challenge facing him. What should I do? What would happen if I just went home - asked her to hear me out - talk things through like adults? He conjured the scene. Helen would be unwilling to listen to him, at least at first - but she might be persuaded. He imagined her expression and attitude transforming from reluctance to acceptance. 'Okay - but this is your last chance, Frank.'

But a more likely scenario replaced the happier one he created. The door would be slammed in his face - or not opened at all. She would not want to speak to me - not out of the blue, unexpectedly, without warning.

What if I wrote to her? 'Yes, that's what I'll do - write a letter!'

An hour ago, as he drove back from the club after his successful meeting with Horse, he promised himself a celebratory lunchtime session in a pub near to his digs. But now, eager to set his plans in motion, he decided to put off his celebration until the evening. He swung himself off his bed. 'Let's get this letter written!'

Later, after a visit to a corner shop where he bought a writing pad and a bottle of Quink ink for his fountain pen, he settled himself on the edge of his bed, balancing his suitcase on his knees as a make-shift desk, and started writing.

But words did not come easily. The wastebasket at his feet began to fill with screwed up sheets of paper. He swore in frustration - it was harder than he expected to convey the right message.

1 o'clock, he noted, glancing at his wrist watch. 'Sod it!' He picked up the writing pad and pocketed the pen. Perhaps a couple of pints–well, no more than three - might help free up his thoughts, he advised himself. Five minutes later, he was ensconced at a corner table, the only customer in the *Shipwright's Arms*, the nearest pub. After two beers, he found the words flowed. Expecting "last orders" to be called, he went up to the bar and asked for another beer and a whiskey chaser. He sat down again to finish the last few lines of his letter.

As he emptied the dregs of his third pint, the letter was complete. He read it through with meticulous care, anxious to make sure he had included everything he wanted to say. There were four key messages he wanted to stand out. First, it had all been a massive mistake - madness on his part. Second, he was truly sorry. Third, he would never behave in the same way again. Fourth, he wanted to be forgiven - to make a fresh start - to be part of the family again.

After studying his script, he concluded all those points were clearly articulated. He nodded and smiled in satisfaction. But a thought occurred to him: he hadn't mentioned Vee. He took a sip of his whiskey and thought about this. Blaming her would not only be unfair but would no doubt be rejected by Helen - sisterly love and all that. And, I've no idea what Vee might have said. He frowned in the sure knowledge Helen would be protective of her sister. He wrote a short paragraph suggesting the fault was all his, and Vee should not be blamed.

'That should do the job,' he whispered. An imagined scene of Helen reading his carefully crafted words appeared through beer and whiskey filters. She would frown and shake her head at his generosity in shouldering all blame - but she would know much of the fault lay with her sister.

For several moments, he pondered what address to add at the top of his letter. Perhaps the Labour Exchange C/O Trevor? No, that would be too tragic, he concluded. He jotted the club's address and then, as an afterthought, he added a few words of explanation at the foot, hinting he had landed a responsible managerial role with significant responsibilities. The images of that morning's introduction to the strippers flitted through his head - Helen wouldn't approve of that! He smiled at the thought.

At last, satisfied all was in order, he folded the letter and placed it into the envelope. As he penned her address on the front, he felt a sudden wave of emotion - his eyes misted. 'Come on - be positive,' he whispered - then glanced towards the landlord who was watching him. He slipped the envelope into his jacket pocket, making a mental note to buy a stamp.

Later that afternoon, he was still sitting at the bar. The landlord seemed eager to keep his only customer and did not call "Time". With his task completed, Frank became convivial and welcomed the opportunity to talk. Bert, as the landlord introduced himself, was a good listener. By the time, he fell out of the pub door, it was early evening and getting dark. As he lurched the few yards to the front door of the boarding house, he remembered the letter in his pocket. He staggered across the road to the post box and, after several attempts, fed it into the slot.

Chapter 68

"THE REACTION"

(Saturday 26th September 1964)

Helen frowned, recognising the unmistakable scrawl. For a few seconds, she considered handing the unwanted envelope back to the Post Office cashier with a curt "Return to sender" - but instead, she paid the sixpence with good grace. Standing on the pavement outside, she ripped it open and read the letter. She took a long time to decipher the words as there were so many crossings out. Some of the text made no sense at all but, eventually, the overall message became clear.

Had Frank seen her expression as she finished reading, folded his letter and slipped it back in the envelope, he would not have bothered writing.

In the safe cocoon of her car, she shouted at the windscreen, 'You absolute, bloody bastard!'

Half an hour later, Helen sat in the *Crows Nest*, already well into a glass of white wine – a highly unusual activity for her as she would not normally contemplate drinking at lunchtime. Nigel, who arrived after her, was reading the letter.

'Well, he's certainly laid his soul bare. He's admitted everything - come clean.'

'No, he hasn't!' she said loudly. Glancing around embarrassed someone may have heard her outburst, she lowered her voice. 'Meaningless platitudes! Complete rubbish! I bet he was drunk when he wrote this.'

She took a sip of her wine. Nigel said nothing. Please say something - *anything*! she thought, studying his face and looking for a reaction.

'He's said nothing about why he started an affair with my sister,' she continued after a pause, 'Does he expect me to think it simply happened for no reason? Just one of those things? A mistake? An accident? How can he believe I might forgive him? And I'm not exonerating *her*, not one bit - but it's obvious he wants me to think she was entirely to blame - that she was a temptress - and he, the poor weak man, fell under her spell.'

'Are you going to reply?'

'No, absolutely not! I'm not going to give him the satisfaction of knowing I've read his claptrap!'

'Look, this is none of my business - but I do care about you, and all of this - well, I know all that's happened must be taking its toll on you, and obviously Peter as well. If there's anything....'

'I know you care about me and Peter,' she said leaning over and kissing him softly on the cheek, 'but this is your business as well - of course, it is. You're with me now. We may not have told anyone yet - apart from Dad - but you are a part of this - and I trust you.'

'I presume your solicitor will sort out access rights, so Frank can see his son.'

'Yes, that'll be taken care of.'

She paused as if pondering this thought. 'But, I'm not ready to let him anywhere near him yet. God knows what he might say to him, and Peter's been hurt enough.'

Nigel took hold of her hand and squeezed it. 'I'll be here for you. Just talk to me. I promise not to interfere, and I'll understand if you want to sort things out with Frank.'

'You must be joking, Nigel. You can't possibly mean that! I will never get back with Frank - Hell would freeze over first!'

'Well, look on the bright side, Helen.'

'What's that?'

'You have a written confession - proof of his adultery. And what's more, you have an address. You've got what you need now to file for divorce.'

'You know what? I think you're right. I've been getting myself worked up and angry when really, I should be happy Frank's dropped himself right in it! I'll ring Eugene this afternoon and make an appointment for tomorrow. Now, how about getting me another glass of wine? I feel like celebrating!'

Chapter 69

"ENTRAPMENT"

(Monday 28ᵗʰ September 1964)

Helen woke with a very rare hangover. Her celebrations with Nigel had progressed into the evening with a sumptuous meal at a restaurant on the High Street, where he played the attentive host, ensuring a steady flow of wine. However, despite the dull ache in her head, which a light breakfast failed to quell, she started her day with a sense of happy purpose.

Soon after, just a few minutes into her appointment with the solicitor, Eugene Morgan, her buoyant optimism had vanished to be replaced with - well, bitterness could only go part way to explain how she now felt.

For a few moments, Helen almost gave in to a primeval urge to launch herself across the desk and slap what she translated as condescending smugness from the solicitor's face. Instead, she fixed him with a stare so filled with loathing, he flinched and turned his head away as though embarrassed. In her mind, the objects on his tidy desktop: a polished brass lamp, the pile of leather-bound books, an inkwell and blotter, all fell to the floor as she dived across to assault him. She added the satisfying scene of the ink bottle splashing its indelible contents to be absorbed by the expensive Persian rug on which his desk stood.

When he spoke, after several seconds, she noted his confidence and assuredness had returned.

'I don't mean to be rude, Mrs Armstrong, but this letter,' he picked up the piece of paper lying on the desk in front of him and held it like an exhibit, 'will not be admissible. I have dealt with many cases of adultery and I can tell you, in my professional judgement, the Divorce Court will not deem this as credible evidence, and...'

'Surely you can see he's admitted what he did! I know his writing's all over the place - no doubt he was drunk when he wrote what he did - but there it is in black and white: he's stated he slept with my sister!'

Her anger now past its peak gave way to frustration and disappointment. Of course, he was right, she acknowledged to herself.

His patient explanation why Frank's semi-coherent ramblings would not be accepted as proof of his guilt, although unwelcome, made sense. But knowing her hopes of being officially rid of her now hated husband lay in tatters, and the remembered recent conversation in this same office, where the suggestion people might consider her at least partially to blame for the behaviour of her errant spouse, compounded her misery.

'Mrs Armstrong, I am fully aware your husband is as guilty as sin. You are the injured party - and I want you to know I am on your side. However, I must abide by professional standards, and it would be wrong for me to give you false hope. The Law is very clear on...'

'The Law is an ass!' she snapped back, rising from her chair and snatching her coat from the stand by the door.

'Mrs Armstrong. Helen, please!'

She paused, unable to turn around, conscious of the tears now cascading down her cheeks, and not wanting him to see them. Suddenly a wave of guilt swept through her. It isn't his fault, he's just doing his job.

'I'm sorry if I appear rude,' she managed to whisper, 'but this whole business is getting me down. I want that man out of my life once and for all.'

He said something in reply, but she was already through the door and running to the stairs leading down to the car park and the safe cocoon of her car where she finally allowed her misery to overwhelm her.

***

Later that morning, her emotions more or less under control again, Helen phoned Nigel at his office. He groaned softly when she told him the outcome of her meeting with the solicitor.

'I don't believe it! Oh, Helen, I'm so sorry. This is all my fault - I shouldn't have raised your hopes like I did.'

'No, Nigel, none of this is down to you. What you said seemed so right. I mean, what else does the Law need as proof of adultery? Apparently, a written confession isn't enough. How crazy is that?'

'Bonkers! Did he tell you what you should do?'

'He didn't get the chance - I walked out before he could advise me. I should call him - no, I will call him to apologise. I can't blame him for just doing his job. Oh, God, Nigel, this is such a mess, and it's not doing Peter any good - he doesn't understand what's going on.'

'So, what are you going to do? I mean, what *can* you do?'

'Nothing! I can't do a damned thing. If Frank won't agree to a divorce, he can drag the whole business out for as long as he likes. And no doubt he will. He's deluded enough, judging by that stupid letter, to think I might consider taking him back.'

'There has to be some way of getting rid of him, I mean...'

'There's nothing. Let's just try and forget he exists.'

***

For several minutes after the call ended, Nigel found himself lost in thought. His anger and frustration simmered: Frank remained the final obstacle to his plans to set up home with Helen.

'I'm going to finish you, you bastard!' he muttered. But how? 'Can a leopard change its spots?' he whispered,

485

without knowing why. But in a flash of awareness, he understood the basis of the notion suggested by his subconscious, and a plan began to formulate.

***

(Thursday 8th October 1964 - 6.30pm)

Nigel studied the photograph held in his fingers then looked up again and nodded.

'That's him - the one in the jacket with the fag in his mouth walking past the newsagents. See him?'

He turned to the young woman sitting in the passenger seat of his Cortina and experienced, not for the first time since meeting her in the pub in the red-light district, a mix of loathing and attraction.

She nodded and smiled. 'I see him. Not a bad looking bloke - a snappy dresser. So, what's he done to you, then?'

'Long story - and anyway, you don't need to know the details. But he's not as nice as you seem to think. He deserves what's coming.'

He stared intently at his adversary striding down the pavement across the road from where he observed. 'True to form, Frank,' he whispered with a satisfied smile. 'Right, he's gone into the pub, the Watney's house - do you see? Over there - the...'

'*Gauntlet*,' she finished for him, 'I know it well - done a bit of business in there. Now, what did you say you'll pay me? Twenty quid now and another thirty once the job's done?'

'Yes, as I promised. So, do you think you can do it?'

'Of course! There's not many men can turn me down. Think I might enjoy this one, though, he's...'

'Right,' he said, cutting her off, 'here's your twenty - and take this.' He passed her a plastic sachet. 'As soon as you get the chance, slip it into his drink, that should make things a lot easier. You'll have to move fast as soon as he drinks it, though - it kicks in pretty quick. You don't want him nodding off in the pub. Get him out and into the hotel room as soon you can. I'll be watching from the car. You've told your man friend I'll be coming in, I hope, I don't want any...'

'Jerry's alright - he won't cause any problems. He knows what'll happen if he did - his wife wouldn't be too pleased if I told her what he's been up to. Now, why don't you just leave it to me?'

Nigel followed her with his eyes as she crossed the road and hurried towards the pub entrance where she disappeared inside. He frowned as, not for the first time, the implications of what he planned to do presented in his mind - and the consequences if something went wrong. A man-to-man phone call to the solicitor had gained his confidence. Helen must not know the entire truth. A subtle bending of the story, he had agreed with Eugene Morgan, would be acceptable. But the solicitor did not know what the full details of the plan entailed - if he did - well, there would be no plan.

'Let's hope this works,' Nigel whispered, as he pulled into the traffic and headed for his next rendezvous.

***

Frank settled himself into his usual seat away from the busy bar area. He chugged a couple of mouthfuls of beer and then, with a satisfied sigh, put his pint down, lit a cigarette and surveyed the room. Even though the pub opened for the evening trade only half an hour ago, a steady flow of punters began to pile in. He surveyed with detached interest as they formed sociable groups, not wanting to join any of them, enjoying his solitude and anonymity. His focus drew inwards, and he reflected on his revived good fortune and what might be described as newfound happiness. Although his positive emotions did not project outwards, inwardly he smiled and

487

congratulated himself on the progress he had made towards gaining his life back. Funny, he mused, how beer and a fag always made things better.

The Gauntlet had become his local since starting work at *Ravelles* two weeks ago. The pub was a short distance from the club. He liked the atmosphere: friendly and non-intrusive - a place he might be alone with his thoughts without the undertow of aggression he had become accustomed to in the dock area pubs he had frequented in what he now considered his former life.

His first pint vanished in a matter of minutes. Glancing back at the table, anxious not to lose his space, he stood at the bar waiting to order a second, wishing he had planned ahead and bought two pints in the first place.

'Bitter and a whiskey chaser, please,' he said, relieved to be served at last. At that moment, he became aware of a woman squeezed next to him. His eyes were drawn to the twenty-pound note, which she waved to attract the attention of the busy bar staff. Must be buying one hell of a round, he thought. For a few seconds, their eyes met. She flashed him a smile before returning to her attempts to be served. In an instant, he had assessed her. Not bad, he thought, not bad at all.

The barman serving him regarded the banknote as he placed Frank's drinks in front of him on the bar and shook his head. 'Sorry, love, I can't take that – Landlord's policy, I'm afraid. Too many fakes about. Don't you have anything smaller?'

'Oh, what a nuisance,' said the woman, 'I'm sorry, I haven't. Oh well, I suppose I'll have to find somewhere to change it for...'

'Please, let me buy you a drink. I'm guessing you could do with one!'

She rewarded him with a smile which made her even more attractive. 'Oh, how sweet of you, but I couldn't possibly. Thanks, all the same - you're very kind,' she purred.

'I insist,' said Frank, nodding to the barman.

***

Rita trained her eyes on his back as he prised himself through the thickening crowd towards the bar area into which he disappeared. Confident she would now be obscured from his vision, she glanced at his glass of whiskey, untouched on the table. With a quick, furtive scan to ensure no one was watching her, she reached into her handbag, pulled out the sachet, which was opened in readiness, and tipped it into his drink. She picked up the glass and swirled the contents, checking the powder had dissolved. Another quick survey of the surrounding space - no one was watching, she noted with a small sigh of relief. She dropped the little plastic bag to the floor and slid it under the table with her foot. With this part of her plan achieved, she began to relax.

Frank seems like an okay bloke, she thought - a real gentleman and not bad looking either. I wonder what he's done to deserve this?

The approach by the man earlier that afternoon had been unusual. She remembered thinking he might be a plain clothed policeman trying to trick her - she had been on the verge of telling him to get lost - but he persuaded her with the offer of easy money, and she dismissed her suspicions. He offered no reason for what he wanted her to do, nor did he introduce himself. Despite her curiosity, she had not pushed the matter.

After spending an hour with Frank, during which time he bought her three gin and tonics, and he had drunk the same number of pints, she was almost tempted to welch on her agreement with the anonymous man, forgo the additional thirty pounds and spend time with this interesting and attractive character instead. Then she reminded herself of her current dire financial circumstances. I need that thirty quid, she persuaded herself.

**

As Frank waited at the bar for the third or fourth time - he had forgotten exactly how many times - a familiar voice of sense chastised him. 'What the hell are you playing at? Thought you'd cleaned your act up. You're not behaving much like a man who wants to win his wife and son back again.'

'Cheers, mate.'

He picked up the gin and tonic and took his change. For a few moments, he stared at the drink as he sought justification for what he was doing. 'What am I playing at?' he whispered. He understood what the darker side of his character intended - that side did not have to try *too* hard to persuade him down the path of temptation.

'Oh, bugger it!' he muttered, picking up his pint with the other hand. 'Come on, a few drinks with an attractive woman is hardly a crime, is it?' He turned and started to prise himself back through the thickening crowd to the table.

**

She shot a smile at him with her nod of thanks. He smiled back, the door to his conscience now firmly shut.

'Frank, I was just thinking,' she said as he resumed his seat, 'it doesn't look like my friend is going to turn up after all, so, if you want, we could go somewhere else. It's getting a bit crowded in here. Do you fancy coming with me?'

'Sounds like a good plan!' he replied without hesitation. 'Why don't we neck these and go?'

After a few moments, he placed his empty beer glass on the table and wiped his mouth.

'Here's to a nice evening,' she said holding out her drink and nodding to the glass of whiskey still untouched.

'Cheers!' he said, picking up the glass and chinking it to hers before swallowing the contents in one large gulp.

***

Rita led the way to the exit, one arm trailing, gripping his hand. He focused on a spot between her shoulders, finding that, if he moved his eyes, his vision dimmed. Bloody hell, he thought, I've drunk more than I thought I had – I'm pissed! A wave of nausea hit with a suddenness that frightened him - for a moment he thought he would throw up, but a sudden rush of cold air swept the urge away.

They were walking along the pavement, at least she was - he moved in a lurching motion. When he collided with a lamppost, for reasons he could not fathom, he giggled uncontrollably.

He tried to speak but words would not form, only an incoherent grunt.

She was laughing. They stopped. Her palm had reached out towards his face and slapped him gently as though trying to wake him. Then they were moving again, and he realised the end of his tie was gripped in her hand and she was pulling him along like a reluctant dog on a lead.

Suddenly she stopped and huddled in close. Her lips covered his briefly before moving to his ear. 'Come on Frank,' she whispered seductively, 'we're nearly there.'

His legs moved as if drawn by some magnetic force without the need for control by his mind. Despite his senses being dulled, he retained one coherent thought: something's wrong!

She was close to him, an arm around his waist, pulling and pushing. 'Come on Frank, you can do it.' Her face drifted in and out of focus. He could feel himself stumbling and sensed she was struggling to keep him upright. His mind appeared incapable of connecting logical thought - he felt compelled to be led by her.

'Here we are! In you go, Frank.'

She was pushing him forward through a doorway. The smell of stale cigarette smoke and oily cooking smells assuaged his nostrils and for a few moments, he was able to make some sense of his surroundings. He registered grimy linoleum under his feet, a door to his left, which was open. She gripped his collar with one hand, an arm around his middle, pushing and pulling him forward to a flight of stairs drifting in and out of focus ahead. He had no idea how he negotiated those stairs, nor how he came to be lying on a bed, staring up at a yellow, nicotine stained ceiling with a single, brightly lit bulb dangling a few feet above his nose. For a few seconds, he thought he was back in the hated room in the hostel for travelling salesmen - his heart lurched. He passed out.

***

The dream was seductive and powerful. His senses revived behind the fug of his unconsciousness and he became aware of her perfume, cheap but alluring, then the warmth of her body that appeared to wrap around him. He willed his eyes to open, but the effort was too much, nor could he move his arms or legs - they felt detached and beyond his control. She was moving, though, he could sense that, and through the slits of his eyelids, he saw enough to realise she was naked, and then, his dulled awareness registered he was as well.

There were voices - muffled and incoherent. A woman's voice - hers of course - said something in an irritated tone. A man's voice responded, indistinct and distorted like a record being played at a slower speed than intended. Unable to move of his own volition, he sensed he was being manoeuvred. A flash of light registered, even though his eyes automatically squeezed shut in response, quickly followed by another, and then another.

***

Frank woke shivering with cold and with an aching head, the pain from which radiated from somewhere behind his eyes, stabbing fingers of pain into the recesses of his skull. After a few seconds, his consciousness returned enough for him to register the unfamiliarity of his surroundings, and for panic to kick in.

'What the hell?' he whispered, staring around him wildly. He spotted his clothes bundled untidily on a chair next to the bed on which he lay. He lifted an arm and stared at the space on his wrist where his watch should have been.

'Fuck,' he groaned.

With considerable effort, he managed to swing his legs to the floor and sit upright. He plucked his jacket from the top of the pile and checked the pocket where he always stored his wallet. Gone - he knew it would be.

***

(The following morning)

Frank put the clipboard down on the bar with a heavy sigh. 'Okay, all done,' he muttered, 'Fully stocked and ready for opening night. Now let's just hope the decorators will be finished on time.'

His bar muster had taken him far longer than it would have done in more normal circumstances. But recent hours had been anything but normal. Memories of the previous evening flashed through his mind in incoherent detail and illogical sequence. The only part of his memory he could piece together with any confidence of reality was the drinking session with the woman who called herself Rita. What happened after that blurred into a confusion of thought and random images which may or may not represent what really occurred last night. He recalled a man's voice, incoherent and indistinct, somewhere in the background, together with a woman's soft tones - Rita's or someone else? And those sudden bursts of light - one, two, three - like a.....? Like a camera flashing! This thought caused his heart to lurch in the realisation of what might have happened. But why would someone...? None of this made any sense.

That he woke in an unfamiliar room, naked, cold and robbed, presented as the one anchoring, irrefutable fact. But the events leading up to that remained indistinct and confused. What the hell happened?

He locked the bar, and with a heavy sigh, weariness making every movement seem heavy and laborious, heaved himself onto a bar stool. Having lit a cigarette, he leaned back and stared at the freshly painted ceiling, deep in thought. Should I contact the police? He pondered this thought for a few moments, imagining the probable response: 'So, you say you were drunk, and you ended up in a room with a woman who you met only a short while before, and she stripped you naked without you knowing.

494

And then some bloke came in and snapped a few photos of you. Oh, and then you woke up later to find you'd been robbed. Well, sir....'

He dismissed the idea with a snort of self-derision. Unable to make any sense of what occurred a few hours ago, he decided to try and forget about the whole confusing incident.

Chapter 70

"DECREE NISI"

(Saturday 7th November 1964 - Opening Night)

'Early days, Frank, just teething issues. Okay, so there weren't as many punters as we'd thought there'd be, but...'

'Twenty-five, Horse, and some of those didn't stay for long. I had to throw two others out because they got abusive towards the strippers!'

'First night - things will get better from here. Word will spread, and before long, we'll be turning people away at the doors because we're so full. This will be the club to be in, just you wait and see. You're worrying too much! We'll work on a marketing campaign - you and me. We're a great team - we can sort this out!'

Frank smiled and nodded despite his disappointment, finding it difficult not to be affected by Horse's enthusiasm and his buoyant optimism. 'Okay, if you say so, Boss. By the way, I've got a few ideas about what we need to do - I'll run them past you on Monday.'

'Brilliant! I can see you're a man with a vision - like me! Come on, let's get pissed!'

They sat in the smoke-filled bar, empty except for them. The detritus from the evening's business: glasses, some still full, and ashtrays brimming with stubs, littered the counter. Horse poured them both a large shot of rum. Frank was about to ask for whiskey instead, but he stopped himself.

The drinking session went on long into the night. After several such occasions shared with him, he anticipated his boss's mood would change, as it always did, once he reached the point where his speech became slurred and he appeared to detach from reality. Horse liked to drink, usually rum, although Frank noticed he never touched a drop during the working evening. Now the evening's work had finished, he clearly relished the prospect of a drinking session.

Later, well into the small hours of the morning, Frank, having switched from rum to beer, remained relatively sober. An almost empty bottle of rum stood on the bar in front of Horse. Their conversation had dried up a while ago. Horse seemed to have disappeared into a private world. He mumbled incoherently, laughing now and again as if in response to a joke only he could hear. Slumped forward onto the bar, he appeared oblivious to his presence a few feet way. Frank tried to make out the words - he leaned towards him and listened intently.

'I know, got to be careful and...' More incoherent rambling. Frank observed him for a while, both bemused and concerned.

'Best make this the last one,' he whispered, picking up his half empty pint and taking a gulp of beer. Fatigue kicked in - his eyes were becoming heavy. He drained his glass and placed it on the bar.

'I'm going to turn in,' he murmured, touching Horse on the shoulder to get his attention.

Horse waved in a vague motion, his face split with an inane grin. Frank took this as assent, slipped off the stool, steadying himself with one hand on the seat, ready to aim himself to the exit door and the stairs beyond leading up to his flat.

As he started walking away, he stopped and considered Horse, who was slumped forward, his forehead resting on the bar surface, mumbling to himself.

'Not being funny, but don't you think you should call it a day? I'll help you up if you like.'

Horse's abode was opposite his on the upper floor of the building, which involved climbing two flights of steps. He doubted his boss would make it unaided.

'Sh'all right.' Horse waved his hand in a dismissive gesture. 'Finish this first,' he slurred, reaching for the almost empty bottle of rum. Frank shrugged and made towards the exit. Horse grabbed hold of his arm as he passed. 'Hang on a sec.' He pulled a crumpled envelope from his jacket pocket and said something which sounded like 'Came this morning - sorry.'

Frank didn't look at it as he climbed the stairs - but his excitement mounted in the sure knowledge it was a response to his letter - it couldn't be anything else - after all, no one knew where he lived. A few minutes later, he was in his room.

As soon as he turned on the light and examined the envelope, his excited anticipation evaporated in an instant. The official wording above the address read "Morgan & Hill Solicitors." Unfolding the letter within, it took just seconds for him to realise his hopes of reconciliation were dashed.

***

Sleep eluded him despite his exhaustion and the effects of alcohol. Printed indelibly on his mind were the words "Decree Nisi" and below that the heading "Formal Notification of Intention to Divorce". As if taunting him, key phrases kept repeating in his head, recalled from the text. "Marriage irretrievably broken down" - "Grounds for divorce have been proven on the basis of the Respondent's adultery" - "Should the respondent wish to appeal" - "Marriage will end formally within six weeks of the date of despatch".

Frank realised all his hopes had been dashed in an instant.

He thought about his own letter and the effort he applied to create the right message and tone. What had been the point? Vague memories of the afternoon when he wrote his carefully crafted, soul-bearing plea drifted around his head. He remembered how drunk he had been. Acknowledgement of this fact prompted doubts as to whether she received his heart-felt rendering at all.

A scene flashed into his mind of his hand attempting to feed the envelope into the post box. A task that would be easy when sober! Did it drop on the pavement? No, I remember pushing it in, he assured himself.

'Bollocks, I didn't put a stamp on it,' he muttered to the ceiling. He imagined his letter sitting in a sorting office somewhere, abandoned and pointless. If she had received it, would I be reading this now? he wondered. But, then again, how did the solicitors find my address? Was it logged in some official document now I'm in work? Yes, that must be it!

Unable to sleep, he got up and went into his small living room where he sat and smoked a cigarette and stared blankly at the wall. The formal notification his marriage would end lay on the coffee table in front of him - he picked it up and then dropped it back. No need to read it again - every word was now imprinted on his soul.

His agitation increased as his mind tried to create a coherent plan. The thought his letter might not have reached Helen created a small spark of optimism. His bitter self-recrimination at his drunken mistake slowly dissipated with the hope that, just maybe, all was not lost. His hands were shaking - misery combined with a desperate urge to do something to save the situation - he needed to move, to think.

He donned his raincoat, went down the stairs and out of the front door of the club into the dark, damp, empty street outside and started walking. After two hours, the faint light of dawn heralded a dank, grey day. His thoughts were now focused on a course of action: a simple plan, but one that filled him with dread. He needed to phone - beg her to stop the legal proceedings and to agree on a meeting. This was all based on the assumption his letter, into which he put so much careful thought, had not been received - the tiniest glimmer of hope.

Now 8 o'clock and a long way from his flat, he stood, hunched into the turned-up collar of his Mac', his hair drenched with the all-pervading dampness of the relentless drizzle. He smoked a cigarette as he stared at the telephone box in front of him.

In his mind he imagined the scene at his home - his former home, he reminded himself, in Fairfield. Even though it was Sunday morning, he guessed she would be up and about now. A vision of her appeared: she was preparing breakfast for Peter, humming along to some tune or other playing on the transistor radio. The happy scene blurred as tears filled his eyes.

Too early to call yet, he advised himself - but he knew the real reason for the delay was fear. He stood outside the phone box, preferring the damp but fresh air to the claustrophobic interior, knowing it would reek of stale tobacco and urine After ten minutes, he took a deep shuddering breath. Time to make that call.

He dialled - a pause - the number was ringing.

'Fairfield 2413, hello?' The familiar voice reached his ears. He hesitated then forced himself to speak.

'Helen, it's me. Please, can I...'

A click - the line went dead.

Chapter 71

"FRANK MAKES A DECISION"

(Sunday 8th November 1964 – early morning)
When Frank turned into the road leading to the club, the rain had stopped, a wintery sun added a little cheer - and he had made a decision. Despair and dejection, his immediate feelings when he left the telephone box, were now replaced with a grim determination not to accept defeat.

He muttered to himself as he trudged back to the club. 'I'll have to fight to get her back. Stupid to think it would be so straight forward. I need to see her - talk it through face to face.'

A hot shower, followed by a mug of coffee and a cigarette, revived his spirits and helped him clarify his plan of action. Within thirty minutes, he was dressed and ready to go. The image he saw in the mirror as he checked himself over kindled memories of an earlier, much happier time when he used to meet with Helen on their clandestine dates at the Crows Nest. Freshly shaved, he applied a light splash of "Old Spice" - not too much. His tie neatly knotted over a country-check shirt, and his sports jacket held over his shoulder created the exact image he wanted. His reflection nodded back to him – 'Just right, but there's one thing missing.'

He walked across the road to a florist and bought a large bouquet. 'She loves flowers,' he thought, smiling. 'Not that you paid much attention to that,' whispered a cynical voice in his head.

With a sense of purpose and grim determination, the flowers resting on the passenger seat, he drove towards Fairfield.

****

Her anger in the minutes after slamming down the receiver earlier had been palpable. She swore and shouted, waking Peter, who appeared at the top of the stairs looking down at her, an expression of frightened bewilderment on his face.

'It's alright, come down - everything's okay.'

The quizzical look on his face told her he wasn't convinced.

'Was it my daddy?' he asked.

She shook her head. 'No, it was no one,' she replied A small stab of guilt at lying to him was quickly quashed - he is a "no one" to me, she thought.

A tiny plastic submarine fell into Peter's bowl when she poured his Rice Krispies from the box - this distracted him. She took the opportunity to phone Nigel.

'Please come over straight away if you can. I need you here with me.'

****

Later that morning, they sat in the living room, though not next to each other. With Peter in the house, they avoided any impression of intimacy.

'Listen, calm down,' said Nigel,' he was bound to call at some point. I would imagine, he would have received the "Decree Nisi" by now - maybe that's why he called. Although how he could possibly bring himself to talk to you after what he was caught doing!'

'Please, Nigel, I really don't want to talk about that. How can he have stooped that low?'

She paused for a moment before shooting a questioning look at him.

'Nigel, I'm not angry, but why did you do it?'

'Hire a private investigator?'

'Yes.'

'Well, I would have thought that was obvious. You were so miserable about the - you, know, the solicitor's dismissal of the letter. I had to do something. And, as it turned out, it took no time at all for Frank to...'

'Please don't! It makes me sick to think the man I once trusted - and loved - is capable of such a thing! Even after I found about his...,' she struggled to keep her emotions in check, 'affair, I at least thought there would be something left in him, something that in time might allow me to - well, respect him, at least a little - but now?' She shuddered before adding, 'How can I let him near Peter, knowing he's been with a...?' She paused before spitting out the word, 'prostitute?'

'Helen, it will be okay,' said Nigel in a soothing tone. 'Leave the details of access to the solicitor - you pay him to worry about that. You're in control now, remember that. You call the shots. You set the ground rules.'

Helen considered this. 'You're right, I know you are. But the thought he expected me to talk to him after...' She left the sentence unfinished, unable to find suitable words to express her anger.

Regarding Nigel, who sat, she noted, with an unexpected twinge of sadness, in Frank's favourite chair, the realisation how much an essential part of her life he had become swept over her. As each day passed, they became closer - and she more dependent upon him. And yet Frank remained in the background, a malevolent presence - first his rambling letter and now his attempt to speak to her.

'Perhaps your solicitor might issue an injunction against him - stop him contacting you?'

She smiled, wondering if he could read her thoughts.

'Yes, I think that's a damned good idea, although I know we've got to talk at some point. There'll be the details over access to discuss for a start. Mind you, he never mentioned Peter in his letter, did he? Didn't ask about him - nothing!'

'Well, I'm sure he hasn't forgotten about his son - he can't be that bad.'

Helen snorted. 'Can't he?'

'Actually, you don't need to speak to him at all, at least not directly. Like I said, that's what you pay a solicitor to do on your behalf.'

'Perhaps you're right- no, you are right. But...'

She stood and walked to the window before turning.

'He destroyed us! Peter and me - and...' Her voice became more bitter. 'Even Vee's life's been torn apart. I can't ever forgive her - nor can Dad - but she's gone now - for good. And he's the reason for that - the inconsiderate, selfish bastard!'

Nigel leaned towards her, his arms wide in a gesture of placation.

'Okay, I take your point. Listen, how about we forget about him for now? Let's go out for the day. Take a drive somewhere?'

He hesitated, before adding: 'Maybe we should take Peter with us instead of dropping him off at your dad's?'

She looked up at the ceiling above which was Peter's bedroom, where he would be playing.

'That's a wonderful idea! Let's do it. I'll get him ready. You can decide where we're going!'

Within fifteen minutes, they were on their way.

**

There had been an accident on the A27. Frank stared at the queue of traffic stretching into the distance and cursed. The stall in his momentum towards Fairfield presented as an omen - a warning he might be, probably was, wasting his time. His determination waned and, for a few moments, the idea of turning around and driving back to Southampton presented as highly tempting - but an element of resolve kicked in and he persevered. The traffic moved again, and he continued his journey and mission.

It was midday when he reached his destination. As he drove past the familiar sights along the High Street and then along the coast road leading to the cottage, he experienced an almost unbearable sensation of nostalgia and longing.

Pulling up outside his former home, it took several deep breaths to calm his nerves. He looked towards the front door and then each of the windows - no movement. Surely, she would have heard the unmistakable noise of the Healey's engine?

His thoughts taunted him. What did you expect? Helen looking out of a window in the hope you might turn up?

Her car was missing from its normal spot outside the cottage, but he noticed a Cortina parked a little farther on. Perhaps she's traded in the Gazelle?

With the bouquet in his arms, he walked up the garden path and, after a few moments of hesitation, knocked on the door. He waited, breathing hard. No response.

Sitting back in the car, the window wound down as he smoked a cigarette, he thought back to previous patterns of activity. She always stayed at home on Sunday mornings - but that had been while he played golf with her dad. Later, they would meet at Bob's house - an extended visit to the Swan would often follow while Helen prepared Sunday dinner, which she always seemed to enjoy doing. Peter would be there, of course, playing in the front room, or in the garden. The memories of the convivial family gathering, which often included Vee, flooded back.

'Christ, if only I could turn back the clock,' he muttered.

Perhaps she's at her dad's already, he wondered. Although she doesn't usually stay over - so she's bound to return at some point today. He noted the time: almost 1 o'clock. If she had gone out, it would most likely be at

Bob's for lunch - no, "Brunch," isn't that what he called it? So, in that case, she's unlikely to be back before three at the earliest. He knew exactly where his train of thought was taking him - and within five minutes, he was driving into the car park of the *Crows Nest*. Shortly after that, with a pint of ale in one hand and a cigarette in the other, he felt much calmer.

***

'Well, I thought it was wonderful!' Helen announced, her voice filled with enthusiasm. 'Did you enjoy the film, Peter? I bet you loved the songs!'

They both laughed when the sardonic grunt from the back seat of the car conveyed Peter's lack of interest in "Mary Poppins," the movie he had been forced to endure.

'Well, that's telling you!' said Nigel chuckling. 'And, to be perfectly honest, I think I share his opinion.'

'Come on, it can't have been that bad!'

'Yes, it was!' they responded in unison.

'But you liked your afternoon tea, didn't you?' said Nigel. A quick glance back into the back seat confirmed that, yes, Peter approved of that part of their trip out.

'Thought you did, judging by the amount of cake you got through!' Helen muttered.

'You're a growing lad, aren't you, Peter?'

Nigel turned around and smiled at him. Peter nodded and grinned back.

Helen turned her head and smiled. 'Thanks for a lovely day, Nigel. It helped take my mind off - well, you know - things.' She adjusted the rear-view mirror, so she could see Peter's face.

'You're welcome. I've enjoyed your company - and Peter's of course!'

She took a hand from off the steering wheel and patted his hand. 'I think we're making progress.'

'I feel the same way.'

The traffic on the A27 slowed their journey considerably. By the time they turned onto the coast road leading to the cottage, the light had faded. But, as they drew up outside, there was no mistaking the Healey parked under a street lamp.

'Oh God!' she whispered. 'He's here - that's his car.'

'Okay, just stay calm - I'll deal with this,' Nigel said, his voice level and just above a whisper.

Parking the car just behind the Healey, Helen switched off the engine. For several seconds, she studied the rear of the car. Although not sure, instinct told her Frank was sat in it. She dreaded the scene that would no doubt follow.

***

Frank woke with a start - momentarily disorientated. Then he remembered where he was and why. It was the sound of the car approaching, he realised, and that had jerked him out of his slumber. The reflection of the headlamps blinded him briefly when he squinted into the rear-view mirror. He glanced at his watch - nearly 5 o'clock.

Car doors were being opened and slammed shut - a glance at the wing mirror confirmed what he guessed. She stood staring at his car, her arms folded in what struck him as a protective motion across her chest. A movement behind her - it was Peter. He pointed at the car and stared up at her no doubt saying something like, 'It's Daddy's car!'

'Okay, let's move,' his inner voice commanded. He almost forgot the flowers and had to duck back in to scoop them up. Emerging, laden with the bouquet, he turned towards where she stood a few moments before. A blur of movement - he spotted her walking to the front door, dragging Peter behind her. He struggled, trying to pull his hand away from hers. 'Daddy!' he shouted.

Frank ran up the garden path after her, a little unsteadily. He reached out his free hand towards her shoulder, but not touching. Peter snatched his hand from her grip and now clung to his leg.

'Helen, please stop! - I only want to talk, nothing else.'

She turned her head and glared at him. In the faint light thrown by the street lamp, he could see her eyes were filled with tears.

'Go away Frank - I don't want you here, nor does Peter. Now leave us alone! Go away!'

She fumbled with a key, unlocked the door and pushed it open. Reaching down, she grabbed Peter's arm and yanked him through the doorway.

Frank's fingers caught in the door as she tried to slam it shut in his face. He howled in pain. Leaning into the gap between the door and the frame, he found her face within inches of his. Despite the throbbing pain in his hand, he forced the words out.

'Please, Helen, let's talk - we can sort this out.' His voice was raised, almost sobbing.

'Go away, Frank. My God - you've been drinking - you reek of alcohol - as usual. Leave us alone or I'm going to call the Police!'

The door slammed.

He stared down at the flowers, the bouquet gripped in his left hand. With a shuddering sigh, he placed his peace offering on the doorstep, knowing this would almost certainly be a pointless gesture. She would, no doubt, throw them straight into the dustbin.

When he turned to walk back to his car, he found the pathway blocked.

'On your way, Frank,' the man said in a commanding tone.

There was something in the way the stranger eyed him: an expression filled with knowing, contempt and - something else - was it disdain?

Frank's right hand curled as he attempted to make a fist - an automatic reaction remembered from an earlier time - but the pain was so bad, he couldn't quite close it.

'Who the hell are you?' he demanded.

'I'm a friend of - close friend. I believe she's asked you to leave, so why don't you do yourself a favour and beat it?'

The pale light from the street lamp outside the cottage illuminated the man's face. He was smiling, his stance relaxed, confident, and his gaze unwavering. Frank understood at that moment this man had replaced him in Helen's life.

His anger exploded, provoked by the knowing look in the eyes fixed on him: a deliberate, triumphant and silent message that said, 'You lost - and I won!' He lunged forward, swinging his not completely closed fist, wanting to hurt, to wipe the smile from that smug face. The man dodged the punch easily - he was grinning.

'Oh dear, that was rather foolish.'

Frank doubled up as a fist plunged into his stomach, leaving him gasping for air, followed immediately by a blinding flash of white-hot pain as another blow smashed into his nose.

When he came to, he found himself slumped half inside the driver's seat of the Healey. He was being pushed in. A waft of expensive cologne assuaged his nostrils.

'Listen to me, Frank - listen to me!' He felt his face being wrenched around so that he stared into the man's face, inches from his own.

'Just so we're clear,' the voice quietly spoken, authoritative again, 'I'm with Helen now - you're not welcome and we don't want you round here again. You're going to leave and don't even think about coming back. Go and crawl back to the sewer where you came from.'

For a few seconds, he sensed the man's head and shoulders inside the car. He heard the ignition and the engine firing. 'Off you go, Frank - and if you come around here again, I will kill you. Oh, and enjoy your prostitutes.'

A hard push - the door slammed sending a jabbing pain through his hip where it impacted. The man stood watching, clearly expecting him to drive away as commanded.

At that moment, Frank's bewildered thought processes suddenly focused. He knew that voice - and he understood what this man had done. The bursts of light - a man behind the camera - it was him, alright! He wished he had a loaded gun to hand in the sure knowledge he would have used it without hesitation - and to hell with the consequences!

A sudden swathe of light shot outwards from the front of the house. He glanced towards it and saw Helen standing in the doorway. She shouted something he couldn't here, gesturing with her arm - a 'come in' motion. Feeling helpless and crushed, he watched as the man turned and walked up the path to the door, noting how she gently pulled him into the cottage and shut the door.

***

'He was drunk, Helen - drunk and incapable. Christ, he could barely stand! I had to help him back to his car.'

'I smelt alcohol on his breath - but, I didn't think he was that far gone. Did he say anything to you?'

'Couldn't make out a word - but I don't think he was very happy about me being there. He took a swing at me, and then he fell over. Quite comical really!'

She walked to the window and pulled the curtain back a fraction, so she could see out into the road. 'You put him back in the car?'

'Well, yes. If I hadn't, he would no doubt have made a nuisance of himself - and I couldn't leave him in a drunken heap on the path.'

'He's gone - thank God!' said Helen. 'I hope he gets stopped by the Police and booked for drunk driving.'

'So, do I. I hate drunks.'

'Anyway, that's decided things - I'm not having him turning up on my doorstep when he feels like it. I'm going to ask my solicitor to take out that injunction against him like you suggested.'

Chapter 72

"DECREE ABSOLUTE"

(Saturday 19th December 1964)

In different circumstances, Frank would be feeling pleased with himself and what he had achieved. *Ravelles* was filled to capacity.

Having returned from his circuit of the venue, taking in the casino, the lounge, and finally, what Horse called the "cabaret area" - he satisfied himself that all was well. Although early, customers vied for space at the bar, others were queuing outside, eager to get inside.

The evidence of his drive and talent for sales was tangible. Not only had *Ravelles* grown to be one of the most popular after-hours night spots in Southampton, the quality of entertainment, the very fabric of its service delivery to the discerning gentlemen customers it attracted, had improved markedly during the few weeks since the club opened its doors for the first time. Frank created the foundations of success - everyone at the club knew that, including Horse, who relied on him as his "right hand man".

The marketing campaign he devised and managed himself, proved to be undeniably successful. He visited many businesses within and around the city centre, and far beyond, armed with advertising flyers. The chance to use his sales skills again provided a useful diversion from the dark depression threatening to overwhelm him when he found himself inactive.

His efforts resulted in a significant growth in visitors and caused profits to soar. Horse acknowledged this and rewarded him both financially and through enhanced status.

Although naturally tenacious, determined, and hardworking, his focus on the job served as a necessary distraction from reality. His ready smile, the relaxed way he engaged with staff, the swapping of jokes, and his willingness to engage in club banter - all this was a façade behind which lay hidden profound misery.

Usually under control, on this night he struggled to hide his feelings. His usual charm and friendliness were absent - he scowled and avoided conversation. The difference in him could be seen - several staff members commented on it. Earlier in the evening, he snapped at Sarah, the Hospitality Manager, when she admitted forgetting to put in an order for wine, leaving the bar under-stocked. Shocked by his unexpected nastiness, she had burst into tears and fled into a backroom, confused and frightened.

The cause of his uncharacteristic behaviour lay on the coffee table in his sitting room upstairs. When the white envelope arrived that morning, he guessed immediately what it contained. Nonetheless, when he registered the official wording "Decree Absolute", it impacted like a punch in the guts. Sent with the formal notification of the dissolution of his marriage was a covering letter - this, more than the announcement his union with Helen was now officially over, had stoked his ire.

From his vantage point, he watched the activities in the club, but with none of the professional interest, he usually showed. Although full of customers and noise, he only partially acknowledged what was going on around him. His vision focused inwards, the words in the letter imprinted on his brain for him to study, digest, and become increasingly bitter.

The house he once shared with his family would now be the sole property of Helen Park. She had cast off her marital name, he noted. More legalese instructions jumped out of the memorised letter: No further claim on any chattels... no claims on the Park business ...any attempt to inveigle business will lead to legal action.

I'm expected to walk away with nothing even though I paid for just about everything in that house! His sense of injustice was profound. He reminded himself that, although her father provided the deposit on the house, and placed the property in Helen's name, this was to have been a temporary arrangement: they were going to arrange joint ownership. But this was before everything changed.

Maintenance will be paid by Mr Armstrong to Helen Park by monthly banker's order at the rate of £50 per calendar month.

As these words played through his head, it took considerable will to stop himself from punching the wall next to his head in anger. The financial dictates created feelings of burning resentment - but the instructions regarding his son made him howl with rage when he read them.

Custody of the boy, Peter, is granted to Helen Park, his mother. Mr Armstrong is to be allowed limited access to his son. Timings will be at the discretion of Helen Park, who has directed that meetings should be restricted to every second weekend - Saturday or Sunday agreed by prior arrangement.

He realised what had once been love for Helen had changed to hatred. As he pondered this thought, the undefined visage of the man who attacked him while he was off-guard flashed into his mind: the man who had taken his place - the man who had set him up. Perhaps he's moved in with Helen - and my son! The possibility of this caused him to clench his fists in blind rage.

Later that night, long after the club had closed, Frank sat at the bar with a bottle of whiskey. Horse was not about - nothing unusual about this - there would be business to attend to elsewhere. Just as well - he didn't want company, apart from alcohol.

Chain smoking, he knocked back glass after glass. But the effect of strong liquor failed to numb the pain and anger. After a couple of hours, he found himself staring unfocused at the row of optics behind the bar. His rage had reached tumultuous proportions. He picked up the nearly empty bottle and, sliding off his seat, hurled it at the opposite wall where it shattered, leaving a dark stain dribbling to the floor. In his mind, he imagined the shape of his assailant at the point where the bottle had impacted. The thought of the missile connecting with that man's head created a momentary sensation of pleasure.

He reached over the counter and plucked another bottle from the shelf underneath. Topping up his glass with a large shot, he downed it in one.

Several hours later he was woken by the arrival of the cleaners. He lifted his head from the dampness of the bar. He saw his face reflecting in the mirror on the wall. Bleary eyes stared back at him filled with hopelessness and misery.

'I'm finished,' he mumbled.

***

Horse demonstrated both compassion and common-sense - surprising attributes in one who, in Frank's view, lacked many typical human characteristics.

In their many conversations - at least during the coherent stages before his boss disappeared into some form of alternative world hidden to others, Horse never mentioned anything about his personal life. He offered no hint of his former existence, nor did he show any inclination towards anything approaching a meaningful relationship. He was a loner, a man with strange charisma that both attracted and repelled, and with no need of affection. Not for him the ties of love nor even close friendship - at least that's how it appeared to Frank.

But the advice Horse gave to him one night provided the prod and the direction Frank needed.

'You're not married anymore. She's gone now - and it doesn't sound like you stand a cat in hell's chance of ever getting her back. But, if you loved her, why did you stray? Why don't you ask yourself that? Were you really in love with her in the first place, Frank?'

He resisted the truth behind the words at first - after all, how could anyone understand how he felt, particularly his strange boss? Perhaps the whiskey helped - but suddenly, it dawned on him, Horse had been talking sense.

'There's no reason why you can't see your son, is there? He means everything to you, yeah?'

He nodded. 'Yes, of course, he does - and you're right, nothing will change that.'

'Use the access they've given you! Fix up a date. Take him out - it's Peter, right?'

Horse pulled out his wallet, and dismissing Frank's polite refusal, pressed a twenty-pound note into his hand. 'Think of it as a little bonus - a reward for everything you've done so far. You deserve it, mate - I'm glad I took you on!'

Chapter 73

"RED MIST"

(Sunday 28th March 1965)

Helen heard excited shouting from outside, followed by a shriek of childish laughter. She smiled - Peter sounded happy. It seemed ages since he showed genuine enjoyment in a game. She scanned the garden through the kitchen window- no sign of him. The timeless game of "hide and seek" was in full swing. Nigel swung his head back and forth with exaggerated bafflement, holding a hand over his eyes as if to enhance his ability to search out his quarry. Peter's face could be seen grinning from his hiding place behind a shrub.

'Ah hah - got you!' Nigel roared.

The adult appeared to be enjoying the pantomime as much as the child, she noted. Seconds later, he held Peter squirming in the air.

'Put me down!' Peter shrieked, adding, 'You bully!' which made Helen shake with laughter.

'Okay, you two, come in now. Yes! Peter, you must get cleaned up before you go out.'

After gulping down the orange squash, she gave him, Peter ran upstairs, laughing as he dodged the hefty slap on his backside she pretended to aim at him.

'I don't want any hanging around - it's hard enough having Frank turn up here - the last thing I need is him waiting while Peter messes about. Can you imagine what it would be like? I have nothing to say to that ...'

'Calm down,' Nigel cut in, 'you shouldn't allow this to upset you. Let's face it, you hold all the cards here. But, why not let me deal with him? I won't take any nonsense, you mark my words!'

Nigel's suggestion was tempting. She had been dreading Frank's first arranged access visit since the date had been agreed after a short, terse telephone call a few days before. Her mind taunted her with several possible scenarios - all painful.

'No, I think I should handle this - at least for the first time. I mean, no point in provoking him is there?'

He squeezed her shoulder. 'Okay, fine – I'm sure you're right. Look, I can make myself scarce for now. I'll come back at about twelve - so be ready! As much as I love having Peter around, it will be nice, for once, to have you to myself.'

She smiled and kissed him. 'Go on, go! Before Frank bumps into you and creates a scene!'

***

Frank woke with mixed feelings, wondering whether he should look forward to the day. The clear knowledge that, to Helen, he represented only an unnecessary inconvenience, filled him with sadness and deep regret. Knowing she was in a relationship with another man created a burning sense of resentment - an emotion that intensified to anger whenever he thought about what that man did to him both before and during that ill-fated visit to his former home. He hadn't told Horse about the attack - an omission, he acknowledged to himself, that was down to personal pride and a fear of being considered weak.

'One day you will regret crossing me!' he muttered, not for the first time.

It took all his resolve to drive to Fairfield. He quelled the intensity of his negative feelings and tried to focus instead on the pleasure he would feel from spending the day with Peter.

Before leaving Southampton, he visited a toy shop, knowing exactly what he wanted to buy with the twenty pounds bonus Horse had awarded him. He emerged grinning, laden with a large colourful box emblazoned with the motif "Scalextric."

He'll love it - what a perfect gift from a dad to his son! A vision of Helen's disapproving expression flashed into his mind - he quashed it. 'You're not going to spoil it!' he said to the fading image. He manoeuvred the box into the small boot of the Healey, relieved that it fitted - just.

At 12 o'clock, as agreed, he arrived at the door which opened a fraction as soon as he rang the doorbell - only enough to allow Peter to squeeze through. Helen's face appeared in the gap.

'Make sure you bring him back by five on the dot.' The door slammed in his face.

Although not expecting a warm welcome, far from it, her abruptness took him by surprise.

'Jesus wept, is this how it's going to be?' he whispered.

A brief recollection of a closeness now lost - an awareness he represented no more than an unfortunate entity in her world - hit him with unexpected suddenness.

'Hello, son!' He kneeled and hugged him. 'Come on, let's go and have some fun.'

As they drove away, Frank shot a glance at his son, and noted how he stared fixedly ahead and seemed reluctant to speak – in fact, he appeared distinctly unhappy.

The day did not go well.

***

They sat near the front of the theatre in the smoking area. The pantomime had finished. Frank enjoyed the show and had laughed uproariously throughout, enjoying the innuendoes, this despite his anticipation it would be something to be endured. Now and again, he had glanced at Peter, looking for clues as to what he might be thinking. His face reflected several emotions, but enjoyment was not one of them. Instead, he seemed bored and miserable. He hasn't laughed - not once – Frank noted.

'What's the matter? You don't seem very happy.'

No response. 'What do you think? Funny, wasn't it?'

Peter turned his head to him. 'I've seen it already,' he said, 'with Mum and Nigel.'

Frank slumped in his seat and gazed at the ceiling. A myriad of thoughts cascaded through his mind, anchored in bitterness, and resentment.

'Why didn't you say?' he said, in a quiet voice, which he tried to control, avoiding any hint of anger.

Peter said nothing - he stared ahead as if wanting to avoid eye contact, but Frank could see he was on the verge of tears. He studied him for a few moments not trusting himself to speak. It was difficult to quell his boiling rage. Getting the tickets had been no easy feat - the show had been sold out and it had taken several phone calls and hard negotiation to procure the tickets, these at an exorbitant rate.

'Right, come on then, let's go!'

By the time they reached the Wimpy on Fareham's high street - the second stage of his carefully planned itinerary, it was 4 o'clock. Peter had not uttered a single word since leaving the theatre apart from monosyllabic responses to his attempts to talk to him.

'A good fry up and a milkshake - that'll put a smile back on your face!'

Frank was hungry - the thought of a burger cheered him.

***

'So, what would you like? How about that mixed grill you usually have - you know the curly sausage and chips?'

They sat at a Formica-topped table. Frank was surveying the plastic menu. The waitress smiled, poised with her notepad and pencil, gazing expectantly at him.

'I don't want anything.'

'What?' He laid the menu on the table top and stared at Peter in disbelief. 'Just give us a few moments, will you?' This to the waitress who nodded and walked back to the counter.

'What's wrong? Are you not feeling well? Aren't you hungry? You are? Well, why don't you want anything?'

Peter was silent - he stared towards the door. Then he turned and looked at him.

'Nigel says fried food is bad for me. He says I should only eat healthy food.'

'What did you say?'

A surging wave of anger, abrupt and severe, flooded through him. He stared unfocused at the menu on the table in front of him, unable to look at his son, knowing he was fighting an urge to hit out. In an instant, Peter ceased to be the focus of his affection - instead, he had crossed the line into the enemy camp and betrayed him. These thoughts were overwhelming. He stood abruptly, knocking his chair backwards.'

'Right, put your coat on - I'm taking you home.'

***

'Why not let Nigel collect him? You shouldn't be driving, Helen, not after two glasses of wine - it wouldn't be safe.'

She frowned. 'I don't know, Dad, it's not fair on him. What if Frank creates a scene - especially after the last, I mean, the only time they met?'

'I agree with your dad. I don't see a problem. That waster is just going to have to get used to the idea of me being around - there's no point in hiding the fact. That is what's bothering you, isn't it?' Nigel said, picking up his car keys.

'But - well, it seems too soon.'

'Come on, Helen, Nigel's right. Stop worrying about Frank - you've absolutely no reason to care about what he thinks anymore.'

'Okay, but please, don't allow him to start an argument with you - just collect Peter and come straight back.'

Bob smiled and squeezed her arm. 'Don't fret, it'll be fine. Now, why not let him go? You can help me put the roast on - and you can pour us both another glass of that excellent wine!'

***

At that moment, Frank and his son were sitting in silence, stuck in a traffic jam on the A27 a mile outside Fairfield. The row of cars ahead had been stationary for twenty minutes. The sound of a pulsing alarm bell throbbed, getting nearer - a glance in the rear-view mirror - a blue flashing light heralded the slow progress of an ambulance threading its way through the rows of cars.

He groaned in frustration and switched off the engine. They would be late, he thought. After another twenty minutes, the traffic moved. He turned on the engine and inched the car forward. The movement was painfully slow.

Not one word had passed between them since they left the café. He glanced at Peter, who was staring through the windscreen, his face blank. Frank could think of nothing to say - instead, he wallowed in his resentment and hurt, sure in his conviction something had been ripped away from him.

Finally, at 6 o'clock, he turned the Healey into the High Street. Free of traffic now, he put his foot down - but then slowed down again.

'Oh, what's the point? I'm late anyway, and no doubt I'll be blamed. I'm not going to dance to her - their tune!'

His bitterness and anger simmered, and he realised he no longer cared.

'Sod them!' he muttered.

Peter scowled at him.

Pulling up outside the cottage at ten past six, he resolved to keep calm and not rise to the expected remonstration from Helen. For a few moments, he considered escorting Peter as far as the garden gate, then directing him to walk alone to the front door. He would then drive away with his dignity intact.

He sighed. 'Okay, let's go.'

As he was about to walk Peter up the garden path, a sound of movement caused him to spin around.

'Where the hell have you been?'

The man emerged from shadows. Frank recognised the hated voice straight away, the one belonging to the man who he now knew was called Nigel.

'You were supposed to be here over an hour ago. Peter - come here!'

Frank said nothing - but he felt his body tensing - a shiver of anticipation - his fists clenched.

'The car's open, Peter, jump in - I'll be with you in a minute.'

Peter did as he was told, pulling his hand from his. Frank watched as he climbed into the Cortina, noting he didn't say goodbye.

The features of Nigel's were clear, illuminated by the light of the street lamp. His eyes bore into his own, glaring and indignant.

'Got nothing to say for yourself? I knew we couldn't trust you!' Nigel stepped forward and stopped in front of him.

Frank remained immobile and silent as he fixed his protagonist with a stare filled with hatred. Nigel stared back with an expression of disdain and, what Frank interpreted as, superiority.

'If you can't be trusted to bring him back on time, then I will make sure you don't get any further access. Do you...'

His arm jarred as his fist impacted with Nigel's jaw. He stepped in closer and followed up his first punch with several more to the head and body, unable to stop the dreadful momentum his rage had ignited. Within seconds, his target fell to the pavement in front of him, clutching his head in his hands.

His attack was frenzied, unstoppable - fists were joined by kicks. Oblivious to everything other than the focus of his bitterness, anger, and hatred, he rained blows at the body now writhing on the ground.

Frank did not hear the car approaching, nor see its lights. A screech of brakes - the opening of doors.

Screaming jerked him from his frenzy.

'For Christ's sake, stop! Stop it, you're going to kill him!'

He felt hands pulling him back. Helen was shrieking at him; Bob trying to pull him back. The rage left him as swiftly as it emerged. He looked at the unmoving body.

'Oh Christ, what have I done?' he moaned softly.

Chapter 74

"GUILTY"

(Friday 23rd April 1965)
He ascends slowly, conscious of the guard's presence behind, watching his back as he climbs the stairs. There is an all-pervading impression of dark wood, witness to many proceedings – an atmosphere of authority and judgement.

Now standing in the dock, he sees his own face reflecting from the polished brass rail in front of him at nose height. His heart aches with loss - a life that can never be returned to - gone forever.

The room is full. Many faces turn in unison to gaze at him. Some are smiling, but not in a friendly way - he knows they are eager to hear what form his punishment will take. Others stare at him reflecting different emotions: sadness; regret; even pity.

There is the judge, crimson-gowned, a shock of white wig in contrast - his face mottled and red - he stares down at the dock, his eyes angry and accusing. He bangs a gavel - and his lips, which seem to grow suddenly to an inhuman size, mouth the unmistakable but soundless word: 'Guilty!'

The court is empty now - except for a couple: a man and woman, not seen for a long time, but recognisable. His mother and stepfather turn their faces towards him. They shake their heads. He senses their sadness and regret.

***

The recurrent dream presented itself in several variations - but they created the same waking sensation: his life could not possibly have sunk any lower.

Frank's trial bore little resemblance to his dreamt imaginings. The first hearing lasted a few minutes. He confirmed his name and address and pleaded guilty to the charge of Grievous Bodily Harm. He was remanded in custody without bail.

A week later, the trial convened. From the outset, it was clear the odds were stacked against him despite the efforts of his barrister, paid for by Horse, who tried to argue mitigating circumstances. With impassioned eloquence, he talked about a crime of passion: a man brought to the brink of madness because he could not cope with the dramatic changes in his life.

He listened intently when Helen and then Bob took to the stand. Unable to meet their eyes, he hung his head in shame. They both gave damning evidence of his guilt. Neither held back when describing the ferocity of his violent attack. Their words would seal his fate, but he felt no animosity or sense of betrayal. Only after would he dwell on the thought, those who once loved him now saw him as a monster.

Nigel provided the undeniable testimony of an innocent victim.

Frank stared at him with loathing, noting with some satisfaction the bruises on his face which, although faded, could still be seen. Even now the blind rage had passed, he understood it was not the damage to this man he regretted but the consequences.

When cross-examined by the Prosecution and then the Defence, he guessed no one believed his version of events. To his own ears, his words sounded lame and contrived.

When the Prosecution summed up the case, he knew he was damned.

'This is an appalling crime: an unprovoked, violent attack on an innocent man. A vicious assault carried out in the full view of a minor.'

The words hit him hard. He discerned expressions of disdain and disgust as the court members stared at him. The Jury reached a unanimous "Guilty" verdict.

'You will go to prison for twelve months,' declared the judge who, unlike the one in his dreams, did not display anger, nor did he appear judgemental. He had been matter-of-fact as if all he wanted was to get the business concluded.

Chapter 75

"PRISON"

The physical privations of prison life did not cause him any real concerns. Although his Army days were long behind him, the memories remained fresh in his mind - so, being confined within a regimented system presented as a not totally unfamiliar experience. The daily routine at Winchester Prison became familiar, perhaps tolerable, despite the unrelenting boredom. His fellow prisoners gave him no problems - they respected him - being banged up for a violent assault afforded notoriety and respect.

The fact of incarceration itself did not bother him overmuch. Neither did he expect nor want visitors - and he received none – at least at first. No one wrote to him, and he didn't write letters to anyone. In effect, he became a willing recluse. Society had rejected him, and he wanted nothing to do with what happened beyond the walls. He shunned communication with the outside world.

Then, six months into his sentence, he received a letter. Noting the Fairfield postmark, but not recognising the handwriting, he wondered who might have written to him. He was surprised to discover it was Gregory.

As he read the opening lines, he was, for a few brief moments, back in Fairfield again. *I've been promoted, Frank*, wrote Gregory. *Bill's retired now, so I've been moved up to Distribution Manager.*

It was clear Gregory had thought carefully about the wording of his letter. Frank knew his former protégé wanted to acknowledge him and the key part he had played in helping him develop from the shy young man with no confidence to the now successful, positive individual with prospects. But, as well as gratitude, the words conveyed another clear message, one that Frank would spend a good deal of time thinking about.

I know you've done some bad things, Frank. Why? Well, only you can answer that question. But, what I do know, is that deep inside, you're a good man – and that's how I will always think of you.

***

One night, as he lay on his bed, staring sleeplessly at the springs of the bunk above his, he remembered Peter's birthday. The thought made him more miserable than normal because he could not think of any way to show he cared. But a sudden realisation made him smile: the Scalextric set bought with the bonus Horse awarded him still lay in the boot of the Healey.

While on remand awaiting sentence, he asked for the keys to his car to be sent to Horse along with a request he arrange for its collection from the police station where it had been taken following his arrest. This presented a neat and tidy solution. In a brief letter, he asked Horse to have the box wrapped and delivered. He received an equally short message back telling him the task had been accomplished.

He wondered whether Helen would allow Peter to accept his gift. The thought of Nigel in the background pulling Helen's strings rekindled the bitter, angry thoughts he tried hard to quell. Oh well, he consoled himself, at least I can't be accused of not trying.

Peter's Birthday passed. Frank received no letter of thanks, nor acknowledgement the present had been delivered. At first, he experienced dull disappointment - then anger when he imagined Nigel's reaction to such a grand offering arriving. He guessed it had been rejected, encouraged by him. Helen would probably sell it at the next church "bring and buy" sale.

Frank needed someone to confide in and to share his inner thoughts. Although not a religious man, he made an appointment with the Prison Chaplain.

'I don't exist in their eyes,' he said finally, after baring his soul.

Expecting kind words of comfort, the response came as an unwelcome surprise and shock.

'You need to put your past behind you now, Armstrong. Your family doesn't want you because you hurt them by what you did. Maybe in time, they will forgive - but you cannot expect them to treat you with any form of respect - not after the way you behaved. Now, you've got to move on - if you dwell too much in the past it will destroy you.'

Although not what he expected nor wanted to hear, the advice helped once he allowed the reality to sink in. Acceptance did not come easy - it took considerable soul-searching and time. But, soon after, he woke to another routine and predictably drab day and realised, without knowing why, he was ready to move on. He developed ways of blanking out thoughts of the past which helped considerably in preventing his moods descending to dangerous levels of depression. By maintaining his focus on the future, he found he could, at least sometimes, rekindle some of his former optimism.

Seven months into his sentence, he was told he would be granted early release on the grounds of good behaviour. He wondered what life outside held for him, and worried.

Shortly before his release date, he received his first visitor: Horse.

'Just two more weeks and you're a free man again!'

'Is there anything for me to come out to? My family's gone now and....'

Horse responded with a familiar crooked, metal-toothed grin.

'I understand how you feel. Spent a few stretches inside meself! Did I ever tell you about that?'

Frank could not recall Horse mentioning being banged up, but it came as no surprise: prison reflected his character.

'You'll be okay. Things are happening, and I need your help. So, hang in there, old son. Your job is waiting for you!'

Horse did not expand upon this announcement, but as Frank was escorted back to his cell from the visiting room, he found himself smiling.

***

(Friday 3rd December 1965)

'The best of luck, Armstrong - and stay away from here!'

'Oh, believe me, I've no intention of ever coming back!'

The warder shook his hand and opened the exit door inside the wooden entrance gate, allowing Frank to pass through. Dressed in the clothes he entered the prison in: flannel trousers, a sports jacket and tie, he felt human again. The door shut behind him with a resounding bang. He walked free.

Horse was waiting for him, leaning against the side of the Healey. He grinned his metal-toothed grin and opened the driver-side door, gesturing for him to climb in.

Frank gunned the engine into life, the feeling of power sending a small shiver through his body. 'Where to?'

'The club. I've got a surprise for you!'

Chapter 76

"DESPERATION"

Horse ushered him into the bar. A huge banner hung from the ceiling: "Welcome home Frank!" A small group of familiar faces greeted him, already armed with drinks and, judging by the fug of alcohol and cigarette fumes, the party started a while ago.

The whiskey hit the mark straight away. This was followed by two more before he switched to beer.

Leaning on the bar, smoking, he cast his eyes around him. Everyone seemed strangely subdued. He registered that, except for Horse, no one attempted to engage him in conversation.

'What's been going on? I know something's not quite right here.'

'Bugger me, you're sharp, Frank,' Horse replied with his characteristic crooked grin. 'A small cash-flow problem - nothing to worry about. Now, come on, let's top up these glasses!'

The face said one thing - but the eyes conveyed a different message: anxiety. Eventually, after several more drinks, with the bar now empty except for himself and Horse, Frank learned the truth.

'There was a problem with the Entertainments Licence. Some arsehole reported us to the Council - told them we were operating an illegal casino and...'

'And what?'

'Well, some of the girls - they were carrying out a bit of extra business on the side.'

Frank did not understand the legalities of the license, but he knew of the extra-curricular activities going on behind the scenes. He had turned a blind eye to this, knowing the strippers had to supplement their low wages somehow.

'What happened?'

Horse stared at him - no longer grinning, his face now serious.

'I got a court summons. The lawyer, the one I hired for you, got me off the charge of running, what was it? Oh yes, a *house of ill-repute.*' He laughed without humour. 'The license was another matter. Didn't come away scot-free- there, unfortunately. Bastards!'

'So, they shut you down, is that it?'

'Not as such. But they slammed me with a sodding great fine - hence the cash-flow situation. I can't pay the wholesalers - alcohol mainly. What you see here...,' he waved his hand towards the back of the bar, 'is all that's left - no more when that lot's gone.'

'So, the club's not been open, then?'

'Correct! I can't because I've barely any booze to sell, and I can't make any money because I can't let the punters in.'

Frank groaned. The faint optimism that had accompanied his release from prison disappeared to be replaced by numbing despair. He glanced at Horse, who was nursing a tumbler of rum and staring at the near empty bottles of spirits hanging behind the bar, and was surprised to note, he was now smiling.

'So, what's your plan? What are you going to do?'

'Well, I'm glad you asked that Frank!' He grinned. 'Let's neck a few more drinks and then I'll tell you what I'm thinking, and how you can help me.'

***

'You've got to be kidding! No way! I'm not doing that! Look, Horse, I don't want any part of it! I can't believe what I'm hearing here! It's a crazy idea!'

'Keep it down,' Horse waved his hands in a placating way, 'Walls have ears.'

'I don't want to be involved - I wish you hadn't told me.'

'Look, hear me out, Frank, okay?'

Frank shook his head, as if unable to comprehend the depth of the disaster being faced, nor the ruse Horse offered as a way out of it. The glass he gripped in his hand wobbled as he tried to raise it to his lips. With considerable effort, forcing himself to calm down, he managed to achieve the task - he swallowed the whiskey in one huge gulp.

'I need someone who can be trusted - like you, Frank.' Horse paused before continuing in a softer, reassuring tone, 'I know you can be relied on to make sure things are done properly. Some of the lads are up for it - but they need to be watched - make sure they don't cock it up.'

'You're talking about armed robbery for fuck's sake! They've only just let me out of prison - I would be looking at a much longer stretch if I get involved with this.'

'Only if you're caught - and that won't happen. You'll be there to make sure everyone does exactly what they're supposed to do. And listen....' He leaned towards him and grabbed his wrist in a firm grip, 'It won't be armed robbery - not as such, because the guns won't be loaded. In fact,' he paused as if for dramatic effect before adding, 'they won't even be real - they'll be replicas.'

Frank laughed mirthlessly. 'Well, I'm no expert on these things, but I reckon the law might not see it that way.'

Horse slipped off his stool and stood next to him, placing an arm around his shoulders - a friendly gesture, but also, he guessed, to hold himself upright.

'One raid - just one! These local post offices keep loads of money in their tills - and they have no proper security - it wouldn't be like robbing a bank. A quick "in and out" job and we'll be laughing! There'll be enough cash to dig us out of this shit!'

Frank said nothing - but in his mind, he explored the significance of Horse's words. The message was clear and stark. They shared a dilemma, he reminded himself. If the club goes belly up then so does my job - and, without a job, I'll have nowhere to live. Memories of the hated guest house flooded back.

Soon, as always when drinking, Horse disappeared into his alternative world. After a short while, apparently oblivious to everything, he began his incoherent, one-way dialogue.

With the whiskey bottle now empty, Frank decided a bed, for once, held greater appeal than more alcohol, and he climbed the stairs to his flat.

***

Proper sleep eluded him, although he lay in a comfortable bed for the first time in many months. Drained both physically and mentally, his head woozy, still, he could only drift between being wide awake for a few minutes and shorter periods of semi-slumber. A myriad of scenes, each underlining the irrefutable reality of his precarious existence, played through his mind, as though presenting to him a morality play. Every vignette emphasised his descent.

'You had everything: a good wife, a son - a career! But you threw it all away, didn't you? Look where your weakness has landed you now!' The words, cynical and unforgiving, were clear, spoken in a familiar voice but one he could not place.

The accuser continued. 'How many other lives have you destroyed along the way? Where's Vee now? You wrecked her life! No doubt she's an outcast now - like you! And Helen! Did she deserve what you did to her?'

He argued with the hateful voice at this juncture.

'Bollocks!' he hissed through clenched teeth, a rush of anger and resentment overriding the sorrow and guilt in an instant. 'She replaced me quickly enough - and allowed another man to steal my role as a dad!'

'But were you a good father, Frank? Were you really?' reasoned the voice in a triumphant monotone.

His thoughts failed to formulate a suitable response. He acknowledged there was more than a small element of truth in what his accuser said - and he knew it. The inner voice took on a more placating, matter-of-fact tone - no longer chiding or accusing.

'They banged you up in prison for a violent crime. You're a criminal now - that fact will never go away. How are you ever going to get another meaningful job? If you don't do something about it, you'll lose the one here at the club as well. So, what are you going to do?'

'I'm not an evil man - I haven't crossed the line yet - there's still a chance for...'

'No there isn't! You stepped over when you showed who you really are. No turning back now - you're a criminal and everyone knows it! Why not accept the fact? And you need to understand, if you're going to survive, you'll have to live by your wits - like Horse.'

Memories of dingy hotel rooms and the all-pervading dankness and hopelessness of the bedsit taunted him.

'I'm not going back to that shitty life - never!'

By the time the early morning light probed weakly through the curtains, marking the start of another day, his mind was almost made up.

The official letter he opened later that morning - the one reminding him that, now he was a free man, he must resume the maintenance payments to Helen, finally prompted him to action.

Chapter 77

"ARMED ROBBERY"

(Thursday 3rd March 1966)

A glance at his watch – he noted he had been parked for seven minutes. He resumed his observation of the post office door. A middle-aged woman exited a short while ago - no one else had entered since. A quick scan ahead along the pavement, then to the rear using the van's wing mirror. Nobody. Two more minutes to be on the safe side.

Lighting a cigarette to calm his nerves, he took a deep drag and exhaled, opening the window slightly to let the fug out.

No more after this. One last brush with danger. He tried to convince himself - but something told him this might not be the case.

His post-raid feelings following the two earlier robberies in which he took part surprised him. Perhaps it was the adrenalin rush he found so invigorating - the daring, the excitement. He experienced huge pangs of guilt in the sure knowledge he would be considered, without a doubt, a career criminal. But now his life of true crime had developed momentum, he found himself sucked in and - well, unable to stop.

On the first raid, he acted as driver and look-out. That robbery went without hitch - but the haul had been small - only fifty pounds and some blank postal orders.

On the second, as well as being the driver, he performed a more active role, although he had not been armed. He had helped carry the contents of the safe and cash till back to the van. The three of them taking part donned black balaclavas with eyeholes cut out.

Everything went well until the elderly lady behind the counter screamed. Confused shouting and panic ensued. They fled the scene with nothing to show for their efforts. One raider had shouted to his mate by name. Frank, a novice in crime of any kind, knew this to be a big mistake. When he told Horse what had happened, they both agreed he would be better working on his own.

Two more minutes passed - time to go. He flicked the cigarette butt out of the window, casting one more glance ahead and behind before reaching inside his jacket, pulling out the balaclava and tugging it over his head. His hand reached under the raincoat lying on the passenger seat and gripped the stock of the sawn-off shot gun concealed there.

***

'Tea's up, Elsie girl.'

'Thanks, Granddad. Just leave the mug on the counter - I'll stop in a minute.'

She looked up, momentarily distracted from her task of counting coppers and small denomination silver to place as change in the drawer of the till open next to her.

'You look tired, Granddad. Why don't you go back inside and put your feet up in front of the fire? I'll be closing for lunch in half an hour - we can have a chat then - if you're still awake that is,' she said smiling.

'I'll finish this first,' he said. 'Don't like leaving a job half-done.'

He busied himself with emptying the small display of Christmas cards left unsold after the festive season. She smiled sadly, knowing he was trying to make himself useful. He didn't want to be on his own that was clear. He always found something to do so he could be near her. Poor Granddad - losing his wife had hit him so hard. Now he feared being left alone.

Finished with counting out change, she closed the till and picked up the mug of tea - dark and strong - the only way it should be made, Granddad would say. She watched him, engrossed in his task, and felt the prick of tears. He's fading fast, she thought, and he knows - and it frightens him.

As she sipped her tea, brief but vivid memories of earlier times flashed through her mind. He had been strong, fit and sharp - quick witted with a sense of humour that made him so popular with the villagers who visited his post office. With her dad clearing off soon after her birth, and her mum dying, Granddad Fred and Nana Marie had taken on the role of parents. Only he was left now - a shell of his former self.

'Come and sit down - the cards can wait, your tea's getting cold.'

He nodded assent and pulled himself up on to the stool next to the post office counter.

'I told you, you'd ordered too many!' he said.

'We can put them out again next year,' she said soothingly, 'Now, stop worrying and drink your ...'

The door crashed open. She gasped and dropped her mug of tea in fright. The figure in a black balaclava mask took a couple of steps towards the counter and brandished a shotgun in her directions. His eyes wide - she saw fear and something else - uncertainty?

'Empty the safe - now!' he roared.

She sensed the almost imperceptible movement behind her. Alarm shot through her.

'No!' she shouted, 'Stay out of the way! I can deal with this!'

'Do it!' the voice yelled with an edge of panic in his voice, which she registered.

Elsie realised her fear was evaporating. His eyes and voice gave away the clear fact he was probably more frightened than her. Even though he waved the gun only arm's distance, instinct told her this man did not have it in him to use it.

What she feared, however, was Granddad getting in the way.

'Stay back!' The man yelled and brandished the shotgun menacingly. But she knew this was an act. This man looked like he wanted to turn and run.

'You're wasting your time,' she reasoned calmly, 'the safe's empty - I took all the money to the bank this morning - so you're too late. Here, take the till - there's some cash - but not a lot.'

She pulled the drawer from its casing and thrust it over the top of the counter towards him, aware all the time Granddad hovered as if ready to pounce.'

'Take it!' she implored, 'Take the money and leave us alone!'

'No, you don't!'

The old man's voice was quavering but loud, full of indignation and anger. She witnessed the scene with helpless horror as he launched himself at the figure standing in front of them, knocking the till draw she had extended across the counter onto the floor where it landed with a crash, spilling coins in all directions across the linoleum.

Like some strange parody, a scene that might have appeared comical in different circumstances played out before her. Granddad held the barrel of the gun in a firm grip and was attempting to wrest it away - or perhaps turn the barrel around back onto the assailant. Any moment, she expected to be deafened by a resounding bang.

Carefully, she unclipped the flap in the counter that would allow her access to the shop floor, determined to intervene before it was too late. Both men were shouting.

Having just squeezed through the gap, she was thrown violently backwards. Her head banged against the edge of the till and she slid down to the floor in a sitting position, temporarily stunned. Coming to her senses, she realised with horror it had been Granddad stumbling into her, pushed with considerable force by the man in the balaclava mask.

Ignoring the apparent threat from the robber, she slid across the floor to where the old man lay immobile. He appeared to be unconscious and, most alarming, a steady trickle of blood oozed from a gash on the side of his head.

'Granddad' she sobbed, her voice strangulated and filled with growing horror.

'Oh God, what have I done?'

His voice was barely a whisper, but she detected something in it and stared back at him. The eyes stared through the holes in the balaclava - she recognised terror.

'You've killed him, you bastard!' she shouted, her own eyes blazing with anger and tears.

'I didn't mean to hurt him - I'm so sorry. Let me help, please!'

'Go away!' she shrieked as he stooped towards where she lay, cradling the old man's head.

They were both distracted by the tinkling of a bell above the front door. A teenage boy walked in and then stopped - his eyes wide in fright.

'Get out Andrew - call the police - and an ambulance. Tell them a robbery's happening. Go, go!' she screamed. The door swung shut with a bang as the boy fled.

She fixed the man with a defiant stare. 'Well, what are you waiting for? Nothing here for you. Why don't you go? Go on - get out before the Police arrive.'

He seemed to hesitate. Then she noticed with surprise there were tears in his eyes. She was even more surprised when he pulled off his balaclava.

She studied his face. He doesn't seem like a robber, she thought. In fact, he looks quite human. In a few seconds, she registered a deep regret and something else - was it resignation? Whatever it was, this man no longer presented a threat - and it appeared he wanted to help.

'Here, use this to stop the bleeding - press it against the cut- like this.'

He knelt beside her and the prostrate body of the old man, pressing the balaclava to the seeping wound. 'Keep the pressure on it,' he said, as she replaced his hand with hers.'

She stared, strangely mesmerised by the unexpected turn of events, as he applied his finger to the old man's neck.

'I can feel a pulse - he's alive.' He paused before whispering, 'Thank God!'

'What's your name?' she asked.

'Frank - it's Frank.'

'Well, Frank, do you not think you should go? The Police will be here any minute now. Why don't you go - get out of here while you can?'

As if to confirm the veracity of her words, the faint wail of a siren could be heard.

Chapter 78

"LETTING GO"

(Friday 4th March 1966 – early morning)

He woke with a start, his heart thumping painfully as though he had been faced with some form of extreme danger - but he could not remember what. Disorientated and confused, he stared around in panic. After a few seconds, he registered the familiarity of the van. He glanced at his wristwatch - eight-thirty.

'Bloody hell,' he groaned, realising he had slept for over ten hours. The view through the windscreen revealed a pleasing vista that, in different circumstances, would have made him smile with pleasure - but not now. A packet of cigarettes lay on the dashboard where he left them following his last smoke before falling into an exhausted sleep. He fumbled around, searching for his matches.

'Shit! Oh, thank God for that!' The box had fallen to the floor between his feet. He picked them up and lit his cigarette, leaning back into his seat and inhaling deeply. After a couple of minutes, he slid the cab window open and flicked the butt out.

A little calmer now, he stared blankly in front as the images and emotions of yesterday returned in a flurry, reminding him of his folly and the desperate nature of his plight.

'What's the point?' he murmured, 'They're going to catch me sooner or later.'

He tried to rationalise his reasons for fleeing the scene. Blind panic, he concluded. I ran away like a coward. 'I wasn't thinking,' he muttered, as though arguing mitigation for his actions. His mind pieced together the facts confirming the certainty of his impending capture.

She's seen my face and will be able to give a detailed description of me, he thought, remembering the girl. Oh yes, the shotgun. I left that on the floor. My prints will be all over it. What else? He struggled to think. Then he remembered seeing the boy in the wing mirror as he sped away - the one the girl instructed to call the police. He would have noted the number plate.

'Why didn't I stay and face the music? I might have helped - done some good.'

Thoughts of the old man lying unconscious on the floor caused him to take a sharp intake of breath.

'Maybe he died,' said an invidious voice in his head. 'Yes, you found a pulse - but he was frail and weak.'

'Oh God, did I kill him?' he whispered.

'Don't come back here, whatever you do, Frank! Lose the motor then lie low. Get back in touch in a week or so and we can plan what to do next.'

He remembered the call made from a phone box an hour after driving away from the post office. *Horse won't help me, he'll be out to save his own skin.* This thought ignited a flash of anger.

His mouth was dry, and a rancid taste lingered from too many cigarettes. He longed for a drink of water.

Just over five years ago, a grey two-tone Rover stood parked in the same place. He would never know this, nor would the fact have sparked much interest at this moment. The fence, a few feet ahead of the van, appeared new - the mesh taut and shining in the morning sun. This replaced the one that failed to prevent Mr Ramsay's car from plunging over the cliff top.

He opened the door and stepped out, welcoming the freshness of the air after the stuffiness of the cab, and the opportunity to stretch, allowing blood to flow properly into his cramped muscles. The early morning frost was already melting in the sun. He moved around to the front of the van and leant back on the bonnet, still warm from the engine left running through the night.

'Why haven't they found me yet?' he murmured.

Yesterday, two police cars had sped past him as he drove away from the post office. He remembered being relieved they weren't aware of his identity and so he had been able to distance himself from the scene of his crime and shame. The sure knowledge there was nowhere for him to run to only occurred to him later.

'He told me his name's Frank,' he imagined the girl saying with a hint of triumph in her voice.

'Only a matter of time now,' he said aloud.

The sea was flat and calm, the horizon a crisp straight line away in the distance where a ship was transiting right to left. The vessel seemed like a toy - but he guessed it was large, a tanker perhaps - and inside it, the crew would be going about their business. He wished he might be transported and planted among them unnoticed, another blameless person with a home to go to at the end of the voyage, where he might adopt a new life to replace the one he lived in now as a fugitive criminal.

'Where the hell are they?' he muttered, looking over his shoulder at the car park entrance as if expecting to see a black car with a blue flashing light turning in. He turned back and stared towards the sea. A notice board hung on the wire fence: "DANGER - CLIFF EDGE".

A sudden sensation of Déjà vu made his heart jolt. Half-remembered images flooded into his mind as though released through the opening of a hidden door.

His heart raced as he leaned back on the van bonnet, staring fearfully at the vista ahead of him. The familiarity of what he saw frightened and bewildered him because he was convinced he had never been in this spot before. For a few moments, he pondered the thought he might be gazing into a previous life. I know what happens next, he thought, his fear rising further.

Despite his reluctance, a compulsive pull made him walk mechanically to the fence. As though in a trance, he stepped gingerly over the wire and leant the backs of his legs against it, the sensation it created strangely familiar.

A narrow stretch of grass curved gently towards the unseen edge, still wet from the melted frost that covered it earlier. He thought, if I were to step on that, I would slip and slide over the top.

Never in his life had he considered taking his own life, even in his darkest, alcohol-fuelled moments. But, as he stared at the grass curve, he wondered if suicide might be justified. He lit another cigarette.

'Is this my last one?' he whispered. A few minutes later, he flicked the still burning butt ahead of him. It followed a neat arc and vanished over the top into the unseen drop. He knew it would do that.

He took short, rapid breaths, and his heart beat wildly in his chest. A weird compulsion made him lean forward, so he no longer felt the tightness of the wire supporting his legs. His whole body shook - through feat or anticipation - he was not sure which. Gripping the wire behind him, he extended his right leg and placed his foot flat on the grassy area in front of him without putting weight on it. That should have been it - a partial re-enactment of his dream. But a strange compunction - he would not be able to describe exactly what - compelled him to go further. With care, he pressed his right foot down on the grass and, as he did this, let go of the wire and moved his left leg forward.

He stood unsupported, swaying a little before steadying himself. Slowly, he turned his head around, wanting to see the security of the fence, readying himself to dive for the wire should he slip. *What the hell am I doing?* The slightest movement, he knew, would cause his leather soled shoes to shoot forward putting him on his back and propelling his body over the cliff edge.

A sharp awareness of his self-imposed predicament caused his heart to pound harder than ever - his terror acute. The anguished thoughts that, until only a few minutes ago consumed him with guilt, were forgotten.

He wondered whether he would be able to grab the wire in time before momentum pushed his body forward. His body shook - tremors travelled down his legs to his feet with their tenuous grip on the ground. He swung his head to the front again. Perhaps because of tiredness, or maybe the effects of the two cigarettes smoked in quick succession - but sudden dizziness caused him to topple backwards.

'No!' he screamed, falling with a heavy thud on his backside and sliding forward feet first towards the cliff edge.

***

'Sasha! For God's sake, where's she buggered off to?'

'I told you not to let her off the lead - you won't listen. Oh God, Henry, what if she's fallen over the cliff?'

'She's got the scent of a rabbit - don't worry, Marj, she won't have gone far. Look, I'm going to go on ahead and catch her up. I'll see you in the car park.'

He strode out as fast as his bad hip would allow him. His reassuring words to his wife in no way reflected his real feelings - he was anxious. At thirteen, Sasha, their golden retriever, was an old girl, but she did not seem to understand this. Wilful as her much younger version, she might chase a scent with no thought of danger.

'Sasha!' he shouted, his voice becoming panicked. Then he spotted the grey Morris van ahead of him - the driver's door was open, he noted with mild curiosity. A sudden familiar noise caused him to spin around and stare towards the cliff edge.

'Oh Christ,' he muttered. The dog was on the wrong side of the wire, facing the unseen drop. Her front end down, she was moving forwards and back, barking furiously at something beyond and out of sight.

'Sasha! Stay!' He shouted, his heart thudding, thinking, any moment now and she'll lose her grip and slide. 'Come! Sasha, come!' he yelled.

She became silent and glanced back, scrabbling fully upright. But whatever had attracted her interest was too interesting - she turned and resumed her frantic barking.

He crossed the car park to the fence and, leaning over, beckoned the dog.

'Come here, now!' A sudden vision of his beloved dog toppling on her unsteady, arthritic legs caused his heart to lurch. He stretched over the fence as far as he could and, as soon as Sasha edged near enough, grabbed her collar and pulled her under the fence wire.

'Have you got her! Oh, thank goodness! I thought she might topple over!' This was Marjory, his wife.

'What got into her, barking her head off like that?' he said shaking his head.

'I heard her from back there. As you said, must have been a rabbit or something. She probably panicked it and the poor sod ran over the cliff top. Oh well, whatever it was, I don't care. Let's go back now. I need a cup of tea to calm my nerves.'

'Okay Marj, take her back. Look, I'm going to stay out for a while - I need the exercise.'

'Well, alright - but not don't go too far. Don't forget, we're meeting Irene and Steve in the pub later and I don't want you making us late!'

Marjory headed back the way they had come. As she turned the corner of the cliff path and disappeared, Henry approached the van. His curiosity had been aroused by the open door and the fact there was no sign of its owner. He frowned when he noted the engine was ticking over. 'What's going on?' he muttered.

'Oh my God!' he whispered - a sudden realisation - a connection of thoughts. He strode back to the fence, gripped the top wire and, leaning over and forward as far as he felt able, listening intently. Was there something? Yes, there it is again: a gasping sound, or perhaps a whimper?

'Hello!' Can you hear me?' he shouted towards the hidden drop.

A tremulous voice, barely audible: 'Hello, yes... Oh shit!'

'Are you alright?' Silence. 'Hello?'

'Not really.' His voice sounded breathless and with a distinct edge of terror. 'I'm hanging onto a root which is holding my weight - but I don't think it will for much longer. Can you go to the van? See if there's any rope in the back? Please be quick!'

There was no rope, but Henry found a reel of heavy-duty electrical cable - surely that will do the job? Moving as quickly as he could, he returned to the wire.

'I've found some cable - I'm going to secure it to the fence post and drop it down to you.'

Silence. 'Are you...?'

'Good - please hurry!' the man's voice cut in.

Henry yanked the cable from the cardboard drum - there was about forty feet. It seemed strong - but he doubled it up to be on the safe side. Taking a turn around the base of the fence post, he gathered the cable into coils and heaved it ahead of him as hard as he could towards where he calculated the man was hanging on.

'Got it! Are you holding on? I'm going to pull myself up!'

'It's tied off! Are you able to climb?'

He heard a scrabbling sound. After a few seconds, the head and shoulders of a young man appeared.

***

He sat in the driver's seat of the van smoking as though it were his last ever cigarette. The door was open - the old man leant on it, smoking a pipe and surveying him with a quizzical look.

'What on earth did you think you were doing? You could have been killed.'

The young man seemed to consider this for a moment and then nodded.

'Thank you for saving me - I really appreciate that.'

'But, why did you risk your life? What were you thinking?'

'I don't know,' he replied truthfully, 'I guess it was a moment of madness.'

***

(Friday 4th March 1966 – midday)

The beer tasted good, and it hit the spot almost immediately. He reminded himself he had not eaten for at least thirty-six hours, and yet he did not feel hungry.

The *Crows Nest* was filling with its lunchtime customers. They gathered in small groups around the bar or at the tables. He studied them with detached interest, noticing how they smiled and laughed, joked and talked. He wished he could be as carefree and relaxed.

Draining his beer, he ordered another. A pint was placed in front of him - he paid and nodded his thanks. After taking a sip, he put the jug down on the bar and heaved himself off his stool.

He paused to listen to the music coming from the jukebox somewhere behind him. *The Spencer Davis Group* were advising "Keep on running". He smiled at the irony.

'Let's get this over with,' he muttered, picking up the telephone receiver. He was about to push a coin in to the slot but then he remembered he did not need money for this number.

His call made, he returned to the bar, hefted himself back onto the stool and resumed sipping his beer.

'Won't be long now,' he murmured.

If anyone were paying attention to him, they might have noticed the dishevelled looking man sitting alone at the bar was weeping.

EPILOGUE

(Thursday 16ᵗʰ June 1966)

'He must be mad,' muttered the thick-set, bald man, dressed in a sharp pin stripe suit and flamboyant tie, 'Could have sold this for him – got a decent price, and invested the cash. He'll need money when he gets out.'

Gregory nodded, glancing at the strange man walking by his side. He could think of nothing suitable to say and realised this bizarre-looking man called "Horse" intimidated him.

'Anyway, if that's what he wants, who am I to argue?'

Horse grinned. Gregory found himself staring at a row of uneven teeth interspersed with gold crowns.

'This is it.'

They stopped in front of a pair of garage doors with grey paint hanging off in strips. Horse fumbled in his jacket pocket and drew out a bunch of keys, one of which he inserted in the rusting lock.

As he struggled to turn the key, he experienced a surge of excitement, and for the first time since receiving the cryptic letter, understood what it was that Frank wanted him to take possession of.

'Bloody stiff! Ah, there you go! Grab that side, will you? It slides.'

They both heaved on their respective door and, inch by inch, they opened, revealing a dark interior and releasing a strong smell of oil.

Horse reached round on his side and flipped a switch. The interior of the lock-up filled with light.

Gregory knew what would be lying under the tarpaulin as they dragged it off.

'Well I never,' he whispered.

Later, halted at a long queue of static traffic, he pulled out the letter Frank had sent to him and read it again.

The message was brief. In it, Frank provided a Southampton address – a club called *Ravelles*.

The manager there, a man called Horse (don't ask!) will expect you. He's been looking after something for me. No use to me anymore. Take care of it, Gregory. I think you deserve it far more than I ever did.

PS: *It's had two careful owners.*

Acknowledgements

My thanks to all those who have supported me in this project – my debut novel. In particular, I would like to thank Mark Rewhorn for his assistance with editing and historical advice, and similarly Jackie Bishop from Oakwood International for her valuable input. Thanks also to Fleur Blanford, Nicole Dixon, and Gina Andrei, all of whom contributed ideas at various stages of writing.

Lightning Source UK Ltd.
Milton Keynes UK
UKHW020637310719
347147UK00011B/522/P